Copyright © 2021 by Chelsea L.L. Bon

All rights reserved. No part of this text downloaded, decompiled, reverse-engineered, or stored in, or introduced into any information storage and retrieval system, in any form or by any means, whether electronic or mechanical, now known, hereinafter invented, without express written permission of the publisher. For permission requests, write to the publisher, addressed "Attention: Permissions Coordinator," at the address below.

Typewriter Pub, an imprint of Blvnp Incorporated
A Nevada Corporation
1887 Whitney Mesa DR #2002
Henderson, NV 89014
www.typewriterpub.com/info@typewriterpub.com

ISBN: 978-1-64434-195-7

DISCLAIMER
This book is a work of fiction. The characters, incidents, and dialogue are drawn from the author's imagination and are not to be construed as real. While references might be made to actual historical events or existing locations, the names, characters, places, and incidents are either products of the author's imagination or are used fictitiously, and any resemblance to actual persons living or dead, business establishments, events or locales is entirely coincidental.

THE WOLVEN KING
The King Series
BOOK ONE

CHELSEA L.L. BONES

typewriter pub

*To my family and my boyfriend,
thank you for supporting me*

Trigger Warning:
The following story contain gory scenes.
Reader discretion is advised.

CHAPTER ONE
Dark Red Eyes

✦◻✦

Alivia

    I crept down the creaky wooden stairs. Every time the floorboards squeaked, I flinched and waited a second until I was sure they haven't heard me. There wasn't a sound of movement so I knew I haven't woken my aunt or cousins, which meant I was free to continue.

    The house was dark as I tried to navigate my surroundings, careful not to trip down the stairs. I sighed as I finally made it to the bottom. Grabbing my cloak, I left the old house. I embraced the sudden sense of freedom. It was pitch black outside. The cold instantly numbed my cheeks and hands but I didn't care. This is what I wanted.

    No one ever dared to venture outside when it was pitch black. The thought of what was awaiting them was too horrific.

    Vampires were the main threat to our lives.

    I have never seen a vampire, but I knew they were out there. From what I have heard, they were beautiful creatures. They have skin so flawless and eyes so captivating you couldn't move—like a deer caught in headlights.

    They may have been beautiful but that was just to disguise their vicious nature. They were cruel beings who didn't feel emotion or pain. They could compel a person to do anything they wanted of them, whether that be to feed or use you as a slave, to serve their king.

However, they also have a main weakness. They could burn in the sun if exposed. There was another way to kill a vampire but it was extremely dangerous because it meant having to be really close to them . . . You could chop off their heads.

Runes were creatures enslaved to the vampires. The vampires used them to be their eyes during the day. The runes were able to glamour themselves into looking like deadly creatures and even pass as a human. They have superhuman speed like vampires.

Apart from that, runes were pretty easy to kill just like humans. But none of them compared to Wolvens—a separate species that could shift into wolves at will.

They were more powerful and have fewer weaknesses than vampires and runes combined. They controlled the entire kingdom and used us to serve them in exchange for keeping the vampires away along with the runes. Humans have known no other way for over two hundred years.

Wolvens were ruled by the Wolven king. Wolvens followed his every command. He was said to be cold and vicious. Still, I have never been close enough to a wolven to know much about them. I have always just watched them from afar. Besides, I didn't think I ever wanted to meet them from the way my aunt talked about them.

The night never seemed to frighten me. I loved the night. It felt serene and calm. My entire being felt powered and my skin tingled with anticipation whenever I would look up to the night sky.

I kept silent as I made my way down the narrow path of our street towards the woods. I listened for anything that could be nearby. I have excellent hearing, better than most people I knew. I could hear the sound of wind blowing through trees. I could also hear the owls and the croaking of frogs, but nothing else that felt threatening. I held my cloak tight around my body to keep myself warm.

Finally making it to the narrow woods, I breathed in the cold, fresh air. A damp scent filled my nostrils. I sighed in bliss. This is where I was supposed to be. I knew it was. I could feel it in my bones.

If my aunt, Helena, knew where I was, she would have had a panic attack. She feared the outdoors more than anyone else. Her husband, my uncle, was murdered by a vampire when he was on his way home from hunting one night. He was the one who found me as a baby, crying in the woods. He had no idea where I came from but took pity on me and took me home to his family.

Since his death six years ago, it was my aunt who took care of me. She took extra precautions with me and my two younger cousins, Avery and Amber. She was always terrified. I knew she was right to be, but this was something I just had to do no matter the risk.

I have taken precautions whenever I went out and made sure to research everything I could about vampires in case I was to ever come across one—which was extremely unlikely. It could also be my foolishness talking.

It has been a while since I left the house. I've been walking for quite a while so I decided to turn back. My boots were now smothered in mud and my dark hair was blowing in all directions. I only made a few steps before I heard it—a growl.

Wolves. I was sure of it but every time I ventured out, I never once saw them. They barely ever left their territory. Out of all the times, why were they here now?

Another growl was heard, only this time closer. Much closer. Starting to panic, I paced through the dark woods. Branches scraped my arms as I ran. I could dwell on why they were here later but right now I needed to leave before they found me.

Minutes had passed. My body was tired from running and I haven't heard anything for a while. All I could hear were my heavy breaths and pounding heart. Adrenaline was still pumping throughout my body as I waited.

I felt relief wash over me. I didn't hear anything anymore. They must have taken a different turn. Turning back towards my home, something pushed me to the ground. Hard.

I yelped as pain erupted in my leg. I quickly kicked out my legs. Something growled as my foot came into contact with the beast behind me. Taking the opportunity, I pushed myself forward and turned myself around so I could face the monster.

I gasped.

I knew Wolvens were massive but this one was easily six feet tall on four legs. Its black fur made it a little hard to see in the darkness if it weren't for the moon glowing brightly.

A growl erupted throughout its body as its eyes locked with my own. Dark, red orbs like none I have ever seen were looking down at me. They were so dark they appeared crimson.

The wolf looked confused, tilting its head. It sniffed the air and emotions I couldn't recognise filled its crimson eyes.

I crawled backwards, my movements slow and steady as the pain in my leg worsened each time I moved. The beast walked closer towards me.

My body ached as the beast eyed me. I was captivated by the beauty of its fur, wanting to go to it, to feel the softness of its fur against my skin—

Wait! What was wrong with me?

"P—please, let me go, I—I mean . . ." The words escaped me as the wolf walked close to me. It's a huge form looking down at me as my back came in contact with a tree.

It whined when it took notice of the wound on my leg, still bleeding. I was too shocked to understand what was happening. Why was it whining?

The monster seemed to realise what it was doing and growled at me once more.

There was nowhere to go. Nowhere to run. I closed my eyes and braced myself for what was to come. I should have stayed in bed.

Who was I kidding? I never would have been able to stay home. The night was too appealing to me. But now look where it led me. Death.

I slowly opened my eyes when nothing happened. The wolf had disappeared as if it were never there. The only evidence I had was the cut on my leg, blood trickling down my leg.

Without wasting another second, I limped towards the town where I lived. Half an hour later, I closed the door behind me as I made my way into the house.

I heard movement coming from upstairs and down ran my aunt, a candle illuminating her face as she held it up high to gain a better view of me. "Liv, what the hell—." My aunt gasped as her eyes locked onto my injured leg and dirty clothing. " What happened to you?" She instantly pulled me into the living room and lit the fireplace to warm me up. I haven't even realised I have been shivering.

"A—a wolven." I managed to muster as my aunt pulled off my filthy cloak.

"I told you, never go outside when it's dark. Do you know how much worse this could have been? You could have been killed, torn apart, and I never would have seen you again. It would be a repeat of . . . of . . ." She began to sob.

"I didn't mean for this to happen. You know how much I love to go out at night, I'm sorry I couldn't help myself."

"Yes and look where it's gotten you." She gestured to the gash on my leg.

I didn't reply as my aunt left the room. When she returned, a bowl of fresh water was in her hand along with some bandages. I yelped when she poured the clear liquid onto my cut.

"This will stop it from becoming infected," my aunt said. I nodded as she then started to wrap the wound.

When she was done, she gave me some fresh clothes to change into. "You're starting to be a bad influence Alivia. What would you do if Amber or Avery tried to follow you?"

"I'm sorry, it won't happen again. I promise," I said.

My aunt nodded. "Go get into bed."

I did as I was told. I finally climbed onto the safety of my bed. I was exhausted but I could barely sleep with all the questions swamping my mind. *Why didn't it finish me off? It could have done so easily, but it didn't.*

Suddenly, I felt like I was being watched. Add that to the list of reasons I couldn't sleep. My eyes went straight to my window. I jumped up, blinking. The next time my eyes landed on the window, they were gone . . .

It was just there . . . the dark, red eyes.

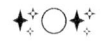

✦○✦

CHAPTER TWO
Ceremonial Preparation

✦▫✦

ALIVIA

I was running through the woods. My heart was pumping extra fast as adrenaline ran through my veins. I couldn't let it catch me.

A ferocious growl echoed through the trees, pushing me to run faster. The branches were reaching out as if to try and grab me. I avoided them as best I could . . .

My bare feet were bloody as twigs and sharp rocks dug into them but I didn't care. The fear of what could happen if I stopped moving was enough for the pain to fade away.

Suddenly I tripped to the ground. I yelped as pain pulsated through my ankle. It was twisted.

I hissed in pain, holding my ankle as if it would stop hurting if I did. I could no longer run. I would have to wait for my soon-to-be demise.

Another growl, only this time it was much louder. Closer. Dark red eyes emerged from the darkness and its entire body soon followed. The wolf looked more frightening and more massive than I remembered.

Please, don't hurt me. I remember thinking this is it before the beast lunged at me.

I bolted upright, screaming as I remembered the vivid details of the nightmare. Sweat smothered my forehead, matting my hair and face.

It has been a week since the incident with the Wolven. Its red eyes have plagued my dreams every night. I couldn't get them out of my head even when I was awake. I have no clue why.

The wound on my leg was now healed. My body was very quick at healing itself. The longest time it took for my injury to heal was two months. It was when I broke my arm, falling out of a tree.

All evidence that I had ever come in contact with that wolf was now gone, except for the nightmares that reminded me every night since

Padding over to my window, I could see the sun beginning to rise from behind the clouds. Soon I would have to start getting ready for the preparation of the Wolven's Ceremonial Shift.

Me and my friend Tristan would be required to help set up. It was the one time in the entire year that matured Wolvens could shift for the first time with the power of the blue moon and we would be allowed to witness it. You had to be at least sixteen to attend and we were both seventeen so we fit the age requirement.

I was honestly excited. I was never allowed to the other celebrations, but this time I have been chosen to attend. Even if it was just to set up and serve them for the duration of the night, it still feels thrilling.

Another reason I wanted to go was that, deep down, I wanted to see those red eyes again. There was a high chance that the Wolven would be there with the others of its kind.

I didn't know why I felt like this. Restlessness grew with every second I didn't get to see those hypnotising eyes. The only way I was going to find out was to see them again.

Finally dressed in a plain green dress and my dark curls tied up I left, making my way to the centre of town where the ceremonial garden was.

"Liv!" Tristan walked over to me when he saw me. I could see the excitement in his forest, green eyes as he embraced me in a tight hug.

Me and Tristan have been good friends since we were little. I watched him grow from a scrawny, little boy with a toothy grin to a handsome, muscled man now standing in front of me.

He was wearing a basic blue tunic with white breeches. I took in my fill of him. His long, blonde hair was in a tight ponytail, and his muscles were poking out of his clothes.

I have always had feelings for Tristan since we were young but never acted on it. We were only friends. I didn't want to complicate things.

"So what do we have to do?"

Tristan just shrugged his shoulders. "I've been waiting for one of the Elders to come and give orders." He crossed his arms over his chest, annoyed that he had to wait. I chuckled at his misery.

The elders were a high up human organisation who worked for the King. They were in charge of keeping the peace between us and them. They dealt with events and ensured everything ran smoothly.

They were the only humans considered important in the Wolven king's eyes.

Me and Tris have been waiting for ten minutes when an older looking man appeared at the entrance. He was easily in his forties and wore a black robe that reached the floor.

"Alivia Harmon? Tristan Sanrio?" The elder's voice was sharp and snappy as if he was trying to speed up the process.

Me and Tristan just nodded when our names were spoken then walked over to him, not daring to speak unless he asked us to.

"Mr Sanrio, you will be needed for setting up the King's banners. Flowers are to be put on every single table, the King's chair must be centred perfectly and coated with fur and I want this all done within three hours, am I clear?"

"Yes, sir." Tristan left me with the old man who stared at me. I didn't know if I was meant to say anything as his eyes scanned my body.

"Hmm, you don't look very strong . . ." he said. I already disliked this man. "Can you cook?"

"I err . . ." I had never really needed to cook before. My aunt always prepared meals with the help of my cousins. I never really had to bother or even try.

"Come on girl, speak up."

"No sir," I whispered. I felt useless. I didn't really have a lot of skills that I was aware of right then.

"I take it you can at least serve, am I right?" I nodded. "Very well, you'll be serving the Wolvens their drinks tomorrow night but for now you may help Mr. Sanrio."

Before he left, the Elder had told me a set of rules I was to abide by: Don't look any of the Wolvens in the eye, especially the king. Don't speak unless spoken to. Most importantly . . . obey any orders given from a Wolven.

✦○✦

CHAPTER THREE
Locked Gazes

✦▢✦

ALIVIA

"Alivia, I like your dress," my little cousin, Amber, said. Her cheeks blushed as she complimented me. I chuckled at her embarrassed face.

"Thank you." I leaned down and kissed her red cheeks.

"I—I wish I could go with you," she whispered so her mother couldn't hear.

We both already knew that her mother didn't want me to go. The thought of being near the Wolvens frightened her. But I had no choice, once you have been chosen you had to go. Disobeying could be punishable by death.

"One day you will, just not today." I smiled at her.

She was so adorable with her innocent brown eyes and light blonde hair that reached the middle of her back. She was only six but could pass as four with how small her body was. She was the complete opposite of Avery who was two years older than her. Avery had darker blonde hair and had more of an attitude. She had to always be right and hated not getting her way. But I loved them both dearly. I had basically helped raise them after their father had died.

Avery appeared at the door. "Mum says you better leave now if you want to leave on time," she said firmly as if she was older than she was. I chuckled.

I told her, "Don't worry, I'm leaving now," then gave them both a quick hug before I made my way to the kitchen.

"Liv, that dress suits you nicely."

"Thanks, Helena."

All women who would be serving had to wear the same. A knee-length white dress. The front of the dress had a red crescent moon which transitioned into a wolf's head to match the same image on the banners placed around the ceremonial garden. It represented the Wolven king. It was his symbol, and I believe it represented how the Wolvens worshipped the moon.

"Please, promise me you will do everything you can to not attract too much attention from those foul beasts," my auntie said, a look of disgust on her face when she said the word "beast."

I rolled my eyes. She was always so cautious and worried.

"Just promise me," she pleaded.

I always pitied that look on her face whenever she got overly worried about something. I always ended up doing as she asked and this, unfortunately, was no exception.

"Okay, I promise."

A while later I was in the ceremonial garden. The Wolvens wouldn't arrive until it was dark out when the garden would be bathed in the moon's light. A full moon.

Banners were put up everywhere, the symbol of the Wolven King placed in the centre of all of them.

In the middle of the garden was a statue of a vampire and a Wolf. The Wolf looked fierce and angry as its claws were buried into the vampire's chest. It was to mark that they were much stronger than the Vampires.

Of course, the Wolvens would want to show off. They were a proud species.

My eyes caught sight of the tall platform placed at the end of the garden. Another banner placed above it. In the middle was a giant throne. It was the size of at least two grown men. The arms and wooden frame were covered in fur as the rest of it was red leather. It was gorgeous, I thought.

Smaller versions which were much plainer than the throne were placed next to it. Two either side. Must be for the King's most trusted guards, I assumed.

"Beautiful." I looked beside me to see Tristan had come and stood next to me.

"I know, you did a good job." I smiled up at him as he put his arm around my waist and pulled me into a hug.

Leaning down to my ear, he whispered, "I was talking about you." I felt his hot breath fan across my face as he spoke, making a shiver run down my spine. He stood up straight again and winked at me.

Today he was wearing a white tunic, the king's symbol on the right side of his chest. His hair was in the same ponytail as the day before but he still looked handsome.

"Not so bad yourself." I felt heat rise onto my neck and cheeks, suddenly feeling very flushed.

"The Wolves will be arriving soon, are you ready?"

I hadn't told Tristan about my encounter with the Red-eyed wolf. I didn't feel he needed to know and he was quite protective. He would have been furious and done something reckless if he knew the monster had caused me pain.

"Yeah, I'll be fine." I felt the need to reassure him that tod0ay I would be alright. I wasn't really sure if it was the honest truth. I didn't know how I would react if I did get to see the red-eyed wolf and if it would even recognise me.

"I don't see any Elders," I said, looking around.

"They're not attending, they're busy dealing with other matters."

"Like what?" This was an important ceremony, it was strange they weren't here to show respect to the king.

"Vampires, I think."

"Vampires?"

Tristan didn't have the time to reply as the horns blew, signalling the arrival of the Wolvens. I waited beside Tristan, his hands running up and down my back in reassurance. It was a long anxious wait before the first few wolves appeared.

They were in their human forms with well-built and tall bodies. They were easily over six feet. I felt small compared to their size. Their faces held no emotion as they took their seats at the white tables around the garden.

Their mates were beside them. The females looked flawless and were slightly taller than the average human woman as they stood next to their partners.

I didn't know much about Wolvens and their mates but I knew it was like their other half. Someone who was promised to them by their goddess.

From what I could see, the mated Wolvens looked affectionate towards the other. It made my chest clench in pain. They were very lucky to have something close to true love.

I didn't dare allow myself to look up for too long. Looking them in the eyes was disrespectful so I never raised my eyes beyond their chests. Tristan did the same.

Another horn blew and came the entourage of younger-looking Wolvens. These were the mature ones and would transform into a wolf. They looked no older than thirteen if I had to guess.

Tonight would be very special for them. A matured wolf could only shift for the first time under the light of the blue moon like tonight. Their faces gleamed with excitement as they made their way to the platform, standing a few metres away from their King's throne.

The third and last horn blew.

My throat hitched as men, stronger than the ones previously, came into view. They were massive and looked deadly. Their faces were stone cold as they walked on top of the platform and sat on the four seats beside the King's throne. After they were seated, he finally made an appearance.

I gasped. If I had thought the other men looked strong and deadly, I was wrong. This man looked ten times more powerful than all of them combined. He had dark, black hair shaved down the sides, leaving it long on top. His facial features were sharp and his expression hard. He wore a metal chain around his neck, the king's symbol placed at the centre of his chest.

But what hypnotised me the most was when I allowed my gaze to lock onto his eyes.

Dark red eyes.

I couldn't look away. I felt a pull towards him, my body wanting to be near him. It took everything in me to stay put.

Before I could even try and look away his eyes found my own. I couldn't move, couldn't look away. I know what I was doing was beyond disrespectful but I had no idea what had come over me. Time seemed to freeze as he stared into my eyes.

Locked gazes.

He was the one I had seen just a week ago. It was the Wolven king.

✦✧○✦✧

CHAPTER FOUR
Impossible

✦▫✦

ALIVIA

    I'm not sure how long we stayed like that, just staring into each other's eyes. His cold eyes were filled with emotions I couldn't decipher. I couldn't move nor speak as I mentally took note of how attractive he was. It was unlike me to feel this way towards his kind.

    Growing up in a home that despised their kind had a massive impact on my judgement towards them. They vowed to protect us in exchange for servitude and yet that didn't stop my uncle from being ripped apart like an animal.

    And yet here I was, admiring not just any Wolven but their king.

    "Liv?" Tristan whispered down at me, worry laced in his voice. It pulled me out of my trance and back into reality.

    I looked around, everything was now silent as all eyes were now on me. Curiosity in every single gaze. I wanted to disappear right then, for the earth to swallow me whole and leave no proof that I was ever here.

    I quickly faced the ground, ashamed of what I had done. I had looked the Wolven king in the eyes. It was starting to settle in, the seriousness of what I had just done. The disrespect I had just shown.

It made it worse that it was him I had kicked back in the woods. It was him who had chosen not to murder me. My thoughts were spiralling out of control as the scene around me took dominance over my mind, bringing me back to reality.

I felt my heart beat faster as my body began to tremble. The King slowly approached, heading towards the spot where I stood frozen. I flinched when a growl reverberated through his chest.

"Get your fucking hands off her!" he growled, which made me flinch. Tristan instantly obeyed, bringing his hand back to his side and staring at this beast of a man with wide eyes.

A wave of warmth went to my core at the sound of his voice, even though it terrified me. I couldn't control my body's reaction to it. His voice was so deep and caressing but in the same instance, I was frightened at how close he was to us. To me.

I felt tingles on my chin as the king's fingers made contact. Gently, he lifted my gaze back up to him. He just stared into my frightened cobalt eyes but said nothing.

My body finally relaxed when he carried on walking to the platform where his throne was set. From the corner of my eye, I could see all the Wolvens bowing their heads towards their King's direction but I didn't dare to look up.

I was confused at how angry he acted to Tristan's arm around my waist rather than at the fact I had looked at him. Instead, he wanted me to look at him.

"Tonight, we are celebrating the first shift of our matured pups under the power of the blue moon . . ."

My stomach spiralled out of control as he spoke, more warmth flooding my core as I felt slightly damp between my legs.

"When the moon is at its highest peak in the sky, the ritual shall begin. But for now you are all welcome to celebrate!"

A horn blew and drums sounded as the Wolvens brought their mates to the centre and began to dance with the beat of the drum.

"What was that about?" Tristan's hands were balled into fists and he seemed furious. His jaw ticked as he breathed out heavily.

"I have no idea," I whispered. "Let's just do what we came here for and then we never have to see them again."

That seemed to work as he visibly calmed down, nodding his head.

"I'll see you after?"

I nodded to Tristan as he left to resume his duties. I quickly grabbed a tray of drinks and began walking around, keeping my eyes to the ground as Wolvens grabbed from the tray freely.

The sound of the drums was lovely as the wolves danced gracefully. I wish I could have joined in but I wasn't here to celebrate.

I felt my body tingling, my muscle beginning to ache slightly as the tray in my hand began to feel heavier. I didn't know what was happening to me and red eyes glaring at me didn't help.

The drums began to quicken as the movement of the Wolvens matched the pace. It was making me dizzy, having all the Wolvens move in a circle as I tried to make my way around them, careful not to drop the tray.

I felt a hand land on my shoulder and I stiffened. I turned expecting it to be Tris but was surprised to see a large, beefy man standing there instead. I recognised him as one of the four men that walked in just before the King arrived.

I quickly bowed my head, waiting for him to grab from the tray so that I could move on.

"Look at me, girl." I didn't dare look at him, I had already broken the rule once and I didn't want to repeat my mistake. "Do you dare defy my command?"

"I—I was told I wasn't allowed to look at you," I said under my breath, with the beat of the drum playing loudly I was surprised he could hear me, even with his wolf hearing.

"You were also told to never disobey a fucking Wolven. Now fucking look at me!" he said. His tone was cold. I couldn't help but feel scared. My heart was racing

I lifted my gaze to his face. He had a scar down the side of his jaw and one across his eyebrow. His eyes were a pale yellow with an orange tinge around his irises.

He gave me a curious look, tilting his head to the side as he examined me. "Your name." It wasn't a question, more like a command.

"Alivia, sir." I didn't know why he was even talking to me, let alone ask for my name.

He ran a giant hand through his brown hair as he regarded me. He looked at me as if I was some sort of disgusting creature that he wanted to be rid of. "You smell . . . strange," he finally said, more to himself than me. "Human but . . . not quite."

I furrowed my eyebrows, confused by his statement. Did I smell strange? What was that supposed to mean?

He sniffed the air once more. "You're coming with me." He grabbed me by the arm in a tight grip as he brought me to the platform.

"What? What are you doing?"

"Don't speak!" He snapped down at me.

I felt my cheeks redden with anger. I had done my best to avoid breaking any rules but I guess this foul wolf-man didn't give a shit.

I trembled in his hold, not understanding what was happening to my body. I began to ache all over once more. My arms and legs cramping as I was dragged by the horrid brute.

"We have a problem." He spoke when we arrived just before the King's throne. The man holding my arm quickly bowed.

The King's crimson eyes flickered between me and his guard. I heard a low growl before he spoke. "What's the meaning of this, Arif?" The king's teeth were gritted as he waited for Arif's response.

"The girl." He gestured to me before he pulled me closer to the king. I trembled all over as I looked at him with frightened eyes.

The King's eyes swelled with emotion and he looked to be struggling to stay still. His crimson eyes flickered back to Arif. "What about her?" He said impatiently as if this topic was boring and wasting his time.

"She smells human at first but when I took a closer sniff." The king's eyes swirled with what resembled anger as Arif continued speaking. ". . . She smelt like a wolf . . . like us, and continues to be getting stronger."

I looked up to Arif, my body starting to tremble more. What was he saying? *I smelt like them? That's impossible.* If I was one of them, I surely would have known by now.

The king's eyes snapped to my own. I quickly looked down, keeping my head low. My form shook under his heated gaze. I flinched when he leant towards my neck and took a sniff. Still shaking as he pulled away, I waited for what was to happen next.

"You're right. I'll have to deal with this later. Leave her here whilst I wrap this up."

Arif bowed and walked away, leaving me standing before the king.

"Quickly, stand here." He pointed to the left of his throne and I quickly followed his command, petrified as to what was happening.

My auntie's plea from this morning came to mind. So much for me not drawing any attention to myself. Now it seemed that I was at the centre of a freak show, free for all to see.

A horn blew as the drums silenced. All the dancing couples looked up to their king. Some spared a few curious glances at me before their attention went back to him, who was now standing.

He was much taller than me. Being so near him gave me a strange sense of comfort but at the same time, he made me feel small and vulnerable.

His power came from him in waves. It forced the Wolvens to bow their heads. I felt a strong urge to do the same but I didn't.

"Pups, come stand in the centre."

Seven Wolvens stepped forward. They held their heads up high as they stood in the glow of the moon's light. The glow filled the entire garden, bathing all of us in its luminescence.

My skin began to tingle. It was more intense than before as my hand and legs began to ache once more. I tried to stand still and ignore it as the King spoke.

"Thank the goddess Elune, for the power of her light shall bathe you and grant you strength, agility, speed like the wolf . . ." he continued the speech. He spoke of their Goddess several times, thanking her for their lives and power.

I couldn't focus on much more than that as my head began throbbing. My hands instantly went to the side of my face. The tingling sensation came back much more intensely that I couldn't ignore it as It covered my entire being, inside and out.

My muscles cramped and my legs buckled. I screamed in agony. The King was instantly at my side.

I noticed I wasn't the only one screaming as the pups in the centre were also in pain.

I screamed once again as another wave of pain washed over me. He didn't seem to know what to do. He looked down at me with worry as if he truly cared about my well-being. I couldn't hold his gaze long as the pain erupted once more.

I felt the bones in my body beginning to snap. With each snap, I screamed. I didn't understand what was happening to me, it was pain unlike I had ever felt before. It wasn't just my body changing. I felt a presence infiltrate my mind, trying to invade my senses and take control. It was excruciatingly painful.

Just as I thought I was going to pass out, the snapping of my bones suddenly stopped as I laid limp on the floor. The tingles are still there but they were slowly fading as well.

I took shallow breaths, too sore to sit up. I heard loud gasps coming from the crowd. I looked up to the King. I assumed he would be as shocked as the others but instead, his eyes seemed pained but he quickly hid the emotion with an emotionless glare.

I opened my mouth to speak but no words came out. Instead, something close to a growl escaped. I tried again and the same thing happened.

Sitting up, I looked down at a pair of dark, brown paws. The white fabric of my dress was shredded next to them.

My eyes grew wide at the realisation.

No, I couldn't be.

It was impossible.

✧○✧

CHAPTER FIVE
Captured

✦▢✦

ALIVIA

 All eyes were on me. Even the other newly shifted wolves didn't look away. I trembled under the pressure of their gaze. This was too much attention that I couldn't bear.

 How could this be happening?

 "Let go of me!" I turned to find Tristan being pulled back by two male Wolvens. They had strong grips on his arms as he struggled against them. "Liv!" I found his green eyes and saw the concern that was written across them.

 I wanted to go to him but I didn't know if they would allow me. I felt a whine escape as I looked back at the male in front of me, pleadingly.

 "Adrenous, what do you want us to do?" Arif was at the king's side.

 Adrenous? It suited him well.

 They were both staring at me, Adrenous more intensely. Arif just looked at me as if I was some sort of abomination and maybe I was. I really didn't like him as I returned a glare of my own. His eyes lit up in amusement but the disgust was still evident.

 How dare he find this amusing.

 My eyes flickered back to Adrenous's. He seemed to be thinking intensely.

I didn't know whether to run or stand still. To be fair, I wanted to go for the former but maybe the latter would be a much less stupid idea.

Adrenous slowly strolled towards me. He leant down and sniffed my neck. Something that resembled lust ignited in his eyes. Without my permission, my body moved towards him on its own. I reached out and inhaled his scent.

What was wrong with me? Here I was randomly sniffing the Wolven king. This couldn't be normal.

But I have to admit he smelt delicious, like the woods after it rained, with a hint of spice. Something inside of me wanted him. I felt desire pool low in my belly at our proximity. He was mine.

Mine? What was I thinking? He didn't belong to me. How could he? We had only just met and already I was an emotional mess in front of him. I had to get my act together before this got out of hand.

I forgot about everyone who was watching us as I and Adrenous took our fill of the other.

"Get away from her!"

I snapped my head away from those crimson eyes in time to witness Tristan being pushed to the ground. The guards held him down by the shoulders to keep him there.

Being a wolf all I could do was whine again. "Arif grab me a blanket."

Arif looked up at Adrenous, surprised. Conflict waged in his eyes before he walked off and came back a few moments later with a thick blanket in his arms. His eyes showed agitation as he handed the blanket over to Adrenous. This Wolven seriously had some anger issues.

The King placed the quilt over my dark fur. "Shift." The simple word held so much power I couldn't resist the command or at least my own body couldn't.

The tingling sensation washed over my body once again. It wasn't as painful as the first time but still caused me discomfort. I felt the bones within my body move once again as the dark fur retreated back to wherever it came from.

    I felt goosebumps as the chilly night air surrounded my now naked body, even under the blanket.

    "We're leaving!" He shouted the command to his Wolvens. Looking back at me, he said, "You're coming with us."

    I violently shook my head. No matter how I felt being next to him, I couldn't leave my aunt and cousins. They wouldn't even know why I haven't come home. This was totally barbaric and outrageous. I don't know how he could think that I would just follow him willingly.

    "I can't go with you. I won't." I slowly stepped away from him. Adrenous was now glaring at me. I stepped away before he could even try to grab my arm. "I'm not going!"

    I quickly ran off the platform and to where I had last seen Tristan. He was a little dirty but was still struggling against the two Wolvens holding him down. I now recognised the two wolves to be the other two who had sat beside the King. They were obviously more powerful than the others just by judging them off their appearances alone.

    "Grab her!" Adrenous shouted to the two beside Tristan. They instantly let go of my friend and came towards me. I dodged in between them and grabbed Tristan's hand, pulling him up off the floor and leading him towards the woods.

    My bare feet were stepping on twigs and stones that laid on the grass floor but I ignored it. We had to get away.

    "Liv, what the hell just happened? You're one of them!"

    "Tris, I'm just as confused as you right now but at this moment we have to run before they catch us."

    I heard the howls of the wolves echoing through the trees. We weren't going to outrun them. The blanket I was trying to keep around me was making it more difficult to run, but I had to try.

    "Liv, stop! They're too fast, we won't make it."

I slowed down to a halt. I stared up at Tris, defeat making its way to my face. "They're going to take me with them," I whispered. The feeling of failure washed over me like a bowl of cold water, shocking me back to the reality of what was going to happen.

I didn't want to be taken. I didn't even have time to adjust to the fact that I had fully transformed into a beast in front of a bunch of Wolvens. It all felt too unreal to me.

"You're one of them, Alivia. You're meant to be with them." His eyes were angry as he looked down at me. His hands formed into tight fists at his side.

"What are you trying to say?" I felt my chest tighten as my friend took a step back. Guilt overcame his expression. He didn't even bother to look me in the eye. His fists loosened, his eyes distant as he thought of how to reply.

Before he could come up with a response, we were surrounded by ferocious wolves. I turned around taking in the sight of all of them. Snarls and growls filled the air, as they trapped us.

The king, still in human form, stepped from behind the wolves. His cold, red orbs looked scary, his anger radiating from him in waves as my body struggled to stay standing.

"You try a stunt like that again and I won't hesitate to kill that fucking boy." He looked at Tristan as if he truly wanted to rip his heart out, right then and there.

Tristan didn't reply but his whole body was tensed and his hands were shaking. From fear or anger, I couldn't tell.

I thought he was going to grab me by the arm again but screeched when he picked me up and placed me over his shoulders. I struggled against him and even tried to pound his back with my fists but he wouldn't drop me.

"Drop me right this instance." He didn't say anything as I still struggled under his firm grip.

"Drop me, you bastard." I tried to pound his back a little harder to get his attention and I guess it worked because he let out one of his deadly growls.

"You are not at liberty to command me to do anything and I assure you my parents were happily married." He continued walking further into the woods, towards the direction of his territory.

I relaxed in his hold as my struggling wasn't working and I was extremely exhausted. I spotted four people ahead of us and had to adjust myself to see who it was.

Arif was standing with the other three guards that were sat beside the King during the celebration. They looked struck as they watched Adrenous walk towards them with me over his shoulder.

"Adrenous, what's with kidnapping the girl?" A dark haired man with green eyes chuckled at the sight of me slumped over the brute's back.

"It's not kidnapping if she's mine."

I snorted at his comment. How dare he call me his.

The man's green eyes glowed brighter as a smile erupted on his face. "Are you saying what I think you're saying?"

Adrenous plopped me on the ground next to the men. I quickly adjusted the blanket in order to hide myself more. "Yes and I'm trusting you four to take her back home, while I handle this."

"Of course."

I quickly narrowed eyes on Adrenous. "Wait! You're leaving me with them?"

"They're my four most trusted generals. They'll make sure you don't do anything foolish," he said. I glared at him as he began to leave again.

Adrenous looked at me once more before he shifted into that frightening wolf I remembered from last week. I felt warmth disappear from my body as he disappeared behind the trees.

I looked back at the tall men staring down at me. Arif's yellow eyes looked cold, his lips in a thin line. I really didn't like him. The man with the green eyes smiled at me, his eyes were much warmer and more welcoming than Arif's.

"I'm Rylan." He offered his hand out for me to shake. My hands being too occupied with the blanket still wrapped around me, I shook it a little. "Umm yeah, you're going to need some clothes." He retreated his arm back to his side. "What's your name?"

"Alivia," I answered.

"Nice. I like it." Rylan gestured to the other two men standing with us and said, "That's Titan and Hunter." The two nodded their heads politely at me but didn't say much more.

Titan had a dark beard which made him look much older than he probably was. His grey eyes looked sad as if he had experienced so much pain. They were a contrast to his light caramel skin that was nicely toned.

Hunter was a slight opposite to Titan. He had dirty blonde hair and sky blue eyes that were much more innocent than Titan's. He was slightly leaner and looked more flexible than the others but was still nicely built. They were all at least a head taller than me.

"And you've already met this moody prick," Rylan said. Arif glared at Rylan, causing me to chuckle. I already knew I was going to like him.

"Nice to meet you all," I said, trying not to shiver from the cold.

They all seemed to notice as they looked at each other. They caught me watching as they turned back to me. Arif was the first to speak. "Let's get the girl back before she dies from pneumonia." Malice laced his tone as he shot me a glare.

I couldn't get over how blunt and rude he was towards me. Maybe it was just the way he was. It wasn't my fault they were stuck with me. I didn't even wish to be here.

"We better get you back home," Rylan said. I knew he wasn't talking about my home back in town with my aunt and cousins. He meant his home. Adrenous's kingdom.

It would never be my home.

✦✧○✦✧

CHAPTER SIX
General Skills

✦◻✦

ALIVIA

"Will I have to be watched constantly?" I asked Rylan. We were currently sitting in front of a fireplace to try and warm me up. I have done nothing but shiver since we've arrived.

On the way back to their kingdom, the four Wolvens had shifted. I had to mount myself on Rylan's back because I was still too sore to try and shift myself. When we reached their home, Rylan quickly brought me a plain white dress to change into. It was very comfortable and soft, much better than the blanket I was forced to hold.

"I'm afraid so," Rylan bent forward, grabbing a stick to poke the fire with. "It's not safe for you to be left alone here yet, and there's still some arrangements we need to figure out first."

Out of the four generals, Rylan was the only one who offered to watch over me for the remainder of the day. I didn't mind though. I felt more comfortable with him than I did with the other three.

"Am I in trouble?" I asked as I gazed into the fire. I was afraid that Adrenous would punish me for being a Wolven that wasn't a member of their kingdom.

"No you're not in trouble, trust me. Adrenous won't hurt you," he sais. I felt my body relax, but I knew he wasn't done answering. "But we still need to know why you weren't born within our borders, even if you only are just part Wolven."

"Well, I never met my parents," I admitted, Rylan staring down at me with concerned eyes. "I was found in the woods when I was just a baby, by my uncle who passed a few years back." Tears brimmed my eyes at the thought of my uncle as Rylan gently rubbed my back.

"Will I be allowed to go back to my family soon?" I truly missed them, even if it has only been hours since I last saw them. They needed to know I was safe before my auntie started to worry about me or begin to think the worse..

I could see Rylan shifting in his spot as he threw the stick into the fire, causing it to blacken as the fire danced around it. He looked to be thinking of an appropriate response, his green eyes looked apologetic as he looked into my frightened ones. "I can't promise you anything. Adrenous is going to have to explain. It's not my place to tell you."

"Tell me what?" The anticipation of it all was too much for me. I couldn't handle not knowing what was to happen to me.

"As I said, Adrenous will have to explain."

I huffed at his response. Standing up, I walked towards the draped window. I needed a quick distraction from the dead-end conversation. As I pulled the curtains apart, it revealed gorgeous scenery. We were surrounded by giant trees with bright green leaves. Flowers were blossoming everywhere, a mixture of purple, pink and blue. A huge empty field was in the centre.

A gorgeous lake split the field in half. A bricked bridge was the only way to get between the two fields. The gorgeous light of the moon reflected off the lake. Their territory was isolated but gorgeous and peaceful. If I wasn't here against my will, I might have enjoyed being here.

I looked further up past the field, a couple of smaller buildings surrounded the area. More trees spaced together tightly were behind them. They must have been some of the other wolves' homes or perhaps used for other purposes.

I was currently in the king's giant estate. It was giant. Many different rooms spread out and at least three floors tall. It was much bigger than any other building I have ever seen.

"Beautiful, isn't it?" Rylan stood next to me. I didn't even hear him walk over. I glanced at him and then back at the gorgeous view, slowly nodding my head in agreement. It truly was beautiful.

"How did you become one of Adrenous's generals?" I didn't quite know why I asked but I was suddenly interested.

Rylan looked taken aback by the question as memories seemed to fill his eyes at the thought. "Me and the other three grew up with Adrenous. We also inherited the titles from our fathers who were Adrenous father's generals before him. We're also the only ones he truly trusts with his life, not just because we grew up with him but we each have great abilities."

"Like what?"

"Well Arif is quite fast and strong whether he's in wolf form or human form and I don't just mean like Wolven strong, he's stronger than anything you might have seen before. Titan is our best fighter and trains the newbies who want to learn. He has excellent vision and can calculate an opponent's next move before they even know what it is. Hunter is our best tracker, he can close his eyes and tell you every single creature in a mile radius."

I felt my eyes widen as he explained. I had no idea what kind of abilities the Wolvens could behold. I don't think anyone did.

"And you?" I said. A smile erupted on his face. I furrowed my eyebrows at him. "What?"

"I'll show you, but I need you to trust me." He said as he offered me his hand for reassurance.

I looked up at him warily. I wasn't sure what he was going to do but it made me curious. I hesitantly gave him my hand as he pulled me closer to him, closing his eyes.

"Close your eyes," he whispered. I did as he said, shutting my eyes tightly. My head started to ache as my mind felt another presence. I could feel Rylan picking at my memories and innermost thoughts.

I began to panic, pulling away from him.

His grip on my arm was tight, I couldn't move away, his hold on me unwavering. I felt a sensation wash over me as I tried to force Rylan out of my mind.

He instantly let go, bringing both his hands to the side of his head and groaning in pain as he fell to his knees.

"What was that?" I accused, he looked up at me with his own baffled expression.

"I was just . . ." He groaned. His hands were still cradling his head as he tried to stand up. "How did you do that?"

"Do what? You're the one who was invading my privacy." I snapped.

"No," He was finally able to stand up again, looking at me in astonishment. "I was trying to help you," he whispered.

Help me? My anger subsided. "How?"

Rylan scrunched his face as he thought for a moment. He didn't answer my question when he finally said, "You pushed me out and attacked my mind. No one has ever been able to do that before?" His green eyes were filled with the same confusion that was reflected in my own.

"What do you mean?"

"Erm, I'm not exactly sure . . ." he said whilst rubbing his head.

The door suddenly opened. I turned my attention from Rylan to see Adrenous entering the room.

His top half was naked, showing off his bulging biceps and muscles which were constantly shifting as he walked. My breath hitched as I stared at his muscled body. His eyes looked angry but instantly softened when they found my own.

33

He looked as if he was holding himself back from speaking as he eased his way further into the room.

Rylan instantly bowed his head. I didn't know if I was meant to but I hesitantly copied Rylan's action. He walked over to me and gently lifted my chin. Tingles erupted at the contact. My eyes met his. They were truly captivating, like two sparkling rubies looking down at me. He gently said, "There is no reason you should be bowing to me."

Butterflies erupted in my stomach as his dark voice caressed the air around me. My cheeks heated, possibly turning a dark red. Rylan awkwardly coughed, making me and Adrenous turn our attention to him. "How did it go?"

"It could have gone better." Adrenous's eyes were angry once again as his body tensed in front of me, his hand releasing my chin.

Rylan frowned. His green eyes filled with dread at Adrenous's response.

"We'll discuss this further once I get her ready for the night."

But I wasn't ready to go to bed.

Rylan nodded his head as he grinned at me. "She looks as if she's going to collapse with exhaustion."

I snorted at his comment causing, Rylan to chuckle and a hint of amusement to dance across Adrenous's eyes. I was too muddled with all that had occurred today that I doubted I would be able to sleep tonight.

Adrenous whispered something to Rylan causing him to nod his head and leave the room. He quickly shot me one of his friendly smiles before exiting the room. What was that about?

I couldn't linger on it as Adrenous unexpectedly picked me up and cradled me in his arms, carrying me out the room and up a flight of stairs. I was surrounded by his warmth and before I realised it, I had leaned further into his chest and breathed in his spicy scent. I sighed in bliss.

Adrenous stepped into a dark room. There was a silhouette of a giant bed in the middle but everything else was too dark to make out. The room was massive, much bigger than the other room we were just in.

There was a door on the left that Adrenous was heading towards. The door opened to reveal a large bathingroom, white tiles covering the wall from the ceiling to the floor and then the floor itself was made up of white tiles. A bath was placed in the middle and was already filled with boiling water.

After putting me down, he started to undo his trousers. I turned away, my face flushing red. "What do you think are you doing?" Did he seriously think I would be comfortable seeing him naked? I felt him shuffle behind me and kick away his clothes that I could just about see, using my peripheral vision.

What have I gotten myself into?

I felt Adrenous move my hair to the side, my heart beating heavily. He leant down and sniffed my neck, breathing in deeply, my entire body erupting with goosebumps at the feel of his breath fanning the sensitive skin of my neck.

This was completely inappropriate but it felt natural and comforting.

As I was beginning to relax, a new terror coursed through my body at his next word. "Strip."

"Ex—excuse me?" I blurted out. I wasn't getting undressed in front of him. I barely knew him. He must have been trying to gain something from me and I doubted my fear and embarrassment was what he wanted.

Adrenous didn't say anything as he drew his hands up my back and halted at the laces of my dress. I felt him tug at one of the knots and I instantly pulled away and turned to face him, no longer caring that his manhood was out for all to see. Just like that part of him, he too was a dick. "I'm not getting undressed in front of you!" I yelled at him.

"You're mine, Alivia," My name passed his lips easily and hearing him say it did things to me which I didn't want to admit. Instead, I glared at him. He said I was his as if I was some kind of possession that he could play with as he pleased. He added, "Let me take care of you."

I didn't know what he meant by that, all I knew was that I had no intention of doing as he had asked.

Instead of getting angry at my clear deviance, he looked at me with a smug smile. At the same time, his manhood began to harden. I quickly shifted my attention back to him in embarrassment. I could feel the heat rising to my cheeks as he looked at me, amused by my reaction to his now rock-hard member.

His eyes watched me intently as he parted his lips to speak. "I am not going to touch you sexually if that's what you're thinking." How stupid was he? Of course that's what I'd be thinking. Why else would a man ask a woman to strip in his presence? He sighed before continuing, seeming irritated that I didn't trust him. " I only want to bathe you."

I looked at him accusingly. He wanted to bathe me? Did he think I was unable to do so myself?

"I am very much capable of doing so without your help, thank you very much," I retorted. Assuming he would leave it like that, I headed for the door to the bedroom. I came to a stop as his arm reached out across my vision, his hand landing on the door as he closed it roughly. All I could do was stare at the arm in front of me, blocking me from leaving this awful situation.

I looked at him, anger rising to my surface, I let out an exasperated sigh and watched him as he stared at me with stubbornness.

It was the same look my cousin Avery would use when she wanted to get her way. I just never imagined I would be seeing it on the likes of a king. He was like a spoilt child.

My eyes watched his arm pulling away from the door. I stared at my escape instead of looking at him. He said, "You can either undress"—I inwardly rolled my eyes—"or I can do it for you." That's when I finally locked onto his face, glaring daggers at him. How could he be this stubborn? He arched a brow in amusement. "It's your choice."

It wasn't much of a choice.

I weighed the options deciding the former one was much less humiliating and at least then I could try and take as much control of the situation as I could.

I slowly walked to the edge of the bathtub, the steam from the water heating my skin. My arm went behind my back, searching for the knot, keeping my dress tight against my body. I tugged on it gently, untying it. Before I allowed my dress to fall to the floor, I said, "At least allow me the decency to do this without you staring."

Adrenous huffed in frustration before turning his back to me, his face now on the door.

I watched him carefully, making sure he didn't peak. I let the dress fall to my ankles and kicked it away. Now I was left in my undergarments. Slowly taking off the two pieces of material, I added them to the pile. I was fully naked as the chill in the air against the steam on my backside caused my nipples to harden of their own accord.

I quickly slipped into the hot water, a soft sigh leaving my lips.

I heard Adrenous's bare feet moving against the hard floor, heading closer to the bath . . . to me. I felt my body go rigid as he gently placed his legs in the water. His hands pushed my shoulders, making my body move forward so he could sit comfortably in the water behind me. His legs stretched out on either side of my body as I tried to shuffle forward and away from a part of him that was poking into my backside.

There wasn't much further I could go and I was still being poked by his member. An irritated sigh left my lips, causing Adrenous's body to shake in silent laughter. Dick.

On the side of the bath, there was a tray filled with different kinds of soaps. I reached for the lavender one but Adrenous got to it first when he realised my intention. I grinded my teeth together. If he could just let me bathe myself, I would feel a lot less uncomfortable.

The soap made contact with my back as he gently massaged me with it, the smell of lavender tingling my nose. My body, betraying me, relaxed, leaning into him for more contact. Adrenous's obliged, pushing the soap harder against my skin as he gently massaged my shoulders and neck.

He was truly gifted with his hands. My core contracted at the inappropriate thoughts crossing my mind. My body was such a traitor. A moan of pleasure passed my lips.

"I'm glad you're enjoying this." And there he went. He just had to ruin it with that smug comment. I snorted, causing him to chuckle. I'm glad someone was finding this funny, I thought bitterly. "Turn around," he said. I moved away from him as my body once again went rigid at his words, anxiety clawing its way up my throat. "I'm only going to clean you, nothing else." He whispered against my neck, the hairs on the back of my neck standing up at the contact of his breath once again on my skin. "Unless you want me to." He smirked against my shoulder.

Yes, I did want him to . . . but I wasn't going to give into him. "No I don't, thanks." My voice was unconvincing and I was sure he knew I was lying.

"Turn around." He repeated, more demanding this time.

I let a defeated sigh pass my lips as I slowly turned around in the tub, bringing my arms to my chest to conceal my breast from his view. I was going to protect whatever dignity I have left, whether it was little or none, I wasn't going to give him the satisfaction of embarrassing me completely.

Adrenous leant forward, moving my dark hair away from my face so that it was only dangling down my back, the tips landing in the water. "Beautiful." He whispered as he stroked my cheek. I was shocked, not knowing how to respond to such a comment, my body responding for me as my core clenched once again at his words.

All my life I have only had feelings for one boy. That was Tristan, but he never regarded me in the same way. Now here I was, naked with the Wolven king, who was commenting on my face and staring at me with lust in his crimson eyes.

The same lust which was beginning to build within me.

His eyes found my own as he retracted his left arm and brought the other up, soap in hand, to begin washing my neck and the front of my shoulders. When the soap could no longer travel down, due to my arms being in the way Adrenous arched a brow at me as if asking me to move them.

I shook my head vigorously, pulling my arms tighter to my chest if that were even possible, the urge to not give up on this one, weighing on my shoulders. I could be stubborn too.

When he realised I wasn't giving up without a fight, he stood on his feet and grabbed a different soap from the tray to massage himself with. My nose tingled, realising that it was the same scent I smelt when I was cradled to his chest.

I came face to face with his member, my cheeks blushing once more. He chuckled at my reaction and continued washing himself. How could he be so comfortable with this?

To distract myself, I reached for the lavender soap once again and this time I was successful. I began to clean my chest, careful to not give him a good view of my breast as I used the other arm to cover myself.

"If you wish to clean yourself properly, I'd advise that you stand up," he commented. I rolled my eyes at him . . .

He was right though, my legs and the bottom part of my body were all submerged in the water which meant cleaning them properly would be difficult. I gripped the soap tightly, angry at my predicament.

He held out his hand. I stared at it hesitantly and then grabbed it when I felt there were no other choices. I faced away from him so that all he could do was ogle at was my backside. That was all the action he was going to get.

I quickly washed myself properly and then we both sat back down when we were done. Adrenous then grabbed a jug from the tray and soaked both our hairs. He messaged some kind of lavender oil into my hair and then did so with his own, using the spiced oil. The two scents mingled together in the air and made quite an appealing scent, I thought.

Adrenous got out of the bath, leaving me in the now lukewarm water. A chill in the air gave me goosebumps once again.

He left the room. When he reappeared, he was now dressed in comfortable bottoms. His top half was still bare, his muscles on full display, shifting as he walked towards me. In his arms were a towel and a nightdress. Placing the clothes on the floor, he held out the towel for me. I stood up, arms still covering my chest and stepped out of the bath. He then wrapped a towel around my body.

"Get changed and then we can get you into bed." He smiled. I nodded. He left the room, allowing me some privacy at last.

I quickly dried myself and then threw the nightdress over my body. My eyes landed on a pair of underwear that was hidden by the dress and I quickly slid them on as well.

I left the room, colliding into Adrenous's chest. I didn't expect him to be right outside the door. He put his arms out and grabbed my shoulders to steady me. "Careful," he said, chuckling at my clumsiness.

Then he knelt down to place one arm around the back of my legs and the other behind my back as he cradled me to his chest like before. He headed towards the double bed.

Adrenous placed me gently onto the covers and tucked me in the thick, warm sheets. I yawned as exhaustion suddenly overwhelmed me. "When can I go home?" I blurted, half asleep. I felt myself succumbing to the darkness. I heard him whisper, though I wasn't sure if I heard him right.

"This is your home."

✦○✦

CHAPTER SEVEN
Keeping up with the Brute

✦▢✦

ALIVIA

    I woke up on my own, Adrenous nowhere in sight. The right side of the bed seemed uncreased like no one had slept there. I fell asleep too quickly last night and had assumed he would get in next to me but I guess he didn't. His actions were starting to confuse me.

    The events of last night tortured my dreams, making sleep unbearable until I was fully awake and aware of my surroundings. Adrenous touching me the way he did both confused me and aroused me.

    He has seen me laid out bare before him but had taken no sexual advances towards me nor forced me to engage in any. Instead, he caressed my skin with a gentle touch and bathed me like he truly wanted to take care of me. To be honest I think I enjoyed it more than I should have.

    The arousal was from the fact that he hasn't made any advances just like he promised. My head didn't want him to but my body was begging for it, making me feel weak. I'm surpised at how I easily submitted to his touch.

    I sat up, my feet caressing the soft fabric of the carpet. I stretched my arms and back forwards, a yawn escaping my already parted lips. I was still partially tired but I felt the need to do something productive. Anything would do as long as it distracted me from thinking of this place as, some might say, a prison.

The room was bigger than I had first thought last night. It also smelt slightly musky, as if no one has slept in here for years. This wasn't Adrenous's room. I took it this was my own and that gave me more relief than I thought it would. Personal space was becoming a big thing for me since meeting Adrenous, considering he has no boundaries.

The walls were cream and the carpet beneath my feet was a light beige, matching the bedsheets. However, the frame of the bed along with the furniture was pearl white. The furniture apart from the bed consisted of a wardrobe and nightstand.

My attention fell to a pile of clothes that was placed gently on top of the nightstand. I walked over to them, picked them up, and threw them on the bed. A piece of white paper fell from the pile and gently glided in the air before I caught it in my hand.

I unfolded the piece of paper and it read:

Get changed and meet Arif at the bridge.
Ps. Try and stay out of trouble.

—Adrenous

I threw the piece of paper, letting it glide through the air once more before it landed on the bed. *How could he entrust me to Arif? The one general who despised me?*

I sighed and grabbed the clothes. Instead of supplying me with another dress, there appeared to be a pair of black bottoms and a matching top with the king's symbol on it. I have always been used to dresses and felt slightly odd with having to change into this two-piece assemble.

Once I was dressed up, I made my way through the estate. None of the other generals seemed to be around, causing me to pout. I was hoping that I didn't have to spend the day with Arif and that I could opt for one of the others. I'd probably choose Rylan; he was much nicer than that moody bastard.

    I huffed as I regretfully made my way outside. Many servants watched me as I angrily stomped my way through the halls but I didn't give a shit. I'd make sure they all knew that their king had taken me against my will. *Let's see how well they'd look up to him then*, I thought smugly.

    Just as expected, Arif was waiting on the bridge, his expression reflecting my own displeasure. He obviously wasn't pleased to be babysitting me, as I was anywhere near him.

    "What took you so long?"

    I glared up at his yellow eyes, shrugging my shoulders. I knew that any response I gave him would be met with a distasteful reply. His expression turned irritated as he crossed over to the other side of the bridge, towards the woods. "Follow me," he demanded when he saw that I was just watching him without moving.

    I dragged my feet, trying to put as much distance between us as I followed him. He too wore similar items of clothing that I was wearing, only his were much larger to fit his bulky form.

    "Where exactly are we going?" I moaned, exhausted. We have been walking in a circle for over an hour and I needed to sit and rest. He finally halted when I decided to stop following him. He watched me in annoyance as I bent forward, hands on my knees, trying to catch my breath. My mouth and lips felt dry as I shot out my tongue trying to moisten my lips. I was thirsty.

    "I'm scouting the perimeter of the estate grounds." His hand fell to his waist and towards a pack that was attached to his belt, digging his hand inside and bringing it back out, he held a water bottle. He took a sip before handing it over to me.

    I hesitantly took it from him, eyeing him anxiously. "Thank you." I brought the bottle to my lips and drank, quenching my thirst. I handed back the bottle and he placed it back into his pack. "Why are you scouting the perimeter?" I asked.

"Fucking hell woman, do you always ask so many questions?" He remarked and then continued walking. This time I tried to keep up with him so that I was beside him rather than far behind.

"As a matter of fact, it's something I've acquired since being taken by your king." I retorted. I couldn't tell but I was sure the edges of his mouth twitched slightly at my comment. "So are you going to tell me why we're out here?"

He stopped dead in his tracks once again, causing me to do the same as I waited for his response. He looked down at me as if he didn't want to waste any more time talking to me. "Very well. We're checking to see if anything other than our kind has approached our borders." He answered. Continuing his walk, he added, "Now please stay quiet."

I bit my tongue at his last request, shutting my mouth and following him once again. Did he always have to be this difficult? It was like he knew how to get on people's nerves and didn't care. How he made it as a general was beyond me. Then I remembered that Rylan had mentioned Arif being abnormally strong and that he must have inherited the role from his father.

Going against his wishes, I opened my mouth once again. "You're very strong, I hear." His eyes flickered down at me for a second and then forwards once again. When he didn't answer I pushed further. "Is it true?"

"Yes," he said through gritted teeth.

Something inside of me warned me to stay silent but I just couldn't help myself. "I'm not sure I believe it." I decided to tease him. Surely I could push his buttons as he was pushing mine.

And it worked . . . a little too well. Before I knew it, he landed a full-blown punch on the tree trunk closest to us. It flew backwards, hitting two more with it at the impact. I just stood there with my mouth open as my eyes flickered from his fist to the trees. Poor trees.

My attention fell back to his hand that was now relaxed once again, with no scratch to be seen. "I believe it now," I said.

His yellow eyes were now fiery orange but slowly soothed back to his original pale yellow, the orange retreating back to just the edge of his irises. He shook his hand and flexed it a couple of times, his biceps shifting at the movement. I couldn't help but stare at his hand, the amount of force that had derived from it was unexpected and . . . amazing, I thought.

"That was incredible." I complimented.

Instead of thanking me, he just shook his head and strolled away from the spot where the tree once was. "Let's head back."

I glanced at the three damaged trees one last time before following him, this time remaining silent.

An hour later we exited the forest and entered the clearing, the giant fields and bridge connecting the two laid out before us.

This time the area was much more crowded, young children were running around near the edge of the lake and splashing each other as they laughed and played. They were all so carefree and I envied it.

Further up from where the children were playing some older males were sparring, their chests bare and sweaty as they tackled each other to the floor. Blood splattered from one of their noses as it came into contact with their rivals fist. I was strangely captivated by the sport, it seemed quite thrilling.

Everyone else was either chatting away or bathing and relaxing in the sun. I couldn't get over how carefree everyone was. Like there was nothing in this world to worry about. I wish everyone back home had that luxury but being human and vulnerable was a curse. A curse that I once shared before I discovered what I truly was.

We passed all of them as we crossed the bridge and headed for the main doors. Two men on guard bowed their heads to Arif, a sign of respect, as he nodded in reply and entered through the doors, which they pulled open for us.

I smiled at the two men politely as I entered and they returned me with the same respectful bow they had given Arif. It was strange having Wolvens show me this type of respect and politeness considering just a few days ago I was just considered a human to them. Now I was one of them. At least physically I was.

"Where are we going now?" I asked, we were travelling down the long hallways. Having no idea where they would lead to, I thought it best to ask.

"Again with the questions." He muttered more to himself than me. I glared at his back as he huffed in annoyance. "We're heading to the kitchen."

My ears perked up at the word "kitchen." I haven't eaten all day and I was beyond starving. Thinking of food already had my stomach growling as I followed close behind him.

Soon the smell of food cooking entered my nostrils, my mouth salivating and my stomach grumbling at the delicious smells that mingled together. The kitchen was hectic, many people shuffling in and out carrying plates either filled with food or dirty, needing to be washed. Some of the cooks and even waiters glanced at me before whispering to whoever they were talking to before we entered.

I didn't like how they ogled at me so openly. Did they have no shame in their actions?

I assumed that we'd stop in the kitchen so it surprised me when Arif carried on walking towards another door. "I thought we were getting something to eat?"

"We are," he answered. I followed, furrowing my brows in confusion. He held the door open for me, my eyebrow arching at the action. Who knew such a foul-mouthed beast could have manners.

I tried to hide my smirk as I thanked him and entered what I could only assume was an enormous dining hall. Three long tables surrounded by chairs were set up with table cloths, knives and forks neatly placed in front of each chair.

Most chairs were filled except a separate table which was smaller than the others but looked much fancier, placed dead centre at the front of the room. All chairs were coated in red velvet and comfortably cushioned. The king's symbol was placed in the centre of only two of the chairs which were much larger than the others, though between just the two one was evidently smaller. As if for a king and a queen.

This was the table Arif walked towards as he halted in his footsteps, he waved his hand to the second biggest chair. "Take a seat." He said before pulling it out for me.

Again with the manners.

"What's wrong?" he impatiently asked when I showed no intention of sitting down.

"Isn't this meant for a queen?" I asked, biting my lip. I didn't want to offend anyone by sitting in something meant for someone of a much higher status.

"You'd think." He retorted as if insulting me causing me to glare daggers at him for the hundredth time today. He was so infuriating. "Just sit down," he said roughly, his arms gripping the frame of the chair a little too much. I sighed, walking to the chair, my arms gripping the seat to pull it forward as Arif left to go sit in his own seat.

He sat on the right of where I assumed the king would be sitting, putting a comfortable space between us. I felt anxiety take hold of me when I realised that Adrenous would most likely be joining us, having not seen him since he forced me to bathe with him. I'd expect some awkwardness between us.

"Is the king going to be joining us?"

"Considering he gets to have the first bite you can count on it." That wasn't the answer I was expecting when he mentioned that the king was entitled to the first bite. I guess it was a Wolven tradition. The king getting to eat before the others were allowed seemed a little too up one's arse If you ask me.

A silence settled between me and Arif as we waited for the others to arrive.

My ears perked when I heard my name being called, my eyes landing on Rylan. He was with Hunter and Titan, the three of them dressed in a red uniform, the king's symbol on their chests. It didn't pass me that many females who were eating stopped to stare at them with appreciation and lust.

However, I noticed that one female who entered in behind them glared at me as I caught her attention. She was rather beautiful in that obvious kind of way, her brown eyes along with her plump lips and other features being framed by long blonde hair that was braided down her back.

She was cut off from my view when Rylan's chest invaded my vision. I looked up, his green eyes gleaming as he smiled at me widely, sitting opposite from me, he said, "Sorry Liv, we didn't mean to leave you with the moody git all day." Arif glared at him and Rylan chuckled, causing my own smile to surface. Rylan always knew how to make me feel comfortable.

"It's okay. In fact, I got to watch, firsthand, as he attacked a tree." I giggled. Rylan, whose eyes lit up with amusement, instantly turned towards Arif, whose glare was piercing the side of my face.

"Arif! What in the world did that tree do to deserve being attacked?"

Arif snapped. "Piss off Rylan!" His hands balled into fists on the table, his knuckles turning white.

Rylan shook his head at Arif as his focus turned to me once again. "Don't worry. I'm free for a couple of days so you can accompany me if you like?"

"That would be nice," I replied eagerly. He was much better company than the brute who was continuing to glare at me as I took up Rylan's offer.

"Have you found any more indications that the vermin have been scouting our perimeter?" It was Titan who aimed the question at Arif, his voice being quite deep as he spoke.

"No, not for a couple of days" Arif replied, his eyes landing on Titan as they stared each other down, their expressions changing in the process as if they were having a silent conversation.

Was that how everyone looked at each other?

Titan cast his grey eyes away from Arif, seeming satisfied. With what, I wasn't sure. Soon his and everyone else's gaze landed on me when my stomach decided to growl for attention, my cheeks reddened. Rylan was amused as always along with Hunter and Titan.

Arif just huffed like always. "How long is he going to be?" The question was for no one in particular as the other three shrugged. "Well, he better hurry the fuck up. I don't want to have to listen to a growling stomach for long," he said. Ass.

As if on cue, Adrenous entered the dining hall, crimson eyes meeting mine. The events of last night crossed my mind, my cheeks flushing at the memory. He smirked at me as if he knows the effect he has on me . . . and my body. I was completely focused on him that I haven't noticed the silence that filled the room. Everyone's attention was on him.

He lifted his arm in the air, hand straight. "As you were," he said. Everyone nodded and went back to their conversations. He was barely able to take a step forward when a woman stood in front of him, cutting him off. It was the beautiful blonde who was glaring at me earlier.

I watched curiously as she placed her hand on his arm, stroking his bicep with her thumb as they engaged in conversation. A feeling coursed through me, which I didn't quite understand, a dull ache coming from my heart. Was this jealousy?

How could I even want him after what he had me do last night? He was forcing me to strip in front of him. As much as I was turned on by his touch, it was still forced upon me.

I watched as he pulled away from her, causing her to pout and stare at his backside as he walked to the table. Her eyes flickered to mine, anger being her dominant emotion as she turned around and stormed back to her seat.

What was her problem?

"What kept you?" Hunter asked whilst Adrenous pulled out his chair beside me and sat down before pulling it to the table.

"The Elders were being rather difficult today." Was his cryptic response. No one questioned him as the food was brought out and placed in front of everyone.

I looked down at my plate of roast chicken, potatoes and various vegetables. My stomach grumbled as I grabbed my fork and stabbed at one of the potatoes, bringing it to my watery mouth. The food didn't make it very far as someone held onto my wrist, pausing my movement.

I looked at Adrenous. "What's the problem?" He uncurled his fingers from around my wrist, his lips twitching at my baffled expression.

He leans over, his lips tracing the outer shell of my ear, his breath on my skin causing me to shiver. "Here, it is customary that I take the first bite." I blush at his words.

I realised everyone have been watching me, all whilst I had forgotten what Arif said about the king eating first. I blushed furiously out of embarrassment. Why me?

I placed my fork back down onto my plate, hoping that Adrenous would hurry up and eat already so that everyone could stop ogling at me. Their gazes put pressure on me, having me wish that they would all mind their own business.

He finally began to cut into his chicken, bringing the food to his mouth and swallowing. "Please,"—he gestured to the plates of food—"enjoy your meals."

I didn't need to be told twice as I finally brought the fork to my mouth with no interruptions, swallowing when the delicious flavours brought pleasure to my tongue. The food was divine as I greedily consumed my meal, not caring that Adrenous was amused by my unladylike appetite.

When I finished, I placed the knife and fork down whilst leaning against the back of my chair.

"Seconds?" He grinned, teasing me with his eyes. I shook my head, I was happily satisfied for the time being. "Well then, I guess it's the right time to warn you that I'll be away for a few days."

To say I was surprised would be a lie. I expected him to be absent more often than not since he was in charge of watching over the entire kingdom. "Where are you going?" I asked, mindlessly tapping my finger against the table. It was something I did when I was uncomfortable.

"There are rumours of an arising threat." My finger ceased its tapping as my eyes and ears were now fully on him. If the rumours spoke of a threat then it couldn't be a good thing, especially if they were true. "I just need to survey the situation and see if it is serious."

"I guess, taking me with you is out of the question?" My eyes were pleading as he nodded, causing me to cast my eyes down at my plate, a sigh leaving my lips. "Is taking me home out of the question?" I lifted my head again, hope surfacing at the thought that maybe, just maybe, he would let me go home.

All that was distinguished when his expression turned dark. "This is your home." His words held finality, a warning not to fight back.

That made my blood boil. This place was a prison after all . . .

✦○✦

CHAPTER EIGHT
Escape

✦ ◻ ✦

ALIVIA

 The last two days were spent with Rylan. He would show me around Adrenous's estate which has twenty bedrooms, all with their own bathing rooms. There were five living rooms, a dining hall, which I have already seen, and three studies plus a kitchen. There were other rooms too for various purposes. But my favourite was the ginormous library.
 There was still much more of the estate I have to explore including the surrounding buildings, the forest, and so forth.
 Other than that I have been kept in the giant bedroom where servants would bathe me and dress me before Rylan would take me out to explore more of the estate. Staying in the bedroom alone could be boring sometimes, and I wasn't accustomed to having people serve me like I was royalty.
 The fact was that I wasn't. I was just a burden that the king has been forced to take on when I shifted at their ceremony.
 Although his actions towards me confused me and I wasn't sure why he wanted me to bathe with him that first night. He said that I was his, as if he owned me, which he didn't. Maybe he was like that with all the females, thinking I would fall at his feet like the rest of them to please him. My heart hurt at that thought. That I was just one of many, who he had tried to seduce into his bed.

Even though he hadn't gone further than to wash me, there was still no other reasons I could put behind it.

He cares about us.

My eyes furrowed. It was such a foreign thought that conflicted entirely with what I was thinking. I was going mad to even think that a king would care about me, the abomination of their kind. A sigh left my lips at the thoughts swirling through my mind.

"Is everything alright?" My eyes found friendly green as Rylan stares down at me with concern. I nodded my head half heartedly but his concern didn't waiver.

Me and Rylan were sitting in the giant dining hall eating breakfast. The cook, Maria served us both a delicious plate of croissants, along with everyone else who was in here, the room being fairly emptier today than the other night.

Only Wolvens with a high status were allowed to use the dining room, I had learned. And with Adrenous absent, we didn't have to wait for him to take the first bite before we could eat.

I decided to change the topic, Rylan didn't need to know about my inappropriate thoughts about his King. "So how come I have never heard about your abilities before?"

It worked as his concern turned into a grin as he answered, "Humans are unpredictable and afraid of what they don't understand. They're already afraid enough without us adding to it with that information." He smirked as he stuffed his face with his croissant, taking a giant bite. I rolled my eyes at him. What an animal.

But he was right. Humans are unpredictable but so is everything else.

"Why did you tell me?" If no one was supposed to know what they could do, why did he even bother to tell me? "Surely you must have thought I might have run off and started telling people?"

Rylan chuckled at my question, giving me a sideways glance. "You really think I'm going to let you run off?"

I narrowed my eyes at him. "Well then why did you tell me?" My patience was wearing thin, whilst I started to pick at my croissant. I was becoming irritated with the fact that some things were being kept secret from me.

"Liv, you're special to the king in a way you can't understand and that's why I told you, but everything else is for him to explain."

I snorted. Adrenous haven't even spoken to me properly since I arrived here and now he had left me here alone with no hope of going home, whilst he dealt with the Elders. "You keep saying that and yet he hasn't had a proper conversation with me since I've been here." I bit into my croissant. The taste of chocolate invaded my taste buds. I moaned in delight. I have never had chocolate before and it was delicious.

Rylan shrugged his shoulders. "He has a lot of issues to sort out first. He's a complicated man."

I rolled my eyes. All men here were complicated.

"Okay well then at least explain to me why you tried to invade my memories two nights ago," I said. He told me to trust him and I wanted to know why he used my trust to look into my most private memories.

He stopped chewing, placing his croissant down whilst glancing at me guiltily. "I wasn't trying to invade your privacy." His expression was genuine. "I was trying to find early memories of your first few days at life. It's a small possibility but I could see if I could find out who your parents are."

I looked at him with shock, my mouth slightly open. "You can do that?" I have never really wondered about my parents. All my emotions towards them were angry and bitter. They abandoned me. If it weren't for my uncle, I wouldn't have survived. I would have died from cold or starvation. I could have possibly even been eaten. Did I really want to know them?

"Rylan, you've been summoned."

I turned to see Hunter. His arms were crossed as he stared at the two of us.

Rylan's features turned serious. "By who?"

Hunter wasted no time explaining. "Arif needs your help at the border. We have company."

Again with the cryptic answers. What was wrong with these men?

Rylan's eyes lit as he jumped out of his seat. Running out the door, he shouted, "Keep an eye on her for me!"

I looked up at Hunter. His eyes were tired as he came and sat beside me. "What's happened?" I asked, losing my appetite for my half-eaten breakfast.

"Nothing you need to concern yourself with."

I narrowed my eyes at him. He ran his hands through his hair and gripped tightly as if frustrated.

"Right." It was all I could think to say. I haven't properly spoken to Hunter by myself and when it came to starting conversations, I wasn't good at it, especially when they spoke to me like I wasn't important enough to explain anything to.

"You must be bored sitting in here all day, want to go outside?" he asked, his hands loosening up on his hair and landing on the table, using them to lift his weight and stand up.

I quickly nodded my head, causing Hunter to laugh a little. "Someone's eager," he mused.

We made our way to the field. It was crowded with training Wolvens . Some were in wolf form while others were in their human form. It was just like how I remembered when I was walking through with Arif. Children running around, having fun and everyone else caught up in their own conversations and activities.

"Is it always like this?" I asked as I watched two strong males fighting quite fiercely. They were surrounded by Wolven warriors who were cheering and shouting encouragements or harsh words. When I had seen this sport a few days ago, it looked thrilling to me, but being close up, it was a lot more brutal at second glance.

"Yeah, pretty much."

The two men circled each other and stared the other down intensely, aiming to intimidate and illustrate some kind of dominance. Finally, one man threw a punch but the other dodged just in time and swung a kick at the other man's legs, causing him to stumble a little, but he kept his ground.

I cringed as the guy who stumbled got a punch straight to the nose, causing blood to drip down his chin and onto his bare chest. Another punch was aiming for his chest but this time he managed to avoid it, throwing his fist at the other guy's throat.

I cringed, looking away. "Can't you do something?" I asked Hunter who seemed to actually be enjoying himself.

"It's just training." He smiled, reassuringly.

One of the men were now on top of the other, holding him down. The crowd roared and counted down to three. When they finally reached three, the man holding the other stood up and lent him his hand. They both shook hands and walked away.

I was finally relieved but the adrenaline running through my body was causing me to become fidgety, my body wanting to release the pent up energy within me.

Hunter looked at me and then to the ring a few times as if considering something. He finally asked, "How about a match?"

I watched him hesitantly. "You want me to fight you?" How was I supposed to even have so much as a chance against him? Compared to him I was no challenge, he would easily beat me.

"I'll fight her."

Me and Hunter turned to the blonde, who had risen her hand to volunteer against me. It was the beautiful blonde from the dining hall, the one who had touched Adrenous and looked at him like he was hers. I felt jealousy and anger surfacing. Mixed with my adrenaline, it wasn't a good thing.

Hunter nodded his head. "Very well, Rita. You'll be the first to train Ali via."

I was at loss for words. My stomach didn't sit right with the situation as Rita looked at me as if she would do more than just train me. I hesitantly walked over to the ring, the both of us stepping inside. The two of us circled each other and observed the other closely. She stood in a fighting stance, her eyes shooting daggers at me as everyone else stood in a circle around us. My eyes instantly cast down as she took a step forward. I quickly took a step back. I dodged and sidestepped to the right as her right fist aimed for my left shoulder. I was a little slow and she managed to kick where I had stepped causing me to stumble to the ground.

I let out a heavy breath and pressed down on my hands, lifting myself up. When I was finally standing again, Rita didn't waste any time running at me. She brought her leg up to kick my stomach, but this time I was able to grab her foot and pushed her leg away from me with force, causing her to stumble back a few feet.

She narrowed her eyes at me and I used this time to take her off guard and landed a fist towards her chest with ease, causing her to gasp for air. She didn't take that too kindly because before I knew it, she had thrown her body at me. She landed punch after punch on my chest and shoulder. I was finally able to deflect one of her punches and lifted my leg, kicking her in the abdomen. We were both breathing heavily at this point.

"You bitch!" She threw herself on top of me. We rolled around in the grass, trying to throw the other off but it wasn't working. I lifted my knees, putting room between our two bodies and turned us on our sides so that I could kick and push her away. It worked!

I was finally able to make it to my feet and quickly straddled her, holding her body down with all the strength I could muster like I had seen the previous guy do.

"Three . . ."

The crowd surrounding us began to count as I continued to force her body into the ground.

"Two . . ."

Just a little longer . . .

"One!"

I released my hold on her but groaned in pain when she lifted her leg and kicked me in my side.

"Rita, that's against the rules!" Hunter scolded. She stood on her feet as I gasped for air and held my side. She glared at me once more and then stormed off.

"Are you alright?" Hunter grabbed my arm and hauled me to my feet, my side protesting as I stood up straight.

I nodded my head, hissing as pain travelled down my side. "Can we leave this area now?" I didn't like that people were still cheering me on and watching me. Hunter chuckled, nodding his head in agreement.

We went for a walk across the field far away from where all the violent training was being held. "I enjoyed the show," Hunter teased as we sat down on a bench, our background being the woods me and Arif walked through. "You were much better than some of my trainees."

"Really?"

He smirked. "Of course most of them are pups . . ."

I slapped his arm, making both of us laugh. I didn't realise he had a sense of humour. "Hunter?" He hummed in response. "Why am I here? I know I'm half Wolven and all but how come I didn't shift until the night the matures pups did?"

His expression became wary as he stared down at me for a second before replying. "The reason you didn't shift until that night is because all Wolvens need to be bathed in the essence of the blue moon to trigger it."

My mind tried to work out everything I had learnt up to this point. I was a half Wolven who wasn't able to shift until a week ago. My real parents gave me up. Tears pricked my eyes as I thought long and hard about why they did.

"What's wrong?" Hunter placed his hand on my shoulder to comfort me.

"I never met my parents," I whispered. "They abandoned me." My hands gripped the fabric of my trousers tightly, frustration creeping its way through me.

Sadness flashed in his blue eyes. "I'm sorry," he said. "I wish I could tell you more but it's not up to me."

"Let me guess, it's up to Adrenous?" I remarked, sarcasm laced in my tone. "I've been here for two days now and not once have I had an actual conversation with him and he's the reason I'm here in the first place." I looked up to Hunter, making sure he could see how upset this was making me. "My aunt and cousins don't even know what's happening to me and it's not like I'm allowed to go see them."

"Look it's for the best—"

"No it isn't." I snapped, a little surprised with myself. I felt the anger bubble up inside of me as I stood up, breathing in deeply to try and think straight.

"Alivia, the king has his reasons for keeping you here."

"Screw his reasons."

Hunter gave me a warning look. "I know you're angry right now but that's no way to talk about—"

"Why should I give a shit?" My tears turned to anger, which was getting the best of me and before I could realise what I was doing I felt a familiar sensation wash over me.

I collapsed to the ground as my legs gave way beneath me. I felt the bones beneath my flesh snap and then rearrange themselves as dark fur erupted from my skin. My nose elongated and I felt all my senses heighten drastically.

Hunter stared down at my wolf, his expression fixed on me, his eyes cautious as he waited for my next move. I didn't mean to shift. It wasn't something I had planned to do but it seemed it was the consequence of my heightened anger.

I look up at him for a while, not knowing how to react before I realised the opportunity laid out right in front of me. This is my chance to do what I've been waiting for since I got here and I'd be damned if I didn't take it.

So that's exactly what I do when I make my way for the woods, running full speed. I escaped.

✦○✦

CHAPTER NINE
Mate

✦▢✦

ALIVIA

    I feel like I've been running forever when I stopped in the middle of the woods, surrounded by giant trees which block out most of the sunlight. I have no idea where I am or how far I have travelled from Adrenous's estate.

    I mentally slapped myself. How could I have been so stupid to have thought that I would be able to travel back on my own? The trees around here were much denser than the ones back home and it was becoming more difficult to weave my way through them.

    I close my eyes whilst heading in an unknown direction. I tried to listen to anything nearby, but all I can hear are little creatures or birds flying over my head. Nothing to indicate where I might be or how far I was from the next town. Just great!

    I started to turn back towards the king's estate. It was a better option than travelling to an uncharted location.

    As I start heading back the way I came unease begins to creep into every fibre of my body.

    Everything within me was invoking me to run but being the idiot I am, I stop. My curiosity getting the best of me as I search the woods, searching for the source of my bodies distress. That's when I hear something wiz straight past me, sending a breeze to swoop through my fur. I stop dead in my tracks and listened in again.

I hear the same as before, just birds, rodents, and my heavy breathing along with the thumping beat of my heart. I was about to run when I heard someone whisper, causing my body to freeze.

"What's a pretty thing like you doing out here all alone?" The disembodied voice surrounds me like a quiet echo. I search my surrounding but there's no indication of who is responsible for the voice.

The fur on my back stood up as a shiver passed my body. My instincts tell me whatever that voice belonged to wasn't friendly. I growl warningly, hoping that will be enough for it to run off and leave me alone. I believe it may have worked as silence settles around me once again.

However, the silence doesn't last long as that voice reverberated around me once again. "Hush now. It's not ladylike to growl."

Something sprints past me again. It was too quick for me to see what it was. I growl again, this time louder. Panic is beginning to settle in my stomach as I wait for any sign of movement.

Something runs behind me. I look back but again nothing is there.

Turning my head back round I jump, my heart missing a beat and beginning to pump fast. A pale-looking man is staring at me with deep black eyes. They resembled pools of emptiness. He inclines his head to the side slightly, his black hair falling over one of his eyes at the action, as he carries on gawking at me.

I growl once again but he doesn't flinch, nor move. I take a slow step backwards.

"Where you of to, little one?" I take another step back, making sure to keep an eye on him.

I don't like the way he's smiling at me. It's sinister. He takes a slow step forward, my eyes honing in on the action and before he can get close enough, I sprint in the opposite direction. I feel the adrenaline coursing through my veins as I quicken my pace, praying that I could at least make it back to the king's grounds.

It was stupid of me to believe I could actually make it back home all by myself and escape this place. I mean look where it got me! I was being chased by what I could only describe as a lunatic.

Without warning, I'm forced to halt in my tracks. Again the mans suddenly standing ten feet in front of me. I stop, my heart pounding in my chest. My legs are shaking at this point as I try to comprehend how he could have outrun me so quick. I had barely made it half a mile.

"Tut-tut, little one. It's rude to run away without saying goodbye."

I didn't move nor make a sound. As I begin to hyperventilate another presence within me was wanting to take over, yearning me to trust them. With the black pools of death examining me as if I was some sort of experiment and the conflict waging in every fibre of my being, I was going to give in.

I'm too scared to even try and run again as my body is struck frozen with fear at what this thing could do to me. That's all I needed to allow whatever was crawling its way inside of me to take over.

I wish I had never been brought here. I wish I wasn't half Wolven. Look at where it had led me. I'm taken from my home and lost in the forest with a lunatic and giving into who knows what to get me out of it.

Fuck it.

The pale man seemed to be sniffing the air. When his eyes meet mine once again a dark smirk had made its way onto his pale lips. "Ah, you're half Wolven." He notes to himself, his movement was creepy as he moved his head from side to side as if to try and understand something. "So you're the one." He comments slyly.

I furrow my brows but can't dwell on it long before I'm mentally pushed to the backseat of my mind and this new entity takes me over.

That's when my body lunges towards him, my jaw snapping shut on his arm, he shrieks in pain as he shakes his arm repeatedly, trying to make me loosen my hold on him. His blood flows into my mouth, the sourness of it causing me to let go. "You stupid bitch!" He cursed at me.

The being within me silently fumes as she communicates with me. It was such a bizarre sensation, to have more than one entity inside of me. She badgers me to attack him again but when I physically hesitate, she growls at me before taking this into her own paws once again.

Only this time he's dodged her attack. He grabs her from behind, gripping our muzzle shut with a powerful grip so that we can't snap at him.

Ouch. I whimper in pain.

"Liv!" I feel relief flood through me as I hear Hunter, calling my name.

The relief is quickly replaced with fear once again. Without warning, he's in front of me, smiling, my muzzle now released. "We'll see each other soon enough. My king would love to meet you." He hisses and just like that, he's gone. Hunter appears from behind some trees, his expression mixed between anger and relief, a white robe draped over his arm. "There you are. You shouldn't have run off like that. Adrenous would have murdered me if anything—" His eyes examined the black blood that had stained my brown fur. He quickly examines my body, looking for what I assume is a wound of some kind. When he steps away, realising it wasn't my blood, he quickly chucks the robe on the floor and turns around. "Change now!" He demands.

I do as he says as I shift back to my human form, the being within me angry that he was sending her away. I then place the robe around me tightly to keep the chilly air at bay. Shifting is still slightly painful as my muscles ache and throb while I place the robe around me.

He grabs my aching arm tightly, making me moan a little and starts dragging me back, once I'm covered. "What the fuck happened?" He snaps. "Who's blood is this?"

"I—I saw someone," I said as he carries on pulling me back to the estate. "Something within me took over and attacked it."

He stops and looks at me, worry evident in his eyes. "Your wolf," he clarifies and then asks, "Who did she attack?"

My wolf? I didn't know Wolvens had a separate being for their wolf. She rolls her eyes at me, calling me stupid. I was loving her already.

"I'm not sure but he was really fast. I couldn't outrun him and I thought he was going to hurt me." Tears swell in my eyes as I remember how scared I was. "And erm he said that er . . . he would see me again soon . . . that his king would like to meet me."

Hunter faces away from me as he begins to think.

"What do you think he meant?" I asked.

He doesn't answer me for a while as he closes his eyes, concentrating. "It's long gone by now." He grabs my arm once again and starts walking. "I'm taking you to Adrenous as soon as we get back."

Hurray! I can imagine that going rather well after I've just tried to escape. My wolf, on the other hand, is excited about it. Why she would feel like that is beyond me. It's not like he would be excited to see her. She growls at that thought and I'm forced to apologise. Again, this is so bizarre.

When we finally reach the estate, Hunter lets go of my arm. He leads me to a study where I could see Arif and Rylan in a heated discussion. Hunter cleared his throat making the two men look back at us. "Did you manage to capture the thing?" Hunter asked. I furrowed my eyebrows in confusion. *Capture what?*

"No" Arif replied bluntly. He looked irritated, his yellow eyes hard as he roughly sat down in a chair.

"We lost track of them near the east mountains," Rylan added.

Tensions seemed to thicken as the two became rather depressed. What would I give to leave this room right now?

Hunter nodded his head, a reflection of the other two's frustration evident on his own face as well. "Where's Adrenous?"

"He'll be here in a few minutes," Rylan replied.

Hunter nodded his head and walked further into the study. I stood awkwardly at the door, I didn't know if I was allowed in the king's study. "Come on in, Liv." Rylan gave me a warm smile and urged me to sit next to him. He was sat on a brown cushiony couch which I found to be quite comfortable as I eased myself down next to him.

When Arif and Rylan finally got a good look at me their expressions shifted. Concern and suspicion took over Rylan's whilst Arif examined my hair which was covered in black blood. I sunk further into my seat, not wishing to explain as I would have to include my failed attempt at escaping.

When Hunter became aware of the fact that the two had noticed my state he took it upon himself to explain. "She had an encounter with someone in the woods." *Snitch*.

"With who?" Arif demanded gruffly, snapping his eyes from my hair to my eyes. I flinched at his tone of voice.

"A Rune." Hunter leaned against the wall, arms crossed as he watched his fellow general's reactions.

I tilted my head curiously at that word. My wolf rose her head with pride that she had hurt a Rune.

Arif clenched his fist tightly at his side. "I'm sick of those savages thinking they can infiltrate our borders. The sons of bitches need to learn when to give up."

"It was a Rune?" I finally said. "It looked nothing like I thought they would."

"Well, what were you expecting them to look like?" Arif huffed. I obviously irritated him with the question. Instead of waiting for my response, he turned his anger on Hunter. "Why was it even able to get close to her in the first place? You were supposed to fucking protect her."

Hunter stepped away from the wall, his muscles tensing and his eyes staring daggers at Arif, causing Arif to sit up from his chair, the two silently challenging each other. "It wasn't my fault she took it upon herself to fucking escape." Hunters hand gesturing in my direction. Rylan's eyes snapped to me, hurt evident in his eyes. Arif's pale eyes fell on me as well, though his were fuming with rage.

"What the fuck is wrong with you?" Arif scowled down at me. I wasn't sure why but I felt he was using anger to hide whatever other emotions he had hidden. Perhaps he feared for my safety as well though that was highly doubtful.

"Arif you should know better than to speak like that to a female." I turned my head to the entrance to see Adrenous standing there looking angry, Titan following him closely behind.

Arif looked up. "Sorry," he growled.

I havn't seen Adrenous in two days but he looked just as handsome as the last time I had seen him. "Now what happened?" His voice made me shiver. I loved the sound of his voice.

My eyes roamed his body. He wore a black short sleeve that clung to his chest, giving me a perfect view of all the lumps and ridges along his chest and abdomen. His muscly arms tensed as he had his hands balled into fists at his sides. He wore tight black breaches as well, hiding his muscled legs.

My wolf eyed him up and down with no shame as she admired his physique.

"Runes were lurking around the borders. We're not sure why but we managed to chase them away. We lost track of them at the mountains," Rylan filled in.

The king nodded his head as he walked across the room and sat at a desk at the end of the room. Hunter looked nervous as he opened his mouth. "Er . . . also, Alivia tried to run away . . ." The king's head snapped in my direction, his eyes furious as he stared me down. I inwardly flinched at the pressure from his stare. "She had an encounter with one of them," Hunter added.

"Right," the king said as he seemed to assess my body for injuries from where he was sitting. " I want you all to leave me and Ali alone for the moment."

I furrowed my eyes at the nickname. No one had ever called me Ali before. I liked it. It felt right coming from him.

They all bowed their heads and left me with him. I shifted in my seat nervously, trying to figure out what I would say. Surely he would punish me after my second attempt to escape him.

"Did it harm you?" he asked when everyone disappeared out the door. I was taken aback by the question. He was asking if I was hurt? I looked into his eyes but saw no anger, just disappointment and sorrow. My heart ached to see it. If possible, it was almost worse than seeing him angry.

"No," I whispered. "My wolf took over and attacked him instead."

I wasn't sure but I thought I saw pride flash across his eyes. "Did he say anything to you?" His eyes were soft but I could see his clenched fist at the corner of my eye.

"Just things to scare me, and then it said that it would see me again before Hunter found me." I didn't mention the "king" bit as I tried to give him just the general information of my encounter with the Rune. Plus,I didn't think it would bode well with him at all. Hunter would most likely tell him later anyway.

The king gritted his teeth. His body was tense as he asked me his next question. "Why did you run off?"

I looked down at my hands as I answered, "Because you took me away from my family." I sighed. "I've been here for nearly a week and I don't even know why I'm here except for the fact that I happen to be half Wolven and it scares me."

"You belong here with me." His voice was dark as he whispered the words.

I looked up at him in irritation. "Just because I can shift into a wolf doesn't mean I belong here." I said. "I have a family that needs me."

"I didn't take you just because of that. Although it surprised me when I learned what you were." His eyes softened at my confused expression. "The night I encountered you in the woods, I thought you were just a human trespasser but then when I smelt you closer I knew you were one of us."

My memory of the first time I had seen his deep crimson eyes and the dark fur of his wolf entered my mind. He thought I was a trespasser that night. That explains why he attacked me at first and then just disappeared.

"If you knew that night, why didn't you take me?"

He leant back in his chair. Conflict seemed to be waging in his eyes as he continues to look at me. "Because I realised you were my mate."

His what? My wolf jumped up at the word. "Your mate?"

"Yes . . . I didn't want to frighten you so I had the Elders arrange for you to be under the moonlight on the night of the pups shift." He sighed as he looked up at my baffled expression. "I thought that if you found out on your own, it would be easier for you to accept."

"I can't believe this." I stood up, tears brimming my eyes. " Easier for you, you mean?" He took my life into his own hands, deciding my fate without my say. That was unforgivable. My wolf on the other hand, loved that he'd done that for us, but then again she wouldn't be here if he hadn't. That still didn't give him the right . . .

"No, it's not like that, Alivia." He stood from his desk, interrupting my thought and walked towards me with pain etched in his expression. "You don't understand how long I've waited to find you— my mate. When I found out you were half-human it scared me at just how fragile you were."

"I'm not fragile." I huffed out. My wolf did the same. She was not weak.

"To me you are. To my enemies you are." He sighed, looking down at me. "I can't have you run off again. Promise me you won't."

I could see in his eyes he needed the reassurance that I wouldn't run away again. I knew deep down we had a strong connection. My body reacted to him in ways I didn't know were possible. It tore my heart to see the disappointment that flashed in his eyes when he had found out I ran away again. I didn't think I had it in me to even try again.

I would do as he asked but if he thought I was ready to forgive him, he was wrong. I slowly nodded my head, looking down at the red carpet. "Fine, I promise. I won't run off again."

We were mates. What that meant I needed to figure out.

✦○✦

CHAPTER TEN
A Heated Discussion

✦ ☐ ✦

ADRENOUS

    I watched Arif, Titan, and Hunter as we sat around in one of my secret studies hidden within the estate grounds. It was only used when severe issues needed to be discussed in secret. I suppressed my growls of frustration as we waited in silence. I didn't miss the way Arif's jaw ticked, his own frustration surfacing.

    We all sat around a fairly large, round mahogany table that took up the majority of the room. The candles illuminated the room but cast dark shadows across our faces and the areas where it couldn't reach.

    Arif snaps. "Fucking hell, where is he?"

    "He'll be here in a minute," I assured, giving him a warning look to remain patient. He took note of my warning as he leant back in his chair and watched the door where Rylan would enter. We were all a little apprehensive but obviously, some hid it better than most.

    Rylan joined us after twenty minutes of waiting for him to arrive. "Is she asleep?" I asked.

    "Yeah, took a while but she's asleep."

    Arif growled, "Took her long enough." Rylan shook his head but didn't retort to his comment as he took a seat, propping his elbow on the armrest and leant on his side.

I let out a sigh of approval as I could finally relax, the tension in my muscles fading. I needed to make sure Ali wouldn't wander the estate groundsand have no idea where we were. I needed her safe and well away from this arising threat. The survival of the kingdom depended on her being safe because if she wasn't, I wouldn't be able to knuckle down and do what must be done.

Hard times bring hard choices.

My gaze drifted between my four generals.

All of them looked tired but this was something we needed to discuss immediately. We had no time to fuck about. "There's been rumours that Krellins been building up his forces—"

"What else is new," Titan growled. Titan was always short-tempered when it came to them. He hated them with a passion for what they had taken from him and his mate. I usually let his anger slide because of his pain but tonight I needed them to all have a clear mind, void of emotion.

"Calm down, we need to get together a strategy."

"He's been trying to take this place down for nearly a decade or so, do you really think this time it's different?" Hunter interjected. He was right. They had always failed to bring us down but that was before. This time it was different.

"Yes," I growled. "He's always tried to find a weakness and this time I have one."

"Do you think he knows about her?" Rylan whispered, his voice echoing around the room.

He had a soft spot for her, I could tell. It slightly angered the wolf inside me at how close they had become in the short time they knew each other. I had to keep reminding myself that Rylan was already mated and wanted to protect Alivia as much as me. She needed all of our protection.

"She was spotted by a Rune, we can't take any chances," I said, leaning back in my chair with a sigh. A king couldn't afford to have weaknesses. I knew that but I couldn't let her go. I wouldn't, not after waiting more than a decade for her.

My whole life has been driven by anger and darkness. I had never cared for much until I saw her in the woods looking frightened and vulnerable. My wolf knew exactly who she was as I was lured by her beautiful, cobalt eyes that held such innocence. How could someone as fragile and innocent as her be paired with me, a monster?

I didn't miss it when Arif gave Hunter a sideways glare. He still blamed him for allowing Alivia to be spotted. Hunter saw the glare from Arif, his eyes withholding guilt as he bowed his head in shame.

"They don't know she's your mate. All they know is that she's half human. That in itself is enough to know that she's the weakest of our kind," Arif commented. "I told you we should have left her where she was."

"I wanted her here safe with me." I snapped, my fist coming down hard on the table, catching all of them off guard as they all stared at me in surprise. How dare he challenge my decision. I was his king. His alpha.

"Well, I hope for yours and the kingdom's sake that she is safest here. Let's hope Krellin doesn't get his hands 'round her fragile throat—"

I bolted out of my seat, and smashed Arif into the wall, my hand gripping his throat tightly as his chair went flying across the room. "Don't you dare speak of such things! She is your future Queen and I won't have you speak of her like that. I don't care if you are my general," I growled, his face now straining as he gripped my hands holding his throat. He may be strong but not compared to me.

"Adrenous just calm down, he didn't mean anything by it." Rylan was at my side trying to relinquish my temper. My temper always brought out a darkness in me that none of them wanted to see.

I let Arif go and he collapsed to the ground coughing. My body still shook as I breathed heavily with anger clouding my mind.

My wolf howled inside me, proud he had showed our dominance. I clenched my fists tightly. Just a few words regarding my mate. That was all it had taken for me to lose my temper. Imagine what I would do if someone actually caused her harm.

"We'll discuss this later." I spat, glaring at Arif's bowed head, his way of showing me absolute submission.

I walked out the room and went straight to where Alivia was sleeping. I stopped outside the door and listened carefully. I could hear the calm, rhythmic beat of her heart as she slept.

I so desperately wanted to join her and have her safe in my arms as she slept but I would have to wait. If I got too close I would most likely mark her before she was ready. I couldn't risk that.

Arifs words rung through my mind. *Let's hope Krellin doesn't get his hands round her fragile throat.* I couldn't let Krellin get a hold on her. However, I knew she was miserable being locked up here that I feared, even though she had promised me she wouldn't, that she'd try to escape again.

There was only one thing I could think of that would make her happier and ensure she keeps her promise.

✦○✦

CHAPTER ELEVEN
Family Reunion

✦□✦

ALIVIA

Since I had tried to escape, I was being followed and watched every day and night. Guards were stationed outside my bedroom door for extra precaution, thanks to Adrenous.

My promise was obviously not enough for him. Considering I haven't given him much reason to trust me, he hasn't given me much either. We were both now wary of the other.

The realisation that I had lost his trust along with the others was hard to bear, I admit, but I couldn't help but feel that way. Even Rylan watched me closely, worried that I would try something. He thought I didn't notice his change in demeanour with me but I did. Whenever I made a sudden move or approached a door I could see from the corner of my eye how his body tensed, making sure he could spring into action if I was to escape again. I hated it.

I trailed along the corridors, Rylan on toe as I navigated my way 'round the estate, remembering the route quite clearly as I made my way up a flight of stairs. I'm sure Rylan took into account the fact that I was able to make my way around without his lead. He may as well believe I would use it one day to run away again. Not that I would. I have learned my lesson.

Continuing along the hall, I took note that the main colour theme for the hallways was red carpets and white stone walls which seemed to brighten the place up and give a decent sense of space even though there was tons of it anyway. It also made it look ancient. I had no doubt it was ancient but the stone walls helped me believe it.

The staircase spiralled downwards as we made our way around. As soon as we reached the second floor, I descended from the stairs and walked forwards.

"You seem like a woman with a mission." Rylan chuckled, cutting into the silence of the hall.

I hummed in response, trying to concentrate on which way to turn as we reached an intersection which split off into two halls. Remembering it was right, I continued along. "I figured since I have a lot of free time on my hands, I might as well make use of it."

"And you think the library is a good use of your time?" He said, his brow arched as he continued to trail behind me.

"Well yes . . ." I was worried that it may not have what I was looking for. " It has books on mates right?"

Realization and surprise swooping across his face, he said, "Adrenous told you."

"Yeah, well it took him long enough." I huffed in response.

We finally stood outside the library doors, my hand barely touching the door handle as I hesitate to open it, turning to Rylan as he seems to have gone quiet. His eyes seem glazed over, his expression changing, while I watch him cautiously.

"Rylan, are you alright?"

He shakes his head as if tuning back into focus, a grin plasters itself on his face as his eyes focus back onto me. "We have to head into the dining hall, Adrenous has a surprise for you."

"How do you know that?"

"He told me." He shrugs likes it should be obvious but my confused expression makes it clear to him that I'm completely lost. "You do know Wolvens can mindlink don't you?"

I shook my head. "No, should I have?"

He grabs my hand which isn't leaning against the door and pulls me away from the library, away from my answers. I guess I'll have to wait. Rylan answers my question as we arrive back at the intersection and head back towards the stairs. "Every member of our kingdom can communicate telepathically, it's to keep in touch in long distances and make sure everyone is safe."

"How come I can't do that?" I ask. It would be incredible to speak to people in that fashion. Maybe because I was only half I was robbed of that privilege. I hope that wasn't the case.

"Your not part of our kingdom just yet. It involves a ritual which binds your wolf with us."

My wolf jumped at the chance to join them, to be close to other wolves. I, on the other hand, was slightly apprehensive at the idea of binding myself to these people.

I decided to remain silent, biting my lip nervously. I figured I would just hurt Rylan if I admitted I wasn't too quick to be involved into some sort of ritual that would connect me to them permanently.

We stepped off the stairs and onto the first floor. Rylan led me to the kitchen, the thought that Adrenous may have cooked for me crossing my mind, making my heart flutter slightly. However it seems no one was around, the smell of food absent as we headed past the kitchen and into the dining hall.

As soon as we turned the corner the air was pushed out of my lungs as small arms snaked around my waist and two heads leant against my stomach. Happiness overwhelmed me as Amber and Avery pulled away just enough for me to have a full view of their adorable little faces. I knelt to the ground to pull them in tighter as tears began to flow from my eyes at how much I had truly missed them. This was the best surprise I could have ever gotten.

"I've missed you girls so much." I cried. They pulled back to wipe the tears from my eyes, making me laugh.

"Mummy said you couldn't come home because you're a wolf," Amber whispered, her eyes looking around to make sure no one could hear. "Is that true?"

I laughed at her innocence. From the far end of the room, I could see Adrenous watching us, his shoulders shaking from silent laughter. He could easily hear her. Beside him was my aunt Helena. Her posture was slightly tense. Most likely because she was uncomfortable being surrounded by so many Wolvens. However, her face was relaxed, her eyes teary as she smiled in my direction.

I was surprised to see that Tris was also here, standing beside my aunt. Adrenous really was full of surprises and it was odd considering how he spoke to Tris the last time. Tris's long, blond hair was tied back and he wore a white shirt and black breeches. Very casual. He smiled at me though his eyes were filled with guilt as he averted his gaze to the floor.

I decided to ignore that for the time being as I looked back down at Amber. "Yes it's true." I admitted, the tears still sliding down my cheeks. "But don't worry, I'm a good wolf." I joked as I poked her nose causing her to giggle.

I stood to my feet and held both the girls hands as we walked up to Adrenous, my aunt and Tris. I smiled up at Adrenous. "Thank you for letting me see them." I smiled up at him.

He nodded. "You needed it. I'll leave you to catch up."

He was right, I did need it.

I watched as he left the room, turning to smile at me before he left along with Rylan. I guess he wasn't all bad.

The girls let go of my hand and stood out of the way as Helena threw her arms around me. I took comfort in her hug and breathed in her familiar scent. She always smelled of baked bread and I loved it. It reminded me of our house which used to always smell of it. "I've missed you so so much." She cried.

"I've missed you more." I said.

"Have they been good to you?" she asked, pulling away to assess me for any signs that I had been hurt.

"Yes they have." I assured her. "I'm one of them and they treat me as such."

"I—I never knew you were one of them. If I did, I would have made sure you knew." She sobbed. I hugged her tight, stroking her back. It wasn't her fault and I didn't want her to feel responsible for any of this.

"I know you would have." She didn't deserve to carry any guilt on her shoulders. I didn't blame her and never did for one minute.

"There's something I want to give you. I wasn't going to but I thought you would want it after everything's that's happened." She explained, reaching into her bag on the floor. I watched as she pulled out a baby blanket. It was white and had blue words embroidered on it.

I gasped in surprise. The words read "Alivia."

"This is where me and your uncle got your name. You were wrapped up in it the day he found you."

How had I never seen this before? Tons of emotions I couldn't decipher bubbled up inside me as I gently took the blanket from her. It was so warm and snuggly and smelt familiar. It was all there was of my parents. It didn't make sense though. Why did they bother to embroider a blanket with my name if they knew they were going to abandon me? It didn't sit right.

"Are you okay?" my aunt asked. I haven't spoken for a few minutes. I was too busy marvelling at the blanket.

"I'm fine," I answered, swallowing the lump in my throat. "Thank you for giving it to me."

"Of course, honey." She picked her bag up off the floor, pulling it over her shoulder. "Me and the girls best get back before it's dark," she explained. "There's a lot of distance to cover."

A frown crossed my lips. "Can't you stay?"

She shook her head, her eyes turning sad. "I don't think that's a good idea. Besides"—she paused to stroke the tears that were falling down my cheek—"Tristan would like to speak to you."

My eyes flickered to Tristan. He shuffled uncomfortably on his feet, casting his head down. I turned back to my aunt, nodding. "I love you guys so much," I whispered.

"We love you too."

I gave her one last hug along with the girls and walked them outside the front of the estate to wave them off. Rylan was standing by and offered to take them home which made me feel better about letting them go. When they disappeared along the path, I turned my attention on Tristan. "Come on," I said. "I know a place we can speak privately."

I can't say I haven't missed Tristan. From the way we left things I didn't imagine seeing him ever again. But here he was.

"Okay." He muttered, following my lead.

I lead him back inside the estate until we exited back out through the double doors which opened up to the two fields connected by the bridge. It was pretty crowded as we walked through until we came across a quiet spot and sat down near the edge. In the distance I could see Adrenous watching us, his body tense as he kept his distance, Arif beside him with constant eyes on Tristan.

I decided to ignore him and focus on Tris. "So," I started nervously. "What did you want to talk about?"

"I wanted to say I'm sorry." His voice was low as he spoke. "I didn't mean to get angry with you."

My eyes softened. "Why were you angry?"

"You wouldn't understand." His eyes met mine. They were shrouded with guilt as he leant back on the bench, assessing my reaction.

"Try me." I challenged, tempting him to explain.

His green eyes were wary. "Alivia there's a lot I haven't told you." I furrowed my brow, urging him to explain. "If I told you everything you would hate me."

I reached my hand out to touch his arm. "I seriously doubt that." I assured him.

We have been friends since I could remember. What could he have possibly done to make me hate him?

Tristan scanned our surroundings warily, whatever he was looking for I wasn't sure. He was hesitant as he continued. "Liv I'm the reason they know about you. It's because of me that you could bring this entire place to its knees." I stared at him dumbfounded.

What on earth was he talking about?

I was about to question him further when he cut me off and continued. "Sometimes your friends aren't really your friends, just enemies in disguise, preventing you from reaching your highest peak."

I frown, his words are confusing as I try to process what it is he's actually saying. Was he saying he wasn't my friend? Why did he have to talk in bloody riddles? He was right, I didn't understand.

"Why are you talking like this?" I snapped, my confusion and frustration turning to anger as I narrow my eyes at him.

He sighs heavily, his eyes flashing at Adrenous as if he disproves of him. "I'm saying this because you need to open your eyes and realise who you can trust."

"Tris, please stop, you're scaring me." I shiver, feeling cold all of a sudden as my eyes follow his line of sight, Adrenous still watching us.

Tristan seemed to be struggling with his inner thoughts and without explaining further he stands to his feet. "Think about what I'm saying. I have to go now." I stand up after him, watching him walk away from me.

"Tristan?!" I called after him but he ignored me, not even bothering to glance at me as he leaves me more confused and frightened than ever.

Adrenous is beside me soon enough, sensing my distressed state. "Did he hurt you?" He growls. "I knew I shouldn't have let him visit."

"No." I said bluntly. "He just confused me slightly." I watch his back as the guards open up the door for him, my mind processing everything he just said to me.

My best friend wasn't who I thought he was, that much was clear.

✦○✦

CHAPTER TWELVE
What is this Pain?

✦□✦

Alivia

    A giggle passes my lips as me and Rylan run from the door, skidding across the room as we jump back into our seats. Rylan sits down a little too violently, almost knocking me out of my chair but manages to quickly reach out, grabbing my arm and pulling me back onto my seat as I try to stifle my laugh. We quickly appear to be eating normally as we try to contain our excitement.
    My eyes scan the bucket gently balancing on the dining room door, filled with water. I try hard not to giggle as Rylan scoffs his breakfast beside me, his eyes on the door as well, a sideways smirk plastered on his face.
    We soon cast our eyes down at our plates to prevent getting blamed as we hear Hunter's footsteps approaching.
    He was going to be furious.
    The sound of water splashing meets our ears and so does a ferocious growl. "Who the fuck did this?" I lift my head up and almost choke on my food at the sight of a soaking wet and furious Arif. His eyes scan the room and the few people who are sitting around glance at me and Rylan, basically giving us away.
    Rylan fakes innocence as he stands and points down at me. "It was Liv's idea."

What? I snap my head up at him, narrowing my eyes as he keeps his finger close to my face. He was such a liar.

"You're such a little shit." I hiss at Rylan as he sits down. I shove myself against him, knocking him of his seat, causing his ass to hit the floor hard. He groans in pain as he rose back up to his feet, rubbing his tailbone which had took the impact of his fall. I burst out laughing whilst he playfully glares at me before laughing himself.

Hunter comes in beside Arif, his surprise evident, but soon a chuckle reverberates through his chest.

"What the fuck happened to you?" Arif shoots him a glare, causing Hunter to cough as he attempts to cover his laughter. Arif raises his finger, pointing it at Rylan and then gestures for him to follow him out the room as he storms off.

Someone needed to learn to take a joke.

"Pray for me." Rylan says, pretending to be terrified and then goes after a mad Arif.

Hopefully he doesn't get beaten up.

This whole prank idea, which was Rylan's idea by the way, was a welcome distraction from everything that had happened since I spoke to Tristan. Plus Adrenous wasn't here either.

Adrenous has been away dealing with a few approaching threats that I wasn't really sure of. It seemed to be that he was always busy. I wanted to speak to him further and ask about the whole mate ordeal but he would always avoid the conversation and then leave for days at a time.

I have already been here for a month and a half and I desperately wanted to speak with him and get some answers.

Hunter sat opposite me, his chest still rumbling with laughter from witnessing a drenched Arif. "Rylan will be lucky if Arif doesn't murder him."

"Where did he take Rylan anyway?" I ask whilst bringing my fork to my mouth and chewing the delicious bacon. I loved bacon.

He shrugs. "I think Adrenous sent a letter for some kind of assignment, nothing they can't handle." He reaches across the table and nicks some of my bacon.

"Hey!" I yell, slapping his hand away with my fork causing him to chuckle again.

My mind lingers on his words. The mention of Adrenous causes my wolf to whine. She's missed him a lot and to be honest I have as well. "Where is Adrenous anyway?" I question, pushing away my now empty plate.

"You know where." He says, glancing at me like it was a dumb question.

"No I don't. I know he's dealing with threats but I don't know what that means or where it is." I corrected him, a huff of frustration leaving my lips.

"He'll be back soon. Stop worrying about it." He answers, practically shooting my question down which makes me believe there was something he was trying to keep from me. What else was new?

"I'm not worrying." I retorted, standing. I brush myself down and headed for the door. My wolf rolls her eyes at me, knowing that I was in fact worrying. Okay, maybe I was a little.

"Hey, where are you going?" Hunter calls after me and soon I can hear his footsteps as he tags along behind me. I make the familiar journey to the library, arriving at the intersection and turning right. That's when Hunter realises where I'm leading us.

"Rylan warned me you might be heading for the library at some point. May I ask why?" He questions as he overtakes me and decides that he'll do the leading. He was a man, what should I expect?

The corners of my lips curl up into a smirk. "Because I'm probably going to get more out of a book than from Adrenous at this point."

Hunter glances at me, not happy with my comment but doesn't argue. He knew I was right.

"And you," I add chuckling, causing his sky blues eyes to darken but again he doesn't argue.

Exactly my point.

I made it to the familiar door of the library, my hand once again wrapping around the handle but this time I open it without hesitation. My lips parted on a gasp at the sight of book after book that lined the shelves as we made our way inside the library. Each section of books were labelled above. There was an isle that said "Wolven history," while another said "The origin of Wolves."

I made a mental note to read up on those later on. Hunter glances at me, silently asking for what it is I'm searching for. "A book on mates." His features shift, confusion mixed with hesitation but he continues along the library anyway. I allowed Hunter to lead me as he clearly knows what it is I need.

Finally we made it to a small isle, labelled "Mates." "Here we are." Hunter said as he grabbed a few books and led us to a small table. "Everything you need to know should be inside these books."

I sit down next to him, reading a few of the titles. My eyebrows furrowed in confusion when I read a book titled *Marking*.

"What's 'marking' mean?" I asked, picking up the book and opening the first page. Hunter ran a hand through his hair nervously, watching me read the first page.

Out of the two mates, the male will be the one to mark his female at the base of her neck. The mark is a small bite, which leaves the male's scent on her body. Unmated wolves who see or smell the mark will know she belongs to another.

"He's not planning on marking me, is he?" I looked up at Hunter who ran a hand through his hair once again and sighs.

"Not right now, he'll wait until you're ready," he explained, his eyes soft.

My teeth fiddle with my bottom lip as I think it over. Would I ever be ready for that? I don't even know what I want any more. My heart and mind are conflicted as I grasp what life with Adrenous would be like.

I carried on reading, changing the page.

> *Once the female is marked by her male, the bond between them will grow and become unbreakable. They will be able to feel each other's presence, even when they are miles apart. That inclu-des strong emotions and pain. Their minds will become one and they will be able to communicate through this connection.*

That sounded so intimate. I let out my breath slowly, processing this whole concept of Adrenous one day marking me. I turn away from the page meeting with Hunter's gaze which appears to be assessing me. "What if I'm never ready for Adrenous to mark me?"

"You will be." Hunter answers, his expression adamant that he was one hundred percent right.

"How can you be so sure?" I ask, my fingers fiddling with the pages.

"You belong with him, Alivia." Hunters seems to plead with me, his eyes soft as he continued. "You have no idea how long this pack has needed a queen, a mother-like figure to keep us functional and connected."

My eyes widen, my brows raised. I didn't even think about that. I was too focused on just me and Adrenous. It didn't even occur to me that I could one day be a queen. I didn't know if I could be given such a role. I was only seventeen. How would I be able to succeed their expectations? "What if I'm no good?" I whispered, my insecurity on full display.

Hunter offers me a smile, placing his hand on my arm in reassurance. "Believe me, the moon goddess wouldn't have made you his mate if she didn't think you could handle it."

My heart melted at his words, his sky blue eyes were filled with hope as he smiled at me. "You were born to be our queen."

"Thanks, Hunter."

"Any time." He smiled. "I need to quickly sort something out but I won't be far so I'll be able to catch you before you even decide to run," he mused, making me chuckle. He headed for the door but turned and added, "And no more pranks." He laughed and I match his laugh with my own.

"I'll be good," I assured him with a giggle.

When he finally leaves the library I turn back to the book, continuing to read.

The bond is everlasting even in death. One will always find the other.

I smiled at that. Wolvens really did have it all.

I could see from the corner of my eye that Hunter sat back down beside me, keeping my focus on the page. "This is where I sit." I heard a feminine voice sneer.

I glanced up to see that it wasn't Hunter who came and sat beside me. Instead my eyes met with brown eyes which were glaring at me. It was the blond who I had fought with before outside on the field. Rita, I believe her name was.

"W—what?" I inwardly cursed myself for stammering like a fool. What was wrong with me?

"I've never seen you in here before. I don't know who you think you are but I've been dying to ask . . ." She smirks. " why are the Generals stuck by your side all of a sudden?" Her voice seemed accusing like she was trying to blame me for something.

"Adrenous told them to." I blatantly reply, my attention returning straight back to the book.

I don't expect it when the book is snatched right out of my grasp, my eyes wide in shock. Did she really just do that? What the hell was her problem? I glare at her as she flips through the pages and then glances at the other books on the table as if piecing together a puzzle. Her eyes narrow before returning her gaze to me. "You're his mate?" She accuses.

"Give it back," I yell at her, reaching for the book. Instead of attempting to give the book back to me and leave me alone, she keeps it In her grasp. I match her glare as she makes no attempt to leave. Her lips curl upwards in a sneer. "You really think that just because you're his mate it means you can take him from me?"

Wait, what? What the hell did that mean? How could I possibly take him from her unless they were together?

A smile forms on her lips when she catches my baffled expression. "What do you mean?" I question demandingly. She best explain to me exactly what she means before I lose it.

"He's mine." She whispers tauntingly. "I'm the female who will bear his mark. You're a nobody here." She sneered loud enough that everyone was now staring in our direction, a mixture of confusion and curiosity among their faces.

"Rita!" I heard Hunter shout. I didn't look at him, a sharp pain making its way through my heart as my wolf whined, her pain reflecting my own.

What was this pain?

I felt betrayed. I know I had no right to but it still hurt and I couldn't help it. Every inch of my being was aching from the sense of...

...rejection.

That's exactly what it felt like.

"Leave now." He snarled at Rita, who was now stood to her feet.

"Hunter darling, do you really think you have any authority over me." She taunts him with a nasty smile. At least it's not just me who she likes to play nasty games with. Hunter growls at her words, making her nasty smile widen. He made his way over to me, trying his best to ignore her.

"Hunter, inform this girl how Adrenous is mine." Her voice is teasing, her brown eyes gleaming with mischief. She must be very pleased with herself.

"I said leave! Unless you wish to be locked up in the cells." He snarls, his voice hard and threatening and I had no doubt his threat was real.

Her smile was now gone. "You wouldn't." She challenged.

"Try me." He raises his head, towering over her as his attempt to intimidate her works. She decides it's best to leave but not before giving me a nasty look.

Now that she was gone I felt tears prick my eyes. "Is it true? She's with Adrenous?"

The guilt that swept through his face was enough to convince me she wasn't lying. That's what I thought. He couldn't even say anything.

"Take me to my room." I sigh, my voice was soft and weak, afraid it'll break if I say any more.

"Liv, it's not what you—"

"I don't care, Hunter." My voice broke slightly, exactly what I didn't want. "Take me to my room." I repeated, more demanding this time.

He didn't say anything more after that. We walked in silence, his eyes glancing down at me every once in a while. I could see his lips parting to speak a few times but he thought better of it and remained silent. When I finally made it to my room I slam the door shut and head for my bed, slumping down onto the soft sheets.

I allowed the tears to fall, my body curling in on itself as I attempt to comfort myself. This pain that I was feeling was so unexpected and to be honest, I don't know why I was so surprised. A king like Adrenous wouldn't want to settle with an abomination like me. He needed a pure breed. Someone who was as strong as him and could protect his people. And that wasn't me. It would never be me.

Adrenous had already said it himself . . . I was weak

✦○✦

CHAPTER THIRTEEN
Desire

✦□✦

ALIVIA

 Numb. Betrayed. Exhausted. That was just the tip of the iceberg with regards to how I was feeling right about now.
 I rested my head against the headboard, refusing to move. My arms were wrapped around the pillow and I had it close to my chest for comfort. My hair was messy and loose as it sprawled around my tear-soaked face. The tears only recently stopped falling.
 How could he have lied to me like that? Telling me he had waited for me and yet he hadn't. Rita was bragging about how Adrenous was hers. I assumed they had fucked too. It was obvious with the way she boasted that she would bear his mark. He must have said something to her to make her believe that was true.
 I know it was ridiculous to feel this emotional over a man I barely knew but I thought he was telling the truth when he said I belonged with him. Though given everything I had learned, it was evident he would need a stronger mate to take my place. Not a weak abomination who knew nothing of their ways, nor their beliefs.
 I was vulnerable. Weak. Too much of a risk to his kingdom. He had already stated it himself. To his enemies I was an obvious target. I was someone they could use to bring this place to its knees, just as Tristan had said, though what he meant exactly still

puzzled me and I hadn't even told Adrenous. Whether that was the right or wrong decision, I would probably find out one way or another.

I didn't really care about that right now, I'm too caught up in my own pain as I let out a shaky breath. I was trying to hold in my emotions to prevent another outburst of tears. That was the last thing I wanted right about now.

"Alivia?"

I was wrong . . .

This was the last thing I wanted right about now.

I looked up to see that Adrenous was standing at the foot of my bed. Being too occupied in my own thoughts, I haven't even heard the door open. I slammed my head back down against the headboard, tuning my face to the side. "Alivia, Hunter told me what happened."

I don't respond as he settles himself on the bed next to my legs. "Ali, please let me explain."

"I'm not bothered, I didn't want to stay here anyway. Soon once I'm done here, I'm going home," I retorted, not even meeting his crimson orbs which from the corner of my, looked regretful.

It hurt my heart to speak the words, but what could I do? I was never going to be his when he had another.

"Don't say things you don't mean," he warned softly. Cocky words for someone who couldn't see what was going on inside my mind, even if he was right. I didn't mean them at all but I was hurt and stubborn. "Me and Rita have been separated for two years now. I never intended to mark her or have her by my side in the future. She knew that from the moment we got together. She's just angry and jealous," he explained, his eyes assessing me closely, searching for a response.

I looked up at him, my eyes reflecting the heartbreak as I spoke. "How do you expect me to believe that? You made it clear that you had waited for me and yet I find out from someone else that you hadn't waited like you had me believe." My voice held a hard edge towards the end as I chuckled. "The funny thing is, if the shoe was on the other foot this would be a whole other story. I saw how furious you acted towards Tris when you thought *we* were together."

His expression shifted slightly, I had clearly struck a nerve when he releases a heavy sigh, running a hand through his ebony hair. "You don't understand, I had just found you and when I watched you run of with *that boy* my wolf took control." His face looked desperate, vulnerable and then just like that it was covered up with his cold facade. "Haven't I proven that I'm no longer bothered? I let him visit you, didn't I?"

He had me there but still, why would he want me? I was weak remember.

"Why do you want me anyway? You said it yourself, I'm weak, a liability here." I remarked, my eyes casting down towards the pillow, drawing my bottom lip in through my teeth.

"That's not what I meant." He sighed, realising how much of an impact his words had on me. "I said you were fragile, not weak. I meant it as in you're my weakness, something I've never had to worry about for a long time." He paused for a moment, watching me lift my head up slightly to look at him. "It's terrifying."

"I'm sorry, Your Highness." I didn't even bother to speak his name, I was still angry but didn't mean to sound as sarcastic as I did. My emotions were still all over the place at the moment, my wolf only just beginning to wag her tail in happiness.

A shriek passes my lips when my legs are pulled straight, causing me to lay flat against the bed, Adrenous straddling my waist and holding my arms down at my sides. He leans over me, his face so close to mine I could almost feel our lips touching.

"It's Adrenous to you." I quickly nod my head in agreement as he whispers the words into my ear. My anger is instantly replaced with desire as I feel the achy sensation between my thighs. The king smiles down at me, his breath fanning my face gently but he makes no move to kiss me.

His entire body is pressed tightly against mine that I can feel a certain part of him poking my thigh as it strained against the fabric of his breeches. "It's only your voice I ever want to hear say it." He whispers against my ear, his breath fanning the side of my face, causing goosebumps to rise along my neck. "Let me hear you say my name." He demands softly, beginning to trail light kisses along my neck, a soft moan drawing from the back of my throat as it sends tingles along my skin.

I try to squirm against him but it only makes his length grow harder, rubbing against me, my underwear becoming wet as his grip on me tightens. "Say my name," he repeats more aggressively.

"Addy." I mocked, my lips curling slightly when he lifts his head enough to glance into my eyes. An emotion I couldn't interpret crosses his eyes. My eyes flash with satisfaction, knowing that I effect him as much as he effects me.

Fuck. Just kiss me already.

Just as I thought he was going to kiss me, he pulls away. A frown crosses my lips as I feel the warmth of his body disappear from my own. My bundle of nerves still begging for attention as I sit up, slightly frustrated.

"We need to talk about you becoming a member of my kingdom." He breathes out, moving beside me on the bed and rests his hand on my thigh, squeezing it gently. The contact felt nice and comforting but I couldn't let him know that. I was still a little upset with him no matter how much I wanted him right now.

"What do you mean?" I question, my brows furrowing in confusion, his crimson orbs seemed a lot darker than earlier but they were still beautiful none the less. I suspected he was just as sexually frustrated as I was.

"Well, it means you'll partake in a ritual which will bind your wolf with us, allowing you to connect with us fully." He paused for a moment, making sure I understood, "But first—"

"You have to mark me?" I scoffed, tearing my eyes away from him. I sit up and kneel on the bed, my ass resting on the back of my legs as I recalled what I had learned from that book before Rita came and distracted me.

Watch. When I see her, I'll . . .

"How do you know about that?" He seems slightly taken aback by my words, his own brows furrowing and his eyes slightly narrowed as I bring my eyes back up to meet his.

"The library." I shrug like it's no big deal. At least it shouldn't be, it was open for everyone here, why not me?

"I should have known." He shook his head but didn't linger on it as he continued, "That will happen after you're a member." He strokes my thigh for reassurance, adding, "And when you're ready."

"Thank you." I smile, not knowing when that time would come but I was beginning to believe it might just happen sooner than I think.

"Adrenous?" He stared down at me with those gorgeous eyes which made my belly flip and desire pool from inside me. I shook my head slightly trying to think back to what I wanted to ask. "Are you sure Rita meant nothing?."

It was a question I needed him to answer. Something inside of me wouldn't relax until then.

"Yes. She was just a distraction, I made it clear to her that she was never going to be my queen."

I slowly nodded my head. Adrenous seemed to be contemplating asking me something as his hands repeatedly ruffled his gorgeous, dark hair.

"What's wrong?" I ask.

His eyes found mine, he looked slightly vulnerable, laying himself bare as he spoke. "Tristan, the one you tried to run with..." he looked to be trying to control himself as he tried to get the words out. "Were you ever together?"

I stared at him, thinking about his question. He was asking if me and Tristan were ever together? Now I knew why he had such a hateful look in his eyes when he looked at Tris. He believed me and Tristan were more than friends and yet he had allowed him to visit me. If that didn't show how much he was trying for me then I don't know what did.

I quickly shook my head, giggling a little. "No we were never together. He was always just a friend." I assured him. I wasn't going to tell him that I had fancied Tristan. I don't think that would have done us any good if he knew and besides I was over Tristan.

I was beginning to fall for Adrenous.

An inaudible sigh of relief left Adrenous's body as he pulled me from my position and onto his lap. "So you've never been with anyone?" He asked gently.

I didn't quite catch his meaning. My innocent mind tried to think for a moment until I realised what he was asking. "I'v never been physical with anyone before," I whispered, feeling my face blush bright red as I averted my gaze away in embarrassment.

I felt his fingers grip my chin gently, lifting my gaze up, causing the now tingling sensation to erupt at the contact once again. His deep, red eyes looked into mine as he brought his lips just centimetres from my own.

"You have no idea how hard it is for me not to mark you right now." His dark voice caresses my face, his gaze locking with my lust filled one.

His lips soon found mine, caressing them in a gentle kiss. The kiss got deeper and rougher as our hunger for one another grew with each passing second. He nibbled gently on my bottom lip, causing me to gasp against him. He used this as permission to plunge his tongue into my mouth, deepening the kiss further. I moaned into him, my mind becoming fuzzy with lust. His rough hands roamed my body, one of them finding one of my breast and squeezing gently whilst the other squeezed my thigh and roamed dangerously up toward the throbbing between my legs.

I had never kissed anyone like this before and yet with him it was so easy. It was so right as my body erupted with tingles all over, overwhelming me.

"Adrenous." I moaned against him, my tongue running over his bottom lip as I drew it between my teeth, sucking it. A groan emitted from the back of his throat as I released his lip and kissed him with more fever.

He growled with approval as his hands trailed down from my breast to my small waist and squeezed it tightly, bunching my dress up into his grasp. He moved his other hand further up my thigh, his thumb running over my clit through the fabric of my underwear as I moaned in pleasure. I wanted him right now.

I felt my underwear grow wetter as I felt his massive bulge poking my stomach. "Ali, I can smell your arousal." He growled into my neck as he shifted from my lips to peck down my shoulder, he lifted me up from his lap and laid me gently down onto the bed, his lips continuing to trail light kisses along my collar bone. I writhed against him, needing more friction between my legs as he leaned over me.

His eyes darkened as he smirked down at me, teasing me. He used his knee to gently push my legs apart, my dress crumpled up to my waist, putting my underwear on full display as he ran his hands along my thighs, gripping them gently. I needed more friction, attempting to rub my legs together but he kept them apart forcefully, his eyes warning me not to move.

He leant down, his lips placing gentle kisses along my thigh, whilst his hand reached and groped my breast gently, his fingers then pinching my nipple, bringing a moan from my lips as I drowned myself in his scent. He smelt so good.

My teeth were beginning to ache, my eyes widened slightly when I felt them elongate and poke out of my top lip. My wolf was nearing the forefront of my mind as she watched through my eyes, our mate bringing us pleasure.

Adrenous glanced up at me, the glow of my eyes reflecting in his, realising my eyes had changed colour slightly. "Is your wolf enjoying this too?" He smirked, his own eyes darkening, shifting in colour as I nodded, my eyes half lidded with lust as I stared down at him.

He paused his movement for a moment, his eyes flashing mischievously, his voice husky with lust as he said, "Let's see if you taste as good as you smell." My eyes widened slightly, excitement bubbling through me as he gripped my underwear, pulling them down my legs in one swift motion and then discarding them somewhere in the room.

My hips rose off the bed slightly when his breath fanned against my throbbing clit, startling me. I was soaking at this point, my arousal dripping onto the sheets as his tongue darted out, running along my slit and over my clit as I buckled beneath him, my chest rising and falling as my breaths came in short pants.

"Please, more," I begged, my voice shaky as I struggled to form a proper sentence.

He did as I asked, his tongue lapping up my arousal as he ran it up and down my slit, running over my clit before he drew it into his mouth, sucking on it gently. Moan after moan stringed together from my lips as I gripped the sheets beneath me tightly, feeling the pressure build within my lower abdomen.

"You taste so good." He groaned against me. His tongue darted into my entrance, fucking me with it as I thrusted my hips upward, begging for more. I whined when he used his strong hands to push me down back onto the sheets, demanding full control as he continued his assault on my body. I haven't experience anything like this in my lifetime and it felt so fucking good.

I yanked my hands from the bed, entangling them in Adrenous's hair. I gripped it tightly as I was approaching the edge. I had no idea what was over the cliff but my body begged for it.

"Oh my god . . . yes!" I screamed as he quickened his pace. I almost shot up when I felt his thumb beginning to massage my clit. "Shit," I breathed out.

I could feel my walls beginning to tighten around Adrenous's tongue, his thumb beginning to massage my clit more aggressively as I screamed with pleasure, all thoughts gone, my mind only focused on the delicious feeling as I became closer and closer to the edge.

"That's right, baby. Cum for me."

That was all the encouragement I needed as I fell over the edge, my hips shaking as my walls clenched repeatedly against his tongue as he lapped up the juices that were flowing out of me. My screams drowned out all other noise, my back arching of the sheets as I rode out my orgasm.

When I finally came down from my high, I looked down at Adrenous, his eyes were dark, his face pulling away from my slit as he climbed up my body, his lips coming down on mine in a soft kiss. I could taste the sweetness of my juices on his lips, causing my stomach to flip with more desire as he pulled away.

"You taste amazing," he complimented, his eyes flashing.

We held each other's gaze for a moment, my eyes soon glancing down to the strain in his pants.

I wanted to taste him just like he had tasted me.

A growl emits from the back of Adrenous's throat when a knock resounds from the other side of the door.

No! You've got to be kidding me.

Adrenous regretfully pulls away from me, pursuing the door as I quickly pull my dress down and cover myself with the sheets. I could hear him discussing something with someone who's voice I recognised to be Arif's.

When he was done he walked over to me, pulling me up to stand in front of him. "I'm sorry I have something to take care of," he said, his eyes pained with his own frustration.

I nodded my head in understanding. I probably won't even see him for at least a few days now and the thought struck me hard as I tried to look calm. "I'll send for Rylan to watch you while I'm gone."

"How long will you be gone for?" I tried not too look too disappointed as I stared up at him.

"Only a few hours, I promise."

"Okay." I sighed as he brought a kiss to my forehead and left me alone once again.

I looked into the mirror near the wall opposite the bed. My dark curls were tangled and my dress creased. I didn't care though. It was a reminder of what had just happened.

I could still feel the soft tingles on my lips from our kiss and the now overly sensitive area between my legs. Right now I was in bliss. True bliss.

✦○✦

CHAPTER FOURTEEN
A Game

✦◻✦

ADRENOUS

We made our way towards the cellar hidden underground in the woods. Arif was walking in sync beside me, his expression dark and angry as we manoeuvred our way through the trees. He had that fury hidden beneath his irises for as long I could remember and right now it was aimed at the situation at hand.

"Where did you find it?" I demanded when we reached the centre of the woods, the air around us blowing rather harshly tonight, causing the trees to rustle above us.

"Near the border, it tried to run but we managed to capture it." He smirked. His clothes were filthy, evidence that he had to get down and dirty with the creature in order to capture it. His hands were curled into fists at his sides, his eyes focused ahead of us.

I nodded in approval, not saying much more as we reached the cellar door hidden beneath the leaf covered floor. I stomped my foot a few times, listening for the sound of metal and looking for the door. When I heard the familiar sound I knelt down, moving a few leaves out the way and then wrapping my fingers around the door handle, pulling it up in one swift motion. We made our way down the steep, concrete stairs that led to where the prisoner was being kept.

When I lay my hands on him he's going to wish he never stepped foot in my territory. We hadn't captured one in years. They had become much more clever and were better at avoiding being seen. *But not this time*, I thought with a dark smirk.

This creature had not only disrupted my evening but had also disrupted an important moment between me and my mate. My still hard cock straining against my breeches was all that was left of that moment and it still ached for a release that never came.

Titan and Hunter were already there with the prisoner in their grasp when I turned the corner, a black bag over it's head, concealing it's features. I signalled for them to take it off. They obliged and revealed a rune with black hair reaching just above his shoulders and black eyes which were glaring at me with the same hatred that reflected my own. It's clothes were torn where it had been slashed by my generals, it's wounds trickling with black blood and its face was covered in dry mud.

He hissed and sneered at us, trying to get out of my generals grasp as they held onto him tighter, maintaining their positions. Arif moved towards the creature before I could say anything and threw his fist into the creatures face, full force.

"Behave in the presence of the king," Arif warned, pulling his fist back to his side.

He screamed and groaned in pain, spitting out blood as he hissed, "Let me go."

"You're not going anywhere," I spat, causing the creature to bow his head slightly when he sensed my dominance. It didn't however stop the rune from sneering once again.

"Master, will not be happy," he said, an underlying threat hidden in his tone as he smirked at us.

"That's too bad," I said mockingly, nodding to Hunter who understood exactly what I was asking before I glanced back down at the rune, "He won't like this either." His face fell slightly, understanding the dark threat hidden in my tone, his eyes glancing around rapidly when Hunter released his grip. Titan held him down by his shoulders, keeping him from running for the exit.

Hunter pulled the metal table beside the rune, his expression revealing his terror as he caught a peak at all the sharp instruments I had at my disposal.

I smirked darkly, reaching out and picking up one of the many knives. I played with it in my hand, the light from the candles on the wall reflecting off of it as the rune eyed it with fear and caution. Hunter moved back into his former position, helping to hold the rune in place.

"Now we're going to play a little game," I circled him as I spoke, his head tuning to watch me but couldn't see me with Hunter and Titan in the way. "I'm going to ask a question and you're going to answer truthfully." I finished when I returned to standing in front of him.

"What part of that is meant to be a game?" He retorted, the unease in his voice strong.

"Simple, if I guess you're lying or you refuse to answer, I get to punish you with one of these." I smirked, gesturing to the tools on the table. He didn't respond as he looked up at me. I took that as him choosing to comply.

Arif's smirk reflected my own as he too took pleasure in seeing the fear beyond the runes eyes. Hunter and Titan remained expressionless, their focus going into keeping the rune still.

"Why are you here?" I demanded. My body shaking as my hatred for their kind surfaced. My wolf wanted to come out and rip the creatures throat out but I remained calm, the knife in my hand twirling in my fingers. "What do you want?"

The rune let out a dark chuckle, his eyes filled with amusement. It looked at all three of us before answering. "We want her," he hissed.

"Who?" My body shook, holding my wolf back was getting more difficult as the creature continued to chuckle, mocking me like I wouldn't hurt him.

Like I wouldn't carry out my promise to punish him.

The chuckling turned to a shrill scream when I threw the knife into his right shoulder, blood dripping down his clothes as he leant forward, gasping for breath. Hunter and Titan hauled the creature back up to his knees to face us once again.

I kneeled in front of him. I narrowed my eyes, plucking the knife from his shoulder effortlessly, emitting another scream from his hoarse throat. "Who?" I beamed, my wolf shining through my gaze, ready to burst if we didn't get the response we wanted.

"Your mate." He spat at me, his lips curling up as he struggled against my generals slightly.

What the fuck? How did they know know about her? I thought I had done a good enough job at hiding her. I grasp the creature by the throat, bringing its face closer. My wolf was in full control as I'm pushed to the edge slightly.

"How does he know about her?" We roared, whilst shaking his form ferociously.

"He's always known about her." He chuckled "We lost her for a good few years but then found her again, keeping tabs on her." He smirked. "And then the night of the ceremony we discovered something . . . She's your mate."

I furrowed my brows in horror. For the first time in years, he finally had something against me.

"I have to admit that was a delicious surprise." He licked his lips as he spoke. I instantly slammed my head into his face, head butting him. The sound of his nose breaking was music to my ears. I leant back, happy to watch the blood dripping from his nose.

"How did he know who she was before I did?" I growled with rage.

The creature didn't reply, shaking his head as if to shake away the pain and instead began chuckling again, his teeth stained with the blood that was pooling from his nose. It's dark chuckle rang in my ears, infuriating my wolf to a new extreme.

That was it!

Without thinking, I grabbed the saw from the table and then crouched back down in front of him, I yanked his hand forward, forcing his body to lean towards me, his chuckling ceasing as fear crossed his features once again. That's what I liked to see.

His expression fell drastically when I balanced the edge of the saw against his pinky finger, my eyes daring him to defy my command. "How does he know?" I snarled, repeating the question, my rapid breathing reflecting his own, his eyes glancing down at the saw and then to me, already deciding for himself what was going to happen.

Realising his answer, I viciously press down on the saw, severing his finger from his hand. Blood squirted out, staining the damp concrete whilst his screams echoed around the room, falling on death ears.

Hunter and Titan didn't flinch or turn away, stomaching the scene in front of them with ease. This isn't the first nor the worst thing they have ever witnessed me do. Arif's eyes continued to dance with pleasure , enjoying the gruesome scene before him. If it were up to him he would rather be in my position, carrying out the torture.

I didn't give a fuck anymore. My patience was long gone as I waited for his wailing to cease. I kept a firm grasp on his hand, not allowing him to retract his arm instinctively to his chest.

"How?" I roared once again. He flinched from the tone I used but again gave no reply except for his raspy laugh surrounding the cell again. He should have been more than desperate to spill the information to us by now but it seemed we would have to take this further.

I gripped the saw slightly and this time levelled it against his wrist. "I won't ask again." I sneered. This time his raspy laugh didn't stop, the fear in his eyes well hidden, trying to make out he didn't care.

Very well then. It was clear he wasn't a compliant player. Too bad for him, I was. This time I sliced through his flesh slowly, his screams echoing around me. Tears had brimmed his eyes, sliding down his dirty cheeks as the blood began to pool from the wound, soaking my breeches and staining them black.

I kept going until the saw met his bone. The Rune's eyes closed and his body slumped back against Hunter and Titan as they kept him from hitting the concrete floor. He had passed out, the pain being too much for him to handle.

"Adrenous that is enough!" Titan and Hunter both warned me.

"You won't get answers if you bleed him dry, he's lost too much blood." Titan's voice was deadly serious, understanding that if I didn't stop the bleeding he would most likely die and we wouldn't get the answers we needed.

"Think about Alivia," Hunter added. I instantly stopped, pulling the saw out of his flesh, his hand still intact. Given some time, he would heal on his own. Runes healed a lot slower than us and Vampires, but they could still heal themselves quicker than the average human.

They were both right. I wasn't going to get the answers I needed to keep Alivia safe if I bled him dry. I suppose if torturing wasn't the way to go we'd have to pull out another tactic. I knew just the guy for the job but whether or not he would be up for it was another matter.

I turned to Arif and said, "Tell Rylan I need to speak to him in the secret study." Arif nodded, his eyes shifting to the rune with hatred before he turned on his heals and ascended the stairs. "Lock him up and seal the wound," I ordered Hunter and Titan. I took one last glance at the filthy creature before he was dragged away. Soon I'll know all his secrets . . .

✦✧◯✦✧

CHAPTER FIFTEEN
Eavesdropping

✦▢✦

Alivia

  Adrenous has been gone for nearly two hours since he left with Arif.
  My jealousy towards Rita had soon faded in that time after what played out between me and Adrenous, my wolf and I satisfied with the pleasure he gave us and the way he assured us he only wanted us. I had to give it to him, he was amazing with his hands and his tongue.
  Of course, I planned on returning the favour at some point. But that would have to wait.
  My eyes lock with Rylan across from me, his body leaned against the back of the couch, his elbow propped on the arm rest as he rests his cheek against his hand, an open book in his other hand. I close my own book I had been reading. I figured I might as well learn more while Adrenous was gone but this book was of no help.
  Rylan follows my actions before his gaze flickers to mine. "Have you learned anything useful?" He nods towards the book in my lap.
  I sighed softly. "Not really. Just vague knowledge." My gaze drifts to the fireplace, focusing in on the flames that are licking at the pieces of wood, turning them black, allowing my mind to become blank whilst I take a break from reading.

Rylan smiled, disregarding his own book onto the cushion beside him. "Don't worry, you'll find out for yourself soon enough," he stated, referring to when Adrenous finally claims me and marks me. That's if I agree. I still don't feel ready but the way Rylan smiled at me, I know he's excited for that to happen. I didn't want to dampen his mood when I responded with, "I guess."

He smiles brilliantly back at me, making me feel slightly guilty for the way I feel towards this whole marking ordeal. Perhaps I just need some time to myself to properly think about it. I suppose only time will tell whether or not I could be ready for such a commitment, though I couldn't deny how much I was beginning to care for Adrenous and the way he made me feel was incredible. Especially earlier.

"Rylan, do you have a mate?" I said, perhaps he could sympathise with me if he had experienced similar insecurities.

He's taken aback for a moment, not expecting the question before his smile widens, his eyes becoming filled with awe when he answers, "Her name's Laurey. She's the most loving, amazing and gorgeous female I have ever met. I believe she'll like you."

"Maybe one day I can meet her?" I replied, thinking whether or not she really would like me. I hope so. It would be nice to have a friend here other than one of the generals for a change.

"Of course." He smiled. "You'll be welcome to my home anytime."

"Thanks." I'm pleased he's so eager to have me meet his mate but now it was time to ask him the question that was beginning to burn on the tip of my tongue, "Rylan were either of you scared when it came to claiming one another?"

Rylan furrows his brows, thinking the question over, he's about to respond when the door bursts open. We turn our attention in that direction to find Arif's bulky form now standing in the door way. I look him up and down, frowning at how filthy his clothes are, dried mud staining the fabric of his clothes.

The scar along his jaw and the one on his eyebrow seem to protrude from the way he's tensing his face tightly. His pale, yellow eyes glance at me briefly before landing on Rylan, "Adrenous needs to speak to you. You know where to go." His eyes flashed. His expression shifted.

I had observed them enough to realise they were mind linking. *Great guys, leave me out of the conversation why don't you?*

I glared at the both of them, not appreciating the way they were leaving me out in the dark. It wasn't fair. My curiosity and frustration building rapidly until Rylan breaks his stare with Arif to glance at me.

"Wait here, I won't be long." He assured me.

I'm not waiting anywhere . . .

I cover up my displeasure along with my hidden intentions, rolling my eyes playfully. "Okay, go on."

He chuckled at my response and then passed Arif, turning the corner. Arif glares at me from the doorway, giving me some sort of a warning look before slamming the door shut. Someone needs to stop with the glaring before the wind changes direction.

I was quick to my feet, quietly heading for the door. I open it so it's slightly ajar, turning my head from side to side to peak at the now empty hallway. Shit. Where did they go?

I step out into the hall, closing the door quietly behind me and then continue to turn my head in each direction, wondering which one they were more likely to go down. I almost jump when someone turns the corner.

I thought it might of been one of the generals but it's just a female who works here. "Excuse me?" Her gaze snaps to mine, startled slightly before she composes herself and gives me a sheepish smile. "Do you know where Rylan or Arif went?"

"General Rylan went that way. I didn't see General Arif with him," she answered, pointing in the right direction.

"That's okay, thank you." I made my way in the direction she had pointed out. I head along the hallway, keeping my ears perked for any footsteps or voices. Over the past weeks I had noticed that all my senses had heightened drastically and when I focussed properly I could hear for miles or see the smallest of details, one of the many perks of being half Wolven I suppose.

I halt my steps when I hear Rylan's voice coming from Adrenous's office. I leaned against the door and pressed my cheek against the wood but all I could hear were muffled words which didn't make sense. If they were in the room casually talking I would be able to hear them much more clearly. I open the door to peak through, furrowing my brows when I don't see anyone.

Where the hell were they? Rylan's voice was coming from this room, I was sure of it.

I was about to close the door and walk away when I heard them again. I strain my ears and catch the end of a sentence. ". . . I don't know abo—" The rest becomes too muffled to hear properly but I could recognise Rylan's voice. It seemed to be coming from the brick wall on the right of Adrenous's desk. I bite my lip, the risk of getting caught weighing on my shoulders when I decide to head toward the wall, pressing my ear against the cold bricks.

"The Rune didn't break under my torture. I believe your abilities will be able to help like last time, whether we'll proceed with this depends on how you feel about it." Adrenous states, his voice reverberating through the brick walls, allowing me to hear him clearly.

A rune . . . ? Torture? Torturing a Rune for what?

"I understand." Rylan sighed. "But I'm still struggling to make sense of all of this, how on earth could they have know about her before any of us?"

They've known about who before them? Urgh! What the hell is going on?

"You know as much as I do at this point. It would be good if you could take Ali away from this, perhaps—"

I pull away from the wall, the end of his sentence cut of from my hearing. I move away when the bricks begin to slide out of place and give way to a small passageway. Before the two can spot me, I bolt to the other end of the room, stepping backwards out of the doorway and closing it behind me as quietly as I can, my back facing the hallway.

They wanted me away? Why?

I allow a small sigh of relief to pass my lips when I'm sure I had gotten away with not getting caught, however, I feel two large hands grip my shoulders from behind. I tense up, my heart thumping fast against my chest when I glance over my shoulder to find a muscled chest. I allow my gaze to hesitantly drift upwards, coming into eye contact with Arif's angry ones.

Oops.

I smiled innocently, hoping to sway him to my side when I said softly, "Please don't tell him."

He shakes his head, not amused with my attempt at charming him. My smile falters, my heart continuing to race with the fear coursing through my veins. Arif keeps a firm hand on my shoulder whilst the other takes hold of the handle, pulling it down and then pushing the door forwards. I'm pushed into the room, staggering slightly before I'm able to catch myself.

Adrenous and Rylan are both surprised at the interruption. Adrenous leaning back in his chair in front of his desk, shifting his gaze between me and Arif whilst Rylan sits opposite him and holds back a smirk. Rylan always did have a good sense of humour.

I turn my gaze on Arif, glaring at him for pushing me into the room. He was such a snitch. He avoids my glare, pretending not to notice when his eyes lock with Adrenous's.

"Someone's been eavesdropping." Arif nods his head to me, his lips turning up slightly as if it brought him pleasure to rat me out like this.

I bet he was enjoying this more than he was letting on.

"Has she now?" Adrenous notes more to himself than anyone else. I avert my gaze to the floor when his eyes snap to mine, my body warming with the intensity of his stare.

Arif responds with, "Perhaps a shorter leash for such a nosy dog." I gasp at his comment, snapping my eyes to his which are completely unapologetic. If looks could kill he would be dead right about now.

Adrenous's voice cuts in. "Arif, one day when she's queen, she could have your head for that." I transition my gaze to Adrenous, his chest rumbling with laughter.

Great, now *he* found this funny?

Rylan is laughing as well, his voice cutting in between laughs when he says, "Arif you better run for the hills."

Damn straight! If I become queen, that is.

Arif leans against the door frame, crossing his arms over his chest, his eyes portraying annoyance rather than fear. "Perhaps. If the girl's got it in her blood to do such a thing."

You have no idea what I could be capable of. Sleep with one eye open, mister.

"I think she's got it in her." Rylan comments, winking at me.

I giggled in response, Arif snorting from behind me but I choose to ignore him.

"Don't think Rylan, it's dangerous when you think." Arif retorts, his eyes flashing intensely.

Rylan's expression flashes with mock hurt. he's about to respond but is cut off. "Right, it's enough of that. Can you guys give me a moment to speak to Ali." Adrenous's tone was more of a demand than a question. Arif pulls away from the door frame, leaving without question. Rylan stands to his feet, winking at me again before walking out the room, closing the door behind him.

Silence falls on the two of us for the moment. Easing myself further into the room, I take a seat across from him and lean back against the chair. My thoughts are returning back to what I had overheard, the amount of questions filing my mind are coming in quick and it's hard to prioritise them properly. Let's not forget I wasn't even suppose to hear anything so perhaps I should remain silent and allow him to do the talking for me.

Adrenous props his elbows on the desk, leaning his chin against his hands as he regards me with a soft gaze. "Tell me, what did you hear?"

I heard more then you probably wanted me to that's for sure.

I think of how I should respond to this, deciding to tread carefully, I said, "I didn't really hear much." I fear my response is too vague from the way Adrenous's eyes begin to darken slightly.

Adrenous is quick with a response, his tone serious. "I didn't ask how much you heard, I'm rather interested in the content." He regards me with an intense gaze, one that causes me to shift uncomfortably In my chair.

I released a reluctant sigh, I suppose I'm not going to get away with faking ignorance. "I heard you two talking about a rune you had captured."

His eyes flash when the words leave my lips, his expression revealing that this is exactly what he didn't want me to have heard.

Too bad for you, I have.

"Right . . ." he muttered to himself. "Is that all you heard?" His eyes were searching mine, most likely looking for a trace of deceit.

"Yes." A lie I hope he doesn't see through. "Why torture it? What were you trying to find out?" I pry.

His gaze hardens, clear he's unhappy with my line of questioning but then again, what did he expect? "I'm sorry, I can't answer your questions."

My anger flares at his words.

"But this isn't something you need to be worried about, nor do I want you to worry." He replies, standing from the desk and then rounding it to kneel in front of me, his hand cupping my cheek while I stare at him confused. "Just know that anything I do from here on out is to keep you and my kingdom safe."

115

Admirable as it is, I've decided not to ask about the girl they were referring to. Sometimes it's best to know more than people give you credit for and I could use that to my advantage one day.

I place my hand on top of his which is gently caressing my cheek, my lips forming a small smile. "I believe you."

And I do believe him. It's clear in the way he regards me and the wolven's aroud him. Especially those closest to him.

He smiles at me softly, my mind fuzzy as I allow myself to be drowned in his gaze. His hand brushes along my cheek when he said, "I need to know if you trust me?"

I furrow my brows slightly. It was a complicated answer, one I haven't had time to put together. He's keeping things from me but it was to keep me and everyone else safe and I couldn't blame him for that.

It's silent for a moment before I smile and breathed out, "I do trust you. I trust you'll keep me safe." *But do you trust me? Obviously not* . . .

His eyes softened, his hand still grazing my cheek. "It means a lot to me, having your trust. But if you want mine I need to trust that you won't sneak around, listening to private conversations, do you understand?" His tone is soft but the way his eyes gaze into mine, it's clear he's beyond serious.

I suppose that's fair. "Okay, I'm sorry."

His lips break out into a smile. "That's my girl", leaning forward, he brushes his lips against mine in a soft and gentle kiss. Before I can keep up, he picks up pace the kiss becoming more firm and hungry as our desire for one another increases at a gentle rate. I tear myself away from him, breathing heavily whilst I use my hand to push against his chest. He arches a brow, a smirk plastered on those gorgeous lips of his.

I decide this is my chance to return the favour and right now I was in need of a good distraction, wanting nothing more but to focus on just the two of us.

Here it goes . . .

"I—I want to taste you." My words are breathy, my eyes glancing down to his already hard length, straining against his breeches. How I'd love to wrap my lips around him, using my tongue to taste every inch of him.

His eyebrows furrow, his eyes dark with desire. He takes a moment to process what I said before he answered, "You don't have to—"

"I'm not asking." Even I surprised myself at how bold a statement that is. Adrenous arched a brow in amusement, a smirk tracing his lips before he wraps his hands around my body, planting them on my arse cheeks, between the chair, and lifts me up in one swift motion, causing me to squeal in surprise.

I wrap my arms around his neck when he releases one hand to open the door. I suppress a giggle when I notice all the confused expressions watching as he carries me down the hallway.

I wonder where he's taking us.

After ascending the stairs and rounding a corner he passes my bedroom for some reason and continues along until we reach the bottom of the hallway, only halting his steps when we're in front of a double door. He releases one hand again, opening the door easily and then carrying me inside.

I took note of the gorgeous red carpeting and the cream walls, squealing again when he plops me down onto a giant double bed. His chest rumbled with laughter at my reaction. And then he begins to trail kisses along my cheek and jaw. He went down my neck, a moan passing my lips as his kisses made my skin heat up and the sensitive area between my legs throbbed.

I pulled away again, my mind slightly fuzzy as our gazes lock. He watched me intensely when my hands trail down his shirt, feeling the bumps and ridges of his toned chest, his muscles protruding through his shirt. I gripped the bottom of his shirt, slowly pulling it over his head. He lifted his arms to help me pull it over him, tossing it on the floor.

I tap into the strength of my wolf to switch our positions and use my hand to push him down onto the bed, his eyes gazing into mine with surprise and excitement, trusting me as his back touches the sheets of the bed. I climb on top of him, straddling his waist as I lean down, my hands travelling up and down his chest, touching and feeling every inch of him whilst my lips begin to trail light, feathery kisses across his jaw, down to his neck and along his chest.

I can feel my fangs protruding out of my top lip, my wolf urging me to claim our mate but I resisted, pushing her to the edge slightly so she can still watch as we bring him pleasure.

"Someone's learning to take control." He teases darkly, his eyes trailing from my eyes down my body, appreciation glistening in those gorgeous eyes as he watches me.

"You're surprised?" I smirked.

He chuckles at my playful tone, shaking his head. "Not at all, I like it."

I'm glad and you're going to like this too.

My fingers began to undo the buttons of his breaches and then pulled down the zipper. I curled my fingers beneath the hem of the fabric, pulling them down along with his underwear. It moved through his thick and powerful thighs, giving me a clear view of his impressive length. Without thinking, my tongue darts out to lick my lips, admiring his hard cock. He caught me licking my lips, his eyes darkening and shifting colour to reveal the wolf within. *Yes . . . I want him to enjoy this too.*

He watches closely when I take his cock into my small hands, having to grip it with both because of how big he is. I smirked at him, my tongue reaching out to flick along the head, rewarding me with one of his groans. I continued to tease him, licking along his head and down his shaft, but never taking him into my mouth. Not yet. I want to see if he's going to beg for it.

I draw back my tongue, opting to press my lips against his cock, kissing and teasing. He groans, shifting his hips upwards, wanting more but I don't give in. A dark growl emits from the back of his throat. "Ali, if you keep up like this, you may find my cock thrusting in and out of you quicker than I had planned on and I don't think you're ready for that."

I feel my core tighten at his words, excitement sparking in my eyes, knowing it was going to be the closest thing to begging I was going to get. I decide to heed his warning, drawing the head of his cock into my warm, moist mouth, sucking on it and tasting the saltiness of his pre-cum. It was enough to drive me crazy.

"Fuck Ali, I want to feel my dick hit the back of your throat." He groans out through the intense pleasure, those crimson eyes of his causing my stomach to flip.

I can't help the corners of my lips curling upwards as I grip his cock harder, running my hand up and down his shaft a few times before I take him into my mouth again. My wolf enjoys how powerful this feels and I can't help but feel the same, bobbing my head up and down along his cock, sucking and gagging against him every time my chin touches down against the base of his cock..

His grunts and groans surround me, giving me the confidence to continue. He soon takes some control, thrusting his hips upwards, matching my rhythm. "I love watching you suck my cock." He groans, his eyes continuing to watch me. I glance up at him, our eyes locking as I continue to suck , my tongue flicking against his head each time my head comes back up.

I can feel his cock beginning to twitch and I quicken my pace, allowing my instincts to take over, knowing he's ready to spill himself inside of my warm mouth. "Yes . . . shit . . . I'm going to cum!" I can feel his cock expanding in my mouth, his cum hot as it hits the back of my throat. I slow my pace, using my tongue to lap up all of his cum and then swallowing it with ease, leaving him clean when I pull away. The taste drives me crazy with desire, my underwear drenched.

When I look down at him, he reaches his hand up to cup my cheek, using his thumb to wipe away some of the residue that had made its way to the corner of my lips. I don't think he expected it when I drew his thumb into my mouth, sucking and swallowing the leftovers. He stares up at me in awe, brushing his hand across my cheek.

"You're absolutely amazing."

CHAPTER SIXTEEN
Distressing News

✦▢✦

Alivia

    I kept my focus set on the marked path before me, excitement bubbling to the surface as I'm set to meet Rylan's mate Laurey today. It was about time I met somebody new. Plus, being cooped up in the estate for long periods of time was doing nothing for my health.
    Adrenous was happy for me to meet with Rylan's mate. He thought it would be good for me too. For once, I was glad we were on the same boat about something. After what had gone down yesterday between us, it was nice that I had the control for once and it was beyond exhilarating for both me and my wolf.
    After that, it was difficult for me to push her to the back of my mind. She wanted to take over so she could be with Adrenous's wolf but he said that she will in time. After that, she calmed down. She will be with her mate soon enough.
    I got beside Rylan as we walk along the path, a smile gracing his lips whilst he glances at me from the corner of his eye. "Me and the other three live in the larger cottages between the front tree line and the dense forest." He explains, pointing ahead where I can the tree line ahead of us, the spaces between them revealing the cottages he speaks of.

"Anyone else might think you live within the estate grounds with how often you're there." I joke, laughing. He joins in, his own chest vibrating with laughter.

I really thought they lived with Adrenous in the beginning with the way they're there all the time, but I suppose that's part of their job description.

"I could never. Me and my mate need our own space. But I suppose you're right. Even Laurey seems to think I'm away too much," he confessed, a sigh passing his lips.

Hmmm . . . I can understand a small fraction of how she must feel. Adrenous is off doing something important more often than not and I can't help but miss him when he's gone. It must be worse for her.

"She just misses you," I said. As smart and lovely as he is, it can be very confusing when it comes to knowing the workings of a woman's mind. Even I don't always know why I act the way I do or think the way I do. It can be very frustrating.

"I know, I miss her too when I'm away." He admits, guilt reflecting in those green eyes of his.

I offer him a small smile before my gaze lands on the massive cottages up ahead, about a quarter of a mile away. Four of them lined up beside each other for each of the generals, lots of land in front of them and behind them before the dense forest takes up the rest of the land.

"Rylan, which one is yours?" I asked, nodding my head towards the cottages.

"The second one from the left," he answered as we pass the front line of trees, the cottages a lot closer.

The one Rylan said was his has one floor and is at least two times wider than the average cottage. The walls are grey stone and the roof a dark slate. The windows are quite long with grey frames, allowing the warm sun to shine through and lighten up the small home. The front garden is professionally tamed, flowers of all variety marking a path toward the black front door.

It's beautiful and cozy, a quiet and peaceful sanctuary for Rylan and his mate.

Rylan unlocks the door, stepping inside while I wait in the door frame. He turns to me. "You don't have to stand there you know, come on in." I do as he says, closing the door behind me and stand beside him in the small hallway. Rylan called out, "Honey, I'm home!" *Such a cliché welcome.*

I rolled my eyes but based from his smirk, I realised he had said it to make me feel more at ease in his home. I appreciated it, smiling as he chuckled and winked at me.

Suddenly, a woman comes bolting through the hall, jumping into Rylan's arms as her legs wrap around his waist. They share a kiss as I stand of to the side, not feeling awkward at all.

When they pull apart, I finally got to see her properly. She's nothing like I have expected. For some reason, I had imagined her to be blonde but her hair is jet black and it barely touched her shoulders. She stares lovingly at Rylan with stormy grey eyes and her skin is a light and creamy tone.

"I missed you," she said to Rylan, her voice soft and warm. Rylan pulls her closer, his arms tightening around her before he finally releases her, allowing her feet to touch the wooden flooring.

"I missed you too," he finally responded, kissing her on the cheek and then taking a step back.

Her gaze suddenly fell on me now that Rylan's muscled frame is no longer blocking her view of the rest of the hallway. Her eyes shift back to Rylan's.

"Of course," Rylan began, ushering me forward. When I stand beside them, smiling at Laurey, he continues. "This is Alivia, Adrenous' mate." Laurey was astonished before she bows her head slightly in my direction. "Alivia, this is my mate, Laurey."

"It's an honour to meet you, Queen Alivia." Laurey bows her head once again, her words genuine.

I would be lying if I said that title wasn't appealing. "Please, just call me Alivia. I'm nowhere near becoming a queen just yet." I laugh softly. She seems slightly confused by that but nods her head anyway, her eyes softening.

"I thought today would be great for you two to get to know each other while me and Adrenous attend some important business," Rylan revealed, my eyes snapping to him. *He was leaving me here? He didn't mention this to me.*

"Rylan can I talk to you for a moment?"

Rylan turned to me. I narrow my eyes at him and it's clear he understood what I was going to say based on his apologetic expression. I quickly offer Laurey an innocent smile before I pulled her lying ass mate outside, gripping his forearm harshly.

"Ouch, easy there, I'm only delicate." Rylan winced. Once we were outside, stroking his arm when I release him.

I rolled my eyes at him before jabbing my finger harshly into his chest, causing him to whine once again. "You told me we were coming here so I could meet your mate, not once did you tell me this was all a rouse to get me away from the estate so you and Adrenous could do whatever it is you plan on doing. I bet it's to do with that rune, isn't it?"

"Liv, I—"

"It is to do with that Rune, isn't it? Why didn't you just say so? Stop tiptoeing around me like I'm stupid enough to not realise what's going on around me," I retorted, my feelings slightly hurt. Adrenous on the other hand will get what he deserves later.

"Fine, you're right but at the end of the day my loyalties lie with Adrenous," he reminded, stroking the area where I had harshly poked him.

"I'll let you off today but we'll be having words later, understood?" My expression serious. He nods his head like a child who has just been scolded for stealing from the cookie jar. It made me roll my eyes once again.

I took some breaths, trying to calm the stress that overcame me before I headed back inside to greet Laurey properly. It wasn't her fault her mate had dragged me here by lying to me.

Besides, a good girl talk is exactly what I needed after only being surrounded by guys since I've been here.

I saw that she was waiting patiently in the hallway, slightly confused that I had dragged her mate outside. When her eyes land on me they soften slightly. "Sorry about that," I said. "Please, I would love it if we could get to know each other." I can feel Rylan standing behind me when I added, "Rylan has told me so much about you."

"Has he now?" She smiles, her eyes meeting with Rylan's when he nods his head.

"Well, I hope you two have fun and I'll see you afterwards." Rylan steals a quick kiss from Laurey and then leaves us alone to get to know one another.

I spend the morning helping Laurey prepare breakfast, the both of us laughing and joking around the kitchen when she tells me embarrassing things about Rylan. I can barely contain myself when I grip the surface of the kitchen side, holding onto my stomach as my body wracks with laughter.

"I ca—I can't believe h—he thought it would be a—a good idea to—" I'm finding it hard to speak through my laughter after Laurey had told me that Rylan had thought it was a good idea to roll down a hill in wolf form for fun only to land in fox shit. He had needed a tomato bath after that to clean the stench which his wolf was not happy about, according to Laurey who had to force him. I wish I had been there to witness it.

Tears had sprung to my eyes from the constant laughter. I used my hand to wipe them away, trying to catch my breath while Laurey attempts to do the same.

"It's true." Laurey said after we've both managed to calm down. She scooped our breakfast onto our plates. The smell of egg, bacon and sausage filled my senses and made my stomach rumble. We both laughed again when hers does the exact same.

We took our plates of food to dining room table, sitting down as we both dig into the gorgeous food. "This food is amazing, thank you."

"Oh please, you helped." She waves the compliment away and then takes her own bite.

I dig in again, chewing on the delicious bacon while Laurey drinks her glass of water before asking, "So how did you and Adrenous find each other?"

I swallowed, grabbing my own glass of water for a quick drink before answering, "I snuck out when I wasn't supposed to and he found me in the woods but of course I believed I was human at the time and thought nothing of it." Her features shifted to confusion as I continued. "Well after that, it turns out he organised the Elders to have me at the Wolven ceremony so I could shift for the first time along with the pups, which as you can imagine was a big surprise to me."

She nods her head, understanding that I'm still new to all of this. "I have to say, this is the first time I've heard of mates meeting like that. I mean not only did you discover that you were one of us but that our king is your mate as well. That's enough to push someone over the edge." She laughs softy.

"Actually, I felt the so called 'connection' to him but I didn't understand what it meant until some time after," I confessed, placing my silverware down once I've finished my breakfast, my stomach now full as I lean back in my chair. She watches me closely, her mouth slightly agape at what I had just told her.

"I'm sorry, I don't mean to stare like this, it's just hard to believe how you and Adrenous met. If you don't mind my asking, where are your parents? Didn't your Wolven parent explain any of this to you?" Laurey asked, trying to piece everything together. "Wolvens don't have human mates so you're the first of your kind it seems."

If I couldn't piece my life story together, there's no way she'll be able to. I suppose I must be the first of my kind, which means my Wolven parent chose to mate with a human rather than their true Wolven mate. It's hard to understand the reasoning behind it and it's something I don't think I'll ever know.

I exhaled a heavy breath, my heart hammering in my chest at the thought of being abandoned in the woods . . . left for dead. I still can't piece together why exactly I was abandoned. I had assumed it was because they didn't want me, yet they had left me wrapped up in a blanket with my name on it. Why would they do that if they were just going to abandon me?

I had slept with that blanket every night since because it was the remnant of something I never got to experience.

I sighed softly, my expression now pained when my eyes met with Laurey's concerned ones. "I was left for dead in the woods, found and adopted by my uncle who found me. He's dead now but I lived with my aunt and two cousins until I was brought here," I said. Her features are stuck between feeling bad for me and holding admiration for the ones that took me in as their own.

"I'm sorry I brought it up," she said, her tone apologetic, placing her hand above mine to comfort me.

I smiled, changing the subject. "What about you and Rylan, how did you two meet?"

She removes her hand from mind, placing a piece of stray hair behind her ear as she recalls how her and Rylan met, her eyes withholding the love she feels for him. "We met around five years ago, I had just passed my medical exams and was now officially a doctor. Well, it turns out the moon goddess has a funny way of bringing mates together as I'm sure you can guess who my first patient was." She giggles, rolling her eyes playfully.

"Oh no." I laughed softly. "What happened to him?"

She shrugged her shoulders. "Just an injury from training." She smiled softly, standing up and grabbing both plates. "Not long after that we claimed one another and have been happy ever since." It seemed like she didn't have any doubts about their relationship like I do with Adrenous.

I followed Laurey into the kitchen. "Can I ask . . . did you and Rylan ever have worries or doubts when it came to claiming one another?"

She seemed taken aback by my question, placing the plates in the sink before her eyes met with mine once again. She sighed. "I was apprehensive in the beginning. The thought of giving myself completely to someone else was difficult for me because I was always so independent, but when I finally stepped over that threshold it was like nothing I've ever felt," she said.

She's right, it is a difficult decision but I suppose if stepping over that threshold is what it takes than I think it's what I want.

"Thank you, you've put my mind at ease more than you know." I want Adrenous more than I think I do and that should be enough for me to take the next step and allow him to claim me as his.

I'm brought back from my thoughts when a loud knock wracks the front door. I don't think it's Rylan because he wouldn't need to knock. I turn to Laurey, silently asking for permission to answer the door and she nods her head, yes. I swung the door open to find two armoured guards, looks of hysteria on both their faces. My anxiety came forward. "What's wrong?"

They both glance at one another. "General Rylan has fallen ill. Is his mate home? She is required in the medic wing."

My eyes widened, panic seeping into my tone. "Laurey!" She rushed out of the kitchen. "Rylan has fallen ill," I said.

"Doctor, your assistance is required immediately," the guards reiterated.

"I'll leave right away." Laurey rushed out the door, the two guards stepping aside to allow her to leave.

"I'm coming with you," I said. She glanced back, giving me a thankful look before I watch her shift before me. Black fur replaced her flesh as her wolf comes forward, bounding past the front tree line and along the marked path back to Adrenou's estate.

I called upon my own wolf, hearing and feeling the snapping of bones as brown fur erupts across my flesh. My nose elongated to form a muzzle. My teeth were replaced with fangs. When I fully shifted, she released a distressed howl, communicating to others what has happened before she rushed through the trees, following the marked path back to the estate grounds.

I just hope Rylan's okay . . .

✦○✦

CHAPTER SEVENTEEN
Brain Damage

✦ ☐ ✦

ADRENOUS

The rune lays sprawled on the floor, unmoving. He had given up the fight and struggling when he came to the conclusion that it was of no use. There was no escaping from me. Three inches of pure silver was the only thing blocking me from reaching him, protecting him from my wrath. For now.

My lips curved upwards. I like that he's vulnerable and weak before me. No shred of mercy from me is going to save him and he knows it. I can't wait to see the look on his face after he realises what we plan to do. This whole time he's managed to conceal whatever information he's hiding in regards to Alivia, but soon we'll know everything. Soon Rylan will retrieve all the information we need to know about what he wants.

I heard the metal doors above open and shortly behind it, Rylan's footsteps can be heard as he descends the stairs and turns a few corners before I see him emerge and stand beside me. His eyes are hard and filled with dread as he comes to understand what is expected of him . . . what he must do in order to ensure everyone's safety, including his own mates.

His eyes skip me, snapping straight towards the rune, which lies limp on the damp floor. "Are you sure you want to proceed with this?" I push, needing to know if he'll be able to handle what has been asked off him. it's critical that he can because he is the only one able to.

Rylan stares long and hard at the Rune before shifting his gaze to me, his usual humorous self gone, his expression and demeanour now completely serious as this is no joke and will not be treated as such. "Yes, let's get this over with." He nods his head, stepping closer to the cell door, mentally preparing himself.

"Do you know what you're looking for once you're inside?" I pressed. It's vital that he uncovers everything I need in order to protect my mate along with everyone else.

"Take hold of his mind, find out how they know of Alivia's existence and whatever else they know revolving around her and then report everything back to you." He repeats everything back to me. Everything I asked of him back when I called him into my secret study. The conversation that sadly Ali had slightly overheard.

Everything I'm doing is for her own good, to protect her and keep her safe from the creatures that lurk within the shadows. I'm well aware Rylan hates entering the minds of murderous beings. He didn't like to see what they have done to innocents that were unlucky enough to come across them. Rylan's body remains slightly rigid as his jaw clenched. He glared back down at the weak form of the monster through the bars of the cell door. He rolled his shoulders back and tilted his neck from side to side, hearing the clicking of his bones. His glare never once wavered.

"Are you ready?" I walked towards him, pulling the key to the cell from my pocket. I was getting ready to unlock it once he responds to my question.

It takes him a moment, keeping his sights set on the the rune. His thoughts calculated whether or not he's ready for this. He finally makes eye contact with me, all doubt vanishing from his eyes. "Ready."

I nodded my head, placing the key into the lock. I open the cage just enough so that Rylan's body can fit through and then locked it once again. The rune's eyes flutter open, looking up at

Rylan in fear as he approaches him. He has no idea how much pain he's going to be in, knowing that Rylan will have to force his way in as the rune won't give in easily.

I smirk at the thought, he deserves every ounce of pain coming his way.

Rylan stood over the creature as I watched, anticipation consuming me as I thought about how this is going to play out. I only required him to do this one other time and it had taken him a week to recover from what he saw. I wish I didn't have to make him do it again but we need to know what they are planning. What *he* is planning.

My eyes narrow on the rune when he crawls backwards, toward the back corner of the cell, hissing at Rylan. I took a step forward but halted when Rylan's words slip through my mind.

"It's okay, I've got this."

I nodded, staying put as I watched him continue to approach the rune, his eyes darkening as his wolf steps forward, demanding the Rune's submission.

My eyes widen when its flesh tore apart, replaced with black leathery skin, the rune revealing his true form. From head to toe, its leathery skin covers him, his bony arms longer than a human's, with talons instead of claws at the end of each bony finger as he lashes at Rylan with them. He almost catches Rylan's arm but he was quick to dodge.

"Do you need some help?" I offered, ready to unlock the cell and help tame the Rune but Rylan shook his head when I approached the cell door. *"Be careful,"* I said.

Rylan's nails are replaced with claws as he lunges at the creature, slashing him across the cheek, a wail being torn from the rune's already hoarse throat. He cowers back into the corner, regarding Rylan cautiously as Rylan continues his earlier approach. Rylan's wolf once again demanding submission and this time the rune bows his head in defeat, too weak to fight, knowing he'll easily lose.

Rylan lets out a sharp breath when he places both hands on the rune's shoulders, his claws digging into the leathery skin to keep him in place, causing him to cry out. The Rune instantly tries to get away but a growl from me stops his movements. The Rune's black eyes snap to me with pure hatred.

Good, he'll hate this even more.

I watch as Rylan begins concentrating on the task at hand, his eyes closed tight as he takes in deep breaths. Once he's certain he has the rune under control his hands move up towards the runes temples.

A burst of electricity runs between them as both there bodies jolt, causing me to take a step back from the impact of energy that surges out slightly. Both their heads tilt back towards the ceiling, their eyes open wide. A pure white glow gleams from both their eyes, appearing completely glazed over.

It's been roughly an hour now, the two of them stuck in the same position as pulses of electric continue to surround them. It was taking longer than I had anticipated, Rylan should have been finished by now. It seemed off. Something wasn't right.

All of a sudden, Rylan's full body begins to convulse and tremble, losing his footing and collapsing to the floor. I rushed forward, digging the key out of my pocket while the rune is still conscious, riving in pain as he begins to claw at the sides of his head. The scream that emanated from its throat is extremely high pitched that I drop the key and instinctively bring my own hands up towards my own ears to block out the sound, collapsing to my knees.

"Please master, spare me!" The rune manages to scream out, the sound piercing my ears. Whoever he was talking to doesn't seem to be listening as the rune's screaming continues, feeling blood trickle from my ears through the pain. I manage to lift my head up, watching his head turn raw red before black blood splattered everywhere, covering nearly every inch of the cell as his head exploded. His body fell limp on the floor, the pain that was resonating through my head finally ceasing.

I immediately rose to my feet, picking up the key and heading towards the iron bars. I unlocked the cell to find Rylan unconscious on the blood-soaked floor. I kneeled down to check his pulse and sighed in relief. He's still alive.

What the fuck just happened?

I picked up his limp body, slumping him over my shoulder and heading up towards the forest. I ran towards the infirmary, startling passing servants. I ordered for Laurey to be summoned to the infirmary right away. Whatever is wrong with him, hopefully she'd know and be able to treat it.

I place Rylan down onto one of the plain beds, his closed eyelids scrunched up. I couldn't understand how this happened. Whatever it was, it was obviously a trap set out by Krellin. He must have known we'd find a way to get information from his minion and found a way to prevent us from doing so.

I growled in frustration, putting my fist through the wall beside Rylan's bed.

"There's no need for that." I turn to find Laurey, Rylan's mate. She walks towards Rylan's bedside, dressed in a white robe and breathing heavily. She had obviously shifted and ran as quickly as she could when she heard of Rylan's state.

Her eyes grow wide, looking at the black blood soaking his clothes, knowing it's not his but turns to me for an explanation.

"The Rune's head exploded," I said bluntly. She shook her head at my answer, turning her gaze back to Rylan. "Will you be able to help him?" I asked, watching her forehead crease in worry while observing Rylan's condition.

"First, I need to run some tests," she answered, worry etched into her tone.

My nostrils flared, smelling the familiar scent of Alivia. I turn my head to the side, seeing her turn the corner. She too wears a white robe and looks completely knackered from having to run.

Her long, dark curls are mangled and matted to her sweaty forehead, her gorgeous blue eyes gaze into mine for a moment before her focus shifts to Rylan, a look of concern crossing her features.

As Laurey gets to work on her mate, I walk over to where Ali is standing, tucking her into my side, wrapping my arm around her small waist and placing a light kiss onto her forehead.

Her voice is soft and quiet. "What happened to him?"

"I'm not completely sure. I had him interrogate the rune to find out what they're planning and after an hour he started to convulse and collapsed to the floor," I explained, keeping certain details a secret. Perhaps sometime in the future when I know she's completely safe, I'll be able to tell her.

"And what of the rune?"

"Dead. I believe somehow when his master found out what we were doing, he managed to kill him with some sort of mental ability." I revealed my suspicions from what I had observed back in the cell. Hopefully, I'll be able to determine the cause later on.

"Oh . . ." she breathes out. "When you say 'interrogate' do you mean Rylan used his special abilities? Is that what I had overheard you two talking about?"

I was shocked that Rylan had told her about that. He was usually quite wary of any one that he didn't really know. I had underestimated how close and comfortable they were with each other. My chest tightened out of jealousy, answering her with a simple nod.

We waited whilst watching Laurey use a variety of chemicals to test Rylan's symptoms. When she's done with her assessment of Rylan's symptoms she turns to face me and Alivia. Devastation is etched into her face, causing anxiety and fear to crash over the both us in huge waves. Ali becoming overcome with worry and panic as I hear her heart rate starting to pick up and a shallow breath escaping her lips. Unease crept into the room like a thick fog.

I looked over at Rylan. His face is still pained as he sleeps, his forehead now covered in sweat causing his brown hair to stick to his face.

"Laurey?" It was Alivia who spoke, her voice soft and gentle.

"He's alive but has gained quite a high fever . . ." Laurey begins, a tear escaping her eye but she quickly wipes it away with the back of her hand. Alivia steps towards her and stroked both of Laureys arms in a comforting manner. My wolf's chest rises in pride at how caring his mate is and I agreed. "I don't know what's wrong with him but whatever it is it's got to be some sort of dark magic."

Fuck!

"What do you mean by dark magic?" Alivia looks towards me for the explanation.

"There are people known as the Wells. They can harness either evil magic, also know as dark, or light magic. It seems that our enemies have the dark kind and are using them against us." It seemed I had one of my answers and I wasn't happy about it.

"Well it doesn't matter what caused it." Laurey said. "If Rylan's fever doesn't break before tomorrow morning, he'll die." Her voice held so much agony for Rylan. "I can feel his pain, Your Highness, whatever's going on inside his head right now is making him frightened and confused"

I already had an idea on what to do.

"Well, lucky for us I know of a light Well who owes me a favour. I'll have her summoned right away." I assure her.

Laurey and Alivia's relief shows strongly. "Thank you." Laurey thanks, hope shining in her eyes as she sits in a chair at Rylan's bedside, taking one of his hands within her own.

Rylan is one of my closest friends and one of my loyalist. I will ensure Raven will use all her power to bring him back to us. She owes me that much.

✦✧◯✦✧

CHAPTER EIGHTEEN
A Revelation

✦▫✦

ALIVIA

Adrenous had sent Arif to retrieve the light Well. Once Arif was clear why he was given the command he wasted no time in waiting around and left immediately.

Me, Laurey and Adrenous had stayed with Rylan, the silence settling in as we silently prayed for him. His condition hadn't improved in the slightest, instead it had gotten slightly worse, beads of sweat had started to drip from his forehead, his face remaining pained as his fever continued to rise.

Laurey remained seated at Rylan's bedside, her hand holding his as her thumb slowly stroked the top of this hand. She holds a damp cloth in the other, wiping away the sweat from his forehead and trying to cool his temperature down.

In the short time that I have been living here, me and Rylan had gotten fairly close. He has become one of my closest friends. I already knew what it was like to lose someone. When my uncle had been murdered by vampires, anger and sorrow had consumed me completely, I had even gone through a stage of learning all I could about Vampires, especially their weaknesses.

If ever the time came that I would be face to face with a vampire, I wanted to make sure I could kill it. I wouldn't care if it wasn't the one who had murdered my uncle, it would still feel like justice to me. Luckily, I've never crossed paths with one. I wasn't prepared to let to vampires take someone else I cared about.

Hunter and Titan entered the room, moving my head up from Adrenous's chest to stare at them with tired and puffy eyes.

"We came as soon as we heard," Hunter said, his expression bleak as he approached Laurey, placing a comforting hand on her shoulder. "He'll be fine Laurey, he's one of the strongest."

"I know, thanks, Hunter." She smiled, removing the cloth from Rylan's head to place it around his neck.

Titan remains silent, standing beside Adrenous and me. Agony contorted his features, keeping his sights set on Rylan's vulnerable form.

Adrenous broke the silence that had settled once again. "Is Arif on his way back?" Arif had left around four hours ago now, the longer we're left waiting for his return the more anxious we become. What if he had failed in convincing this "Well woman" to come back with him? I don't think Laurey would be able to handle that. I didn't know much about what happens when a Wolven loses their mate but judging from what I did know, it was beyond heartbreaking. *Please don't let that happen.*

Hunter closed his eyes, concentrating. He stayed like that for less than a minute before opening his eyes back up again. He gave a reassuring smile. "I can sense that he's no more than a mile away. It shouldn't take no more than half an hour for him to arrive."

I instantly relaxed in Adrenous' hold, feeling his own body relax as he exhales in relief. Finally we have some good news.

As if on cue, Arif arrived within the hour and he wasn't alone.

Standing beside him was a young woman. Her hair was a midnight black and her eyes were big, blue orbs with long, thick eyelashes. She was stunning with a flawless, pale complexion. A slight contrast to her dark hair.

I didn't know who I was expecting but it certainly wasn't a young, beautiful woman. I was probably thinking of someone much older like mid-fifties or something.

Her gown was a gorgeous forest green and was made from equisite fabric. She was clearly very wealthy, but with the powers she supposedly had, I wasn't surprised to find she had expensive taste.

Adrenous pulled away from me, his posture tense as his face held admiration, walking across the room to greet the beautiful woman.

My chest tightened at how he looked at her. He walked ever so slowly as if he thought she'd disappear if he didn't. My whole body sat rigid as I was consumed by the similar feeling that I felt when Rita told me Adrenous was hers.

The black-haired beauty smiled up at Adrenous in a loving way when he leant down to kiss her hand that she held out for him. "Raven, thank you for agreeing to come."

"Please, I owe you this much for what you went through for me. I will be forever grateful, Adren." Her voice was barely above a whisper but I could hear her perfectly. I heard the way her nickname for the Wolven king slipped past her lips in a gentle and caressing way.

It didn't pass me that she didn't greet him by his title. They must have been close for her to be able to have had her own nickname for him. I wonder if they had been lovers. The thought forced a sharp pain to course through me as I struggled to breath. I took in a sharp breath to try and fill my empty lungs as I watched their interaction reluctantly.

"Alivia?"

My eyes snapped up to meet with Adrenous's. His crimson orbs were staring into mine, holding out his hand, beckoning me to walk to him.

I slowly made my way towards the two. When I came beside Adrenous, he placed a hand on my back and used his other hand to force my line of sight towards the young woman.

"This is Raven, she's one of my closest friends. She's like family to me." Adrenous explained, his voice reflecting the admiration in his eyes. I suppose I had assumed too soon. If he thought of her as family then they couldn't have possibly been lovers. The pain in my heart lessened and I was finally able to smile at her, a real genuine smile.

"Raven, this is Alivia. My mate and future queen." I was instantly overwhelmed by the pride in his voice as he said those words and I wanted to kiss him for it.

Raven seemed shocked by this information, "You finally found her." She stated, looking me over softly. "May I?" She asked, looking up at Adrenous.

I wasn't sure what she was asking but it couldn't have been anything bad because Adrenous nodded, accepting her request. She stepped towards me. "May I hold your hand?" she asked.

I was confused. I looked up to Adrenous for support but he just smiled and said, "You can trust her." If this woman had earned the Wolven king's trust, then I suppose she deserved mine.

I gingerly held out my hand to her and she took it with a look of fascination and interest. She stared into my hand, tracing the outlines of my palm and then touching and prodding each fingertip. As she did so, the palm of her hands illuminated with a soft glow. My jaw dropped at the sight.

She giggled at my reaction as she continued to trace the lines in my hand. Each line lit up in a different colour, there was red, green and blue.

Suddenly she gasped. "You're only half Wolven."

I looked at her with wide eyes. "How did you know?"

"I can look into people's souls just by touching and examining their hands. It's one of my many talents," she answered, her eyes dancing with mischief. "The green one is what tells me you're half Wolven."

"What do the others tell you?" I question, fascinated by her gift.

She was about to answer but was interrupted by Laurey's urgency. "I don't mean to interrupt but Rylan seems to be getting worse." Her voice was shaky and she seemed close to bawling right there and then.

My smile dropped as my heart clenched seeing her so vulnerable. My eyes turned to Rylan, his body now boiling as his face dripped with sweat, his features filling with agony.

Raven walked towards a distressed Laurey, placing her hand on her shoulder. "I'll see what I can do." And then she walked towards Rylan, his body now shivering.

She placed her hand on his forehead. We all let out a soft gasp as her palm glowed and radiated through his body. It was a different glow compared to the one she used on me, being much brighter and had a calming aura about it.

The glow illuminated his skin until it only remained on his forehead. The glow grew brighter until it aggressively changed colour from a pale yellow to a sinister red before it soon faded.

Hunter let out a low whistle only to be nudged by Titan. I would have giggled at the two if the situation didn't seem so tense. Instead I rolled my eyes at Hunter who shot me an apologetic look.

"What's wrong with him?" Adrenous being the first to question what was on all our minds.

"It seems my brother is behind this," Raven answered, her voice pained as she shared the information.

My eyebrows furrowed in confusion. "How can you be a light Well but your brother be dark?" I asked.

She stared at me, contemplating my question. "You have to choose to be dark. Any light Well can choose to be nasty if they wish it."

"You never told me Draven was working with Krellin." Adrenous sounded slightly angry when he accused her of keeping this information from him.

"I'm sorry, Adren, but I didn't know myself. All I can say is that this is his work." She was apologetic and the disappointment in her bother was very much obvious in her features.

Adrenous relaxed slightly. "Is there anything you can do?"

"He's trapped in his own mind whilst his body heats up until his mind finally bursts," Raven explained. "If he had been anything other than a Wolven, he would have been dead long before now."

"That must be what happened to the Rune," I surmised, looking up at Adrenous as I spoke the words. He nodded.

"I see. It looks like my brother's been busy," Raven said, a look of disgust on her face. "I'm sorry . . ." She looked at Laurey this time. "I'm afraid there's nothing I can do for him," Raven said softly.

Laurey began to cry. Her form beginning to shake as her tears fell to the floor and her wails of agony pierced the ears of everyone in the room. I instantly ran to comfort her, my own tears threatening to flow. Laurey sobbed into my chest as all three generals looked down with woeful expressions.

Raven quickly put her hands in the air and lit up the room with a soft glow, forcing our attentions back to her. I looked at her through tearful eyes. "Just because I said there's nothing I can do doesn't mean there's not someone here who can."

We all looked up at her, unblinking and confused. "Who?" Titan demanded.

"None of us here have the ability to heal," Adrenous confirmed.

"You're right about that, but your mate here is able to deflect someone else's power." Her eyes snapped to mine as she finished the sentence.

Adrenous's red orbs turned to me, disbelief crossing his features. He stalked towards me, grabbing my arm to pull me up and away from Laurey. "Why didn't you tell me?"

"I—"

"She didn't know, Adren." Raven revealed.

He let go off my arm and I held the spot that he had been holding. I shot him a glare as my arm ached slightly from his harsh grip. "She has no idea what she can do nor how powerful she is." Raven continued.

"I don't have any gifts and I'm definitely not powerful," I argued. I was about to storm out of the room when I bumped into a unknown force, some sort of visible wall. Raven was serious about her 'many talents.'

"Believe me when I say that I only speak the truth." She looked desperate as she tried to convince me that her words were true.

I looked at her, my features beginning to soften as I gave her the time to convince me. Raven recognised this and didn't hesitate to continue, "When I touched your hand"—she started gesturing to my hand that she had been studying—"the red glow was your link to Adrenous whilst the blue is your power, your life force even."

I contemplated at her words. Why would she lie to me? It seemed ridiculous that someone would go out of their way to explain something like this to me if it wasn't true. I looked back up at her.

"Alivia, I'm going to need your help or I'm afraid we'll lose Rylan." Her words hit me like a ton of bricks. How was I suppose to save his life?

"How? I don't even know how to use this gift that you seem to think I have." I argue, however my voice is soft. I don't want to upset Laurey even more by sounding as if I don't want to help her mate because I do.

I just don't understand how.

"I can get you into his mind but the rest is down to you. You need to deflect my brother's energy out of him or soon he'll die."

She must be crazy if she thinks that I will be able to do this.

Adrenous walks across the room. "Is it dangerous?"

Raven frowns as she lets out a soft sigh. "If she's in there when Rylan dies, then it could kill her as well."

I considered her words. There's no way Adrenous will let me do it.

Adrenous shakes his head but before he can forbid me from doing it she grabs his arm. "She's powerful, Adren. Believe me, she can do it." He stares at her for a minute and then lets out a defeated sigh, his eyes shooting up to meet mine.

He's giving me the control by letting me choose for myself.

I don't let any of my fear show. If Raven seriously believes that I can save Rylan's, life then I will try.

Adrenous pulls me into his chest. "You don't have to if you don't want to." He whispers gently, placing his forehead against mine.

I kiss him gently before slowly pulling away. His crimson orbs swirl with admiration. "I know, but I'm going to try."

I release myself from his hold and turn to Raven. "Let's do it."

✦✧○✦✧

CHAPTER NINETEEN
A State Of Mind I

✦◻✦

ALIVIA

I joined Raven next to Rylan's bed. "So how does this work exactly?" My voice was shaky, having no clue what I was doing. Raven mentioning that I could die if I fail while inside Rylan's mind doesn't make any of this easier.

"Place both your hands beside his head," Raven instructed, positioning herself on the right side of the bed. I did as instructed.

Rylan's head felt extremely warm and sticky as I gently settle my hands on his temples. My arms were shaking in fear, but I did well to calm my breathing and stop my anxiety from getting the best of me. *This needed to be done . . .*

"That's good. In a moment, I'm going to use my energy to place your consciousness within Rylan's subconscious state," Raven explained, studying whether or not I understood what she is telling me.

I nod my head, looking around the room. My eyes instantly found Adrenous's gaze. He gave me a reassuring smile and mouthed the words, "You can do this." His eyes however, showed pain and his body remained extremely tense. I knew he didn't approve with this but it was the only way to save Rylan.

I turned back to the task at hand. I could worry about Adrenous after this was over. If I survive that is. *Breathe . . . happy thoughts.*

Raven's voice is hard as she explains the risks to me. "When you're there, you must look for Rylan right away. There will be obstacles and challenges which will try and prevent you from doing so but you mustn't get caught up in it. You must remember why you're there or you will get trapped. They will use your worst fears and insecurities, but ignore them and you will be fine."

That's easy for you to say. "What about when I find him? I have no clue how to use this gift." I voice my concerns before she can proceed further.

"It's in your veins. It's your instinct. When it comes to it, your body will know what to do," Raven assures, her voice gentle. I pray she's right about that. "You ready?"

I swallow the lump in my throat. "As ready as I'll ever be."

Raven got to work straight away, her hands beginning to glow brightly. I had to squint my eyes at the blinding light as she placed her hands on the sides of my head. "You'll begin to feel a little woozy but it's nothing to worry about."

"If you say so," I mumble, Raven letting out a small laugh at my reaction causing me to smile as well. I didn't know what it was but she had a way with calming my nerves and helping me feel at ease.

She was right about the wooziness. My head began to swim as my eyes became heavy, yearning me to close them. I could feel my consciousness drifting away unnaturally, almost like my very being was being ripped apart from my body.

My physical body was left paralysed. Pain began to override my senses, my screams unheard because I couldn't do anything physically. Raven didn't tell me how painful this was going to be.

Everything went black as I was consumed with pain. It was almost like a soaring heat making its way through every fibre of my soul and pulling me apart, unravelling my essence as it poured into Rylan's. Suddenly I was numb.

It felt like my numbness lasted forever, until a cold shiver coursed through me, forcing me to jump at the shock. I was cold, very cold. The black abyss that surrounded me was endless. I felt as though I was floating weightlessly, travelling to an unknown place.

I couldn't even tell in which direction. Up? Down? I had no idea.

Just as I thought that this endless pit wouldn't stop, warmth began to flood through me. It wasn't painful like before but actually kind of pleasurable. I revelled in the sensation as it made every nerve ending within me tingle with life.

A bright light burst through my vision, blinding me. I shut my eyes tight until the brightness faded.

When I opened them again, I gasped.

I have never seen anything like this before. There were trees everywhere I looked; however, every single leaf was rose red. The leaves which fell created a gorgeous carpet of flowers on the floor. Everything was illuminated in a red aura-like glow. It was all so breathtaking.

I spun around, noting that everything was the same. Nothing but trees could be seen for miles.

My mind still felt fuzzy, recollection of why I was here coming back to me . . . Rylan! I had to find him quickly before it was too late.

Breathing in the humid air, I suddenly felt like I was enveloped in a sticky heat, the rising of Rylan's temperature manifesting itself into his subconscious. It was uncomfortable, causing my clothing to stick to me like a second skin.

I began to walk forward, no weight to my step at all, an unsettling sensation causing my stomach to flip. I have no clue where I am and it unsettled me further, everything was the same. Nothing was out of place or gave any indication as to why I was here.

"Rylan!" I called out, hoping he would hear me but there was no reply, the silence deafening as I glanced around.

My head whipped to the side when I heard something zap past me, the hairs on the back of my neck standing to attention.

I didn't have time to think of what it might have been before something with great speed lunges itself at me. I find myself gasping for air as I'm lifted from the ground by my throat. Eyes wide with fear, I stared into the dark abyss of black eyes.

It was the same rune that I had encountered from the woods. I begin to struggle, lifting my weak arms to scratch at the claws which were suffocating me. "Let . . . me . . . go!" I croaked.

"I said we would meet again." His head lulls to the side as his sinister eyes inspect every inch of my face. "My king wants to meet you."

"No . . . thanks." I continue to lash out, catching his groin with my knee, forcing him to drop me as I land on my ass, crying out from the pain that erupted from the impact.

He cries out, cradling his manhood as his dark gaze pierces through me. I attempt to crawl back whilst slowly rising to my feet, continuing to face him. I go to shift but my wolf is absent, her essence left behind, leaving me vulnerable and weak. *Shit . . .*

The rune captures the vulnerability that causes my demeanour to shift before he stalks forward like the predator he is. I take a step back but stumble over a log and land once again on the ground. "Tsk, tsk . . . can't beat me without your wolf now, can you?" He crouches down in front of me, capturing my chin as I try to pull away, my fear reflecting in my eyes as he studies me.

"You're nothing without your wolf," he chuckled, edging closer towards me.

Panic takes hold of my chest, feeling as if a pair of hands are squeezing the air from my lungs. He's wrong . . .

I think back to what Raven had said to me. *You must remember why you're there or you will get trapped. They will use your worst fears and insecurities, but ignore them and you will get through.* I have to ignore him.

I closed my eyes, mumbling to myself "This is not real!" Over and over again until I forced myself to believe it.

Something inside me began to build up to the point that it became unbearable. Without thinking, I was forced to release the pent up energy. A glow of blue burst out of me, turning the rune to dust before me.

"Shit . . ." I breathed out. Raven was right! *It's in your veins. It's your instinct. When it comes to it, your body will know what to do.*

I have to find Rylan.

The air seemed stuffier now as sweat started to drip from my forehead. My hair stuck to my face in an uncomfortable way.

I rose to my feet, the pain from when I had fell now completely gone as if it had never happened . . . because it didn't happen. It was all just a figment of my imagination. My fears came to life to distract me from my one goal.

Perhaps that's all I need to do. I have to remain focused on my goal. Closing my eyes, I think of Rylan, remembering everything about him, bringing him alive within my mind, wanting it to become my reality.

Opening my eyes, I watch as my surroundings start to ripple away like water. The scenery around me no longer solid, transforming and moving to form something completely different to the forest that had once been.

I now found myself standing at the entrance of a dark cave. It was sill humid but the sinister feel the cave gave caused the hairs on my neck to rise. My breathing was now ragged, my mind and body tired from wielding this place into existence.

I marched forward, ignoring my fear. My need and desire to save Rylan is my driving force. I can hear a pained cry echoing around me when I took a step inside, almost as if the cave had prevented all sound from travelling outside.

I continue on down, the darkness making it hard to see how deep the cave goes. It doesn't take me long however, seeing the source of the crying as relief floods through me. Rylan was in the distance, facing away from me as he continues his tormented cries.

I walk towards his kneeled form, only now noticing that a limp body lays in his arms, a pool of blood surrounding him, turning the concrete damp and crimson. I refrain from gasping at the sight, realising that this must be some kind of fear though it isn't mine. It's Rylan's.

"Rylan." I whisper but he doesn't seem to hear me through his cries of pure anguish. The sound of pain coming from him is enough to pull at my heart, bringing me to my knees as I crouch down next to him.

My eyes widened when I catch the face of the person lying in his arms, tears wanting to form. Laying limp and lifeless in his arms is Laurey. Laurey's dead . . .

✦○✦

CHAPTER TWENTY
A State Of Mind II

✦▫✦

ALIVIA

The tears cascaded down my cheeks before I could stop them, the scene in front of me too realistic.

Laurey's neck was ripped, blood still oozing out of the wound that resembled a bite mark. Now that I was closer, I could make out a few more bite marks across her thighs and wrists, blood pouring from them in an unrealistic manner, soaking Rylan's breeches in the process. Placing a hand on Rylan's shoulder, I attempted to gain his attention, tearing my gaze away from the horrific sight to look at him. "Rylan, what happened here?"

Rylan shook his head. "I—I heard her screaming. S—she called out to me and I couldn't . . ." His voice broke, a sob wracking his body as he struggled to breathe. "Vampires . . . th— they killed her."

That was his worst fear? He was afraid that he would fail to save the one person he loved the most, Laurey. Vampires, the one thing that they have spent their whole lives protecting everyone from, killed the one person he wanted to protect the most. They wanted this to be his fear. It was a warning, threatening to harm the ones he loves.

"Rylan . . ." I said but he doesn't look at me. I tried again, my voice harder as I attempt to break through his pain. "Rylan listen to me. This isn't real, Laurey isn't dead. She's waiting for you, this is just your worst fear coming to life."

"No! She's gone. The pain I'm feeling is too unbearable . . . that can only be caused by her death. The loss of my mate." He breathes harshly, trying to focus on anything but the pain that is continuing to overwhelm his senses. It's stopping him from realising that none of this is real.

"Rylan! The pain is not from her death. It is caused by a dark Well who wants you dead. You have seen the inside of the runes mind and he doesn't want you to tell us what you saw."

I know I don't have long to convince him but I have to let him understand what would happen if he doesn't listen to me. "We have to wake you up before the pain your feeling becomes too much. If you die . . . I die."

His pained cries halt for just a second, finally focusing in on me when I place my hand on his tear-soaked cheek, turning his head to the side to look at me. I then move my hand away from his face, tears still falling from his eyes as they trail down and fall to the ground. I hold out my hand to him, urging for him to offer me his own. "Take my hand."

He's reluctant to pull his hand away from Laurey. His eyes shifted back to her body, gliding his fingers across her pale cheek. My voice is soft but urgent when I reiterated. "Take my hand Rylan and I promise you'll see her again."

He nods his head, his eyes still on her when he takes the hand that is wrapped tightly around Laurey's lifeless form. He finally took my hand.

A light blue glow illuminates the cave. Rylan's eyes widened. He glanced my way and I offered him a smile and a wink.

Our surroundings started to ripple away. The solid, damp floor beneath us shifted and crumbled. Rylan held my hand tightly. "It's okay," I assured, even though I have no clue where we'll end up. Without warning, a flash of light blinds us as we hold onto each other instinctively. When the light dispersed, we opened our eyes.

It's dark out. A few scattered torches lit up a certain area as the flames cast dark shadows in the deepest corners of the small town. The moon is plastered high in the sky, helping to illuminate the houses that surrounded us. Me and Rylan stood at the edge. A dark tunnel was behind us, too dark to see what's on the other side.

The houses are fairly small and made from old, dried wood. The roofs were made from dark crumbling slate. I glanced in a few of the windows. There was no light or movement to be seen. Silence also settled in. Nothing could be heard but mine and Rylan's heavy breathing.

Everyone must have either evacuated or were fast asleep. The former made me panic because I recognised this street. Just around the corner is where my home was.

"Where are we?" Rylan broke the silence, his hand leaving mine as he took a step forward. "I don't recognise it."

"I do." I follow behind him, pointing forward. "Just around that corner is where my aunt and cousins live." There was fear laced in my voice, knowing that nothing good can come from being here.

I frowned when I noticed how Rylan broke out in a sweat, his features contorting in pain as he tried to force himself forward. "Are you okay?" I took a step towards him, but he held up his hand.

"I'm fine." He doesn't sound convincing as he walks in the direction of my house. "Come on, which one is your home?" he asks, his hair now matted to his head. He presses his hand to his head, trying to ease the pain as he faces away from me.

"That one," I whispered, pointing forward when we reach the middle of the street. I have a bad feeling about this. This must be another one of my own living nightmares. I had already seen that sinister rune. Now I was even more fearful of what to expect next.

Rylan suddenly collapsed to his knees, I quickly kneel down beside him and check his fever, his forehead coating my fingers in the sticky heat. He was boiling. We don't have much time left . . .

"I'm going to save us both," I whispered to Rylan but I doubt that he could hear me through the pain that has consumed him once again. He curled up, his body convulsing. There's nothing I can do to help apart from facing my fears . . . Whatever that may be.

I started to walk towards my home. Each step I made echoed around the street, causing a shiver to run down my spine. When I reached the front door, I took a deep breath before entering the threat that awaited me. But not before I checked on Rylan's state one last time, turning to see he was still curled up on the cold path. This was all for him. I have to save both of us.

The house was dark but I could see the silhouette of all the furniture in the living room, along with the stairs that led to our rooms. Everything seemed to be where it should be. The only thing out of place was the sinister aura that surrounded and suffocated me, causing my chest to constrict with fear.

"Hello?" My voice echoed around the empty room. "Auntie Helena? Avery? Amber?" Nobody answered me.

I made my way up our creaky stairs, the sound ten times louder with the silence that enveloped the house. The first door was my aunt's bedroom, left ajar which she never did when she slept. The door was always shut tight whenever she went to bed. I felt my heart begin to quicken as I pushed the door until it was wide open.

I instantly collapsed to the floor, crawling to the lifeless body at the foot of the bed. A scream was lodged in my throat as my chest constricted, making it almost impossible to breath.

I took my aunt's body into my arms, blood from a stab wound on her stomach soaked my clothes but I didn't care. My tears flowed onto her pale face, her brown eyes wide open in horror, knowing the last thing she saw was her killer. I gently closed her eyes, moving the strands of her blonde hair to the side so that I could stroke her cheek, holding her closer to my chest so that I could bury my head into her shoulder.

What sick bastard could do this? They deserved a fate much worse than this. Then I heard it . . . Muffled cries coming from my cousins's bedroom.

I placed my aunt gently onto the blood soaked ground, kissing her cold forehead before I ran to the bedroom. My eyes flashed with horror, adrenaline pumping in my veins, pushing me not to panic as I took in the sight before me. A man I had never seen before had each arm wrapped around each of my cousins in a tight grip, his giant hands muffling their cries.

He had pale white hair that flowed down to his shoulders, his unsettling blue eyes looking straight through me, causing me to shudder under his haunting gaze. His whole attire was black and his hands were gloved with black leather.

I had no recognition of him and right now the anger bubbling up inside me made him the person I hated the most.

"Let them go!" I basically demanded, my eyes hard as I held his gaze, not showing an ounce of vulnerability. My expression faltered when he snickered at my futile attempt at forcing him to let go of my cousins.

"Hush now, we're having fun. Aren't we?" He used his hold on my cousins to force them to nod their heads. They continued to cry, begging me with their bloodshot eyes to help them.

I've never felt so helpless in my entire life.

"You don't want to do this." I said, my eyes shifting from Amber to Avery before lifting my gaze back towards him. "Take me instead."

"Oh please." He mocks, his eyes flashing with dark intent. "Why give up your life for something that isn't even real?"

I furrow my brows, not understanding what he plans to do. His eyes flash, a smirk playing on his lips, unease settling within the centre of my chest. My heart broke the moment he broke both of my cousins' necks, a blood curdling scream tearing from my throat as he tosses them to the floor like they mean nothing.

I collapsed to my knees, the broken pieces of my heart shattering. My body trembling with the realisation that I was a failure. I will never be able to protect the people I love. I'm weak . . .

In a flash, he's kneeled in front of me, capturing my chin between his fingers before forcing me to look up at him, his eyes studying me. The air around us felt suffocating, struggling to breathe properly. My body was slowly heating up as I sat there exhausted, my face blank as I stared back at him, his face distorted by the tears in my eyes.

"My sister was foolish to send you in here." He smirked, gripping my chin tighter. "Did she really think the likes of a mutt could stop me? You're not even a full mutt which makes it even worse." He kicked me while I'm down, taking pleasure in my agony.

At least I know this is Raven's brother. Draven, I believe she called him. Her brother is a sadistic bastard.

I didn't reply to his mockery, not wishing to give him the satisfaction of toying with me but he takes my silence as a cue to continue. "Don't worry though, soon all you mutts will be either dead or bowed down to my king, leaving Adrenous for last. And it will all be thanks to you one way or another."

What does he mean by that? The mention of Adrenous causes something within my chest to tighten. My heart hammering at the thought of what could happen to him if these monsters did win whatever war they're waging.

I was beginning to remember why I was here in the first place, my eyes shifting to the lifeless bodies behind him. *They're not real. They're not dead and if I allow myself to die here then I'll never get the chance to protect them from the war that is coming.*

My lips turn up in a mocking smile, causing confusion and slight fear to cross his eyes for a split second. "But that's not today and I won't be preyed on by the likes of you," I whisper in his ear before an explosion of dark blue burst out of me, wiping out everything in sight. It made the building to begin collapsing.

I stand to my feet, my feverish body beginning to cool down as everything around me begins to spin like a tornado, the gust of air picking up the strands of my hair when it picks up speed. When everything finally halts to a stop I find myself in the middle of a field, a cool breeze sweeping through, blowing on the variety of flowers that surround me.

I hear someone grunting from behind me, turning to find Rylan on the floor. He's in the same curled up position as before but this time he's not in pain, looking up at me with the same surprised look as me. "Rylan!" I shout, so happy to see that he's okay and no longer in pain.

My hand instantly land on his forehead when I sit down next to him, finding that his fever has broken. I sigh in pure relief. "How do you feel?"

"The pain is completely gone, I don't know what you did but thank you." He smiles, bringing me into his chest, wrapping his arms around me, hugging me tightly.

"Anytime," I replied, hugging him back just as tightly, feeling so overwhelmed that tears escape my closed lids.

Just as we begin to enjoy this moment of relief and happiness, our surroundings begin to transform once again, feeling Rylan's grip on me disappearing as I lift my head from his chest, my eyes growing wide with fear. He looks down at his body, staring at his arms in disbelief as his form turns to dust, blowing in the direction of the wind as I watch him disappear completely.

What on earth is happening?

I feel everything around me tear apart including myself, my own body transforming into dust as my essence once again unravels itself before I'm smothered in darkness.

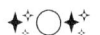

✦○✦

CHAPTER TWENTY-ONE
Awake

✦□✦

ADRENOUS

    I watch as Raven starts the process, pouring Ali's consciousness into Rylan's subconscious. Fuck.
    I couldn't move at all or speak. Raven had taken away my ability to move, ensuring that I wouldn't try and stop this from happening. To be honest, knowing how protective my wolf was over Alivia, it was highly likely I would have stopped it. Raven was incredibly clever . . . *and fucking sneaky*, I thought bitterly.
    Alivia's eyes found my own, her gaze soft. All I could do was offer her a reassuring smile and mouth the words 'You can do this.' She smiled back at me and then focused back on Raven who was explaining the dangers to her. I wanted to protest but nothing passed my lips. I was left to brood in silence.
    Alivia is hesitant, trying to understand exactly what she's getting herself into. "What about when I find him? I have no clue how to use this gift." She's underestimating her capabilities. Her powers are new to her but they're a part of who she is . . . Her instincts will take over when the time is right. Just like me when I discovered my own.
    Raven voiced exactly what I'm thinking. "It's in your veins. It's your instinct. When it comes to it your body will know what to do."

I never thought my mate would possess any gifts, it was unheard of that anyone outside of mine and the generals lineage would posses abilities.

It made me more curious about who her parents could be.

I was brought back to the room when Ravens hands began to illuminate, placing them on Ali's temples. Even I had to squint my eyes as the glow brightened, encasing the room in a bright light, feeling the energy pulsate around us, causing the hairs on my arms and neck to stand to attention.

Ali's eyes soon glazed over, Raven continuing to work her magic.

When the light that came from Raven's palms finally dies down Alivia stands motionless, her hands still firmly attached to the sides of Rylan's head. Her eyes completely glazed over.

I felt my body relax, movement coming back to me. I rushed to her side, sighing in relief, the shallow sound of her heartbeat audible. Her breathing was also shallow, her senses dulled down, unaware of everything around her.

My wolf paced back and forth inside my mind, cursing me for allowing this to happen. I growled out causing everyone in the room to take a step back, especially Raven. I turned sinister eyes on her, hissing beneath my breath. "You best fucking hope she doesn't die."

"She's strong, Adren. Believe me she'll be fine." She shrugs it off like Ali's life isn't a big deal, her confidence catching me off guard. How could she be so sure?

My teeth grind together, trying to control my beast. Titan stands beside me, placing his hand on my shoulder, trying to console and calm me down. "Why don't we go and train?" He offers, wanting to distract me from the prospect of not only losing Rylan but Alivia as well.

If that was to happen . . .

Let's just say I'd feel bad for the poor souls who come across me.

I'm hesitant, my wolf couldn't leave his mate and I didn't want to leave Alivia either. If anything happened to her and I wasn't here beside her, I don't know what I would do. I wouldn't be able to forgive myself. "Raven will watch her," Titan added, noticing my inner turmoil.

"Me and Laurey will watch her for you." Raven agreed, the guilt in her eyes noticeable but I decided not to acknowledge it.

I directed my next words to her, putting as much power in my voice as I could muster. "As soon as anything changes, you get me straight away, do you understand?"

She nods her head, obeying my command, walking around the side of the bed to sit beside Laurey, the two of them beginning to converse as they watch over Rylan and Alivia.

Me and Titan make our way to the training grounds, Hunter and Arif on our trail.

We trained for about twenty minutes, my anger pushing me to be more aggressive as I fight against all three of my generals at the same time. They did their best to take me down.

First, Hunter came at me, trying to force me to the ground but I was faster, side stepping out of his way, his momentum causing him to stagger forward. I turn round when I'm fully behind him and then lift my leg, kicking him to the dirt aggressively.

"Shit." He yelped before landing face-first into the floor, spitting out grass and dirt that made its way into his mouth. "Gross!"

Next came Arif. He was extremely strong but I was stronger and faster. He threw a punch towards my face, full force, his aggression matching mine, not holding himself back as I ducked and then threw my right fist into his stomach, making him groan and instinctively hold onto his abdomen. I then swiped my leg out, catching his ankle, making him lose balance and fall to the ground with a hard grunt.

"Fuck!" he breathes aggressively.

His aggression poured out of him, his wolf erupting as the clothes on his back tore to shreds. His brown wolf now stood before me, his top lip reeled back, showing me his fangs as he snarled at me, watching me closely. My eyes darken as my wolf reveals hisself, staring Arif's wolf down. I watch as he bends his back legs, putting all his weight into them before lunging forward, snapping his jaw.

Before he can clamp down on my arm, I punch him square in the muzzle, a whine escaping him as he spiralled towards the ground.

I'm breathing harshly at this point, sweat embedding my forehead, trailing down my face and beading of the tip of my nose.

In a swift second I can sense Titan behind me before his arm hugs my throat in a death grip. He was the only one who ever came close to beating me, being extremely observant and calculative, picking up on your moves within seconds but I was just that bit quicker. He rarely knew what I was going to do next.

"Big mistake." I smirked as my claws elongated within seconds, digging my claws into his thigh, making him growl on pain and lose focus and then I threw my head back, popping his nose.

"Bastard," he growled, holding his bleeding nose. "You fucking broke it."

"It will heal," came my simple response, unsympathetic to his injury. After all, this was his idea.

Hunter and Arif gather themselves, rising to their feet. Arif now shifted back to human, a servant is quick to supply him with new clothes and he's quick to get dressed. "Wow, that looks painful," Hunter notes, pointing at Titan's nose, mimicking a pained expression.

Titan stares daggers at him. "Shut it, mutt." Hunter's expression shifts, bringing his hand to his chest in mock hurt before poking his tongue at Titan. Titan takes a step forward, threatening Hunter to carry on.

"Okay, okay, I'm sorry," Hunter chuckled, backing away from Titan.

I shake my head at the two of them, they could be amusing at times. This was a good distraction but I'm still anxious, feeling the urge to go back to her side. We still haven't heard anything from Laurey or Raven so I suspected things were still the same as when we left. *Draven will pay for what he's done. I'll make damn well sure of it.*

"They'll be alright." I was surprised to hear those words coming from Arif, glancing up to find that he noticed my distress. "As much as the young wolf infuriates me, she's the female version of you, strong and stubborn."

I smile, acknowledging his words. She was a strong wolf for certain and more stubborn than I sometimes. I only hope she realises how strong she is, I don't want her to doubt her strengths when there's no need to.

"Can you believe that after ten years you finally found her?" Hunter commented in disbelief.

Has it really been that long?

I suppose it has been. When I turned eighteen, I awaited the gift that all Wolvens were given—our mates. The other half to our souls. My parents were killed two years prior and I was all I had, apart from my generals of course.

I watched as one by one they each found their mates, their reason for living.

I slowly became angry and bitter, sinking into any woman that offered themselves to me and there was a lot of them. But nothing worked to fill the ache in my chest. It was of the reasons why I ended it with Rita. She expected too much for a female who wasn't even my mate. And even though I explained to her several times that she would never be my queen, I think deep down she assumed I would eventually change my mind. But I didn't and I ended it with her because of that. I remained single for two years after that because I knew this ache could never be filled . . . until I found her. Finally!

Now I regretted my actions. Alivia deserves so much more than what I have to offer and I'm not even sure if in the end it will be enough. The only thing I can do for her after this is over is keep her safe, prevent something like this from ever happening again.

"Arif." He caught my gaze, my demeanour and tone signalling that now I wish to talk strategy. "The Elders need to be briefed on what is happening, I would like you to go and meet with them so that I can spend some time with Ali once she wakes up." And she will wake up.

"What am I to tell them?" he questions, wanting to know whether I wish to tell them everything or only what they need to know.

"Tell Victor the basics, the vampires have a dark Well on their side and a war is brewing. Make sure they put the safety measures we agreed upon into effect." Arif nodded. "You'll leave tonight and get back here as soon as you can."

"We should keep Raven here as well, when her brother tries anything else it'll be good to have her here," Titan advised.

He's right, Raven can't leave yet. We need her here, where her powers can be of great help. "I'll speak with her later and ask her to stay," I said, glancing towards the estate where I can see Laurey in the distance.

She rushed towards us. "Rylan's fever has been broken!" She screams with happiness, tears of joy in her eyes as she gestures for us to follow her, rushing back toward the medic wing.

I feel my own muscles relax In relief, making my way towards the infirmary. My wolf howls in joy, his tail metaphorically wagging.

Thank the goddess!

When we got there Raven's hands were glowing once more, working on bringing them back from Rylan's subconscious.

I waited anxiously, wanting to shroud my Alivia with admiration. The pride I felt was overwhelming, admiring how brave and strong my Ali was overwhelmed me and my wolf. A gasp of air leaves Rylan's mouth, his body bolting upright from the bed. Laurey was quick to suffocate him in a tight embrace causing him to wrap his own arms around her instinctively, tears welling in both their eyes.

Rylan leans back, caressing Laurey's cheek with the pad of his thumb. "I thought you were dead, if felt so real." He breathes out, Laurey's gaze shifting at his words.

"It's okay, I'm still here. I was so scared I would lose you. Don't ever do that to me again." She cried, scolding him before they share a gentle kiss.

My attention shifted to Alivia, her eyes becoming focused, blinking a few times as she wobbled on her feet. I was at her side in the next second, catching her before she fell to the ground. I held her tightly, breathing in her scent. She mumbled into my chest, "Adrenous, I can't breath." My chest rumbled with laughter, loosening my grip before I kissed her forehead gently.

"I'm so proud of you, but don't think you're ever doing that again," I said. She giggles, nodding her agreement before tilting her head up to kiss me. Our lips moving in sync before she pulls away, checking to see how Rylan is doing.

"Rylan," I said. He pulls his head back from Laurey's shoulder to meet my gaze. "I'm sorry for being the reason this happened to you."

He gave me a soft smile, his gaze shifting to Ali. "It's okay. Liv saved my life. She was badass." He smirked, causing Alivia to smile and shake her head in amusement.

Raven walks towards me and Alivia, remembering I needed to ask to extend her invitation. "Raven, your brother may try something like this again, will you stay and help us?"

"He's dangerous." Alivia interjects. "He threatened my family, please stay Raven."

"Okay . . ." Raven said, her eyes shifting to mine as they harden. "I won't leave until I've made sure he's no longer a threat. I've been running from him most of my life, it's about time I faced him."

It's true, her brother is power-hungry, killing their parents when he was younger for their powers. He was the devil's spawn, no conscience to speak of. Raven escaped and ever since he's been after her, greedy for her powers.

"Thank you." Alivia beamed, a smile on her lips.

I mind link one of my servants and within minutes, they're at the door. "Your Majesty." The woman bowed, waiting for her orders.

"Do you mind showing Raven to her room?" She nods her head, a smile gracing her lips. Raven follows her out the door, heading to her room that she'll be using whilst staying with me.

"I'm leaving to prepare for my departure."

Arif's words slip through my mind, nodding my head in acknowledgement. His gaze pauses and soften's on Alivia. When he captures her gaze, he says, "You did good today." Her eyes widened and she became speechless. He didn't wait for a response, nodding at me before leaving the room.

I turned back towards Ali who's biting her bottom lip nervously. "Adrenous can I ask . . ." She shifted on her feet as I arched a brow at her. "My family . . .when I was in Rylan's subconscious, I watched Draven murder them. He knows where they are. Can you have someone bring them here? It'll help me sleep better at night."

"Anything for you." I smiled. "I'll have it arranged," I assured, watching as her eyes gleam with happiness, a tear escaping. She's been through a lot today, she must be overwhelmed. "Come on, you need rest." She squeals slightly when I pick her up, cradling her small frame in my arms as we leave the infirmary and descend the stairs towards my bedroom.

✦˚○✦˚

CHAPTER TWENTY-TWO
Safe With Me

✦ ◻ ✦

ADRENOUS

Alivia giggled, snuggling into my chest. I was kissing her forehead as I carried her in my arms, taking her up to my bedroom. Hopefully sometime soon it'll be our bedroom.

Once in my room, I place her gently down on the bed, pulling out the covers before climbing in next to her, bringing her to my side. She places her head on my chest, listening to the sound of my heart beating against her eardrums.

I stroke her hair, admiring the dark, brown strands. "I was afraid I was going to lose you today." She lifts up off my chest, her cobalt orbs glancing up to meet mine, concern hidden in the depths. "I don't want to ever have to feel like that again," I admit, my desire to keep her safe weighing heavily on my shoulders.

"You won't have to," she whispered, her hand cupping my cheek, drawing me closer to her. "I've been thinking and I've decided that I'm ready." She strokes my cheek with the pad of her thumb, a small smile forming on her lips as I come to understand what she's meant. She's ready for me to claim her.

"Are you sure about this?" I ask, my eyes shifting to reveal my wolf, his excitement coursing through my veins at the thought of being able to claim our mate as ours forever.

Her own wolf steps forward, her eyes darkening, nodding her head. "I've never been more sure of anything."

I crashed my lips against hers, that one sentence ringing in my ears. It put my mind at ease as I once believed she would never accept me. Pulling away slightly, I trail heated kisses along her jaw and down towards the soft spot of her neck. My fangs ached to mark her right now but I resisted the urge. I want to wait until she was fully mine. I want to take my time and savour this moment.

I drew myself back, her eyes fluttering open as they had closed from the pleasure. She looked up at me with glassy eyes, not knowing what It is I plan on doing to her.

"Stand up and take off your clothes," I ordered, my words dripping with the alpha influence that I possess, making it hard for her to disobey. However, based from the smirk that made its way onto her lips, she's more than happy to oblige, her eyes glowing with the essence of her wolf.

I watch her stand, her eyes locking with my own as she slowly undresses before me. The fabric of her clothes piled onto the floor around her feet.

I marvelled at the sight of her gorgeous body. Her breasts were perfectly plump. I licked my lips at the thought of drawing one of her nipples into my mouth and then tasting every inch of her. My desires sent a shockwave through my body, a pulse of that trailing down to meet my cock, causing it to harden against the fabric of my breeches.

I moved away from the bed, walking towards her with a spark in my eyes. She watched me carefully, following my movements before she takes a step back suddenly, her breasts bouncing at the movement. "Are you afraid, little wolf?" I tease her, her wolf coming forward as a small growl emits from the back of her throat.

"No, I want to watch you undress first." She smirks, her eyes glistening with desire, trailing down to lock onto the bulge between my thighs.

"You don't tell me to do anything." I scold her, my voice dark as I usher her forward, my wolf demanding our mates submission, wanting to dominate every inch of her.

I've given her control before but this time I'm going to have full control.

She shakes her head, her eyes widening when I continue to stalk her, my eyes trailing up and down her delicious flesh, my eyes flashing with the lust that is trailing down toward my cock as it continues to pulse, yearning to be buried deep inside her. I reach out and cup her cheek, drawing her closer towards me until her breast are pushed up against my chest, my lips capturing hers once again as my other hand trails down to rest on her hip.

She moans against me when my teeth capture her lip, drawing her lower lip into my mouth as my tongue licks over it causing her to moan again and this time I release her lip, diving my tongue into her mouth, tasting every inch of her as she grips my forearms in an attempt to remain stable.

I turn our bodies, our tongues moulding together as I walk her towards the bed until the back of her knees feel the bed behind her. A groan emits from the back of my throat when she takes it amongst herself to palm my bulge, rubbing her hand up and down causing me to hiss through my teeth when I break apart from the kiss.

"You're treading over a dangerous line, little wolf." Her eyes spark with excitement, palming my cock harder. It takes everything within me to resist pounding into her right now. "Lay back down on the bed."

She does as she's told, her back hitting the sheets as she scoots back up to rest her head against the pillows. I crawl between her legs, my wolf's desire reflecting my own when we breath in the scent of her arousal, pushing him back down when his urge to fuck her becomes hard to ignore.

She wants us just as much as we want her.

I trail my fingers up her thigh until I'm close to her entrance, my eyes capturing her own as she yearns for the pleasure only I can provide. I comply with her wishes, leaning down to run my tongue along her slit, her eyes rolling back as she moans out, fisting the sheets and bucking her hips upwards.

"Are you enjoying this." I smirk, running my tongue up against her slit, swirling it round on her clit, causing her to cry out. "Well?"

"Y—yes." She moans when I stop my assault against her clit, her arousal dripping onto the sheets.

That's it, my little wolf.

I pump a finger inside her, her moans echoing around the room, bringing music to my ears as I add another, stretching her further as she coats my fingers with her arousal.

Her walls tighten around my fingers when I add a third, pumping harder as a string of moans and curses pass her lips, her pussy heating up as her orgasm begins to build. "That's it, cum for me, Ali."

It's not a second later that I feel her walls contracting around me, her back arching of the bed as she rides out her orgasm, my fingers continuing to pump in and out as my thumb strokes across her clit, her hips bucking at the sudden sensation.

I pull out my fingers, missing the warmth of her pussy as she slumps against the bed, her eyes half open as she glanced at me. "I want you to fuck me." She breathes out, her voice soft, causing my cock to twitch.

I stepped away from her, our gazes remaining locked while I unbuttoned my shirt. I shrugged it from my shoulders as it fell to the floor. She licked her lips, her eyes averting from mine as she admired my muscled chest. My breeches are soon to follow, being added to pile of fabric and then my underwear saved for last.

My fingers grip the edges of my underwear, pulling them down my thighs just as her eyes land on my thick cock, causing him to twitch under her intense gaze.

She crawls up onto her knees, approaching the edge of the bed and grabbing my cock, wrapping her fingers around the length gently before bringing the head toward her succulent lips. I groan, closing my eyes when she lays her tongue flat against the head before drawing him into her warm mouth, emitting a groan from the back of my throat. I tangle my hands into the strands of her dark hair, controlling her movements as she begins to suck.

Oh fuck . . . Her mouth feels so fucking amazing wrapped around my cock. Her tongue is laid flat against the underside of my cock, flicking across the head every time her head comes back up before burying me back down her throat, causing her to gag around me whilst my cock twitches, enjoying the vibrations made by her gagging and moaning.

I can feel my balls beginning to tighten before pulling my cock away from her mouth. She tilts her head to the side, a pout forming on her lips as she glances back down to my cock, wanting more.

"Patience." I warned. "Lay back down on the bed like a good little wolf."

She held my gaze, her eyes igniting with desire as she lays down against the soft sheets, watching me as I lean over her, using my arm to hold most of my body weight. I once again trail hot kisses on her body, down her neck and across her chest before taking one of her nipples into my mouth, nibbling and sucking gently, a moan leaving her lips. I then lift myself up, staring deeply into her eyes as I grip my cock, aligning him up against her entrance, knowing she's more than ready for me.

"If this ever becomes too much for you or you need to stop then you let me know," I warn her, my eyes soft. She nods her head in understanding, the anticipation noticeable in her gaze.

I begin to push my cock against her entrance slowly, feeling her walls stretching to accommodate my size. She exhales sharply, hissing through her teeth when my head enters her. I continue, burying my self inside her until my cock is all the way inside and then stop, allowing her to get used to the new sensation.

After a while, I begin to move my hips, slowly pulling out before thrusting back in. Alivia moans gently, gripping my biceps tightly as she adjusts to my movements, feeling her pussy grow wetter around my cock. I continue with the slow thrusts, remaining gentle as her moans start to increase, panting beneath me. When her eyes meet with mine, my cock twitched at her words. "I need more. I want you to fuck me harder."

I obliged, hearing her cry out when I thrust harder, pounding into her relentlessly. I lifted her legs further up my hips, allowing me deeper access. I can feel her walls beginning to tighten as her hips thrust upwards to meet mine, the two of us in sync with each other.

Her orgasm is once again building, her fangs breaking through her top lip, her wolfs instincts taking over as she pulls my face closer to hers before sinking her fangs into my neck, claiming me as hers. She then shatterers apart, pleasure coursing through her when she reaches her peak.

I continue to thrust when her fangs dislodge from my neck, feeling my own fangs breaking through. Just as I'm about to cum, my fangs pierce through the soft flesh of her neck, her emotions and essence mixing with mine. I pull away, grunting and groaning as i spill myself deep inside her.

I pull out and lay in the spot beside her, pulling her to my side as we both attempt to catch our breath.

"You'll always be safe with me."

Her eyes widen when my voice slips through her mind, catching her off guard. She glances up at me and I wink down at her, a knowing smile on my face.

"I love you." I could hear her thoughts, her lips smiling as she snuggles into my chest.

"I love you, too."

She was shocked, her eyes widening once again in embarrassment. "Y—you heard me?" she said softly, her cheeks colouring with embarrassment.

"Yes, we're one and the same now."

She smiled, snuggling into my chest once again as a yawn passed her lips. I kissed her forehead. "Get some sleep," I said.

It's not long until she's fast asleep, the steady rhythm of her heartbeat is evidence of that. I stare at her for a moment, admiring my mark on her neck. Finally she was mine, always and forever.

Reluctantly, I untangle myself from her gently before tucking her into the warm sheets. I then stood on my feet, getting dressed as I have one thing left to do tonight.

"Rylan meet me in twenty minutes."

✦◯✦

CHAPTER TWENTY-THREE
Protect Her

✦▢✦

Adrenous

"I'll be right there."

Rylan was quick to respond, knowing this conversation was coming sooner.

I made my way towards my study, wanting this to be a completely private conversation. At least this time I don't have to worry about Ali eavesdropping. She was completely exhausted and had fallen into a deep sleep after our session. The sensitive mark on my neck is a permanent reminder that I'm hers now, just as much as she is mine.

Once inside my study, I find Rylan already waiting for me. I nod my head towards the wall beside my desk, pressing my palm against a particular brick. When the wall moves to reveal the passageway, we make our way inside, the wall moving back into place behind us.

I sit in my chair, Rylan opting to sit opposite me so that we are facing each other. His expression is blank but there is so much going on behind those eyes of his, his mind in turmoil.

He's nervous to tell me what I want to know and that isn't a good sign.

I begin with an easier question. "How are you feeling?"

Rylan smirks, rolling his eyes. "As good as can be expected but we both know you aren't here to ask about my health."

I chuckle, he knows me too well. I'm glad to see he's back to his normal, humorous self. I finally get down to business, asking the question I was really here for. "What do they want with her? What did you see?"

He's hesitant, exhaling sharply as he watches me warily. "You're not going to like it." My body tenses at his words, leaning forward to rest my chin in my hands, silently urging him to continue.

He sighed, continuing cautiously. "They need her. They believe that because she is half-human, they'll be able to compel her in order to control her. Their plan was to use her to infiltrate us."

What? Wolvens were immune to the vampire's compulsion, but if Alivia being half-human means she's susceptible to it then I suppose they would be able to control her. However, that doesn't explain how this plan of theirs came about. How did they know Ali was half-human or know about her at all?

I rub my temples in frustration, breathing in deeply to calm my wolf. He wanted to tear them limb from limb before they could even attempt to touch Alivia.

I continued my queries, my tone hard. "How did they know about her before me?" I was desperate to know the answer, whatever it may be.

"They were there when she was born. Her father made a pact with Krellin that he would sire a half Wolven for them in exchange for god knows what." He cringed when my demeanour shifts, my jaw clenching, slamming my hands down on the table in rage. Rylan doesn't even flinch, being too used to my outbursts.

What piece of shit could do that to their own pup? Her father is one of us and when I find out who, he's going to beg for mercy!

"Her mother saved her life, taking her and hiding her in plain sight." Rylan continues when I remained silent. "They tortured her for months but she never told them the whereabouts of her daughter so they killed her. Her mother died saving her."

At least Alivia could be proud of one parent but one thing's for sure . . . Alivia is a child born of rape.

I have never suspected one of my kind could be part of such a vile act. Forcing a human to bear his pup just to try and then use them as a bargaining chip. It was fucked up. How am I suppose to tell Alivia this?

"Who is her father?" I growled, my wolf coming forward.

Once again Rylan hesitates. "That's the thing . . . you already know him."

I was taken aback by his statement, my eyes widening at the prospect. I knew Alivia's father? "Who?" I question, ready to fly off the handle and rip their heart from their chest without an ounce of regret.

"He . . ." Rylan trails off, his eyes averting to the ground.

"Tell me now!" I demand, anticipation setting my blood aflame, heated rage coursing through me.

"The one who betrayed your family, General Alijah Sanford."

I bolt out of my chair, the chair flying back from the impact. I'm beyond livid, my body shaking, my claws elongating as all the emotions and memories that I've buried over the years come straight to the surface. The anger that had remained under check was now consuming my senses, feeling my wolf wanting to erupt right here and now.

Alivia was a Sanford? I couldn't believe that fucker had not only stabbed my father in the back and ripped my family apart, but had also sired Alivia for some sick gain. The same man who my father had once trusted with his life, the same one who took his and my mother's life has now found a way to fuck with my life again.

How will Arif take this? Alijah had killed his mother right in front of him and then badly abused him. I can't tell him. Fuck! What am I going to do?

I'm breathing roughly at this point, trying to calm down. Rylan's voice pierced through my thoughts. "Adrenous." My eyes snapped down at him as he continues. "Are you going to tell them?"

Alivia has been through a lot lately. I'm afraid this will destroy her if she finds this out. She had never met her father thanks to her human mother who had sacrificed herself for her. Alivia had no idea how lucky she was to have a mother who was willing to do that for her. However, at the same time she was equally as unlucky to have a foul father who would give her away to the vampires.

"It's best to keep this from them for now." I sighed, running a hand through my hair.

"You know you can't let them get her, right?" Rylan mumbled. "Once they have her, who knows what they'll try and do."

I nodded. My mate's a bigger weakness to my kingdom than I had first anticipated. Yes she has powerful abilities but they could easily be turned against us if she were to come under the control of that bastard Krellin.

However, I didn't have it in me to kill her and eliminate the threat of that ever happening. The moon was truly cruel at giving me a mate who had the capacity to bring down the entire kingdom. My ancestors had kept it running for two thousand years but it could crumble all because I couldn't harm my mate.

Instead I was going to do the opposite.

"In a weeks time she will officially be joining the pack," I state. The quicker she's one of us, the stronger she will be and the quicker her coronation will follow.

"Good choice." Rylan agrees.

I head towards the door as our conversation has come to an end. I glance at him just as the wall is sliding to reveal my office. "One last thing. Nobody else is to know any of this or so help me . . ." I threaten.

"As you wish." He replies bluntly, no questions asked. I was going to protect her. Moon goddess save us all.

✦○✦

CHAPTER TWENTY-FOUR
Questions

✦▫✦

ALIVIA

I stir in my sleep, waking up from the light streaming through the windows. I try to move in order to shield my eyes from the blinding light but find two arms restricting my movement. They tighten around me, pulling me into a muscled chest, feeling a nose skimming along my ear before sighing. "Good morning." Adrenous's husky voice mets my ears, the memories of last night coming back to me.

"Good morning." I smiled, snuggling into him further, my naked back pressed firmly against his chest.

Adrenous's nose leaves my ear to be replaced with his lips, pressing light, hot kisses along the back of my ear down to the fresh, sensitive make on my neck. An involuntary moan passes my lips when he begins to gently suck on his mark, pleasurable heat trailing down to my core from that small action.

"I can smell my scent all over you, it's driving me crazy." Adrenous mumbles against my skin. I can't help but moan as he continues to suck on the mark, sending me into a heated frenzy.

I turn in my spot, his lips forced to pull away from my neck as I look up into his gorgeous, crimson eyes. His ebony hair is in disarray from having been asleep and if it's possible he looks ten times more gorgeous than before. My eyes soon trailed down to his neck, catching my mark, the one that I had made last night with the help of my wolf. She's proud of her work, holding her head up with pride.

    I touched it gently with my fingertips, Adrenous shivering at the action. I instantly pulled them away, a frown gracing my lips. "I didn't even know that I could mark you too. The books said nothing about it." My eyes met with his, silently asking for an explanation.

    His eyes briefly darken before softening on me. "Before my father changed the laws, females weren't allowed to mark the males. We were only allowed to mark them to stop other males lurking around our mates. However, males were allowed to be with multiple females but only their marked mate would bear them pups. That was all the mark used to signify." Adrenous explained this to me with displeasure and shame.

    "What made your father change the law?" I said, admiring his father's decision. For centuries, women have always been treated lowly, expected them to marry and have children. But his father made them equal. He must have been a good man.

    "My mother." Adrenous smiles wistfully, his voice soft. "She was his everything, he didn't need anything more." There's a burden of hurt hidden in those crimson debts, one I never knew he carried.

    "They must have really loved each other," I whispered, hoping to make him feel better. He's never spoken about his parents before so I assumed it's because it's too hard for him to talk about. "What were their names?" "Wyatt and Claudia."

    "Your mother's name is lovely."

    Adrenous nodded his head in agreement, his fingers gliding beneath the chain around his neck, the one he always wears and holds his symbol. "This was my father's and his before him. It's the only thing my father left to me apart from the throne. It's the Claxton family crest, my family crest."

Claxton? "Your family name is Claxton?" I question, surprised that nobody knew that. Not even Rylan or Hunter told me. I didn't know the Wolvens had family names, believing that was just a human tradition.

"Yes." Adrenous smiles with pride. "And soon it'll be yours." Adrenous sits up onto the bed, bringing me with him as I lay my head against his chest, the idea of one day having his name has me smiling with happiness.

Adrenous's tone takes a serious turn, his body now feeling rigid beneath me. "Today I'll be arranging for the ritual that'll join your wolf with us to be prepared in a weeks time."

What? That's sooner than I would have thought. I look up at Adrenous, confused. "Why so soon? We have plenty of time."

"The sooner you're one of us, the better your wolf will feel, and the more powerful and connected you'll become," Adrenous said, no room for negotiation. He lifted me up and placed me down gently on the other side of the bed so that he could stand on his feet and start getting dressed.

I furrow my brows slightly but now that I think about it, it does sound like a good idea. My wolf is already wagging her tail at the prospect and the doubt I had once felt towards the idea seems to have disappeared, agreeing with my wolf for once.

Once Adrenous is dressed, he took a seat on the bed beside me. "Laurey and Raven have both volunteered to help prepare you for next week. They'll answer all your questions and Laurey will teach you the ritual step by step."

"When does that start?" I asked, knowing there are many questions dominating my mind waitng to be answered.

"While I'm off organising, you'll be meeting them in the downstairs lounge." He leaned forward, capturing my lips and kissing me gently before pulling away. "Get dressed and meet them downstairs, I'll see you later, okay?"

"Okay." I smiled. He returns my smile and heads for the door.

He's about to walk out but stops himself short, turning to me to say, "I almost forgot, your family are being escorted here by Hunter. They will be set up in one of the cottages near where my generals live."

"Thank you." I'm grinning now. I felt relived and happy that I don't have to worry for them. Adrenous winks at me, leaving the room to go and organise the ritual.

It's not long until I'm out of bed, my hair having been brushed and my face and body washed. I get dressed into a cute light blue dress that flows to the ground.. I quickly put on a pair of matching flats and tie the laces, leaving the room once I'm done.

I head downstairs, stopping a passerby to ask directions to the lounge. They point the way and I head in the direction, stepping into the room to find Laurey and Raven causally conversing on the sofa until they spot me.

Laurey smiles, waving me over to come and join them. When I take a seat, she says, "How are you feeling?"

"I feel okay." I answer honestly, understanding she's referring to my time in Rylan's subconscious. "Your brother is very intense," I added, glancing at Raven with a small frown on my lips.

She sighs, sadness and anger crossing her features at the mention of her bother. "He's a lost soul, too far gone to be saved from the sins he's committed. When the time comes, it'll be me he'll answer to." She seemed to detach herself emotionally, saying the last part with ease.

"Why did your brother turn dark?" I ask softly, not wanting to push her too hard. I'm not certain how touchy this subject may be for her.

"I have no idea. One night, out of the blue, he murdered our parents, absorbing their powers for himself. He came after me that same night but he didn't realise I was watching him from the doorway, watching what he did to our parents." Raven paused, her voice shaky as she recalls her parents being murdered. "I ran as fast and quickly as I could, using my powers to cover my tracks. I didn't think I would survive until Adren found me, showing me how to survive on my own."

That's why she helped us save Rylan, she owed it to Adrenous for helping to save her life.

I lean forward, placing my hand over hers for comfort and Laurey does the same. Raven smiles at us, appreciating what we're trying to do for her but her smile falters, her eyes widening before they fill with awe and happiness. "You're bonded now. I can sense it. It's very powerful." She breathes out.

It's then that Laurey's eyes widen as well, her excitement shining through as she looks to me in question. "It's true." I move my hair out of the way, showing them Adrenous's mark. "It was a long time coming but I was ready for him to claim me." I tell them, not bothering to hide the love I feel towards Adrenous.

The love I feel for him is pure, with no doubts or regret tainting it. It's simple, I'm his and he's mine now.

"I'm happy for the both of you." Raven beams, not taking her eyes off the mark. "We've been waiting for this day for a very long time."

My eyes met with hers, showing her my appreciation before changing the subject. "Anyway, Adrenous said that I could ask you questions about the ritual?"

Laurey nods her head. "That's right. Please, ask us anything."

I try and think for a moment, too many questions tumbling through my mind, making it hard to choose which one to ask first.

Raven noticed. "There's no rush, take your time." She assures me, both of them remaining patient with me.

I admire how they allow me to take my time, organising my thoughts and choosing which questions are at the top of my priority list. I exhale softly, glancing between them as I ask, "What happens to me during the ritual? Will I feel different?" My voice is soft, afraid that this ritual will hurt like the first time I shifted beneath the blue moon. That pain was unimaginable and I don't want to experience it ever again.

Laurey furrows her brows slightly, unsure of how to answer. "You'll still be you and feel yourself. The only difference that will come from the ritual is your increase in strength, your responsibilities to the pack. You and your wolf become one with us." I take in what she's saying, understanding and accepting what may be expected from me. "The ritual is for your benefit as well as ours. The generals and King Adrenous especially, will pledge their lives to you, swearing an oath to protect you. You must swear by the same oath, offering your own life and protection in exchange."

I take a moment to process the information. Whilst I'm silent, Raven makes sure to add in. "A Wolven who is connected to a pack is considered untouchable as far as other packs are concerned. Right now, you are what others consider a rogue."

A rogue? I've never heard that term before. "What's a rogue?"

"A wolven without a pack or home. They're very rare and considered dangerous. They don't follow any pack laws and do as they please, including threatening the safety of packs." Raven glances at Laurey, an understanding passing between them as Laurey nods her head, granting permission for Raven to continue. "They only follow their leader, calling him their 'King'."

"What's his name?" I press, fascinated but also wary of this new realisation.

"No one knows." Laurey interjects before Raven can answer. "We'll answer the rest of your questions but first, it's time to find you a dress." They both stand to their feet, their excitement for dress hunting prominent. I match their excitement, following them out the room and down the hall until we're standing outside a pair of double doors, both of them pausing their movements to look at me.

They glance at each other, a mischievous smile pulling on both their lips. I furrow my brows, slightly wary. "What?"

"Close your eyes," they both said in unison.

I'm slightly nervous but I trust them, doing as they ask. Once my eyes are shut, I hear the sound of the doors being pulled open. They each take one of my hands into their own, leading me into the room until I'm sure we're standing in the centre.

"Open your eyes," Laurey whispered, hearing the smile in her voice.

My eyes flutter open, a soft gasp passing my lips as I glance at the rails filled with all kinds of dresses. There must be at least thousands lined up in here, appearing to be unworn and of expensive taste. I'm left speechless, turning to the two grinning at me with wide eyes. "Wh—wha—?"

"Adrenous had this room set up the first day you arrived on his estate. They're all yours," Laurey said.

I walked through the centre of the room, reaching out to touch the different materials and fabrics, tracing them with my fingertips. It warms my heart that Adrenous did this for me even when he barely knew me. I'm completely blown away by how beautiful the collection of dresses are, not sure how I'm going to pick just one for the ritual.

Raven breaks the silence that has settled over me. "Let's find you a dress, shall we?"

✦○✦

CHAPTER TWENTY-FIVE
A Successful Beginning

✦▢✦

ALIVIA

Breathe . . .

I found myself standing in front of the mirror, staring into my frightened, blue eyes through my reflection. The ritual is set to start soon, time passing by, knowing that soon I'm going to be standing in front of Adrenous's people. The closer that moment approaches, the faster my heart beats.

My gaze trails downward, analysing my dress for the hundredth time, hoping I made the right decision.

It's a long sleeve, mid-thigh dress, the sleeves and top half transparent except for the chest area, embroidered with a floral pattern whilst the skirt has two layers of thin material, allowing the top half of my thighs to remain hidden under the fabric. My waist can be seen through the threaded pattern that connects the skirt to the top half. The same threaded pattern runs up between my breast and then down my back on either side along my shoulder blades. The centre of my back is on display, a string tied behind my neck to keep the front half of the dress tight around my chest.

The dress is white, signifying a successful beginning.

That's what today will be, a start of a new life within the pack, among Adrenous's people, protected and cherished by them.

I go over the steps in my head, knowing the ins and outs of how I take part in the ritual. Laurey later explained that me, Adrenous and the generals will have to shed a few drops of blood each, signifying our devotion to protect and offer our lives for one another. I would call it barbaric but here it is normal and if I'm going to live with them, I have to accept their strange traditions.

The sound of heels clicking across the wooden floor, meets my ears, Raven and Laurey appearing in the mirrors reflection. I turn in my spot, my gaze travelling between them, admiring their dresses.

Raven's black hair has been placed in a gorgeous bun and she adorns a short, forest green, lace dress. The neckline is very deep, showcasing her breasts and the material that does cover her actual breast is transparent, barely covering them. It's short-sleeved, the straps that go over her shoulders are thick and transparent like the rest. The whole dress is covered in a floral pattern and the colour suits her skin tone very well.

Laurey has her hair straight down her back and has chosen to wear a strapless, pink, straight dress which reaches her knees. The neckline is deep enough for her cleavage to show but not too revealing.

"You both look beautiful." I compliment them, a grin on my face.

"So do you," Laurey said, waving her hands and gesturing to my whole outfit. Raven nods her head, agreeing with Laurey as she smiles at me.

"Thank you." I turn back towards the mirror one last time before saying, "Let's not keep them waiting." I exhaled a sharp breath, trying to relax my nerves before I stepped away from the mirror.

"Are you sure you're ready?" Laurey asks gently, seeing the fear in my eyes.

"I am," I assured. I headed for the door, Raven and Laurey following closely behind.

The ritual is being held at the centre of the two field, where the bridge connects them, under the full moon. I haven't notice it before but at the base of the bridge is a sacramental stone, one that I have passed many times without realising it was a special tool for this kind of ritual. The stone is where they're blood will be spilled while I stand on it, pledging their lives to me before I do the same and then the rest will follow.

We reached the exit, standing in the open. My gaze fell on the crowd. In the distance, the moonlight bathed the land in its light, Adrenous and the generals hidden by the mass of people. My nerves are on edge. People's gazes fell my way. Children pointed in my direction, their little faces lit with excitement. I can't help but wish to be invisible. I'm not used to being the centre of attention.

My legs feel slightly shaky, making my way towards the crowd, my heart pounding in my chest. My wolf tries to console me, allowing her courage to wash over me, her head held high as she enjoys the looks of awe and admiration.

At least someone's enjoying the attention.

I walk through the crowd, people stepping back to make a path for me, revealing Adrenous and the generals who are standing on the bridge, their heads held high, smiling at me. Even Arif has a smile just about touching his lips.

Laurey and Raven join the crowd as I walk towards the bridge, my eyes meeting with crimson orbs. I breath in, my wolfs courage helping me to relax, taking in deep breaths as I stand before them, stepping onto the marked stone, Adrenous's family crest carved into it.

Breathe . . .

My eyes narrow on the knife in Adrenous's hand as it reflects the moonlight. It's not an average kitchen knife, it has strange carvings and symbols which I've never seen before.

You look beautiful. Are you okay?

Adrenous's voice slips through my anxious mind, my eyes lifting from the knife to meet with his.

Thanks and I will be once this is over.

I respond to his question, the words filled with humour. Adrenous chuckled and nods his head, turning to the crowd to get this thing started. "Wolvens, we are here to welcome a new addition to the pack, Alivia Harmon. Our goddess Elune will bathe us in her light." Adrenous gestures to the moon in the sky. "Her light will guide and assist in the ritual, accepting Alivia as one of her own."

Being accepted by a Goddess does sound like a big deal.

"The generals and I will pledge an oath to Alivia on your part." Adrenous is referring to all of them, their heads nodding as they accept what their king is telling them, their protection extending to me.

Everyone went silent, watching the moon. They waited for it's glow to fall on me and the stone. It's a matter of a few minutes, the moon's light washed over me. I felt a strange energy course through my veins as Adrenous's crest on the stone lights up. I gasped at the sight.

And so it begins . . .

Adrenous, being the king, is the first to swear an oath of loyalty and protection whilst slicing the knife through the palm of his hand, not even flinching. "I, King Adrenous Claxton, promise to protect you with my life so long as you promise to offer your own protection and life in exchange, to never do anything that would put everyone's life here in jeopardy."

Adrenous's blood drips onto the stone. Once his oath is finished the blood turns to red dust, lifting upward towards the moon. Laurey explained that this is a sign of the Goddess Elune accepting the oath.

Adrenous passes the knife to Titan and then walks towards the crowd, standing at the front.

Titan runs the blade through the flesh of his palm, his grey meeting with mine. "I, General Titan Kramer, promise to protect you with my life." The blood drips and turns to the same red dust, floating up towards the moon.

Titan places the knife in Hunter's hand before walking into the crowd to stand beside a brunette, his hand wrapping around her waist. She has brown eyes and is snuggling into Titan, I assume she is his mate. Next to them is a young girl around six and a boy around five, they both have brown hair however, the girl has her mothers brown eyes whilst the boy has Titans grey ones.

My attention is soon drawn back to Hunter, slicing the knife through his palm, his blood dripping onto the stone. "I, General Hunter Callan, promise to protect you with my life." It's no different, his life source rising up to meet the moon.

The knife is soon passed to Rylan, Hunter walking towards his mate as well, a red head with blue eyes, two little girls standing with them. They both have blue eyes the same as their parents though one has her mothers red hair while the other has her father blonde hair.

Rylan slices his palm. "Ouch." He moans like a child, pretending to be hurt. I find it amusing but gave him a scolding look, telling him to hurry along. He pouted at me but got the message and becomes serious. "I, General Rylan Fayne, promise to protect you with my life." He winks down at me, a smile forming on my lips before the knife is placed in Arif's hands, Rylan walking away to stand with Laurey.

My gaze locks with Arif's, his eyes soft for once, not hesitating to slice his hand with the knife. "I, General Arif Sanford, promise to protect you with my life."

Kramer, Callan, Fayne, and Sanford. It's nice to finally know their family names, ones I didn't realise they held until recently.

I smiled at Arif, appreciating that he's finally softening up to me. As soon as his blood raised to the moon, the knife is given to me. I could feel the pressure weighing on my shoulders. Arif offered me a comforting smile before walking away to join his family as well.

His mate is blonde with warm, brown eyes, staring down at the little girl on her hip. The little girl has her mother's blonde hair but Arif's pale, yellow eyes; however, they're filled with more warmth than her father's. Two boys stood with them as well, both of them have their father's brown hair and their mother's brown eyes.

I watch over all of them, seeing the generals in a new light as they stood with their families, my heart warming at the sight.

My eyes fell on Adrenous as I remembered my part. My gaze drifted to the knife in my hand, turning it a few times as I hesitated to slice my palm.

"You can do it Ali." Adrenous's voice soothed my mind, looking back up at him. A smile graced his lips as they all waited patiently. I look back down at the knife, slicing my hand without a second thought to stop me. I hiss through my teeth, the wound slightly stinging as I hold my palm down, letting the blood drip onto the stone before I recite the oath I've come to learn. "I, Alivia Harmon, promise to protect everyone here with my life, promising to never do anything that will jeopardise the lives of the pack."

The light of the stone intensifies, the wound on my hand slowly healing until it's completely closed. I watch as my blood rises up to the moon, my body, mind, soul and wolf connecting with the people before me, a rush of energy travelling through my body, my wolf excited to be connected with the other wolves. I can feel the life force of everyone before me, my mind linked with all of them.

"Yes Liv, you did it!" Rylan's excited voice filled my mind as everyone chants and cheers, accepting me as their own.

I walked towards Adrenous, the hard part now over but we're nowhere close to being finished yet.

Everyone around us removed their clothes, bones snapping and fur erupting as they all shift to release their wolves. They all sit patiently, waiting for me and Adrenous to shift and begin the pack run in celebration.

Adrenous's voice is playful as it slips through my mind, a smirk forming on my lips at his words.

"Are you ready to run, little wolf?"

✦○✦

CHAPTER TWENTY-SIX
Running Free

✦▢✦

ALIVIA

Adrenous is the first to shift, black fur erupting all over his naked body. His bones snapped and rearranged as his nose elongated to form a snout.

I'm in awe of his wolf, recalling the moment I first laid eyes on him. The only difference is I'm no longer afraid. He's massive, a head taller than me even in wolf form. I placed my hand on his fur, remembering when I had the urge to feel it's softness. Now, my fingers are finally running through it. It's softer than I could have imagined.

"Shift, little wolf." Adrenous's demand washes over me. He's my alpha now and his words have a strange power over me which I've never experienced.

I did as I'm told, allowing my dress to fall to the ground once I've untied the knot. I slowly shift, my wolf coming forward, seeing through my eyes as my body rearranges itself, my snout forming and brown fur erupting. She stretches her limbs once were fully transformed, arching her back to stretch before we lay our eyes back on Adrenous.

"Beautiful," Adrenous said, his wolf looking down at us with pride. My wolf tilts our head to the side, assessing how strong and powerful our mate is and she is beyond pleased with what she sees.

"*So are you,*" I respond playfully, and I mean it. His wolf really is beautiful.

His wolf's eyes smiled at me as he turns his head towards the pack. We're all waiting for Adrenous's order now. We lean our weight on our front paws, waiting to run free. He lifts his head up toward the sky, howling to the moon. It's not long until we all join in and then before we know it, we're running after Adrenous as he speeds off through the woods.

My wolf was running just behind Adrenous's wolf, slightly to his right. I allow my wolf to run as fast as she likes, revelling in the feeling of the wind in our fur. This is the first time I've ever allowed her to have full control and she's doing the most with it, moving us at a speed I didn't know we could ever achieve.

Adrenous is slightly faster, remaining in front, looking back now and again to check if we're keeping up with him as he manoeuvres through the trees. My wolf keeps up easily, propelling us forward with mischievous intent. I'm unsure of what she's planning but I don't take back control, allowing her to remain at the forefront of my mind as I take the backseat.

Before I realise it, she's leaped into the air, pushing off her back legs at incredible speed. She lands back on her paws just before Adrenous, forcing him to halt to prevent himself from colliding into us. She lets out a playful bark, now taking the lead, leaving him behind.

"*That's cheating, little wolf,*" Adrenous mused, his wolf running after us at quick speed. He nipped at our back legs playfully as he came up behind us. My wolf kicks her back paws out, pushing him away before propelling herself forward, leaping into the air again.

"*You're treading on a fine line, Alivia!*"

"*Says the one who's being left behind to eat my dust.*" I can't hold back the remark, my confidence increasing as my wolf keeps well ahead, not looking back to check if Adrenous is behind us. Although it's clear that he's close, his wolf growling dangerously at us in response. My wolf yelps slightly at the sound but continues to run away from the giant wolf chasing us, crimson eyes burning holes into our back.

After a few minutes of running, my wolf is unsure whether Adrenous is still following us, turning her head to find Adrenous gone, her claws digging into the ground to bring us to a stop, releasing a small whine. The other wolves continue forward, Arif's wolf taking the lead alongside his mate.

She searches our surroundings, tilting her head up to sniff the air, searching for Adrenous's scent. The breeze is blowing to our right, making it hard to find and we come up empty, another whine leaving her.

Why would Adrenous just leave us? It doesn't seem right.

We turn back to the direction that the other wolves had taken, pushing herself forward once again. Something collides into our side all of a sudden, the force forcing us to the ground, a large furry body pinning us to the floor as they lick at our face playfully. We opened our eyes, a growl forming in our chest when we came face to face with those crimson irises.

"*What the hell Adrenous?*"

"*Payback's a bitch.*"

Adrenous's wolf tilted his head to the side, amused by our irritation as we try to escape from beneath him. His wolf doesn't let up though, keeping us in place as we release a huff of air, staring up at him in frustration.

"*Get off!*"

"*Why should I? You look amazing where you are.*"

He did not just say that!

My wolf growled again, nipping at his neck in the hopes that he will release us. His wolf shook his head in amusement, lifting up onto his legs and then stepped away, allowing my wolf to rise back on her feet as well. Her eyes narrowed on him.

"*Calm down, little wolf. I have something to show you.*"

My wolf tilted her head to the side, curious. His wolf nudged to the right before walking in that direction. We followed closely behind him, excited to find out what he wanted to show us.

We follow Adrenous, walking out into an opening. We're amazed by the sight, a gorgeous lake laid out before us, the moons light reflecting off its surface, creating a gorgeous scene. However, the thing that attracts our attention is the area of grass with a blanket and picnic basket laid out. Two robes are also visible.

"*You did this for me?*" I said.

"*I thought you might like it.*"

We padded over to the blanket, the both of us shifting and placing the robes around our bodies as we relaxed. "It's really beautiful," I said, marvelling at the serene view. The lake was completely mellow, not a ripple in sight.

Adrenous smiles at me, opening the picnic basket and grabbing a bottle of expensive wine along with two glasses. "I thought we should have our own little celebration, just the two of us."

"I'd like that." He passes me a glass, filling mine and his own with the red liquid. I look down at it with curiosity, wondering how it tastes. I've never had alcohol before.

Adrenous holds his glass up in the air. "To you becoming one with my pack." I smile at him, clinking my glass against his before taking a sip. "Finally, might I add."

I rolled my eyes at him, pushing his shoulder playfully, making him chuckle and smirk. "I had to give it some thought," I remarked playfully, placing my glass down and laying my back against the blanket as the alcohol warmed my skin.

Adrenous lays down beside me, his crimson eyes staring softly at the side of my face. "I love you, Ali."

"I love you, too."

He leaned in closer, capturing my lips with his own. He kissed me gently, his hand running up the inside of my thigh beneath my robe. His touch made my skin ignite with fire, heat coursing through my veins until it mets that sensitive nub between my thighs.

 The pace of the kiss increases, Adrenous's tongue demanding entrance and when I moan into him, he's given exactly what he wants, diving his tongue into my mouth to meet with mine. Our tongues move in sync as his dominates mine, setting the rhythm.

 I can feel his hand continuing to glide along my thigh. I shiver beneath him when his thumb brushes against my clit, my walls clenching at the action. He then moves his fingers toward my entrance, groaning against me when he comes in contact with my moist arousal. He pulls away slightly, leaving me breathing heavily as he says, "Such a good little wolf, already wet for me."

 I glanced up at him with my half open eyes, begging for him to satisfy the ache between my legs. "P—please, I need you, Adrenous."

 He smirks at my words, crashing his lips against mine once again. I can feel two of his fingers enter me, my walls hugging them tightly as he begins to pump them at a soft rhythm. My arousal soon intensifies, moaning against his lips as my walls clench and unclench, feeling the wetness between my legs grow.

 It's not too long until I'm arching my back, my orgasm washing over me relentlessly. Adrenous pulls away, glancing down at my face as I cum. His eyes are filled with lust and desire, feeling his hardness press against my hip.

 I want him so bad, bringing him closer between my legs. "Fuck me."

 He's shocked by my boldness. His expression shifts after, nodding his head. "Spread your legs."

 I do as I'm told, spreading my legs further so that he can lay comfortably between them, his irises dark as his wolf comes forward. I allow my own wolf to come forward, greeting his as a smirk makes its way onto my lips.

I can feel the head of his cock pushing against my entrance, my body expanding to allow him to fit through, nowhere near as painful as before. Once the head of his cock has entered me, his shaft soon follows, giving me a sense of fullness. My walls hugged his cock tightly as I moan out in pleasure.

He glances down at me, his eyes dark as he begins to move his hips at a gentle pace. My hands are on his back, digging my nails into his skin as the pleasure continues to course through me. I could feel the tightness in my abdomen waiting to explode, but I need more. "Adrenous, please . . . more." I'm barely able to form a sentence. I've become a panting mess beneath him, begging for my release.

I cried out when he shoved his cock into me, his hips moving at a faster and rougher pace. My hips rose to meet his hard thrusts, allowing our bodies to move in sync.

Soon, I'm shifting my hips, placing my legs high up around his waist, allowing him to fuck me even deeper. I could feel his cock pounding deep inside me. At this angle, his cock is able to rub against my G-spot even harder, making my orgasm grow rather rapidly. Soon, I was shattering apart. My walls are now clenched around his cock forcefully, making him grunt and groan as his cock expanded, releasing his seed deep inside of me.

He collapsed against me, his head buried into the side of my neck as we both attempt to catch our breath.

I want to stay here. Just like this, with him, forever.

✦○✦

CHAPTER TWENTY-SEVEN
An Old Frenemy

✦◻✦

ALIVIA

It's been a a month since I've become one with the pack, the connection between me and them growing stronger, feeling the life force of everyone around me. If one of them were to be under threat or hurt I would know about it, same goes if I was to be hurt.

Adrenous has been a little busy lately, giving me some time to spend with my aunt and cousins. While my aunt is cooking with Avery and the twins, Tess and Tate, I'm watching Amber play with Cammie in the garden.

Tess and Tate are both five, their parents being Titan and Trinity. Cammie is only two and she is the youngest of three children belonging to Arif and Sylvia.

It's been nice getting to know the generals families, building trust and friendship with the generals mates is also nice. I was also surprised to learn that Rylan and Laurey are expecting their first pup. I was beyond happy for them and I can't wait to meet the little one when they're born.

My attention is soon drawn back to the present as I watch Amber and Cammie play, "Amber, be careful with Cammie, she's only little." I scold her, seeing her playing 'Tag' with Cammie a little too rough.

"I am being careful, Alivia. Promise." Amber says softly before going back to playing with Cammie.

"Amby." Cammie squeals with laughter, running away from Amber, who's chasing her, trying to tag her.

Cammie stumbles over a rock, her little body tumbling to the ground. I quickly rise to my feet and walk towards her to help her but she lets out a loud cry, the sound forcing me to cover my ears and crumble to my knees. What the fuck? Why is it so painful?

Amber seems unaffected by the sound, frowning at me and wondering why I'm covering my ears. Sylvia comes rushing out when she hears her little one's cry. "Baby, what happened?" she asks, picking Cammie up and placing her on her hip whilst inspecting her small body for injuries.

The sound stops, feeling a little bit of blood trail from my ears before the wounds heal.

"She fell over a rock," Amber murmurs. "I'm sorry, it was my fault." Amber's sad face is cast down, feeling guilty for hurting Cammie.

"It's okay, she'll be okay. It was no one's fault," Sylvia assured Amber softly. Cammie was now back to her laughing self. "Sorry if her cries hurt you Alivia, she inherited the ability from Arif's mother," Sylvia explains, looking at me apologetically.

"It's okay, I'm fine," I assured, rubbing my ears softly. There's a slight ring resounding in my eardrums but nothing painful. "Does it only affect other Wolvens? Amber wasn't effected by it."

"Pretty much, and anything else that may have enhanced hearing." Sylvia said, looking down at her daughter. "It's meant to paralyse and cause severe pain to an attacker but she hasn't learnt how to harness and control it yet."

"I'm sure she will soon enough," I said.

Sylvia nods whilst Cammie yawns in her arms. "I best get this little pup in for a nap, I'll see you later, Alivia."

"Bye, Sylvia." I smile, waving goodnight to Cammie, who is rubbing her eyes.

I stood on my feet, needing to wash the blood away from the sides of my face. That little girl had a powerful voice at such a young age. I feel bad for anyone who she uses it against once she knows how to control it. "Come on, Amber, lets go in and see what your mum's prepared for dinner."

Amber licks her lips and nods, starving as she rushes to the kitchen. When I enter the house I'm enveloped with the smell of beef stew, my stomach rumbling as I come close to drawling. Before I join the others, I grab a wet wash cloth, cleaning the blood away.

Everyone is already sitting at the table, a bowl of stew in front of them as they each dig in. "I saved you a bowl in the kitchen." My aunt tells me, a smile on my lips as I grab the bowl and join them at the table. Tess and Tate are seated next to each other, Amber and Avery are opposite them while me and my aunt sit at each end of the table.

I place a spoonful of stew into my mouth, nearly spitting it back out when it burns my tongue. I should have blown on it first.

Everyone around the table giggles, finding me nearly burning my tongue off amusing. "You're so silly Alivia," Tess said, digging her spoon into the stew. "Watch me." I watch as she blows on her spoon and then shoves the spoon into her mouth, speaking with her mouth full. "See, that way it doesn't burn."

I can't help but find her little demonstration cute. "Thanks, Tess, and yeah I can be silly sometimes." I smile and she returns my smile with a toothy grin, proud of herself for helping me not to burn my tongue again.

This time when I bring the stew to my lips, I blow on it gently before placing it into my mouth, savouring the gorgeous taste. "This is really amazing, Helena."

"Thanks, Avery and the twins helped," Helena said, smiling at them as she shares the credit.

"Yeah, mummy always lets us help in the kitchen at home," Tate said and his sister nods her head, confirming what her brothers said.

"Well she's very lucky to have two amazing cooks helping her." I praise, making Tess's grey eyes and Tates brown ones light up with happiness.

Once dinner is finished, I help my aunt with the dishes. Tess and Tate have already been picked up by Trinity twenty minutes ago and Amber and Avery are in bed, most likely pretending to be asleep.

Those two probably wouldn't be asleep for a few hours. They could be a handful sometimes but I loved them more than anything. I was beyond happy that Adrenous allowed them to stay here and remain protected within his territory.

From what I've seen, my aunt is grateful too. She was adjusting better than I could have hoped. Her anxieties towards Wolvens have decreased drastically since she found out about me and got to know some of them better. She was trying and I loved her for that.

As I'm drying a plate, I'm taken off guard by a sudden cramp in my abdomen. It intensifies slightly and I'm forced to bend down, wrapping my arms around my waist instinctively as the plate crashes to the floor.

"Are you alright?" My aunt is at my side, rubbing my back, worry dominant in her brown eyes.

I breathe through the pain, feeling it subside before it's gone completely. I'm able to stand up straight once again. "Yeah, it was just a stomach ache. I'm okay." I assure her.

She doesn't seem convinced. "Do you need to sit down?"

"No, I'm fine." I held my palm out to her, needing some space. "I best be leaving now anyway, Adrenous will be expecting me back home soon," I said while getting ready to leave, determining whether I should shift and run or just walk. I think shifting will be much quicker. I don't want to leave him waiting for long. Besides, I don't know what brought on the cramp, but I want to go home in case another one starts.

"Okay, no problem sweetie." She brings me in for a hug and I kiss her cheek before pulling away. We carefully step around the broken pieces of the plate and approach the door.

"I'll try and visit you again soon," I said, walking out the door.

"Okay, I love you."

"Love you, too." I head towards the path that lay between the trees, stopping to hide behind a few trees and quickly take my dress off. The chill night air touches my skin, the hairs along my neck and arm standing as I allow the shift to begin, my wolf coming forward. The woods are quiet apart from the snapping of my bones as they rearrange themselves.

The brown fur of my wolf keeps the cold air at bay as we place the dress in our mouth and begin running along the path. My wolf catches sight of a few rabbits bouncing through the trees, her tail wagging as she's tempted to chase them but I pull on the reigns of our mind, keeping her focused on the path. She obliges, though she's not happy about it. I promised I'll let her hunt some other time and that seems to lift her mood. Once again, we're running along the path.

We're almost smack dead in the middle of the woods when my wolf came to an abrupt stop. She sniffs the air, picking up an unfamiliar scent a growling. She placed the dress down on the floor, the growl still settling in the centre of our chest. I can't tell what we're smelling but her instincts tell us it's something to be wary of.

I soon find the smell to be human, trying to reign my wolf in so she doesn't hurt an innocent life but she doesn't let up, persistent that they're a threat. Why would a human be in Adrenous's territory? It's forbidden unless you have his permission.

My wolf forced me into the backseat of our mind, her protective nature coming through. She releases the growl that has been forming, facing the right as the sound of a twig snapping meets her ears. Her eyes narrowed, trying to find the trespasser. It's too dark to see. Her defence went into overdrive as she leans back on her back legs, ready to pounce and strike whatever approaches us.

Something breezed past us at unnatural speed. My wolf barked angrily at it, her top lip reeling back to reveal her sharp fangs. I could swear they had smelled human, so how had they moved so fast?

My wolf whined when a strong force collided into our side, throwing us into the air. Our back hit a tree before we fell to the ground hard. We hit our head, blood pooling from the wound as it had been cracked open. We try to rise and stand but a sharp, unimaginable pain travelled up our back right leg. It must have broken from the fall.

A silhouette of a man begins to approach, their face cast with shadows making it impossible to see their face. We try and scamper away, our paw continuing to throb, the pain causing us to feel sick as the urge to pass out washes over us. My wolf can't take it anymore, a shift being forced upon me, reverting back to human form.

I'm laying on my stomach naked, my ankle searing with pain. I'm completely afraid, wondering what's going to happen to me as tears threaten to spill.

"Adrenous?" I try and reach Adrenous, knowing he'll come to my aid when he realises I'm in danger but something appears to be blocking our link. My heart begins to beat erratically, I'm completely on my own. The figure steps forward, my dress in their hands as they kneel to the ground before me, my eyes widening up at him when his face becomes clear.

Tristan?

"Wh-why?" I blurt out, my voice strained, the pain continuing to run up my leg, forcing me to grind my teeth. My wounds are healing but slowly, too slow for my liking. It's as if my healing abilities have been weakened.

"I—I didn't mean to hurt you like this. I knew if I appeared, your wolf would attack me without thinking. I needed you to shift back before I revealed myself." His voice is low, his eyes apologetic. I'm completely lost and confused, the pain too unbearable that I can't think straight.

I watch with wide eyes as he brings his wrist to his lips, fangs protruding from his top lip before he sinks them into the flesh of his wrist. Blood pools from the wound, outstretching his arm towards me. I shake my head, my face contorted in horror, disgusted that he wants me to drink his blood. What the fuck is wrong with him? What is he?

"Drink and I promise you'll feel better." He says, his words genuine.

I'm still apprehensive, reluctantly closing my lips around the wound, closing my eyes tight as I wait for the horrid taste to fill my mouth. However, I'm surprised when nothing but sweetness touches my tastebuds, my eyes fluttering open in surprise as I pull away.

I can slowly feel the pain from my ankle disappear, the bones sowing back together along with the wound on my head now healed.

What in the . . . ?

He places the dress next to me and turns around, waiting for me sit up and dress myself. I quickly shimmer myself into the material, thankful for the covering. "What are you? Why can't I reach Adrenous?" I snap, anger simmering in my expression as I stand to my feet.

He stands along with me. "I made sure to spill liquid silver around this area, I needed this conversation to be completely private. Once you step out of it, you will be able to contact him again. Your healing and strength will be restored as well," he explains.

Liquid silver? Is that some kind of weakness?

"I'm . . ." he trails off, his eyes cast down as he tries to build the courage to tell me what he is, my noticeable anger not making it easier for him. He brings his green eyes back up, staring into mine warily as he said, "I'm half human . . . half vampire."

"What?" I can't help but exclaim, my emotions spiralling out of control. My best friend has lied to me. "But I've know you my whole life. How could you not tell me any of this?"

"Liv—" Secrets he wanted to spill overwhelmed him. "You've only known me for a year."

What?

"We grew up together," I said, my mind trying to process what he's saying. It doesn't make any sense.

Tristan seems stressed, his voice soft and serious. "Liv, you and your family were compelled to believe that. In reality, I've only been in your life for a year."

A year? "Why?" I sob, my chest constricting, feelings of betrayal consuming me. Our whole friendship was a lie. The feelings I once held for him were also a lie.

"Do you remember when I told you that because of me you could bring Adrenous's entire kingdom to its knees?" I nod my head, remember thinking how strange he was being that day, not realising the true meaning behind his words. "I was ordered to watch you by Krellin, my king. I had to report back to him everyday, letting him know your strengths, weaknesses and so on. Soon I had become to care for you, a genuine friendship forming." His eyes lock with mine before he continued. "I can't let what they have planned for you happen."

"Why would they need you to watch me? What plans?" I ask, not understanding how they knew about me. Even I didn't know what I was back then.

"Ask Adrenous. He knows who your parents are, he should be the one to tell you." Tris reveals, my mind becoming numb at his words.

"He would have told me if he knew who my parents are." I retort, not believing a word he's saying right now. Our friendship has been a supposed lie and he expects me to believe him now.

"Rylan told him." He states as if I should know that.

Rylan told him?

Seeing how I don't trust him, Tristan sighs, seeming frustrated. "You have no reason to trust me but trust when I tell you not all vampires are bad. Some of us are forced to follow Krellin, me included." He stops speaking, glancing past me, hearing a wolfs howl. Adrenous. He must be looking for me.

"Liv," Tris said, bringing my attention back towards him. "My mother was killed, used just to give birth to me. Trust me when I say I want revenge on Krellin as well. I have to go, think about what I said and make sure to ask Adrenous about your parents. He knows more than he's letting on."

Within the blink of an eye, Tris disappeared. My heart sank at all the things I've come to learn. I'm still trying to process it all.

I turned my head back around, my gaze locking with the crimson eyes of Adrenous's black wolf. I stepped forward, feeling as if I'm crossing over an invisible barrier as I approach him. It must be the liquid silver Tris was talking about, finally feeling my mind linking with Adrenous's.

"What the fuck happened? I couldn't connect with you. I was so fucking worried."

✦○✦

CHAPTER TWENTY-EIGHT
Don't Lie To Me

✦▢✦

ALIVIA

It's not long until we're back in the estate, Adrenous closing his bedroom door as I settle myself at the edge of the bed.

I had told him that I hurt myself earlier and blocked the connection on purpose so he didn't know I was hurt and worry about me. It was a strange lie but he seemed to have bought it and it gave me some time to build the courage and ask him the question that has been constantly simmering at the edge of my tongue, my palms sweating with how nervous I am.

Adrenous walks across the room, a robe tied around his naked body. He catches my gaze, his brows furrowing. "Is everything alright?"

I breathed in deeply, shaking my head and exhaling the air from my lungs. I need to know whether what Tris said is true or not, praying for the latter. Me and Adrenous have been so happy lately and it would kill me to learn that he's kept the knowledge of my parents to himself. It's unfair and selfish.

"What's the matter?" he questions, his gaze soft. His lips pulled into a tight line as he searches my expression, most likely seeing the hurt that I can no longer keep hidden.

"Do you know who my parents are?" I whispered, praying he doesn't. I can't stand secrets, especially when I've already given myself to him completely.

My heart sank when his eyes widened in surprise before his expression shifts to that of a guilty person caught in their lie. I drop my gaze to the floor, feeling the tears that want to fall. "Wh-why didn't you tell me?" My voice cracks, a sob wracking my body at the betrayal.

The second betrayal in one day . . .

I couldn't take it.

"How did you find out?" He asked, guilt now mixed with confusion swirling in his eyes.

"Does it matter?" I snap, angry that he's more worried about how I know rather than the fact he had lied. "Why the fuck didn't you tell me?" Tears were streaming down my eyes now but they were angry tears.

"I . . ." He trails off, running his hand through his hair in frustration. I should be the one who's frustrated, not him. "It's complicated. I knew the information would hurt you."

"No, this has hurt me." I stand to my feet, not wanting to be so close to him as I gesture with my hands, signalling that this situation has hurt me. "You don't get to decide what I can and can't know regarding my own life. Keeping this from me was selfish and you know it."

"I'm trying to protect you, Alivia!" His outburst catches me off guard, abruptly standing to his feet, his body tense and his jaw ticking. I've never seen him this angry before, the look in his eyes has my wolf bowing her head with her tail in between her legs but I don't easily give up.

"You protect me by not lying to me!" I shout back, not allowing him to have the upper hand in this situation. What he did is wrong and he needs to know and understand that or he'll just do it again.

I begin to feel slightly warm, my cramp from earlier returning as he speaks, his temper consuming him as his eyes darken, the beast within him coming forward. "Okay then, your father was a sadistic fucker who raped your mother to have you! Is that what you wanted to know?"

What? I can't breathe. How could he say something like that?

"Your father murdered my parents for their position but he didn't count on me, Titan and Rylan walking in. He would be dead right now if it weren't for the fact he managed to fucking escape!" Adrenous shouts, his eyes glistening with unshed tears but he holds them back, his eyes narrowed on me.

I can't believe what I'm hearing, my head and heart divided, feeling the anger and pain settle in the centre of my chest. I want to scream and shout at him for blurting out such sensitive information, learning my father was a rapist and a murderer sent me into shock, knowing I'm related to such a monster.

However, I can see the hurt in his eyes, my wolf wanting us to comfort him but I'm too stubborn and angry at the things he's said.

The tears are still falling, my heart skipping a few beats as I continue to control my shallow breathing. "I can't deal with this right now." I cried, my face heating and body boiling with what I can only assume is rage. I need to get away from him.

I sink to the floor when my body continues to heat up, another cramp overwhelming and forcing me to cry out in pain. What's wrong with me?

Adrenous is no longer angry, his features filling with panic as he walks towards me. But I held up my hand. "P—please stay a—away from m—me." It's hard to speak through the pain, feeling as if I'm going to pass out soon.

"What's wrong?" His nostrils flared, his eyes darkening as realisation mixed with horror contorts his expression. "You're in heat." The words are barely audible through the sound of my blood rushing through my ears as my heart pounds against my chest. *What's a heat?*

I cried out when a wave of pain erupted across my skin, feeling as though fire is coursing through my veins. The muscles in my stomach clenched as the cramps are thrown in as well.

Adrenous hovers around me, not knowing what to do because I won't let him touch me. "At least let me carry you to the bed," he urged, his voice desperate.

The pain is too much and I'd rather bear it on the soft sheets of the bed than on the hard floor. Adrenous is relieved when I nod my head, giving him permission to pick me up and carry me to the bed.

When his arms wrap around me and my face is pressed against his bare chest through the opening of his robe, I'm given a slight reprieve. The skin to skin contact cools the fire spreading through my veins but it's not enough, the cramps in my abdomen unbearable and I continue to cry as he carries me to the bed.

Is this what dying feels like? I'm certain I must be dying with how painful it is.

He places me down gently, my head resting against the pillows as he tucks me into the soft covers. I curl up into a ball, bringing my knees against my chest as if it will relieve the stomach cramps but it doesn't. If anything, they're getting worse and more intense by the passing minutes.

"Ali, your in heat. It's your body pushing you to want to be close to me, only my touch can relieve the pain." He explains but I'm in too much pain to fully pay attention.

"P—please l—leave," I begged.

His expression drops, the hurt in his eyes noticeable but I'm in no mood to care about his pain. I'm in too much physical and emotional pain of my own, being left alone is the only way to process everything.

He reluctantly pulls away from me, hovering close a moment longer until he sighs and heads for the door. When the door closes, I bury my head into the pillow, my body urging me to bring him back but I don't.

He should learn one thing from this . . . Don't lie to me.

✦○✦

CHAPTER TWENTY-NINE
Forgive Me

✦◻✦

Alivia

I buried my head into the tear-soaked pillow, muffling the sobs wracking my body. I tremble as I grip the edges of the pillow tightly.

I've been lying and crying here in pain for about two days now. Adrenous has kept his distance, having Rylan keep guard outside my door during my vulnerable state. I'm still not completely sure if I understand what I'm going through. Rylan told me it's only a Wolven thing, that my body is calling out to Adrenous in an attempt to get pregnant.

He also said my scent is intoxicating to not only Adrenous but any unmated wolf that happens to be near by. That's why Rylan was given the task of keeping me safe since he was already mated to Laurey.

The room is currently encased in darkness; however, half a moon is plastered in the sky casting only my distressed body in its healing light as it shines through the window. If only it could alleviate all my pain . . . I don't know how long I can go on like this. I don't want another few days of this, it's too much. If the pain isn't bad enough, the emotional pain is.

Adrenous betrayed me! And if it didn't make it worse he had told me my father was a sick bastard who murdered his parents. How could he disclose such sensitive information like that to me without considering how it would come across or make me feel?

I barely acknowledged the sound of someone knocking on the door, keeping my head buried in the pillow, hoping they will just disappear and leave me alone. The knock soon fades but I don't hear the sound of footsteps walking away. I groan when the sound of the door opens. "Can you just fuck off?"

"Woah, that's not very nice language for a young lady," Rylan said, his tone soft but playful as he strides across the room. I feel the bed dip slightly as he sits beside me.

"I'm not in the mood Rylan," I muttered into the pillow.

"I know what Adrenous said to you. He had no right—"

"No he didn't!" I cut in, lifting myself up off the pillow so he can see my bloodshot eyes and the fury behind them. His eyes visibly soften for a moment as I continue. "Do you realise how painful this is? I feel as if I'm burning from the inside out and then every now and again a cramp is thrown in. I shouldn't have to deal with what he said to me on top of what I'm already going through."

I sit up and lean against the headboard, gripping the pillow against my abdomen as I struggle to stifle the cries and control my shaky breathing. I draw in a deep breath, closing my eyes and then breathing out slowly as the wave of pain washes over me once again and then dulls back down.

This is what I've been having to put up with for three days straight.

"He betrayed me." I cried, my voice shaky as I try to speak between the waves of pain. "H—he told me—he said that my father murdered his parents." I lifted my gaze to stare into Rylan's eyes so he can see how truly hurt I feel. "And you already knew that." My voice has turned hard, my expression portraying the anger I feel.

"I told him what I saw in the Rune's mind," he said, his eyes cast down in guilt. "Adrenous wanted to know how they knew about you, that's the reason I entered his mind in the first place."

That links to what Tris said. He said he watched me for his king, that they had plans for me. *What plans?*

Another wave of heat coursed through my veins, the thoughts forgotten as I grind my teeth and grip the pillow tightly. My vision is blurred and more tears fell. Why does it have to hurt so much?

When the wave of pain dulls down, I ask, "W—why didn't you tell me?"

"I told him not to tell you."

I snapped my head to the door, hating that he had the absolute nerve to show himself. I clutched the pillow tighter as a new wave of pain crashes through me at the sight of him. My wolf yearned to be near him but I fight back the urge. I can't give in to the pain.

When I can finally speak through the pain, I hissed, "Get away from me."

But he doesn't listen. "Rylan leave us, I'm sure Laurey will want you home."

Rylan nods his head. "Yeah I bet. She's been quite impatient and snappy since she became pregnant," he mused, an attempt to alleviate the tension growing between me and Adrenous. I can only fake a half-hearted smile before he takes his leave, passing Adrenous on his way out.

Adrenous strides across the room, taking a seat at the foot of the bed. As if on cue another wave of pain floods my senses, a cry passing my lips. Adrenous attempts to lean towards me but I push myself back into the headboard, my eyes ablaze with fury. "S—stay a—away."

A flash of hurt crosses his features as he pulls away. At this moment in time, I don't care that I've hurt his feeling. I can only worry about the pain, focusing on how it's driving me towards him, using all my remaining energy to fight it. I can't give in . . .

"I'm sorry." He begins, his voice sending shivers down my spine as I cling the pillow to my chest, refusing to look at him. "I should have told you. I didn't mean to tell you the way I did, I-"

"I don't care anymore," I mumbled into the pillow. My voice was small and hoarse from crying. "I'm in too much pain to talk."

"So listen." He breathes slowly. I glance up at him, his face blurred through my bloodshot eyes as I stare at him expectantly. I'm listening. What could he possibly say to make me forgive him? I was too tired for excuses.

"When I found out who your father was, the reasons behind why you were born, I couldn't bring myself to tell you. I knew the reality of what your father did would crush you and I didn't want that for you." I glance up at him, seeing the guilt he doesn't try to hide. "I was trying to protect you in my own way. To save you from the pain but I realise now I've only made it worse and for that I'm sorry."

At least he was owning his mistake rather than going out of his way to justify and guard his lies.

"There is one thing you should know." He continues, his eyes locking with mine. "Your mother is the reason you're safe, she sacrificed her life in order to save you."

My mother saved me?

"She was a brave woman." He adds, having absolute respect for my mother.

"I—"

I'm cut off when the pain returns with a new intensity, a scream clawing it's way up my throat as I struggle to breathe. "I c-can't t-take it no-no more." I sob, giving in to the pain. There's only so much I can take and it hurts so much. *Please make it stop*!

Without my permission, Adrenous lays in the bed beside me, pulling me into his chest as his arms wrap around me. I'm in too much pain to protest, my body trembling in his hold as the cries wrack my body. He wipes away a few tears with the pad of his thumb, his touch numbing the pain just a little and I soon find myself leaning into his touch. I just want the pain to stop . . .

"*Alivia, please let me take away your pain. Don't let yourself suffer because of my mistake.*"

His voice is a caressing whisper in my mind, my wolf pushing me to give in. The pain is too much for her as it is for me and soon I find myself subconsciously nodding my head, giving him permission to take away my pain.

He continues to brush away the tears with his thumb before leaning down to press his lips against my cheeks, placing a few soft kisses until my breathing is calm again. The pain started dulling back down. A moan passed my lips as he began to trail light hot kisses along my jaw and neck, his touch replacing the searing hot pain with a warm, pleasurable heat that travels to my core, the pain of the cramps easing away too.

He gently cups my cheek with his hand, leaning down so that his lips are now touching mine, our lips moulding together as the rest of the pain begins to perish, a sexual hunger taking its place.

I place my hand against Adrenous's chest, feeling his muscles ripple beneath his shirt. I need more skin to skin contact, my fingers working to unbutton his shirt. When the last button is undone, I push it away from his shoulders and then down his arms until it falls to the floor, his chest now bare before me.

Adrenous pulls away from my lips, understanding that my body needs more contact, he lifts my dress away from body, his eyes darkening with hunger. His nostrils flared as he breathes in my intoxicating scent, his wolf coming forward. My wolf pushes through my mind to greet his, my own eyes darkening as he grazes my thigh with his fingers.

When his fingers make contact with my clit, my back automatically arches, my clit demanding more friction. I need it now.

My mind is caught up in a haze, not even remembering when Adrenous's breeches came off. His fingers probed my tight entrance, a frustrated whine leaving my lips. I needed him to pump them inside of me. When he begins to thrust them inside and then back out again, I grind my hips against his fingers, feeling his own arousal poke my hip as his cock begins to harden.

My body is calling to him, his touch is our salvation from the pain. He continue to thrust his fingers in and out until I'm a moaning mess, the sheets beneath me soaked with my arousal. I can feel my orgasm building, my hips jerking as my core tightens, ready to release. My walls tighten around Adrenous's fingers, his voice gruff as he says, "Cum for me, little wolf."

I shatter right there and then, gripping the sheets beneath me as my back arches of the bed. I slump back down but my body is calling out for more, needing him to fuck me.

I won't be satisfied until he does.

He climbs over my body, making sure to be gentle, his eyes soft and gentle as he gazes down into mine, the guilt still visible. He keeps the top half of his body from pressing against mine, leaning his head down to press his lips against mine once again. "I love you." He murmurs against me, swiping his tongue against my bottom lip before I allow him to dive his tongue inside.

The kiss is soft and gentle as he carefully aligns his cock with my soaked entrance, my hips arching up, needing him more than ever. I gasp against him as he presses himself inside, the head of his cock entering me fully as my walls constrict around him, hugging him tightly.

Once he's all the way in, he slowly pulls back out, taking his time as his lips meet mine once again, panting against him as my body becomes to glisten with sweat. I feel as if my body is on fire though it isn't painful like before, this renewed fire is pleasurable and it has me craving him like my life depends on it.

"M—more." I breathe into him, wanting more of him. I need more of him.

"What do you want?" He groans against me, his cock twitching within my walls, pulling his lips away to press his forehead against mine, gazing down into my eyes with a hot intensity.

"I want . . . you to . . . fuck me harder . . . faster." I manage to say between pants.

He pulls out of me, placing both of my legs onto his shoulders before roughly pounding back in, his cock thrusting in even deeper every time he pounds back in. I used my hips, thrusting upward to meet with his, a tightness forming in my abdomen once again as pleasure continues to travel through me.

Before I can shatter apart, he pulls away from me, my heart beating erratically as I grind my teeth in frustration, glaring daggers at him. He smirks, gesturing with his hand for me to turn around. I furrow my eyebrows at him but do as he says, pressing my stomach against the sheets as I arch my back, my arse on full display to him.

He grips my arse cheeks tightly as he pounds into me from behind, feeling his cock pound deeper than I've ever felt before, a scream of pleasure leaving my lips every time he pounds back in.

I can feel my abdomen tightening once again, feeling as if I'm close to the edge. I just need a little more. I find myself meeting his rhythm, pushing back against him as he thrusts in, my walls constricting even tighter.

I'm so close . . .

I can feel his cock expanding as I finally fall apart, my claws elongating of their own accord, tearing into the sheets of the bed. "Adrenous!" I scream into the sheets as he strokes himself inside of me a few more times, spilling himself deep inside of me before my body slumps onto the bed, my orgasm now finished. I could feel him resting his forehead in between my shoulder blades as he tries to catch his breath.

I can feel my senses returning, silently thankful that the pain is gone. He pulls out of me and I move to lay on my side, laying against the pillow that I was not long crying into. He lays down behind me, pressing his lips against my shoulder. "I'm sorry for what I did, please forgive me."

The lies. The betrayal. I close my eyes, sleep creeping in as he wraps his arm around my abdomen, pulling me into him. His touch is still cooling, a relief that my body is still desperate for. I'm thankful he took away my pain even though I know . . . I'm not even close to forgiving him.

✦○✦

CHAPTER THIRTY
Fight Me

✦▢✦

ALIVIA

I stir in my sleep, trying to cuddle into Adrenous but there's no one there. My eyes snap open, finding his side of the bed empty. Where is he?

The sheets beneath me are slightly torn, a reminder of last night. I blush at the memory. I rub my eyes, sitting up to lean against the headboard and that's when I spot the pile of clothes at the foot of the bed, a note on top of the pile. Lifting the note, it reads:

Get dressed and meet me outside.
— A

I furrow my brows, looking at the clothes. It's the same black bottoms and matching top I had to wear when scouting the perimeter with Arif. I pray I don't have to do that again. It was extremely tiring and I am not in the mood.

The memories of last night are blurry, the pain a distant one. I do, however, remember Adrenous's touch, the way it relieved the burning heat and cramps that plagued my body. If he hadn't taken me the way he did, I would still be in pain now.

I'm grateful but he still has a long way to go before I can fully forgive him for lying to me. Perhaps that's why he wants to meet me outside.

It doesn't take me long to get dressed, tying my hair into a high ponytail before I leave the room. The clothes as I remember are just as comfy as before, moulding around my body perfectly as I head towards the exit. Stepping outside, it takes me a while to spot Adrenous. He's standing with Titan, the both of them only wearing black bottoms. It was the same as mine, their chests on display as they stand in the centre of the field.

Walking towards them, Adrenous asks, "How are you feeling?"

"Better," I answered, feeling the strain in our relationship creeping in. Deciding to take the initiative, I ask, "What are we doing out here?"

The tension seems to lift, Adrenous's expression shifting as a smirk makes its way to his lips. I don't like the look on his face, my eyes narrowing suspiciously. Adrenous steps towards me. "I'm going to train you."

"Train me?" That sounds worse than scouting the perimeter. He nods his head and then gestures me closer. I'm still wary but take a small step forward, still unclear as to what we're doing.

Titan stands off to the side, studying me and Adrenous carefully.

"I'm going to teach you how to fight," he explained, watching me closely as I frown up at him. *He wants me to fight him?*

"Why?" Surely this is some kind of joke? He can't seriously expect me to fight him.

"It's my way of making it up to you, allowing you to take your frustrations out on me." I look up at him dumbfounded, watching as he continues with, "I lied to you to protect you and I know now it's wrong to keep you in the dark. Training you, however will help to keep you safe." His expression is completely serious.

I study him cautiously. Was he really that sorry he would change his tactics in keeping me safe? I agree with him. Training me and helping me to defend myself is much better than keeping me in the dark with no way to protect myself if things go sideways.

"I agree," I said softly. This is a strange way of making things up to me but I like it. He won't always be able to protect me by keeping me away from things At some point, I will only have myself and that can either be a good thing or a bad thing.

He takes a step towards me, my breathe hitching as he looks down at me. "Good, little wolf." I rolled my eyes at him. From my peripheral vision, I can see Titan smirking, his gaze still studying us. "Now try and hit me."

I sighed, uncrossing my arms. I decided that if he's going to let me do this, then I'm going to do it properly. I've watched him and the others spar a few times and I've caught a few tricks which I'm sure will catch him off guard. My first advantage is that he'll underestimate me.

I quickly step my foot out to the side, his eyes shifting to the action. That distracted him as I throw a punch to his chest. He staggers back slightly. His expression lit up in surprise, not expecting me to actually hit him.

I lean back, glancing at him smugly. Titan's chest is rumbling, his shoulders moving up and down as he tries to stifle his laughter. "She outsmarted the king."

I did and it actually felt quite good.

My smug smile drops when Adrenous begins to circle me. I follow his movement, turning in my spot so I can continue to face him. He smirks down at me, edging slightly closer. "Don't act too smug, too much confidence can be a disadvantage."

I frown up at him, watching him closely as I continue to follow him. What is he doing? Not a second later, he kicks his leg out, catching my ankle and causing me to stumble forward. I landed on the floor, just catching myself with my hands. I glare up at him from the ground, rolling to the side before he can climb on top of me. I climb back up to my feet, taking a few steps away from him.

He stalks towards me with mischievous intent. "You're quick but you need to be quicker." Before I can take a few more steps away, he's in front of me faster than I can blink, striking me in the shoulder with his fist. It's not hard enough to hurt but enough so that I stumble back, nearly falling to the ground before he captures my wrist and pulls me into him.

I glare up at him. "I'm starting to think you only wanted to do this for your own amusement."

"Perhaps." He releases my wrist. "Make a fist."

I do as he says, curling my hand into a fist for him to see. His fingers curl around my wrist again, pulling my hand towards him so he can study my fist before making changes and repositioning my thumb. "Make sure your fingers are tightly clenched and that your thumb is securely locked over your second and third knuckles." I nod my head, doing as he says.

He spends the next ten minutes teaching me how to punch effectively. Then, he moves on to my footing, telling me to keep my right foot forward and lean back on my left.

Titan stands in front of me, padded gloves on his hands for me to practice punching. I lean back on my left foot and then shift my weight to my right as I throw my fist at the pads. Titan almost staggered back, a proud smile forming. "She's getting better." He boasts to Adrenous.

"She certainly is," Adrenous chuckles, watching my progress. "Practice on my again, little wolf."

I turned to him. I was feeling slightly tired, my body coated with sweat. "I think I need a break," I said, wiping away the sweat on my forehead with the back of my hand.

"If I was a vampire, do you think I would allow you a break?" He stalks towards me, looking down at me as he waits for me to respond.

"No." I breathe out, reluctantly making a stance.

Adrenous nods his head in approval, I shift my weight forward, kicking my leg out to strike him just below his knee but he quickly moves his leg back, leaning his upper body forward, capturing my ankle. I kick my leg out, trying to keep balance whilst struggling to free my leg. I kick even harder, almost capturing him in the stomach before he's forced to release me, my foot landing back on the floor.

He circles me a few more seconds, my senses on full alert, catching his left arm flexing out, his fist almost striking me in the side before I can jump to the right. However, I don't have time to deflect his next strike, his right arm shooting out as his fist catches me in the chest before he lifts his knee up and kicks his leg out, catching me in my chest again. I fly back, landing on the floor with a hard thud. Now I'm pissed!

I jump back to my feet, my wolf coming forward as I glare at him, her strength rushing through my veins. I run at him, full speed, lifting in the air and I kick with my left leg and then my right, hitting his chest twice before I land back on my feet, watching him stumble to the ground.

He lays down on his back, watching me with pride rather than embarrassment. He's proud that I was able to do that, knowing I'll be able to watch myself if someone twice my size tries to hurt me.

"That's me done for the day." I smirked, holding out my hand to him.

He takes my hand but instead of lifting me up, he pulls me on top of him, his arms wrapping around me tightly. "Is that so?"

"I'm going to take my leave," Titan announced before walking away from us, obviously feeling awkward. I chuckled at him, understanding that it must be awkward before turning my attention back on those crimson eyes.

I wriggle out of Adrenous's grasp, sitting up as my thighs rest either side of his body. "I know you only want to protect me.

Can you just promise you won't lie to me again?" I whisper softly looking down at him. My once playful demeanour now gone as I stare down at him expectantly, waiting for him to respond.

His expression shifts, a smile making its way to his lips. "I've learned my lesson, I promise I won't lie again."

"Good." I stood on my feet. "Now that's settled, I need a bath."

"There's one more thing I need to tell you," he said, standing on his feet.

"What do you mean?" I thought he told me everything last night.

"Follow me."

✦○✦

CHAPTER THIRTY-ONE
Blood Is Thicker Than Water

✦☆✦ r

ALIVIA

I lean back in my chair, staring at Adrenous expectantly as he rests back in his own chair behind his desk. "What else do you need to tell me?" I press, not understanding why we're sitting in his office.

"Just a second, he'll be here in a moment." He answers. I roll my eyes and sigh, waiting for him to turn up.

Adrenous mindlinked Arif to join us in his office but I had no idea why. What could he possible have to tell me which involved needing Arif present?

"How long is he going to be? He's taking ages." I sighed.

"He'll be here soon. You need to learn to be patient, you're going to need it one day," Adrenous said as he watches me, his eyes dancing with amusement.

"Perhaps, but that day isn't today," I remarked, shooting him a cheeky smile. "Besides, I feel gross and just want to hurry this up so I can have a bath."

"I promise to help you with that after this." He smirks. I roll my eyes at him, my lips twitching upwards, enjoying his playfulness. My memories rewind to my first night here, being forced to bathe with him. Back then it was rather humiliating and confusing but I would give anything to bathe with him right now . . . Arif better hurry his arse up.

It's not ten minutes later that Arif steps foot into the office, turning my attention on him as he strides to the seat next to mine and sits down. "What took you so long?" I question.

He shakes his head, nodding at me as he addressed Adrenous. "Your mate loves to ask questions." I narrow my eyes on him before he releases an exasperated sigh and answers the question, "I was stopped by Rita on my way here."

Rita? That manipulative bitch? I haven't seen nor heard from her since she tried to turn me against Adrenous in the library and I was happy for it. Now out of the blue she weasels her way back into my life? I don't think so.

"She has been asking for an audience with you but I told her that isn't going to happen," Arif adds.

"Good." I blurt out, not even apologetic. I don't want her anywhere near him.

Adrenous catches my angry gaze, "I won't let her ruin what we have." The anger disperses from my eyes, softening as I smile back at him. "Now, there's something very important that the both of you deserve to know."

The room thickens with tension, hearing the seriousness that drips from Adrenous's tone. Arif gives me a sideways glance, equally as confused as me, the same question wanting to pass his lips . . .

What secret could there be that involves the both of us?

"You'll need to remain calm Arif and realise that Alivia has never done anything wrong," Adrenous tells Arif softly, my eyebrows furrowing as Arif leans forward.

"What are you talking about?" Arif demanded. I'm with Arif on this one. What did I possibly do that would anger him?

"Arif this involves your father," Adrenous reveals, watching Arif closely as he visibly tenses, his eyes hardening.

"Don't speak of that bastard," Arif growls, his hands forming into fists, anger consuming his being. I remain silent, not understanding what Arif's father has to do with this. I'm completely lost, my attention shifting between the both of them as I wait for Arif to relax but he doesn't, remaining stiff as he glares warningly at Adrenous.

Adrenous doesn't stand down but he remains silent for a few moments. Perhaps Adrenous was hoping that Arif will relax as well but as expected, Arif won't relax. Adrenous continues slowly. "This isn't just about you Arif, Alivia has to hear this as well."

"Anything regarding my father doesn't concern her." Arif snaps, his nostrils flaring. Why is he so angered by the mention of his father? I've never seen Arif this mad before. He's always been snippy but never furious like he is now. Perhaps his father was the reason behind why he's so moody all the time.

Adrenous shakes his head, evidently becoming frustrated with Arif, "It does concern her, he's her father too."

What? Arif has gone completely silent, his fist trembling as he grasp what was just said. I feel the atmosphere thicken, my hands becoming clammy as I struggled to breath properly. "B—but you said my father killed your parents?"

Adrenous nods, keeping a wary eye on Arif as he tries to alleviate my confusion. "Your father is Alijah Sanford."

Sanford . . . ? That's Arif's name.

I'm completely speechless. There's so much to this man I've never met. I don't know how to feel knowing that Arif is my brother. Will he even accept me or will I suffer the consequences of this man's actions even though I've never met him?

"I—but I'm not full Wolven." I managed to get out. "That means our mothers are—"

Arif's fist comes down hard on the table. I leaned back in my chair as I flinched at the sudden outburst, my fear spiking. When Arif speaks, I've never heard anyone sound so broken. "Alijah killed my mother right in front of me because she was going to warn Adrenous's parents of his plans. I tried to save her but my father knocked me out and then it was too late." I felt a tear make its way down my cheek, watching him closely when he turned to look at me. "I would be ten when you were born. That means my father cheated on my mother, breaking their bond before he killed her. She was always in pain, not physically…" He can't bring himself to continue.

I feel my chest clench, my heart thumping loudly as I try not to break. "Breaking a bond is more torturous than burning someone alive. It tears apart their soul." Arif reveals in distaste, his gaze distant but angry. "I need to go."

"Arif—"

"Don't Alivia!" Arif growls, heading towards the door. "I can't look at you right now, knowing . . ." He trails off, a heavy sigh passing his lips before he looks away from me and walks straight out.

I'm left hurt, tears sliding down my cheeks. I hear shuffling behind me before Adrenous is in front of me, kneeling down as my gaze remains fixed on the door. "Arif is angry with me," I mumble while Adrenous wipes away my tears with the pads of his thumb.

He shakes his head, the action drawing my attention before I stare at him, "Did you not just hear what he said to me? He's angry that my conception broke his mother apart. How can he ever forgive me for that?"

Adrenous releases a soft sigh, his voice soft as he consoles me, "He's hurt Alivia. He needs time to heal and come to terms with the fact that it isn't your fault. His father's actions have hurt us all. Give him time, this is where patience comes in." Adrenous smiles softly, his earlier advice becoming relevant to the current situation. How ironic . . .

"I need to know more," I said, yearning for all questions regarding my parents to be answered. I want to know every little detail before the unknown drives me crazy.

"You will, but first let's get you cleaned, okay?" I nod, complying as I stand from the chair, following him to the bedroom as my mind remains elsewhere. It is often said that blood is thicker than water . . . but with me and Arif, I fear that will never be the case. Our relationship damaged way before we even knew of each other. Our father made sure of that.

I remain silent, laying down on the bed as a few maids fill the bath with hot water.

Adrenous doesn't force me to talk, understanding that all I need is his company to soothe me as I allow him to lead me to the bath tub, the steam rising up to warm my skin. I release a soft sigh, lifting my arms so that Adrenous can remove my top along with my bottoms afterwards.

I sink into the hot water, the tension in my muscles dispersing as the water relaxes them. Adrenous lowers himself in the water from behind me, his legs stretched out on either side of my body as he pulls me into him, my head resting on his chest as he places his chin on my shoulder.

The water pours warmth into my being, replacing the coldness that is my emotions. I'm hurt, my emotions taking control of my mind as I try to focus on the warmth of the water. It's not enough to soothe me completely, knowing Arif is most likely blaming me for his mother's torment.

I hope he doesn't shut me out forever. I need to talk to him now more than ever.

Adrenous begins to squeeze my shoulders, massaging them, his touch relaxing my mind and body, "Hmm that feels good." I smile, leaning into his touch.

"You shouldn't be so surprised." Adrenous chuckles lightly, "I'm pretty good with my hands."

I giggle, rolling my eyes. A moan is pulled from my lips as he continues to expertly relax the muscles in my shoulders. After everything that's happened in the last few days, from Tristan warning me to today with Arif, I needed a break. I need some time to focus on something else and not have to worry. "I want to get away from here for a little while," I said, turning to face Adrenous, his hands stopping their movement as he looks down at me closely.

"That might not be a good idea right now." Adrenous cautions softly, his hand cupping my cheek as he strokes it gently with his thumb.

"Please, just for a little while. I don't even care where we go as long as it's not here." I plead, looking up at him through my eyelashes.

He releases a soft sigh, deciding whether or not to give in. "I'm due to meet the Elders along with Rylan," Adrenous finally says, "I suppose we could take you with us. It might be good for them to meet you now, considering you'll be their queen soon."

"I've met one of them, just before the ceremony where I turned. I can't say it was a good experience," I said, remembering how rude he was to me.

"Don't worry, I'll make sure they have the upmost respect for you." he whispered into my ear, wrapping his arms around my abdomen to pull me in closer.

"Thank you," I whisper back, my worries fading away as I look forward to officially meeting the Elders and getting away from here . . . away from my problems. It should be interesting . . .

✦○✦

CHAPTER THIRTY-TWO
Rogue Attack

✦▢✦

ALIVIA

"Can I come in?"

I turn my head to see Raven standing in the door frame, "Of course." I turn back round to continue packing away my clothes, almost ready to leave for the Elders meeting with Adrenous for a few days.

"That's a lot of clothes for a few days." Raven comments, chuckling, "Even I haven't packed that much."

I smile, shrugging my shoulders, "You can never be too careful."

Raven is coming with us to the Elders meeting too. Adrenous decided her presence would be beneficial to me and him. I would have a friend to accompany me when he and Rylan are busy and for him, she's the best person to caution the Elders about her brother's power and his intentions.

Raven sits down next to my bags at the edge of the bed, "Really . . . ?" She reaches into my bag and pulls out a paper bag of treats, holding the bag up to me with an arched brow.

"What? I might get hungry on the way there." I say with an innocent smile, taking the bag back from her to put it back in my bag.

"It's only a few hours"—Raven laughs—"and you've got enough to get you through a whole day."

"What can I say?" I shrugged, giggling. "I'm feeling peckish."

Raven shakes her head and laughs. My attention is brought back to the door, seeing Rylan standing there with his arms crossed over his chest. Raven follows my line of sight, becoming amused at the look on Rylan's face.

"What's taking you ladies so long? We have to leave soon," Rylan said, looking between us and then at my bags. "My lord woman! Do you really need that much stuff?"

"Yes." I giggle, grabbing the bag with my treats inside and then walking towards him, "Grab the rest of my bags, will you?" I playfully ask before passing him, Raven following me.

"Urgh, women shouldn't travel . . ." Rylan grumbled, his voice trailing off as me and Raven walked further away from him, heading towards the doors that will exit the estate.

Breaching the exit, my attention is drawn to the gorgeous carriage. It's carved out of fine wood with four giant, golden wheels, a golden door and Adrenous's family symbol plastered on the back, chiselled out of gold as well. Two gorgeous, black stallions, twice my height, are standing in front of it, ready to pull when the coachman gives the order.

I approach the horses carefully, admiring them. They truly are magnificent animals. I place my hand on the right horses side, feeling the silky hair against my fingers as I pat him gently, "Aren't you a gorgeous horse?" I coo, smiling as he sniffs at my hair.

"So you like horses?" Adrenous asks, coming to stand at my side as he pats the other one.

I nod my head, smiling up at the horse, "What's his name?"

"Shadow," he said. "And this one is Eclipse," he added, looking up at the horse he's patting gently.

"They are beautiful," I comment, still admiring them.

"Fuck!" I heard Rylan, turning to find one of my bags on the floor as he struggled to carry the rest.

Adrenous looks over at him as well, chuckling as he walks towards him and picks up my bag from the floor, "Need a hand?"

Rylan narrows his eyes, "I don't understand why Liv needs so much stuff." Adrenous grabs a few bags from him and places them in the back of the carriage, his lips twitching in amusement.

I roll my eyes at him and walk towards Adrenous, "Are you joining me and Raven in the carriage?"

He shakes his head, "Me and Rylan are going to shift and keep an eye out just in case anything goes wrong."

I frown up at him, "I hope that won't be the case."

"Don't worry, I'm sure we'll get there smoothly." He places a light kiss on my cheek and said, "Now go and join Raven so we can leave."

"Okay." I give him a quick hug and then join Raven, Rylan closing the carriage door once we're inside.

The ride is mostly uneventful, me and Raven sitting in comfortable silence as I snack on the treats and keep my attention on the scenery going past. We're still surrounded by trees but they're much denser than the ones around Adrenous's estate. They block out most of the sun, making it appear dark but through my wolf's eyes I'm able to see wildlife that takes residence in the woods. It's mostly just rabbits or small rodents but every now and then I catch sight of a deer.

Adrenous is at the front of the carriage while Rylan is at the back, keeping us protected on either side. So far everything has been smooth and with some luck we'll be there within the hour.

I've finished my snacks at this point, my stomach still growling for more. Raven laughs at the sound, "Seriously? You've just eaten all that food."

"The stomach wants what the stomach wants." I joke, watching as she playfully rolls her eyes. I return my gaze to the window, my eyelids soon becoming heavy as I lean back in my chair. My eyelids are almost closed when I catch sight of something in the distance, my eyes opening fully.

    I move my face closer to the window, trying to see if I can see it again. Raven looks at me strangely, asking, "What are you looking at?"

    I shake my head, "Nothing really, just my mind playing tricks." I downplay my thoughts though I was sure I could see a few wolves in the distance. I disregard the thought, even if there were wolves I'm sure they're just from another pack or something.

    I relax back into my chair, feeling my eyes close once again as I welcome sleep. The sound of growling can be heard, my eyes snapping open as my heartbeat accelerates, "What's going on?"

    Raven shakes her head, equally as confused as me, "I don't know but we've stopped moving."

    I reach for the handle of the door but halt when Raven cautions, "I don't think that's a good idea, Adrenous and Rylan can handle it."

    "I just want to see what's happening," I whispered, opening the door against Raven's judgement. Growling can be heard, my eyes widening at the sight of Adrenous and Rylan fighting off other wolves. "I don't understand . . . Why are they fighting other Wolvens?"

    "They're rogues," Raven answered.

    Oh! I remember now. They're wolves without a pack, the few who don't answer to Adrenous, instead they fight against packed Wolvens.

    There are at least five of them growling at Adrenous and Rylan while two are limp on the floor, their coats stained with blood as it flows from the wounds on their necks. I can sense Adrenous's fury flowing out of him, the rogues tempted to submit but they don't, pouncing at him instead. Adrenous continuously snaps his jaw at them, catching one on the leg while the other is behind him, snapping their jaw at his hind legs.

"Raven, can't you use your powers to help them?" I ask her, hearing my heart pounding as I watch the gruesome fight.

Raven nods and pokes her head out the door, holding her hand out, her palm facing the fight as she closes her eyes. I watch her palm glow before the rogue, that is attacking Adrenous's hind legs is left frozen in place.

This gives Adrenous the time to finish the other one off, pushing him to the ground with his paws before sinking his fangs into their neck, a high pitched whine resounding from their throat until they lay limp. The frozen rogue then unfreezes, looking at their dead friend before anger rushes through them. Adrenous and the angered rogue resume their fight.

Raven then turns her attention on the other three wolves that are snapping their jaws at Rylan. She shoves her hand forward, forcing two of the wolves to fly back, one hitting their back on a tree while the other rolls back a few feet. Raven then looks back at me with a smirk, "Is that what you wanted?"

I smirked back at her, nodding my head and look back in time to see Adrenous had shifted to human, watching as he looks down at a wounded man, the last living rogue, "You tell your leader that if he sends anymore of your kind my way I'll hunt him down personally and make him wish he was dead!"

The fury in Adrenous's eyes catches me off guard, the rogue nodding his head vigorously as he crawl-runs away from him before disappearing into the woods with Adrenous's threat.

I step out of the carriage and walk towards him, seeing his body shake with anger as I approach closer and place my palm on his cheek. He looks down at me, his expression softening as he leans into my touch, visibly relaxing.

Are you okay?

He nods his head, bringing me towards him as his arms wrap around me, releasing his tension as the feel of my body soothes him and his wolf.

I soon feel him pull away from me before gesturing to the carriage, "Go back inside, were only a mile away from the Elders estate now."

"As you wish." I quickly reach up with my toes and kiss him gently before heading back towards the carriage.

Please let that be the only drama we'll have today.

"Raven?" I question as the carriage begins to move again. She hums in response and turns her gaze from the window to look at me, "Who is the rogues leader? I mean, I know Laurey said that nobody knows it but I can't help but feel that, that's a lie."

Raven finds it hard to look at me, not expecting the question as she struggles to respond. When she does, she says, "I'm not really good with Wolven knowle—"

"Raven please, I know you mean well but you're a terrible liar," I mused before I become serious once again. "I'm just asking for a name here, it's not like I'm asking for your deepest, darkest secret."

She bit her lip, thinking about it for a moment before she finally gives in. "I'm not sure but I think his followers call him King Marx."

Hmm . . . catchy name I suppose. "See, was that so hard?" I smirked, arching a brow at her.

She shrugs her shoulders. "Perhaps not."

The last part of the journey runs smoothly once again and it's not long until the carriage becomes to an actual stop. Adrenous and Rylan open our doors after they are properly dressed from the bag of clothes they had stored in the back of the carriage along with the rest of our belongings.

I take Adrenous's hand as I step down from the carriage and step onto the gravel floor. Looking up at the building, it's bigger than I expected but definitely smaller than Adrenous's. The building was only two storeys but made up for it in width, reaching at least the length of at least four houses put together. The windows weren't floor to ceiling but were quite wide and made from expensive glass, framed with steel.

Approaching the entrance two men stood there, heavily muscled but it was obvious they were human by their scent. Both men bowed when they saw Adrenous, showing their upper most respect before asking, "Would you like assistance with your bags?"

"Please." Adrenous answers kindly. One of the men call to a few other men who quickly head towards the back of the carriage and carry our belongings inside.

Now I feel bad for packing so much stuff.

"Victor sends his apologies for not welcoming you personally but he's currently busy dealing with a few protests due to the new lockdown rules." The man explains.

"It's quite alright, I'll go and help him." Adrenous states before walking inside the building, me beside him as I link my arm in his, becoming slightly nervous now that we're here.

Raven and Rylan aren't too far behind us, Adrenous turning us to face them quickly, "Why don't you two go and set up while I introduce Alivia to the Elders."

"Sure, no problem." Rylan and Raven head of down one of the intersections that separate from the corridor Adrenous and I are walking down.

We stop outside a nicely carved double door, another muscled man standing outside. He quickly bows to Adrenous, "Your Highness, it's good to have you here."

"Thank you, may I have entry?" Adrenous questions and the man nods his head, opening the door for us.

"Thank you," I murmur and it's as if the guard has seen me for the first time.

These guards are obviously too stuck up Adrenous's arse to notice the woman clearly standing next to him.

Entering the room, the first thing I notice Is how big the room is. The room was pretty much an open floor plan with steps that lead onto a platform. Five chairs carved expertly out of fine wood along with gorgeous, red cushioning are mantled atop the platform, facing the room.

The chairs are currently occupied with who I assumed are the Elders, the men dressed in black robes while the woman wear long black dresses. In the first chair on the far left, a woman who looks to be in her early thirties with red hair and brown eyes is seated, her expression appearing bored as she watches a man protest to the Elder in the middle seat.

The second chair seats a man appearing to be in his early thirties as well with blonde hair and grey eyes however, unlike the woman his eyes are lit with amusement.

Next in the chair on the far right is another woman appearing to be the youngest. She has to be at least in her early twenties, her hair a light blonde. She appears to be daydreaming, her brown eyes distant as she's pulled away from the room at the moment.

The chair next to hers seats another man, his hair a similar blondes to the woman next to him, though his eyes are green instead of brown. Nonetheless, if I didn't know better I would say they are related but he must be older, looking as if he's in his late twenties.

Finally, the middle chair seats a man with greyish brown hair, his brown eyes narrowed as he listens to the man protesting about something or other, I assume the lockdown Adrenous mentioned. Even so, I could swear this was the Elder I have seen before. The night before the ceremony where I shifted, he gave me and Tris tasks to carry out, though he was quite rude the entire time. I wonder how this next encounter will go.

"It's unfair, I have to work and supply food to my family or we'll starve. I can't afford to stay home and do nothing." The man's protest continued. From the looks of it, he is most likely a cook. An apron is tightly wrapped around him and it's stained with food. It appears he had no time to change and came here quickly to beg for work.

Before the Elder in the middle seat can respond, Adrenous cuts in, making our presence known as we walk across the room, now standing in front of the man. "Food banks will be set up, nobody will starve."

The man looks to him in shock, almost unsure if what he heard was true. When he finally snaps out of his state of shock, he quickly bows his head, "T—thank you, Your Highness."

The Elders straighten up in their seats at the presence of Adrenous.

"You are dismissed," Adrenous said, holding his hand out to the door.

The man gets the message, continuously bowing, "Of course, thank you, thank you."

When the man is gone, Adrenous turns his attention on the Elder seated in the middle. The man looks down at him, a look of relief plastered on his face, "Thank god you shut him up. We've been dealing with complaints like that for the past few weeks."

"That's your job, Victor," Adrenous states, crossing his arms over his chest, appearing displeased.

The man nods his acknowledgement of Adrenous's statement. He then changes the subject when he spots me, his eyebrows furrowing, "Who is this woman? She seems rather familiar."

Here we go . . .

"We've met before," I answered before Adrenous can. "It was at the preparation for the ceremony of the pups's first shift."

"Ah yes, the woman with no skills." He smirks to himself, causing me to narrow my eyes at him.

"Is that how you speak to your future queen?" Adrenous interjects this time, seeming just as angry as me.

All five sets of eyes widen. Victors mouth was left agape. *Let's see you backtrack out of this one . . .*

✦○✦

CHAPTER THIRTY-THREE
A Memory

✦◻︎✦

ALIVIA

"My apologies Your Highness, I had no idea you have found your mate," Victor blurt out, his tone apologetic. The fear in his eyes is decipherable. My lips wanted to curl into a smirk but I hold it back. Who knew I'd have an Elder fearing for his life?

Adrenous once again crosses his arms over his chest, displeased and angry. "It's not me you should be apologising to."

Victor seems taken aback, his eyes snapping to mine. It's almost as if he's embarrassed to apologise to a woman. I bet he believes it to be beneath him, anger rising to the surface of my face at the thought. "My apologies my future queen."

"That's better." Adrenous approves.

"May I ask, when is her coronation? I believe my invitation must have gotten lost in the mail." His tone has once again become snarky, my dislike for him growing by the second.

How easy it was for him to go from being a frightened, little man to now being a snarky prick.

"It won't be for a while." I interject before Adrenous can respond, "There's lots to be discussed before it can be decided." I add, the words more meant for Adrenous than Victor. I'm not entirely sure if I'm ready yet but it's something me and Adrenous definitely need to talk about some time soon.

Besides, it's nothing to do with Victor.

Adrenous gives me a look but doesn't say anything, returning his attention to Victor, "Shall we get on with this meeting now, there's lots to be discussed."

Time flies by rather quickly during the meeting that is currently being carried out in a different room. It's still a big room considering it's only used for this exact purpose. We are all currently sat round a mahogany table which has been carved by the most skilled craftsmen and takes up the centre of the room.

Me and Adrenous sit at the head of the table while Victor sits at the opposite end. Sophia, the woman with red hair, and Carlos, the man with blonde hair and grey eyes are sat on the left side of the table. On the right side, Henry and Eliza, who I now know are siblings, are sat on the right side.

There's not been anything too interesting said during the meeting. They've mostly been talking about the people that are protesting about being kept in their homes and whether they should throw in more measures to keep the Vampires at bay.

You would think people would be more grateful for the measures going into keeping them safe. Instead, they are becoming part of the problem.

Victor leans back in his chair, a golden goblet filled with wine in his hand as he takes a sip. "We've ensured their safety as much as can be done. If they want to go against it further then that will be their own suicide. We won't take responsibility for that." He has a point.

"They are ignorant," Carlos added, his anger contorting his expression. "If it weren't for your people my King, we humans as a race would have all been slaughtered and extinct thousands of years ago. Just because we have kept the Vampires away from them doesn't mean they are no longer a threat. They should understand that we know better."

Ignorance is bliss. If it weren't for the fact my uncle was murdered by Vampires, I too would have been ignorant. It doesn't seem to exist to the eyes of others unless it has personally affected them. If they carry on like that, they may soon face the consequences.

"It seems the rogues are becoming much braver too, we were attacked on our way here." Adrenous informs, Victor and Carlos looking at him with shock.

A rogue attack must be rather rare then for it to incite that kind of shock from Victor and Carlos.

"They dared to attack the infamous Wolven king," Henry chuckled, him and his sister exchanging amused smiles. "I bet they soon realised that was a mistake."

"They did but it didn't stop them from attacking in the first place." Adrenous's words causes Henry's chuckle to cease. "I left one of the rogues barely alive with a threat for their leader."

"Do you think that will be enough?" Victor wonders before taking another sip from his goblet.

"There's no way to tell," Adrenous admits.

"Can't you just take out their leader rather than threaten him?" I blurt our before I can stop myself, "Surely then they'll have no one telling them to attack packed Wolvens."

If their leader was the one infiltrating these attacks then taking him out would stop the threat rather than waiting for it to become too big to handle. Wouldn't that be the obvious solution?

The Elders all look at me as if I've grown a second head, "What?" I snap, becoming slightly paranoid.

"That would be easy if anyone had ever laid eyes upon their leader." Sophia elaborates for me. *At least someone is being helpful.*

"How is that possible?" I said, my eyes narrowed in confusion. Surely someone must have seen his face. He's the rogue's leader for heavens sake.

Adrenous is the one to clarify this time. "Anyone who does see him never lived to tell."

"Oh . . ." I breathed out. That kind of makes sense then. I would hate to know what sort of man is capable of such. Anyone who can murder innocents with no justification is a man worthy of hell. Something I hope he gets a taste of one day.

The thought of murder makes me feel slightly sick, my stomach feeling upset which is rare for me. The need for some air becomes apparent. I have no wish to throw up and I'm sure everyone here will feel the same. "Adrenous, I'm not feeling to well, may I be excused?"

He furrows his brows with concern, "Do you want me to go with you?"

"No I'll be okay, I'll go find Rylan and Raven whilst you finish here." He nods his agreement and I give him a quick peck on the cheek. "It was nice meeting you all," I tell the Elders politely, standing to my feet.

"Likewise," Victor responds, though I can't help but hear a hint of displeasure in his voice. It's clear he doesn't like me at all, but I feel exactly the same way about him.

Exiting the room, I take in a few deep breaths as I walk down the hall. My unsettled stomach soon eases and I'm grateful I no longer feel the need to throw up.

I've never been here before so I use my wolfs sense of smell to sniff out Raven and Rylan. Picking up their scent, I find myself walking down the hall until I reach a wooden archway, finely crafted. Past the archway is a cozy looking lounge, a comfortable, 'U' shaped sofa is centred in the middle facing a beautiful fireplace where flames are already dancing, coaxing the room in light.

Raven and Rylan are seated comfortably on the sofa conversing about one thing or another until they spot me walking in.

"Did you get bored at the meeting?" Rylan smirks up at me.

I roll my eyes and shake my head, "No. I felt a little sick and needed to get out."

"So you came here to throw up on us instead." Rylan leans away from me, a look of fake horror plastered on his face.

"If I was going to throw up you would know it." I remark and walk towards them to sit down on the sofa, the soft cushioning really comfortable against my back as I lean against it. "What have you two been talking about?"

"Raven was going to tell me about her brother but I told her instead of telling me, she could show me," Rylan explained, looking at Raven with a sad smile. I assume the look he is giving her is because he's already seen what her brother has done.

I remember the first time he tried to do the same to me. When he tried to see my memories of my parents. I can't believe I forgot about that, maybe if he does that it will unlock so much more answers that I'm dying to know. Answers that not only I need but I'm sure Arif needs them too even if he doesn't know it.

"Rylan do you remember when you tried to find my memories of my parents?" He looks at me with curiosity, nodding his head, trying to figure out where I'm going with this, "If you do that, will I be able to see the memories for myself too?"

"Yeah it'll be like we're standing right there, only you can't touch or interact with anything." He explains. Understanding where I'm going with this, he asks, "You want to know what happened between your father and mother, don't you?"

I expelled the air I have been holding from my lungs, nodding my head. "I know it'll be painful to see but I'll regret it if I don't."

"You understand that you'll have to be compliant and not push me out like last time?" Rylan warns, his tone serious.

"I won't."

"Don't you want to tell Adrenous before you both do this?" Raven cautions, her eyes shifting between us. She believes I'm being too impulsive and should consult Adrenous first.

"It'll be okay," I assured. "When he leaves the meeting, just tell him what's we're doing and I'm sure he'll understand."

Raven isn't convinced but doesn't protest when Rylan instructs me. "Close your eyes and relax."

I do as he says, my eyes fluttering shut as I breath in and exhale to relieve any tension In my body. Rylan places his index and middle fingers against my temples, that familiar feeling of when he first did this to me appearing.

I do my best not to fight it, not wanting to push him out like I did last time. I need to know whatever I can find out about my parents.

If not for me then for Arif as well.

I feel a pulling sensation filter it's way through my mind, the feeling of Rylan's fingers no longer there. I furrow my brows in confusion.

Why did he let go? Did it not work?

I hesitantly open my eyes, the air catching in my lungs when I find myself in a dark, damp cell. The only source of light is from the moon beams shining through the cracks in the bricks. There is no toilet, just a bed that isn't currently being used. The iron bars appear to be locked as my eyes narrow on a very familiar Rune.

His black hair is neatly combed back, his pale white face causing my stomach to churn, seeing his lips set in a grin as he keeps guard of this cell. He doesn't notice me, evidence that this place is just in my head, some sort of illusion.

I turn my attention back towards the cell, a sense of relief washing over me when I see Rylan leaning against the right wall. He smiles sadly at me before looking away. I follow his train of sight, my eyes widening when I find a woman curled up in the corner, cradling a baby in her arms.

Is that . . . my mother?

✦◯✦

CHAPTER THIRTY-FOUR
Truth Be Told

✦ ☐ ✦

ALIVIA

"Mum?" I breathed out but she doesn't hear me, looking down at the baby in her arms with pain and sadness. The baby is obviously me.

My mother looks no older than twenty with dirty, blonde hair tied into a messy bun. Her eyes are a cobalt blue like mine, once filled with colour, they are now dull and pained. She wears a white, tattered dress, stained with dirt.

How could they put her through this? No one deserves to live like this. They've forced her to not only bear a child but to live in these horrible conditions. My heart breaks for her, tears forming in my eyes, wishing she could hear me, see me. This is more painful than I could have imagined.

My eyes drift to the baby that is making cute, little sounds. She was wrapped in a blanket which I recognise to be the one my aunt gave me. She has a patch of dark hair and is looking up at my mother with bright, cobalt eyes that reflect my mother's. I look back at the blanket wrapped around her little form, seeing the familiar embroidery that spells my name. I wonder if my mother made it for me. She rocks her baby gently, "I'm sorry I allowed this to happen." She sounds broken, a sob wracking her body as she struggles to breathe through the tears. *Please don't cry . . .*

Rylan doesn't say anything, knowing I need this time to concentrate on the memory. I walk towards her, kneeling down in front of her. I reached out my hand to touch her cheek but she doesn't feel it. "Don't be sorry." I cried. "Because of you, I had a normal life."

She continues to cry before we both flinched, the sound of someone pounding against the cage echoing around the cell. "Be quiet Asmara!" The Rune shouts, making me angry. My mother's name was Asmara? It's beautiful.

She looked up at him in anger, the baby starting to stir in her arms. "Go fuck yourself Tyke." Even though she's broken, a fire still burns within her. The Rune, I can name as Tyke, sneers In anger as she glares at him, the baby beginning to cry out as she quickly rocks her gently.

"As soon as that child no longer needs you, my master will no longer need you." Tyke beams with a nasty smile. "Then he will be able to punish you for that nasty, little mouth of yours."

I'm going to kill that bastard!

It's now that I realise Tyke is the same Rune I met when I almost ran away from Adrenous estate. He looks exactly the same with eyes that resemble black pits and black hair that makes his pale skin appear paler.

My mother doesn't respond but a tear trails down her cheek as she looks down at her baby, trying to calm her little cry.

I can't bear to see her in this condition, my whole life I've grown up to never know this woman. I grew up hating my real parents because I believed they abandoned me, my father is worthy of that hate whereas, this broken woman in front of me deserves so much that I can no longer offer.

If one day I have the misfortune to meet the people who did this to her, they'll be in a world of hurt. That much I can promise.

"Are you okay?" Ryan finally says as my gaze remains transfixed on my mother.

I can just about nod my head, my focus still on her. I want to study every detail of her beautiful face so I can remember it for the rest of my life.

Me and Rylan look back when we can hear footsteps approaching, our heads turning towards the cell door where Tyke is unlocking it for three men.

The first man causes my eyes to narrow, realising it's Tristan. He looks exactly the same, considering this must have been at least seventeen years ago.

However, that isn't why my eyes are narrowed on him. He's here, meaning he knew what they were doing to my mother and he did nothing to stop it. He told me his mother went through the same thing so how could he sit back and let it happen again? He told me to trust him, that he wanted to help me but that was all a lie. I'm so stupid!

Rylan catches on. "You know him."

"He was my friend, he's a half-Vampire." I whispered. "I'll explain later, just don't tell Adrenous," I pleaded.

"I'm not going to tell him anything, you are." Rylan's tone is completely serious.

I don't respond as we watch a second man walk in behind Tristan. He is quite tall but perhaps an inch or few shorter than Adrenous. He has beautiful, fair skin and bright, blue eyes that hold a sinister coldness to them. His facial structure is similar to Tristan's, framed with blonde hair that is in disarray, a black, steel crown centred atop his head. He can't be . . .

When my gaze drifts to the last man entering the cell, I almost stop breathing, my blood running cold. His hair is the same shade of brown as mine with pale, yellow eyes that match Arif's entirely. Even their facial structure is identical. I have no doubt that this was our father.

Anger bubbles as I wish he was really here so I could make him pay for everything he did to my mother and to Arif's.

My mother brought the baby closer to her chest as she glared at the men. "Get the fuck away from us!"

"I'm sorry Krellin, I thought she would have been tamed by now." Alijah apologises to the man with the crown atop his head, my blood running cold as my assumption is right. That man is the infamous Vampire king.

Krellin waves him off, a grin pulling at his lips. "They're more fun when they fight." Alijah and Krellin laugh together, though Tristan remains silent, catching Krellin's attention. "What's the matter boy, have you no sense of humour?"

"I'm sorry father, I didn't realise you made a joke," he remarked, my heart stopping at how he addresses Krellin.

Krellin is Tristan's father? What the actual fuck?

Urgh that's a hundred reasons in one not to trust him. He's a total traitor and this makes it ten times worse.

Krellin sneers at Tristan before turning his gaze back towards my mother and then towards the baby, his eyes narrowing in curiosity. "A tiny, little thing, isn't she?"

"Don't worry, she'll grow up to be big and strong like her father." Alijah beams as he walks towards my mother. She turns away from him, holding the baby even tighter to her chest as fear contorts her features. "Don't be difficult Asmara, give me my daughter."

My mother shakes her head vigorously, looking past Alijah towards Tristan, her eyes pleading as if she's asking him to help her. Why would she think he would help her? Tristan looks away, his eyes pained as my mother loses hope. "I won't let you hurt my baby." She snaps at Alijah.

"She's my baby, not yours," Alijah corrects as he continues his pursuit for the baby. "Give her to me or I promise you'll regret it." She looks down at her baby, her eyes filling with tears as she's given no choice but to hand her over. Alijah holds out his arms as my mother places the child into them, her body wracking as she sobs and looks away. She shouldn't blame herself. She did what she could.

Alijah rocked the baby in his arms, turning towards Krellin. "Meet your saviour." *I think not.*

Krellin looks down at the baby and nods his approval. "Indeed she will be. May I?" Krellin holds out his arms and Alijah hands the baby over. Krellin examines her with fascination as he coos darkly. "You'll bring the Wolvens to their knees, little one. You have no idea how important you are."

My hands turn to fists as his words. "I will never be your saviour!" I yelled, knowing he can't hear me. Rylan doesn't respond to my outburst but he does stand beside me. "I don't know how I'm suppose to accept that this was the reason I was born," I said, Rylan's eyes drifting to the side of my face as darkness makes its way through my mind, filling me with doubt. What if I am the reason the Wolvens could be slaughtered? How am I suppose to trust people?

"You don't have to accept it Alivia," Rylan tells me, his voice soft and low as we watch Krellin smirk down at the baby. "You're not supposed to accept it. Get angry, let everything out because I promise that this is not why you were born. Everyone is born for a reason but bringing Adrenous and the rest of us down isn't one of them, being mated to Adrenous proves that. You were born to complete him."

I suppose he's right. I offered him a thankful smile, not realising how good he was at giving advice.

We both pay attention on Krellin as he grimaces when the baby begins to wail and cry. "Give her back to her mother." He orders as he passes her back to Alijah. Alijah nods and takes the baby back to my mother who takes her eagerly, bringing her back to her chest.

"She's hungry. If you wish for her crying to stop you'll give me some privacy." My mother glares at them, her tone cold.

Krellin glares daggers at her, "Whatever." He turns on his heels and walks out of the cell along with Alijah. Tristan stands around a moment longer as he and my mother exchange a look before he's forced to follow Krellin and Alijah.

"We should go now." Rylan advices but I can't leave just yet.

"Can I just watch her for a little while longer?" I pleaded.

"Okay"—Rylan nods—"but just for a little while."

"Thank you."

I walk back towards her and watch as she feeds the baby, the cries now ceasing as the baby drinks from her breast that is covered with the baby blanket. How she has survived this long is beyond me. She is so strong and brave and I admire her for it. I wish she was still alive, to have the chance of a happy life.

My ears perk when the sound of Tristan's voice can be heard, "Let me in the cell and do nothing, don't even speak." Tristan's voice sounds persuasive. It appears Tyke followed his order, the sound of the cell door opening echoed as my mother looks towards the door with hope in her eyes.

Tristan walks inside, his movements urgent as he says, "Quick, get to your feet."

"What are we doing?" My mother did as he said, lifting herself up from the floor as she holds the baby close to her.

"We're not doing anything, you're getting out of here." Tristan corrects as they both exit the cell.

I'm about to follow them but an invincible wall stops me, the illusion beginning to fade. "No! I have to know what happens!" I shouted, but it does nothing. The barrier continued to prevent me from moving forward. *No!*

My eyes are forced to close as darkness ensued before I open them again, sitting back down in the lounge with Rylan's hands pulling away from my temples. "I'm sorry, that's all your subconscious remembers."

I look at him with wide eyes. "Tristan helped my mother escape, I have to tell Adrenous."

✦○✦

CHAPTER THIRTY-FIVE
Be Careful Who You Trust

✦◻✦

Alivia

"Alivia wait until he's out of the meeting." Rylan cautions, stopping me from leaving the lounge. "If the Elders hear you say that a Vampire set your mother free and you want to contact him, they'll believe that you're trying to side with them without listening to reason. Tell him when he's alone."

Are the Elders that narrow-minded they would really think that? Dumb question, judging from what I've seen from Victor so far, I suppose they are that narrow-minded.

"Okay." I sigh, the urgency to go to Adrenous dying down as I remain seated next to Rylan.

Raven looks at both of us, eager to know what's going on. "What did you see?" Her question is directed at me as her eyes lock onto my own when I turn my attention towards her.

"I saw my mother, my father and even Krellin." Her eyes widen as I pause before adding, "I also saw Tristan, someone who I once believed to be my best friend. I only recently found out that he is actually a half-Vampire and now I know he's Krellin's son too . . ."

Before I can add any more, Raven blurts out, "Wait, you're saying Krellin's own son befriended you?"

"Yes. He compelled me to believe we have been friends when in reality, I had only known him for a year." I pause a second time, making sure she understands this time. "The memory that me and Rylan saw showed Tristan setting my mother free. That means he can be trusted, he might be able to help us infiltrate Krellin."

Rylan gives me a look, telling me he doesn't believe this is a good idea. "Liv I know what we saw happen was promising but you didn't remember enough for us to be able to follow them. Let's not rush in without further evidence and trust him freely." Rylan warns me, his voice soft but serious. "In days like this, we have to be extra careful with who we trust."

I didn't think of that.

Raven butts in. "He has a point Alivia. He may have been on your mother's side but that doesn't necessarily mean he'll help us defeat his father."

"What do you suppose we do then?" I ask, looking between them.

Raven shakes her head, whereas Rylan takes a moment to think, his eyes narrowing. Soon a smirk pulls at his lips, an idea entering his mind as he suggests, "Tristan will want us to trust him, right?"

"Yes," I replied, wondering where he's going with this.

"Then if he is truly genuine, he won't have a problem with me picking apart his brain." Rylan smirks again, looking pretty impressed with himself as he leans back on the sofa.

"Good plan, however, how do you suppose we contact him?"

He tried to respond but came up blank, shutting his mouth as he tried to think again.

"Guys, you do realise you have a very powerful white Well on your side." Raven cuts into the silence, her brow arches as her eye shift between us, amused by the look on our faces.

"You can contact him?" I question her, hope that this plan could really work setting up a new spark of excitement.

"I have my ways"—she nodded—"but we'll have to consult Adrenous first."

"I can't see why I won't be able to sway him." I shruggeda, standing on my feet. "He should be out of his meeting soon. You guys get some sleep and I'll tell you what he says tomorrow."

Rylan yawns, nodding in agreement. "I don't know about you two but I definitely need it."

Raven chuckled. "I bet I'll be asleep before your head even touches the pillow."

"Good night you two." I rolled my eyes at them, slightly amused by their interaction before I head towards my own bedroom, my own eyes becoming heavy as I stood outside the bedroom door. I stepped into the beautifully decorated bedroom.

The walls are covered in tanned wallpaper, a pattern of golden flowers mixing with the tanned background nicely. The floor is made from a dark, oak wood with a tanned rug cantered at the foot of the bed. The bed is centred in the middle and is draped in gorgeous golden, silk sheets. The bed looks rather inviting, calling out to me.

I removed my dress and head towards the wardrobe, assuming my clothes have already been put away. I was right, seeing our clothes all hung up. Even the dresser is filled with our clothes. I quickly dress into a nighty and climb onto the bed, now waiting for Adrenous to return from his meeting.

I lean back against the headboard, an hour already passed as my eyes continue to grow heavy. I continue to evade sleep.

I've almost given up, my eyes closing before the sound of the door opening registered in my mind. Adrenous walked into the bedroom. He looks at me with an apologetic smile. "Sorry, I didn't mean to wake you."

I shake my head. "You didn't wake me." I lift myself up to lean against the headboard again. "I was waiting up for you. There's something I have to tell you."

I watch him as he quickly pulls his shirt from his body, his muscles now in view as I openly gawk at him. He catches me and chuckles in amusement. "What did you want to talk about?"

Oh right, the plan. He pulls down his breeches and climbs into the sheets beside me, patiently waiting for me to speak. I take a moment to recollect my thoughts before I clear my throat. "Do you remember my friend Tristan?"

His eyes noticeably darken but he doesn't say anything, nodding his head in response. I have to be very careful how I word this next part, needing him to stay level headed so he doesn't disregard the plan. I watch him cautiously, something he notices as I can see his guard coming up. "Promise me you'll remain calm when I tell you this."

"What's going on Ali?" His tone noticeably shifts, causing me to inwardly flinch. This is going to be a lot harder than I thought.

"I recently found out that Tristan is a half-Vampire," I mumbled slowly, my heart beginning to race as I fear his reaction to this news.

He remains silent, his silence more frightening than his words. I glimpsed the storm waging behind in his eyes as he looks down at me in disbelief. He stares directly at me, putting me further on edge as I grow anxious for a response. "Say something," I urged, my anxiety upsetting my stomach.

"He's been watching you for Krellin." He assumes, his eyes becoming hard. His tone had me flinching once again as I bit my lip. "When did you find this out?"

I have to be truthful, lying will only make me a hypocrite. "A week," I mumble, my eyes shifting to the sheets in front of me. "But there's more." I quickly add before he can get angry with me and lash out. I need him to hear the plan so he can understand what I'm trying to achieve for not just him but everyone.

Hopefully, this will be the start to stopping Krellin.

"Rylan showed me a memory of my parents and it revealed a lot that might help us to infiltrate Krellin and remove him as a threat." I breathed out slowly, taking my time to explain everything.

His brows furrow slightly, his eyes softening. "You saw your parents?"

I'm surprised he's more concerned with that rather than the idea that there is a way to take down Krellin. "Yes."

He nodded. "I knew you would want to know more about them than I could offer. Did you get all the answers you wanted?"

I smile softly at him. "Yes and more, like I said there is a way we can infiltrate Krellin but you have to trust me on this one."

His tone softens. "Of course I trust you. I just wish you told me about Tristan a little sooner. I won't let him near you ever again." He assures me.

If only he knew what I was about to say.

"About that, I saw my mother kept in a cell. She was in a bad condition, treated terribly by the scum who put her there." My tone shifts to anger. "My father, Krellin, and Tristan were also there."

The anger returns, contorting his features. "Go on."

I better say this now. "Tristan is Krellin's son."

"What?" He snapped, his eyes shifting as his beast steps forward. "That bastard had his own son watching you?"

"Calm down, please. Tristan is our way in, he set my mother free. Tristan is the reason I was kept safe."

His beast takes a step back at he narrows his eyes in confusion. "Krellin's own blood set your mother free?"

"Yes, and I believe we can trust him," I said before explaining mine, Rylan and Raven's plan. I made sure to explain every little detail of our way in to stop Krellin. When I was done, he remained silent for another few minutes. "Tristan's own mother was raped and treated like mine, I believe that's why he despises his father."

"Okay," he finally breathes out. "We'll leave tomorrow and have this plan set in place."

"Really?" I'm in disbelief, not expecting him to want to do this so soon.

"The sooner the better." He concludes. "Krellin's forces are continuing to grow stronger. If we do this now, we'll have a better chance at it working."

"That makes sense." I agree, climbing into his lap as I wrap my hands around his neck. "Thank you for trusting me."

"Always, little wolf." He presses a soft kiss against my lips, my tiredness soon forgotten as my body begins to ache for his touch. I kiss him back with more fever, drawing his lower lip into my mouth, sucking it gently.

I begin grinding my hips against him, feeling him harden beneath me as he groans at my action. He pulls away from the kiss, looking at me suspiciously. "Are you trying to tease me little wolf?"

I nod my head, a smirk pulling at my lips as my hands loosen from his neck, trailing down his body until I reach the hem of his underwear. I lightly tug at them, waiting for him to get the message. Understanding what I'm trying to do, he lifts slightly off the bed, allowing for me to glide his underwear all the way down his powerful legs.

My eyes instantly snap to his hard length, feeling his heated gaze watching me closely as I take his cock into my hand, running it up and his down his length ever so slowly. His eyes close of their own accord, a deep groan resounding from his throat as he relaxes beneath me, allowing for me to have full control.

I lean down, bringing my lips to the head as I kiss it gently, feeling it pulse against my hand. Adrenous's voice is dark as he warns, "Be careful, little wolf or I'll have you beneath me quicker than you can blink." I feel my underwear grow wetter at his words, that bundle between my legs pulsing uncontrollably.

I heed his warning, taking his cock into my mouth as I begin to bob my head up and down, sucking gently on his head every time I come back up. "Fuck." He groans, tangling his hand into my hair, forcing me to go slightly deeper. I feel his cock pulse every time I gag on his length, my chin touching down on his balls.

I take my free hand, using it to massage his balls softly, feeling them tighten in my hold. "Good girl, just like that."

I pull my mouth away when I can feel he's about to cum. He looks at me in frustration as I smirk down at him. I don't tell him what I'm doing, allowing him to see for himself when I begin to trail my own underwear down my legs, throwing them somewhere in the room.

I take his cock into my hand again, pumping it gently as I place both my thighs on either side of his, aligning his cock with my entrance before I ease my way down his length, feeling the head of his cock stretch out my opening, the sensation of fullness coming forward as the rest of his length follows.

I don't move yet, slowly pulling my dressing gown up and over my head, his hands instantly taking hold of my breast as they come into view. I moaned against his touch, slowly shifting my hips forward as I begin to ride him.

My moans become more frequent as he continues to massage my breast. My movements became quicker, his cock thrusting in and out of me as I move up and down. My clit grew more sensitive as it rubbed against the length of his cock.

"You such a good . . . little . . . wolf." He groaned in between thrusts, his cock growing harder as he moved his hands to my waist, gripping tightly so he can take control of my movement. He thrusts upwards, pounding into me harder as I cried out, my arousal reaching its peak. I shatter apart, continuing to ride him as my orgasm forces my walls to convulse around him. "Addy!" I screamed out.

He switched our positions, my back hitting the mattress as I gasped, my legs now supported by his shoulders as he thrusts harder into me.

I can feel my claws elongate, my wolf loving the domination as he looks down at me through his own wolf's eyes. I dug my claws into the skin of his back, a second orgasm beginning to build as I cried out again. His eyes lock with mine, his grunting beginning to increase as he's close to his own release. "Come with me, Ali."

His voice pushes me over the edge, my claws digging deeper into his back as I scream out his name. I can feel his cock expand within my convulsing walls before he spills himself inside me, grunting my name as he grips my body tighter, holding on for dear life.

We both lay there for a few moments, trying to catch our breath as he buries his head into the side of my neck, our bodies still connected. He pulls out of me once our racing heartbeats have slowed down, pulling my back into his chest as he wraps his arm around my abdomen. "I love you." He breathed into the side of my neck, kissing his mark gently.

"I love you too." I manage to say before sleep encases the both of us.

The next morning, me and Adrenous are seated in the meeting room with the Elders. However, this time we have Rylan and Raven joining us as they sit opposite each other at either side of the table.

Raven is the one talking at the moment, taking the time to warn the Elders about her brother. "He has no morale compass, if he sees you as an obstacle in his way, he won't hesitate to take you out."

Victor has his elbows propped on the table, his chin resting in his hands as he takes in everything Raven has said. "Does he have a weakness?"

Raven smirks at this. "Me." That is all she says, taking Victor off guard before he quickly composed himself.

"You?" Carlos remarks in disbelief.

Raven narrows her eyes on him, her hand beginning to glow as it turns into a fist, Carlos' airways now constricted as he struggles to breathe, clawing at his throat. Raven soon releases him, smiling proudly. "You were saying?"

Carlos coughs a few times, holding his throat as he broods in silence.

Victor seems amused by Raven's show of power, asking, "How do you suppose you'll take Draven out of the equation?" He inquires, seeming quite intrigued with Raven.

"That part doesn't matter, all that matters is when the opportunity arises, I will make sure he's no longer a problem." She states, her demeanour very confident.

Victor seems impressed. "Very well, I'll trust you know what you're doing." Victor inclines his head towards Adrenous, addressing him. "We did as you advised at yesterday's meeting. There are now free food banks set up and we have sent more Wolven soldiers to scout the perimeter more regularly."

"Good, it seems our presence is no longer needed." Adrenous exhales, satisfied that everything he came here for has been carried out successfully.

However, Victor seems confused. "You're leaving already, Your Highness?"

"Something came up back home but I'm certain everything here is now under control, am I right?" Adrenous arches a brow at Victor.

Victor nods. "Of course Your Highness. It's just I didn't think you would leave so soon. I figured you would want to visit the human villages to ensure everything is definitely running smoothly."

"I'll leave that to you," Adrenous states, Victor's eyes flashing with displeasure.

I rolled my eyes at him. How hard is it to check on the village that you're in charge of. He should look at it as a great responsibility rather than an inconvenience.

"I'm sure the villagers would love to see more of you," I comment slyly. Victor's eyes meet mine. Seeing his displeasure, I'm confident that I got under his skin, smiling as I held his gaze.

His tone is snarky as he nods his agreement. "I suppose you would know after living there for some time."

I can't help but take his response as an insult. Did he deem it a bad thing to have lived amongst the people? If anything, it should be considered a good thing having experience living in a human village. I know what the people want and expect. I understand their fears and wants, unlike this stuck up bastard.

Adrenous cuts in before I could respond. "We best be off, until the next meeting," Adrenous said. Everyone around the table stands on their feet, Adrenous and Victor shaking hands before the Elders each say their goodbyes, seeing us out.

The sooner we get back, the sooner we can get this plan of ours into action. Please let Tristan be trusted . . .

✦○✦

CHAPTER THIRTY-SIX
Friend Or Foe

✦▢✦

ALIVIA

It has been two days since we arrived back home, taking our time to explain to Hunter and Titan our plan regarding Tristan. After they were both on board with the plan, the rest of our time has been used to choose a place to conduct it. Raven has been warming up her powers, preparing herself for some sort of spell that will summon Tristan to us.

We decided to leave Arif out of this, considering the tension that remains between me and him is still fresh. I've already promised myself that once this is over, I'm going to sit him down whether he likes it or not and explain everything to him that Adrenous was unable to. Whether he continues to hate me after that, it will be up to him. At least I can leave him alone knowing I've done everything I could to fix the possible brother-sister relationship that could have existed between us if it weren't for our father. It's up to me to fix my father's mess and I will do so with determination.

I wrap my cloak around my body, a cold breeze sweeping its way through the forest, the leaves now red and orange with the approach of autumn. The five of us stand together, waiting for Rylan. He's due to arrive after he has ensured that Laurey and the baby are both safe.

It's so sweet and considerate of him to do so, my excitement growing for the happy couple. I can't wait to meet the newborn.

Adrenous pulls me into his chest, running his hand up and down my arms, helping me to keep warm. "Thank you." I smile up at him, leaning my head against his hard chest.

The wind is continuing to pick up, the evening sun begins to set in the distance, soon we will be welcomed with darkness. Adrenous turns me in his arms, pointing in the distance as Rylan's wolf comes into view, a bunch of clothes in his mouth as he pads behind a tree.

When he emerges, he is breathing heavily. "Sorry, I lost track of time. My pup kicked for the first time today, it was the most amazing thing I've ever felt."

"Look at you"—Raven smiles—"such a proud father already."

"Of course I'm proud, there's nothing my pup will ever do that would disappoint me." Rylan beams with happiness.

"How is Laurey doing?" I pry, wanting to know how the new mother to be is getting on.

"She's doing pretty well, just a little morning sickness that comes and goes." He shrugs. He turns in his spot, taking note of everyone here before asking, "When do we start?"

"Now," Raven announces, her hands emitting a bright glow as she begins to chant words in a foreign language that I don't understand.

Rylan takes a step back, looking at Raven sideways as he whispers to me and Adrenous, "How is this suppose to bring Tristan here exactly?"

I and Adrenous shrug our shoulders, just as lost as him. Whatever Raven's doing, I'm sure it will work. I have complete faith in her abilities, she's earned that much of me in the time I've come to know and care for her as a friend.

However, there's one question that I wish to ask her once this is over. I lean further into Adrenous, my anxiety surfacing as I try to clamp it back down, the thought that Tristan will take this as an act of aggression putting me on edge. The more time that has passed, Raven continuing her chant, I become more doubtful of our plan. I'm afraid Tristan will attack first, believing that he is being lead to the slaughter. If he were to act accordingly, I have no doubt that Adrenous and the others will take him out. However, a more worrying thought that surpasses everything else. What if Tristan can't be trusted? Where do we go from there?

Everyone moves into place, preparing ourselves for Tristan's arrival when Raven takes a pause from her chanting. "He's close, get ready." She reverts back to the foreign language, her palms growing brighter the closer Tristan is to our location.

I swallow the lump In my throat, using my wolf's sight to allow me to see at a greater distance, locking onto Tristan who appears from behind a few trees. His eyes are glassy, clearly in a daze, Raven having full control of his movement, forcing him to continue walking towards us.

I wonder if he is aware that he is being controlled. It's very unlikely, the more plausible being that he is in a dreamlike state, unable to distinguish between what is real and what is not.

Adrenous addresses Hunter and Titan. "You know what to do."

They both move towards Tristan as he stops his movement at the centre of the clearing, his eyes still glassy, not yet aware of those around him. They each stand on either side of him, gripping one of Tristan's forearms each, restricting him from running away when he is brought back from his trance.

I remain close to Adrenous, not ready to make a move yet, opting to wait until the trance is broken and his initial shock dyes down.

Raven becomes silent, the glow of her palms fading out until it's completely gone, everyone waiting in anticipation for

Tristan's trance to break. Tristan's eyes become clear, the sound of his heart racing loud in my ears as he takes in his surroundings. His fight or flight instincts take over as he tries to run, finding it impossible to do so with Hunter and Titan holding him back.

Fear becomes anger when he snaps. "What the fuck is this?" He bares his fangs at them, Titan forced to grip the back of Tristan's neck to stop him from biting them.

Tristan scanned his surroundings, his eyes locking with mine as they flashed with the hurt he must be feeling. He must be believing that I've betrayed him, that I've given him up to Adrenous. "You ratted me out," he said. I flinched, the tone of his voice causing my heart to lurch. "How could you after I helped you?"

His pain affected me more than I'd like to admit, still seeing him as the boy I once believed I had grown up with. *That boy isn't real, is he?*

I took a step forward but feel Adrenous's arm quickly snake around my waist. I turn to look at him, his eyes soft as he warned, "Be careful."

"He won't hurt me," I assured, feeling his arm release me.

Tristan reverts his attention from Titan and Hunter's hold on him, lifting his head to see me approaching him. "This isn't an execution . . ." I start, ensuring I have his fullest attention. "I know you're Krellin's son."

His eyes widen. "How did you f—"

I put my hand up. "It doesn't matter, I'm not mad at you for keeping it a secret. If you had told me earlier, I would have reacted much different than I have now." It's true, if I had known Tristan was Krellin's son without evidence that he could be trusted, I would have rejected him completely.

Tristan appears to be confused, not understanding how that fact alone hasn't earned him a death sentence.

"Tristan, I know what you did for my mother. I know that because of you I was taken away from Alijah and Krellin. You tried to save her, didn't you?" I finish, seeing his eyes flash with dark memories that he'd rather keep hidden, not understanding how I came to know such information.

I witness before me Tristan's barriers crumbling one by one, his eyes watering as his past is brought to the forefront of his mind. "I helped her escape, I fell in love with her and I couldn't stand to watch her being treated like that. My efforts weren't enough in the end, she died anyway."

I've never seen him so broken, pain settling at the centre of my chest as I fight back the urge to go to him.

As much as it pains me, we have to be sure we can trust him before we can progress forward. *Friend or foe . . . ?* That's what it comes down to.

"All that matters is you tried. That's all anyone can ever ask of us." I attempt to comfort him whilst maintaining a serious demeanour. We don't have a lot of time for me to waste just comforting him, this needs to be done quickly so that everything else can be set in motion depending on the outcome. *Can he truly be trusted? I hope so.*

"There's a reason why we brought you here Tristan." Tristan looks up at me, his eyes still glassy with unshed tears as he patiently waits for me to explain. "Rylan here"—I usher Rylan to stand beside me as Tristan glances at him warily—"has the power to see your past, your memories. With your permission, he will delve into yours, allowing for us to decide whether or not we can trust you."

"And if I say no?" I knew this question was coming. He's smart, already knowing that if we decide he is untrustworthy, we won't let him go. What he's really asking is, what are you going to do to me?

I release a heavy breathe, my eyes telling him all he needs to know before I say, "We'll assume you can't be trusted and I'm sure you can imagine what will occur after that's decided." *Don't let me down, Tristan. Just say yes.*

He's silent for a moment, weighing his options as his gaze shifts from person to person, lingering a little longer on Adrenous. The two exchanged looks of displeasure before he finally turns back towards me. I can see his resolve waver, admitting defeat before he's forced to answer, "Very well, do it."

I can almost feel the tension that's been weighing on my shoulders lift. I can't help the smile that graces my lips at his answer, watching as Rylan steps into my line of sight, making his way towards Tristan.

Tristan is still apprehensive, not a hundred percent sure what he's gotten himself into.

"This won't hurt," Rylan assures Tristan. Tristan is still unconvinced but he doesn't protest when Rylan places his fingers on either side of his temples.

Let this be a start . . . With luck, the end of Krellin's reign is coming.

✦✧○✦✧

CHAPTER THIRTY-SEVEN
Memories I'd Rather Keep Hidden

✦▫✦

TRISTAN

    I feel the grip on my upper arms disappear, my reality distorting as everything around me changes. Memories I'd rather keep hidden climbing their way up to the service of my mind, forming the illusion that I now see before me.
    The wolven, Rylan I believe his name was, stands beside me, having chosen this as the first of many bad memories to witness... The day Asmara was captured.
    "Why this one?" I questioned Rylan, keeping my sights set on the scene in front of me.
    It's only me and my father we see for the time being. "I want to see how you regarded Alivia's mother before you decided to set her free," comes Rylan's answer.
    I suppose that's fair but it doesn't remove the pain I know I'll feel from seeing her again. I wish I could take everything back, to not have to bear this pain but that is only selfish on my part. If I hadn't done what I did, Alivia would have been under my father's full control by now.
    I shift my gaze, zeroing in on my father. He's dressed in formal attire, his blonde hair combed back as his steel crown sits neatly on his head, his eyes hard as he regards me, the me that is seated beside him. They both sit in thrones, my father's much

bigger, which are placed atop a platform, steps leading down to open spaced flooring, chandeliers overhead.

"You really think the Wolven can be trusted, Father?" the me seated beside my father asks.

My father shrugs his shoulders. "He's power-hungry, people like that can never be trusted; however, a lot can be gained from them."

"If you say so," past me remarks.

Both their gazes are drawn to the double doors at the end of the room, the doors opening, two guards walking beside a man who strides with purpose, distinct, yellow eyes staring back at them.

"Alijah," I breathed, anger coursing through me at the sight of him.

Rylan gives me a sideways glance. "Not a fan, no?"

I shake my head, silently watching the exchange of false pleasantries.

Alijah stops a few feet away from the thrones, standing at the bottom of the stairs. "Your Highness." He bowed. "It is a great honour to finally meet you."

Cut the crap.

My father leans against his throne, his arm resting on the arm rest as he leans his cheek against his palm, eyeing Alijah with intrigue. "I have to say, your proposition was quite intriguing but the thing I'd like to know, what do you have to gain by helping me take down your fellow species?"

Alijah exceeds confidence, already knowing the answer to the question. "Control. In exchange for bringing down Wyatt Claxton, I ask for power over the remaining few. I'll ensure they obey you as their king of course, but I want to be the one who controls them."

My father smiles brilliantly at Alijah, enjoying how the conversation is going however, there's one last concern, "What can you possibly offer that will send the Wolvens to their deaths?"

Alijah turns in his spot, facing the doors in which he entered. "Bring her in."

One of my father's guards walks through, pulling on a pair of chains connected to a pair of cuffs that are locked around a young girls wrists. My heart plummets all over again, my temper flaring as I go to step forward only to be stopped by Rylan. "Remember, this is only a memory."

I take in a soothing breathe, remaining still as I watch with great sadness Asmara being dragged to her fate. Her cheeks are stained with tears, her eyes still puffy from crying as the guard drags her to the centre. She wore a plain beige dress, now filthy and tattered from the struggle. Her skin is bruised and bloodied, possibly being punished for disobedience.

Considering she's in a nasty state, she's just as beautiful as I remember. Old scars surfaced as I forced myself to watch the guard bring her to her knees.

"What is this?" my father questions Alijah as the other Tristan's gaze locks with Asmara's. I remembered how disgusted I felt seeing a girl in such condition, the sight bringing back memories of my mother. My mother was often punished by my father for being rebellious. After my father was done with her, he killed her.

I was always scared of my father. I'm a coward when it comes to him.

Alijah stands before Asmara, she quickly casts her gaze to the ground, her heart racing for everyone to hear. Alijah grabs her hair, forcing her gaze back up, earning him a nasty glare from her. Alijah smirks down at her. "This is a human girl I took from one of the local villages . . ." The girl tried to pull away from his hold, only for him to grip her hair harder, a scream tearing from her lips.

Pain and anger I had tampered down begin to unravel like a vortex, consuming my mind. I could feel my hands ball into fists. I regret not doing anything, the other Tristan remaining seated, displeasure was written on his face but he does nothing to help her.

My father doesn't see how this girl will help him, his tone bored when he asks, "How exactly is a human girl going to help?"

"Wolvens can't be compelled but humans can." Alijah begins, his sights set on Asmara as if she is the key to his answers. "A half Wolven, half human can be compelled, used to infiltrate the others. My gift to you will be the first half breed Wolven, sired by me."

My father leans forward in his throne, completely blown away by the idea of having his own Wolven that he can control. As much as Alijah is already fitted for the job, he can't be fully trusted. A half Wolven will be one hundred percent loyal to him.

"You have yourself a deal." My father claps his hands together, rather pleased with the conclusion of tonight's meeting.

The room shifts, a soft glow illuminating as everything begins to disappear. "What's happening?" I begin to panic, not sure what's going on.

Rylan is completely calm. "I'm picking out a different memory, hold on tight." He winks at me, the glow getting brighter until I'm forced to clamp my eyes shut. My stomach flips when the ground beneath my feet disappears, the feeling of floating apparent until the light fades, my feet touching solid once again.

My eyes snap open, the urge to vomit very much present until my eyes narrow in on me, walking down a dimly lit corridor, his movements silent.

I remember this. The day I realised I was falling for Asmara five months after the day she was captured.

Me and Rylan follow him, sadness and pain constricting my chest, asking, "Why this memory?"

Rylan gives me a sideways glance. "This was an emotionally intimate moment between you and Alivia's mother, not only will it help me decide on whether you're trustworthy but it will help me understand why you chose to help her."

"That should be obvious by now." My tone is clipped, taking my anger out on Rylan when in reality, I'm angry that I have to relive the pain all over again. My biggest regret, heartbreak, and failure. I should have done more for her. It's my fault she was killed. I'll never forgive myself.

"Not everything is as obvious as you might think," Rylan remarks with a smirk, provoking a glare from me.

We wait whilst the past me knocks on the door, three soft knocks followed by two hard knocks, a coded rhythm so that she knows it's him knocking.

There were no guards by the door. Asmara was already compelled not to physically leave the room. This was before she was sent to live in the cells after the stunt she will eventually pull. I'm already cringing at the memory.

The past Tristan opens the door, me and Rylan walking in after him, coming to stand at the edge of the room. Rylan's eyes narrow on Asmara's swollen belly, now five months pregnant.

She's seated on the bed, knitting a soft blanket, gorgeous embroidered lettering running down it spelling "Alivia."

I watch my past self sit beside her on the bed, his fingers gliding on the gorgeous lettering. "I didn't realise how talented you are."

She gives him that heartwarming, beautiful smile of hers, telling him, "My mother taught me, she's a seamstress." She pauses from her knitting, holding the blanket up. "I thought the baby could have this to keep warm."

"It's beautiful," he said, admiring the colours before tracing his fingers along the lettering. "What's with the name?"

"Well, don't judge me"—she smiles, embarrassed—"but every firstborn in my family has always been a girl and I don't think this little one will be any different." She places the blanket back onto her lap, adding the finishing touches. "Alivia was my younger sister's name, she died from a fever when she was five." Her gaze turns distant, her eyes watering, a tear sliding down her face before landing on the blanket.

I feel my heart clench all over again, remembering how often she would talk about her sister.

He wraps his arm around her, and she does the same as she buries her head in his chest, sobbing. "I—I can't d—do this, Tristan . . . I w—want to go back h—home."

His arms tighten around her, his eyes closing as he tries to soothe her with the embrace. "I'm so sorry."

Rylan clears his throat, capturing my attention. "Why didn't you help her escape now, why wait?"

"I was scared." I said, turning to look at him. "I was afraid for myself, of what my father would do to me if he found out. A coward being the correct term for it." My cowardice killed her.

Past me closes his eyes, moving up on the bed, bringing Asmara with him as he continues to comfort her, his eyes closing.

This is when I began to realise how much I truly cared for her, I didn't want her to come to the same fate as my mother. My worse fear came true.

Rylan brings me from my internal torment. "Come on, time for the next memory." He smiles softly, beginning to understand how painful these memories are for me.

"Okay."

I have time to prepare myself for the change of scenery, the flip in my stomach not as effective as the last, expecting it this time. I wait for the air beneath my feet to solidify, my eyes closed softly until I hear a load of commotion, the ground returning to normal.

Me and Rylan found ourselves in a crowd of Vampires surrounding a room, all of them gossiping amongst themselves, wondering what's happened.

No . . .

I slowly walk to the room with Rylan on tow, his confusion evident. I halt at the edge of the doorway, my eyes zeroing in on the dead Vampire on the floor. The floor was soaked with blood as the life within his eyes is diminished. His body is slowly decomposing along with his head which is on the other side of the room, having been decapitated from his body.

Asmara is curled up at the edge of the bed, frantically sobbing. Her dress and hands were soaked in blood as the knife she had used is laid beside her on the bed.

"Move! Now!" I cringed at the sound of Alijah screaming at the crowd of Vampires, the past me following him closely behind. I see both their eyes widening at the horrific sight before them, Alijah snapping his gaze from the dead Vampire to Asmara, his body trembling with fury. "What the fuck did you do?"

She moves back against the bed, trying to get away from Alijah as he stalks towards her. "P—p—please, he tr—tried to h—hurt me."

"And that gives you the right to kill him?" Alijah snapped back, grabbing her upper arm painfully as she cried out. He attempted to pull her off the bed but she grabs the bed post.

"I was just protecting myself!" She held onto the post for dear life.

I looked away, the past me doing the same. I can remember how painful this next part will be to watch.

Alijah grips the back of her head, pulling on her hair. Her screams filled the room after he backhands her across the face. "Stop fucking screaming!"

Past me sniffs the air along with Alijah. Asmara's screaming was now aimed at the pains that come with labour. The bed was now soaked after her water had just broken.

"Fuck!" Alijah snaps, picking her up and placing her back on the bed. "The baby's coming, get the midwife," he ordered to the past me.

Me and Rylan are forced to follow past Tristan out the room, watching as he rushes to the infirmary, grabbing the midwife and then escorting her to Asmara's bedroom. She visibly pauses, screaming at the sight of the dead Vampire before Alijah snaps her out of it. "Hurry up and do your fucking job or it'll be you dead on the floor."

She trembles at Alijah's warning, rushing towards the bed as she sets up her equipment with trembling fingers. Asmara is still screaming, her hair matted to her face as she fists both sides of the mattress. Her chest heaved up and down, unable to control her breathing.

"Should I call my father?" past me asked Alijah, visibly frantic as he hadn't expected the baby to arrive this soon.

Alijah shakes his head. "No, he can wait. There are too many people in the room, you should go."

"But-"

"Get the fuck out!" He snaps, glaring at past me, my anger apparent.

Rylan turns back towards me, the space shifting before the floor once again becomes air. My eyes snapped shut, waiting for the next memory to unfold, hoping this is the last one.

This time we're in my bedroom, past me sitting on the bed with his head in his hands. This is after we were forced to visit Asmara in her cell. My father met the baby there for the first time, showing his approval before we left.

He pulls his head out of his hands, his eyes filled with determination. This is the moment I decided I didn't give a fuck what happened to me, I was going to save her. If only I knew . . .

He rushed out of the room. Me and Rylan are forced to match. We arrive at Asmara's cell, listening to past me compelling Tyke. "Let me in and do nothing, don't even speak." Tyke is forced to comply, opening the cell before Tristan rushed inside.

His movements are swift. "Quick, get to your feet," past me said.

Asmara stands up, the baby held close to her chest. "What are we doing?"

"We're not doing anything, you're getting out of here."

She looks up at him in shock, hope shining through as she follows him out of the cell, the baby now asleep in her arms.

We don't stop walking until one of my father's guards stops them, Past me grinding his teeth in frustration whilst Asmara looks between them with wide eyes, scared that she's going to be punished again.

"What's your business with the breeder?" The guard questions, glancing at Asmara, her head bending down as she casts her gaze to the floor in fear.

Even in my own home, I was never considered a prince, being half-human and all.

"With all due respect, you were never a good guard." The guard looks at past Tristan with confused eyes before I watch myself tear the head from the guard's body, using nothing but mere strength.

Asmara is close to screaming before he forces her along, me and Rylan following them until we're are outside.

"You really wanted to save her." Rylan comments, referring to me killing the guard.

"I loved her," I state, Rylan showing that he understands.

"You're free Asmara, there's a human town not too far from here, you can make it." I watch past me tell her, placing urgency into his tone so she'll get the message and hurry up.

She looks at the forest before turning back to him. "T—thank you." She places a gentle kiss against his lips. "I'll miss you, Tristan."

He doesn't respond to that, the emotions too painful to think about. "You have to go, stay safe."

She nods, smiling softly before turning on her heels and rushing into the forest until she's out of sight.

"No." I scream, catching Rylan off guard. "Follow her you, idiot." He doesn't though, turning to go back inside.

"No . . . no . . ." I crumble to my knees, the pain too much. "I—I should h—have f—followed her." I let the tears fall, my body wracking as I'm wrapped like a cocoon in the pain that continues to torture me.

I barely notice when the air around me and Rylan shifts once again, finding myself still on my knees, only this time Titan and Hunter's hold on my forearms is there again, Rylan stepping away from me, his fingers no longer held against my temples.

"What's the verdict?" Adrenous's voice rings out through the clearing, asking Rylan who is looking down at me with sadness, understanding my pain.

Alivia is on the edge, holding onto Adrenous as she waits for Rylan's response. Rylan shifts his gaze to them. "He can be trusted."

Alivia let out a sigh of relief, pulling away from Adrenous to walk towards me. "Will you help us take down your father, Tristan?"

I turned away from her. I failed my mother. I failed Asmara. I can't fail her daughter as well. I'm a failure. I'll just get them killed.

"I'm sorry, I can't help you."

✦○✦

CHAPTER THIRTY-EIGHT
Challenged

✦☐✦

ALIVIA

My heart breaks, being forced to watch Hunter and Titan force Tristan into a cell. I don't understand why he doesn't want to help. He has to know he's the only person who knows what's going on behind his father's walls, he could have been a great ally.

He's lucky he's only being locked up, Adrenous had ordered Hunter and Titan to go ahead with what was planned in the event Tristan couldn't be trusted but I had persuaded Adrenous and the others that Tristan is better of alive than dead.

If he can't help us then he can at least be used for leverage in the event his father attacks or worse.

Once Tristan is out of my sights, I turn in the direction of the estate, Raven beside me. She had placed a small cloaking spell around Tristan so he couldn't be tracked by Vampires, Runes, or even her brother.

It won't be long until Krellin realises his son is missing. The consequences of taking Tristan as a prisoner rather than killing him will soon come to light when Krellin takes action.

We'll see how much he truly cares for his son.

The night is long, having tossed and turned all night thinking about Tristan, my mother, and everything else I've had to deal with as of late.

I yank the sheets from my body, running to the bathing room before throwing up the contents of my stomach, my hair matted to my face.

The stress of everything is beginning to cause physical effects on my body, no longer feeling my best. I wash the remaining sick from my mouth before splashing my face with water, needing some air.

I head back into the bedroom, Adrenous sound asleep as I get dressed and wrap myself in a cloak before heading outside. Breaching the exit, I look up to the sun slowly rising, the moon and stars still visible as I marvel at the gorgeous view, my mind now clear as I take in the breath of fresh air.

Now would be a good time to shift but my wolf is hesitant, residing at the back of my mind. I frowned. She's usually happy to shift for me but now she seems off. I can sense a hint of excitement from her, hiding something from me that I'm not able to access with my mind, her presence blocking me from knowing.

I saw many people exiting certain points of the estate, some preparing to train while others take off, shifting towards the surrounding forest in order to patrol the perimeter, allowing the night shift to take a break.

I catch the attention of Rita. She's standing with a few others who are sparring. I can see her eyes visibly narrowing on me before smirking at the sight of me alone before she saunters towards me. I groan in displeasure, not in the mood for her. I've managed to avoid her this long, what could she possibly want now?

She stops a few feet away, her hand on her hip as she regards me distastefully. "The-queen-to-be all by herself," she comments, igniting a fire within me. "I wonder why that is."

I huff in response, appearing unfazed. "It's nothing to do with you."

A spark of triumph flashes across her brown eyes. "Is life with the king not as easy as you thought it would be, a half Wolven like you," she looks me up and down before smirking. "I'm not surprised you can't hack it properly."

I grind my teeth, my temper flaring. "And yet, I managed to knock you on your arse."

I can see the shift in her demeanour. Knowing I've struck a nerve, I move past her only to be shoved from behind, almost falling forward before I'm able to catch myself. I spin on my heels, turning to glare at her. "What the fuck is your problem?"

She takes a step forward, her eyes flashing with hatred before she snaps. "You stole my place, I should have been queen!" People turn our way, the attention of everyone around me is more unsettling then the girl who is screaming at me.

Her wolf comes forward, seeing her eyes darken. "Let our wolves settle this."

"Excuse me?" I blurt out, my gaze shifting from the people watching to her dark and angry gaze.

She doesn't give me a chance to respond, her clothes ripping as the sound of her bones snapping rings in my ears. I now face a golden wolf. She's leaning back on her legs as she snarls at me, her fangs on full display. I take a step back, the action making her angrier as she pounces forward. I barely manage to dodge her strike, pushing myself to move at the last possible second, seeing her land in the place I once occupied.

I stumble back, my arse painfully landing on the ground. I call for my wolf to surface, an urgency building when Rita's wolf sets her sights on me again. A growl resounded from her chest. Meanwhile, my wolf growls at me, refusing to shift at my command. After fighting with her and coming up empty-handed, I focus back on Rita just as she strikes again.

Quickly rolling to the side, I stand on my feet. "Stop, this isn't how you get what you want!"

Rita's wolf shifts her stance, continuously growling as a connection forms between us when she mind links with mine.

"*Honey, you know nothing about wolves. I've challenged you for your position. If I win this fight, I become the alpha female in the eyes of those around you. You will lose all respect and loyalty. Adrenous will have no choice but to label you a rogue.*"

My heart skips at her words, panic seeping in. I struggle to breath, my gaze shifting between her and the crowd surrounding us, realising there's no way out of this. This is the moment my wolf chooses to abandon me? Doesn't she realise we could lose Adrenous?

I'm forced to move into a protective stance, forced to take her on in my most vulnerable form. The odds are against me but I'm not going to give up everything I've built just for it to crumble before me.

I can sense Rita's amusement, her sly remark resounding through my mind as I attempt to stare her down.

"*Is your wolf too frightened to face me herself, too scared of the humiliation that will come with her loss?*"

"*Go fuck yourself.*"

Her wolf doesn't take too kindly to that. She runs at me, full speed, before jumping up, her jaw almost snapping shut on my arm and almost knocking me to the ground before I'm able to move out of the danger zone. I tap into my wolf's strength, punching her full force in the muzzle. She whimpers, momentarily in shock, allowing me to move further away from her.

I might not be able to shift but I'm not entirely useless.

"What's all this commotion?"

I was taken off guard, hearing Arif's forceful voice as he appears from the woods, glaring at the crowd of people.

"The future queen has been challenged, General." A man from the crowd explains.

"What?" His anger comes forward, the man flinching away from him. His gaze shifts to me. Our eyes locked for a second before I felt a sharp pain in my side. Rita's wolf knocked me to the ground. I instinctively put my arms up, keeping her jaw from snapping at my face and neck. I continue to channel my wolf's strength, just about keeping her from biting me long enough for me to bring my legs up, kicking her in the stomach.

I roll out from under her, hearing her stumbling back before a darker, angrier growl erupts from her chest.

She runs and jumps at me again but this time I'm able to duck, her momentum carrying her all the way forward until she's all the way behind me, giving me time to turn around, seeing her crash into a nearby tree.

"Give up yet?" I can't help but taunt her, a smirk curling its way onto my lips.

She growls again, leaning back onto her hind legs. I appear unfazed, driving her even angrier. I'm about to avoid her strike when I'm overcome with nausea, my body becoming unbalanced as my stomach cramps up. I'm knocked to the ground, screaming after Rita's wolf locks her jaw at the top of my shoulder.

I grip hold of the fur on her chest, trying to push her away as the pain burns its way through my body. More pain erupted from where her fangs are buried into my flesh, tearing as she shakes her head aggressively at the same time. My clothes are now stained with my blood. The sight would have made me feel sick if I weren't so distracted by the pain.

"Your Highness." I hear the crowd erupt with shocked gasps, knowing Adrenous must now be present. He must have ran towards me because I can hear Arif stopping him.

"She's been challenged, you can't interfere," Arif said.

I can hear a growl emitting from Adrenous's chest. "Fuck!"

I need to do this for him . . . For us.

I allow adrenaline to course through me, numbing some of the pain. It gives me time to focus, curling my hands into fists as my claws elongate. I throw a punch at the side of her face, hitting her in the sensitive area of her ear. I feel her fangs lodge themselves from my flesh, a groan escaping my lips as she whimpers.

I'm not done, taking my claws and burying them deep within her chest, blood staining her golden fur along with my hand. She pulls away from me, clumsily running backwards until she's no longer standing over my body.

"Why aren't you shifting Alivia?" Adrenous's mind links me, his voice feeling my pain through our connection.

I tried to catch my breath as I struggle to my feet. Rita's wolf still hasn't given up, getting ready to strike at me again. I'm not sure how much longer I'm going to be able to hold out. The exhaustion was already taking its toll on my muscles. It doesn't help that pain is continuing to radiate from shoulder, the adrenaline gone as the pain becomes more intense.

I use the small amount of time between now and Rita's next strike, replying to Adrenous. *"My wolf won't let me, something's wrong."*

I catch his eyebrows furrowing, horror and confusion contorting his features as he tries to grasp what I've said.

I take a few steps back, trying to ignore the pain when I see Rita make a small step forward, sensing my weakened state. She runs at me, full speed, my movements delayed as I move to the side, dodging her body but her leg knocks me to the ground. I scream when my shoulder hits the ground, not having the strength to climb back to my feet. The pain has won, despair overwhelming me.

This is it . . . I'm going to lose everything. Adrenous. Arif. My place here. I'll be forced to become a rogue.

Rita sets her sights on me again, baring her fangs, her muzzle stained with my blood. *"Show me your submission and accept your fate now."*

I lift my head, glaring at her. "You'll never have my submission."

Her head tilts to the side, mocking me before she makes her next strike. Through unbearable pain, I lift my arms, her fangs just a few centimetres away from my neck. I groan and scream, the pain winning. It made me too weak to keep her at bay. I'm about to slump my arms down when Arif's voice climbs its way into my head.

"Don't let her win Alivia, you're so much stronger than she is. Believe me, I've seen it."

His words took me off guard, filling me with strength that I didn't realise I needed until now. I gripped Rita's fur, screaming as I push her away, my body becoming consumed by a wave of power I've only ever felt twice.

A blue glow surrounds me I watched as Rita's fur becomes flesh, fangs and claws residing until I'm looking at a nude and very frightened Rita. I heard gasps coming from those around me, Arif and Adrenous completely shocked. The blue aura that surrounds me hasn't faded yet. My power had not only affected Rita but other shifted wolves around me. Naked men and women who were forced to shift as well were looking at me in awe.

"Ali." Adrenous draws my attention. "Your eyes . . . they're glowing."

I can't see for myself but I'll take his word for it. Rita covers her crying self, completely humiliated. "You're a fucking monster!"

"No," I remarked, slowly standing on my feet "I'm the future queen and luna of this pack."

She looks up at me horrified, my gaze shifting from her to see everyone else on their knees, their heads bowed, showing me their utter respect and submission. My wolf doesn't take the credit for this one, my own wolf bowing to me, praising me.

The blue aura fades, exhaustion now consuming me, collapsing to my knees. Adrenous grabs me just before I hit the ground, bringing me to his chest.

I can hear Rita frantically sobbing, now realising the consequences of her actions. "Please Adrenous! I—I can't be a—a . . ." Her cries take over and for once I feel sorry for her but this is her doing, she chose this.

Adrenous doesn't look at her, addressing Arif. "Lock her up, she'll be cast out tomorrow night."

Arif takes his cloak and wraps it around Rita's naked body before pulling her up. "P—please don't do this! Adrenous, please! After everything, I gave up so much for you . . . my mate . . . my home . . ."

"I never asked you to." Adrenous glares at her. Her eyes widen in shock, her heart visibly breaking as tears continue to fall down her cheeks. She slumps in Arif's arms, no longer fighting her fate as she disappears out of sight.

Adrenous's gaze softens, looking back at me. "I'll call Laurey to check on you, there must be a reason why you couldn't shift."

I nod my head but my thoughts are elsewhere. I thought I would be happy to beat Rita but I can't help but feel guilty. It's funny though, if the shoe was on the other foot, she would have no problem watching me be cast out.

I have to remember . . . This was her doing, not mine.

✦✧○✦✧

CHAPTER THIRTY-NINE
Congratulations

✦◻✦

ALIVIA

    I've been resigned to bed rest while I wait for Laurey to come and check on me. I feel guilty pulling her all the way over here considering her condition but she was the only one Adrenous trusted due to her medical background.
    My shoulder is slowly healing and has already been bandaged by one of the servants but of course, that isn't my or Adrenous's biggest concern right now.
    I'm praying my wolf will be fine but even so, I don't sense any pain coming from her. All I can feel is her excitement and some irritability but I don't understand why that is. Perhaps, she wanted me to fight on my own so I can trust in myself on the occasion that I might not be able to shift.
    Something tells me I'm wrong.
    I rest my head back on Adrenous's chest, listening to the rhythmic beat of his heart as we wait for Laurey's arrival. He dips his head down, placing light, hot kisses on both my cheeks, bringing a smile to my lips. However, I can't help but wonder. "What's going to happen to Rita tomorrow?"
    His lips pull into a tight line, his gaze becoming distant when he responds with, "She'll be stripped of her connection amongst the pack and banished from ever returning here."

I can't help but think their ways are harsh when it comes to their own pack members. I remember how distraught and scared she was when she tried to beg Adrenous to stay, the things she said made my own heart ache. "Did Rita really give up her mate for you?"

"What she said is true." He doesn't elaborate further. The sound of someone knocking on the door drew both our attention away from the subject. Adrenous moves me to the side and openings the door for Laurey. "Sorry, I wouldn't have called you if I didn't think it was urgent," Adrenous said.

Laurey's stomach has grown twice its normal size, the mother to be glowing as she walks past Adrenous. She has a wide smile on her face as she waves him away. "It's no problem. I needed to get out of the house. Rylan has been driving me crazy."

"Has he been a little overbearing?" I guess he has, assuming Rylan's been holding onto Laurey's every need and whim. I know how he can be a little too much sometimes. Seeing how excited he is to meet his pup, I can only imagine that's increased tenfold.

Laurey shrugs and chuckles. "Men, what can you do?"

I can't help but laugh and agree. Seeing Adrenous shot me a look, I quickly cover up my laugh with a cough. "When is the little one due?"

"Only another month or so. Wolven pregnancies aren't very long," she said, my eyes widening. She can't help but giggle at my reaction before she eyed my bandaged shoulder. "How's the wound?"

"It's okay, slowly healing."

After setting up her equipment, she asks, "Adrenous explained that you couldn't shift?" I nod my head, confirming what he told her. "Has this ever happened to you before?"

"Not that I can recall but to be honest, I've not tried to shift since the run after my acceptance into the pack so I can't be sure how long she's been like it." Even so, I believe it is only recently that my wolf has changed her attitude, becoming much more irritated. It could be because of the stress I've been under, stress can have a surprising effect on one's body.

Adrenous takes a seat at the other side of my bed, silently watching as Laurey asks me all sorts of questions, taking notes as she goes along. "When was your last heat?"

The question took me off guard. What could my heat have to do with my wolf? It takes me a moment to calculate, remembering the night me and Adrenous had that massive argument. "Just over a week ago."

Her next questions had my cheeks burning red. "Were you active during that time?"

Adrenous can't help but smirk, finding my embarrassment amusing as I struggled to respond, biting my lip. "Er, y—yes." I shoot Adrenous a glare when I see his chest rumble with silent laughter before turning back to Laurey. "Why do you ask?"

Laurey glances up from her notes. "I believe I may have the cause narrowed down, there's just one more thing I need to check." I watch as she stands up. "May I?" I'm not sure what she's going to do but I nod and watch as she presses her ear to my stomach, my eyes narrowing in confusion.

I shoot Adrenous a look, silently questioning him. He shakes his head, just as confused as me until we hear a soft giggle pass from Laurey's lips, her eyes flashing with excitement. "Congratulations, it looks like I'm not the only one who's pregnant."

Adrenous is beyond shocked, his gaze shifting to my stomach and then to me when I burst out laughing. "You're messing with me, right?"

"I never joke when it comes to my job," Laurey assures me, my amused smile dropping when I realise she's being completely serious. "When a Wolven is pregnant, shifting can be dangerous for the unborn pup which explains why your wolf refused to do so."

I can't be pregnant now. How can I bring a child into this world when I'm in the middle of helping Adrenous stop Krellin? It's a dangerous time and now I fear Adrenous will treat me like a delicate flower when now more than ever, I have to be on the frontline.

I jumped when Adrenous growled, his expression furious but distant when he snaps. "Rita challenged you when you were pregnant!"

I can't help but defend her, she's already being exiled. "She didn't know Adrenous. Gods, even I didn't know."

Adrenous shakes his head, laying his head against my abdomen, I assume to listen to the heartbeat. "If you didn't win, she would have forced me to exile you as well as our pup. When she realised you couldn't shift, she should have concluded you might be pregnant. It's against our laws to challenge a pregnant wolf." Even though he's angry, he smiles when he hears the rhythmic beat of our unborn pup.

"You have no idea how long I've waited for this moment." He chuckles, reluctant to pull away from my stomach. "I'm sorry I couldn't do anything earlier, challenging someone for their position is an old rule that still holds value."

"It's okay, I'm fine," I assured, cupping his cheek so he can see that I am perfectly fine. "I don't blame you."

He nods and rises from his chair, my heart racing when he heads for the door. "Where are you going?"

He turns to face me, his expression softening. He quickly approaches the bed and kneels down towards me, his hand on my abdomen. "I'm going to prepare Rita's exile for tomorrow night. I'll make sure she pays for this." He places his forehead against mine, looking into my eyes for a second before placing a kiss on my forehead. "I love you so much."

"I love you too." I stared after him when he leaves the room, my thoughts muddled as I start to reel over what could have happened if I had lost the fight.

Adrenous is right. If she had won, it wouldn't just be me left without a pack and a home but also a pup without a father and a home. I know she didn't know I was pregnant but when she realised I couldn't shift, she should have considered me being pregnant as a possibility.

Laurey sat awkwardly and I feel obligated to apologise. "I'm sorry, you shouldn't have to listen to our problems."

"It's okay, I heard what happened. Everyone has been talking about your gifts. Did your eyes really glow?" She seems rather intrigued, wanting confirmation for the gossip which I'm sure has already travelled to everyone in the pack.

"It's true," I confirm.

She looks like she's bursting to ask another question only to be cut off when someone racks their knuckles on the door. I turn my head to find Arif standing in the doorway, his gaze shifting between Laurey and me. "I'm sorry, is this a bad time?"

The tension between us is still present and it's clear that Laurey can sense it. She stands on her feet. "No, I was just leaving." Arif gives her a thankful look before stepping to the side, allowing her room to leave. "I'll see you later Alivia."

I'm not thrilled by the idea of being alone with Arif at the minute but better now than later. "Goodbye Laurey, tell Rylan I said hello."

"I will." She promises before going out of sight, Arif closing the door after her.

I inhaled sharply as Arif awkwardly walks to the side of the bed. "May I?"

"Yeah, of course," I blurted out, nervously smiling as he takes a seat.

He shifts his gaze to his hands which are placed in his lap, releasing a heavy breath when he meets my gaze and says, "I'm sorry for how I reacted before. Learning you have a half-sister from a father you despise . . . it isn't easy." He paused for a moment, all sorts of emotions surfacing as he looks away again. This is the first time I've ever seen him this way and it pulls at my heart. "I know what our father did isn't your fault but all I can think about is how much my mother suffered before he took her from me."

Alijah killed his mother. His own mate. "I'm sorry. I can't understand how anyone could do that to their own mate." My throat dried up, struggling to find comforting things to say.

Arif sighs and nods. "I was only young. He killed her when I was eleven. I suppose you would have been one by then." Arif runs a hand down his face. "My father has always been violent, especially towards me. Whenever my mother tried to stop him, he would turn his attack on her." A single tear slides down his cheek which he quickly wipes away, clearing his throat. "To everyone else, he was a perfect father and mate. People respected him which is why my mother never felt safe telling people the truth, afraid of the disbelief and judgment that would ensue."

I lean over and place my hand on his arm. "I'm sorry you had to go through that," I said. He doesn't pull away, which I take as a good sign.

It's about time, I need to tell him the things I learned about my mother and our father.

I retract my hand and take in a deep breath, capturing his gaze when he looks up at me. "I saw our father. Rylan showed me one of my earliest memories of him."

Arif's eyes narrowed and I can clearly hear the pain and hesitation in his voice when he asks, "What did you see?"

Anxiety claws its way up my throat, my hands gripping the sheets tightly to my chest. "I saw my mother in a cell, holding me as a baby while Krellin and our father forced her to hand me over." Arif's mind reeled as I breathe out deeply. "My mother didn't choose to be with your father. He forced himself on her just so he could give Krellin a half Wolven slave." I can't help the anger brewing with the last sentence.

Arif is overcome with guilt from assuming my mother went along with his father willingly. His voice almost breaks. "I just assumed. I'm sorry, I didn't realise."

"I didn't expect you to." I half smiled. He puts in the effort to smile back.

This brother-sister thing is going to take some time for the both of us to get used to.

I go on to explain everything that he's missed these last couple of days, his expression continuously shifting between anger, confusion and understanding as I explain how Tristan saved me. When I explain how Tristan refused to help us, Arif offers to persuade him but I shake my head and kindly refuse the offer.

Torturing Tristan won't get us anywhere.

However, his expression brights up when I tell him I'm pregnant, the happiness on his face takes me off guard. He thinks for a moment, piecing things together. "That's why you couldn't shift."

I nodded. "Yeah, Adrenous is already taking care of Rita's departure, she'll be leaving tomorrow night."

Arif's nostrils flared, a smirk on his lips. "The bitch will get what she deserves."

I'll take his word for it . . .

✦○✦

CHAPTER FORTY
A New Rogue

✦▢✦

ADRENOUS

    I can't stop the anger from surfacing as I storm down the damp and dark corridor, heading towards Rita's cell.

    I understand she's upset and angry but challenging Alivia, especially when she's pregnant with my unborn pup, has taken it too far. I've already arranged for her so-called 'departure' to be held tomorrow night, not wanting to prolong the inevitable and make her believe she's staying when she isn't.

    I won't allow any threat no matter how minor to remain within my pack and risk Alivia and the pup.

    I can still hardly believe it . . . I'm going to be a father. There was a time I thought I would never find my mate let alone have a family. Now that it's happening, I'm struggling to believe it, afraid that I'll wake up and discover it's all a dream. It's a blessing that I'm not sure I deserve.

    With Krellin's next attack on the horizon, I need to protect Alivia more than ever. I won't risk her life, she's too important to me that if anything were to happen to her, I wouldn't be able to survive. That's something I'm certain of.

    I find myself outside her cell, dismissing the guard who was standing by the door. I take my time unlocking it, hearing Rita shuffle from inside. When my gaze lands on her, I find her pressed against the back corner of the room, looking away from me. I close the door behind me and step in, my lips pulled in a tight line.

"Look at me," I order, my dominance pulling at her willpower, forcing her to lift her head and look at me. Her eyes narrow on me, her anger surfacing as she captures my equally angered gaze.

"What you did was outright despicable and stupid." I scowl at her, my tone dangerously calm. "You broke the law, Rita . . ." I said. Her eyebrows furrowed.

She quickly defends herself, snapping out of her silence. "I didn't break any law, it is perfectly acceptable to challenge another." She catches the darkening of my eyes, changing her tone with me. "I was supposed to be queen, I gave up my mate for you . . . I left my family . . ."

"I never asked you to." I snap, causing her to flinch. "As for being my queen, I never offered you the title, you just assumed—"

"Do you blame me?"

"Yes!" I growl, a whimper passing her lips at the anger in my voice, my wolf coming forward. "I made it clear that me and you were temporary. How you've treated Alivia since she's arrived is unforgivable, let alone breaking the law . . ."

"B—but I didn't b—break any law . . ."

"You challenged a pregnant Wolven . . ." I can barely stand to look at her, my wolf wanting to end her now. I force him back, knowing there's a more fitting punishment that won't involve having to get our paws dirty.

Rita's eyes widen in horror, her voice breaking when she breathes out, "She's pregnant?"

"Your actions would have made an unborn pup homeless and vulnerable, my pup. Alivia is a much better fit for a queen and you are beyond lucky she won that fight." I take a moment to pause, Rita's heart beating erratically as she listens to every word.

"Believe me, if you even won, I wouldn't have hesitated to kill you. Fuck old traditions!"

Rita doesn't respond, her gaze following me as I make my way toward her, forcing her to her feet. She cries out. "What are you doing?"

"I'm not going to kill you Rita, but you will pay for your stupidity." She attempts to pull away, her eyes swelling as tears begin to fall down her cheeks. I pull out a small, silver dagger from my back pocket, the dim light reflecting off its surface, attracting her attention before her eyes grow wide.

"Stop . . . please . . ." she said as I bring the dagger closer to her right shoulder, just above her shoulder blade.

A scream tears from her lips, her body becoming coated with sweat as I pierce her flesh with the dagger, the silver burning her skin. A scar would be left when the wound heals. I place three-lined wounds right next to each other, a symbol recognised by all packs. If Rita approaches another pack's territory and they see the marks, they'll kill her on sight. This will be her full punishment aside from being banished from my pack.

Rita collapses to the floor when I release her, her voice now hoarse when she sobs. "How am I going to survive on my own? You might as well just execute me yourself, you coward!"

"See it as you will, this is your punishment. After tomorrow, I better not see you ever again, am I clear?" I head for the door.

Instead of answering my threat, Rita uses this last private moment to jest. "Karma will come for you Adrenous . . . believe me . . ."

I close the cell door behind me, the guard returning to his post as I take my leave, ignoring Rita's sad excuse for a threat.

✦▢✦

The following evening

ALIVIA

    I walk with Raven towards the bridge in the centre of the field, the place that once made me a pack member now being used to make another a rogue.
    The wind is strong today, enveloping my body with a horrible coldness as I bring my cloak around my body to try and keep the coldness at bay.
    Everyone else is already present, apart from Adrenous and the generals. Titan, Hunter and Arif are helping Adrenous with Rita while Rylan is remaining home to look after Laurey now that she is close to her due date. Everyone moves to the side, showing me respect with the bow of their heads as they make room for me and Raven to pass. It appears we have front row seats to this show.
    Silence falls over every single Wolven here, the air becoming thick with tension. Adrenous appears from the woods on the other side of the bridge, his eyes scanning over everyone here, including me. Even with the distance, I can tell he's angry, his body tense and his expression dark, pulling at my anxiety.
    Behind him, Titan and Hunter appear, holding onto Rita's forearms as they walk her toward the bridge. Lastly, Arif stands behind them, extra force in case Rita tries to run before the ritual is complete.
    Rita's head is cast down, her hair falling over her shoulders in tangles. She's dressed in an oversized rag, not sitting on her body properly as it slides down her shoulders. My eyes narrow on some sort of mark on her right shoulder. At first, I believe it may be some sort of tattoo but now that she's closer, I'm surprised to learn that it's a scar.
    It must be new, the scar still red and raw, having only just healed. I can't recall ever seeing it on her before so I'm certain it's new.

What's the purpose of this mark? Is it part of her banishment?

They all stop in the middle of the bridge, forcing Rita to stand on top of the engraved stone as Titan and Hunter step back. She's visibly crying, her shoulders trembling up and down as she looks away from everyone watching. Adrenous stands before her, his eyes flashing and I can see his wolf surfacing, realising he's angrier than I thought.

I place my hand against my abdomen for comfort, reminding myself what could have happened if Rita succeeded in her plan. She deserves this.

Adrenous's voice rings out in the clearing, capturing everyone's attention. "Rita Sutton is being judged before the moon goddess today, guilty of not only losing a challenge that she provoked but for also breaking the law and challenging a pregnant Wolven."

Everyone around me gasps and I inwardly cringe when they come to realise the pregnant Wolven he is referring to is me. I can feel their eyes piercing my form as I attempt to remain calm and collected, keeping my focus on Adrenous and Rita. I appreciate it when Raven glares daggers at them, people turning back to the king in fear of her.

"Thank you," I whispered to her and she returns it with a smile.

Once silence has settled once again, Adrenous continues. "Rita will become a rogue, a wolf without a pack. She will not be accepted by others, left to fend for herself, a just punishment for the crime she's committed."

Rita's sobs become louder, her heart racing as she comes to realise the severity of her actions. "Just kill me . . . please." Her voice was hoarse

A just punishment. The way Adrenous says it, it's clear the punishment should be considered merciful. She could have had it a lot worse, I'm sure of it.

Adrenous pulls out a dagger from his back pocket. It's similar to one that was used to welcome me into the pack; however, this one has different carvings. One of them is similar to the scar on Rita's shoulder. Her scar must be some sort of symbol that marks her as a rogue, I assume.

Rita glances up, her puffy eyes wide when they land on the dagger. "Please . . . n—no . . . not again."

Adrenous grips her wrist, forcefully opening her palm so he can slice the dagger right down her palms centre. Her scream echoed around the fields, causing birds to fly out of the trees.

Just as her blood fell onto the engraved stone, the moon that is now appearing from the clouds shines its light down on Rita's form. She's now shaking, Adrenous still holding onto her wrist to ensure her blood continues to fall onto the stone. His voice is cold and distant when he says, "The blood that was once offered is now being taken back. The protection that was once given will no longer be yours. The moon goddess, who once connected your wolf with ours, will now be severed by her power alone."

The stone beneath Rita's feet starts to glow, the connection between us all and her starting to snap apart, almost like a cord being cut. Only this is much slower and a tad painful though it's nothing compared to the pain Rita must be experiencing.

Now that Adrenous is no longer holding onto her palm, she collapses to her knees. The screams and cries that leave her body are enough for me to understand how intense and excruciating the pain must be. If I think losing one's wolf connection is painful, imagine losing hundreds of connections, each individual cord being cut.

It's been quite a while. Rita's screaming only just died down as she's left lying on the ground, barely conscious. Hunter and Titan once again grab hold of her forearms, hauling her back up to her feet. I suppose the show isn't over just yet.

Adrenous waited until Rita is looking back at him, Her body was drained but even she knows this isn't over yet. "Shift rogue!" Adrenous beamed, Rita's heart once again beating fast.

She shakes her head. "I—I c—can't."

"Shift or I'll take it as an act of defiance." Her heart skips a few beats, tears welling once again. "Which would you rather, rogue?"

She nods her head in defeat, Hunter and Titan letting go of her. She wobbles slightly on her feet, her wolf coming forward as her eyes darken, forcing the shift onto her drained and defeated body.

Another scream tears from her lips, her bones snapping as blonde fur erupted. Her screams become whimpers and whines of her wolf, once again collapsing to the ground, just about looking up at Adrenous.

He looks down at her in disdain. His wolf came forward to show his dominance for the last time. "You will leave my territory and never come back, do you understand?" A whimper leaves Rita's wolf's lips with a small nod of her head. "Go!"

Rita's wolf struggles to rise, still wobbling slightly even when she does stand. She glances at the crowd one last time before she turns and heads towards the woods, her new life as a rogue waiting for her.

When she's out of sight, the crowd disperses. Adrenous and Arif make their way towards me. Now standing beside me, Adrenous pulls me to his chest. "How are you feeling?" he said. I'm not sure how to respond. I can't help but frown. "Rita's punishment was justifiable, you shouldn't feel bad for her."

I glance up at him, finding his gaze to be reassuring. "You're right."

Adrenous moves forward, taking me with him. "Come on, let's get you out of the cold."

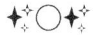

✦✧○✦✧

CHAPTER FORTY-ONE
My Coronation

✦▢✦

ALIVIA

I take in a few deep breaths, my heart racing as I make my way towards the ceremonial garden, Arif on my arm as he attempts to reassure me. "You'll be fine, it'll be over before you know it."

"I hope you're right. I already feel like I'm going to throw up." He chuckles and shakes his head as we continue to make our way across the field, heading towards the platform where I shifted for the first time.

Tonight I will be named the Wolven queen and what better place than the place where this all began.

For the occasion, I adorn an elegant sequin gown that flows out towards the floor. The colours range from a dark blue to a reflective silver that is decorated with blue, embroidered flowers. The dress is off the shoulder and has been made specially to accommodate the bump that has now formed on my stomach.

Another few months and my pup will be here.

I and Arif halt at the beginning of the path that leads towards steps going up to the platform where Adrenous and the other three are standing in front of their chairs, looking down at me. They're all finely dressed, including Arif, with Adrenous's family symbol embroidered into their shirts.

I catch Adrenous's gaze and I can see the pride and admiration he holds for me, placing a smile on my face. He, himself, is wearing a finely made blue shirt to match my dress, his necklace still around his neck as the pendant with his family's symbol is centred perfectly against his chest. A massive golden crown is placed on his head, decorated with red rubies, allowing his eyes to stand out.

Everything else is just as I remember only this time there is an extra seat up on the platform. It's similar to Adrenous's throne, decorated with lovely fur as the seat part is adorned with red leather, finely pleated.

On either side of the path, chairs are neatly lined up and every single one is filled. Even my aunt is seated at the front, her gaze softened as she, like all the others, turns to watch me and Arif walk along the path. I'm surprised to see that Amber and Avery aren't with her, I would have thought they'd enjoy seeing this as well. I'm also surprised to see that the Elders are also present. I suppose Victor got his invitation after all.

Laurey and her newborn pup, Reagan, are also present as she rocks Reagan in her arms gently whilst smiling over at me. Raven is next to her, cooing at Reagan. Laurey had only given birth to Reagan last month and the little pup was already so filled with life.

I can feel my heart continue to skyrocket, Arif being my only stable anchor in a situation where I'm afraid my legs will give out beneath me. I focus the rest of my energy on walking up the steps without tripping over my dress, afraid of the humiliation that would follow if I was to embarrass myself like that.

Don't trip . . . please don't trip.

I finally make it up the steps and wait until I'm beside Adrenous to release Arif's arm. He places a quick kiss on my cheek before walking towards his own seat and stands in front of it like the others.

I make the mistake of looking out toward the audience of people watching me. Please don't let me throw up.

I welcome the distraction when Adrenous's voice echoed through the clearing, capturing everyone else's attention too. How does he speak out in front of all these people so easily?

"Alivia Harmon, my mate and the future mother of my pup will from this day forward be known as Alivia Claxton, my Queen as well as yours." His words take hold of me, surrounding my being along with my heart, a smile pulling at my lips as I can't believe this is really happening.

Adrenous turns towards me, taking my hands into his much larger ones. His touch bringing me comfort as he continues with. "As queen, you will be expected to uphold all traditions and laws set by those before you. You will be expected to protect and mother those who look up to you. You will be expected to serve and guide the pack using your better judgement and the power you hold to do so." Adrenous pauses and I find myself using the time to go over his words over and over again, realising what it means to really be Queen. Adrenous finishes with the question I've been waiting for. "Do you accept? Will you stand by my side and rule with me?"

My answer slips past my lips with ease, not an ounce of hesitation in my voice. "I accept what is expected of me and I'll happily rule by your side."

The crowd erupts in applauds and encouragements but my coronation isn't finished just yet. Adrenous turns towards his throne and bends forward, picking up a crown that I've only just realised was there. "Then with the power I hold, I rightly announce you Queen of the Wolvens, mother and Luna of the pack."

I hold his gaze as he places the crown on my head. It's a lot heavier than I thought, made out of gold and decorated with rubies, a smaller counterpart to the crown that sits on Adrenous's head.

He takes one of my hands in his as we both turn to the crowd, everyone bowing their head like me and Adrenous take our seats. The generals each bowing in mine and Adrenous's direction before taking their own seats.

The night is still far from over as the sun begins to set, everyone moving from their seats to dance and drink the night away in celebration of their new queen.

I have to say, I'm enjoying this moment more than I thought I would.

Me and Adrenous make our way through the crowd, many Wolvens taking the time to congratulate me on being queen.

I catch Arif and Rylan making their way towards us and it appears Arif is speaking to a very tired Rylan. "Welcome to fatherhood." He smirks, causing Rylan to glare at him.

Adrenous catches on. "Has the pup been keeping you up all night?"

"Yes." Rylan sighs, rubbing his eyes before looking back at Adrenous with a mischievous grin. "You're just as doomed as me."

Adrenous becomes visibly worried, causing me and Arif to break out in laughter.

I'm pulled from the conversation when I see my aunt calling me over. "I'll just be a moment," I said before making my way towards her and pulling her in for a hug. "I'm so happy you could make it, where's Avery and Amber?"

She frowns, causing me to become worried as she takes a while to answer. When she notices me staring and waiting, she quickly said, "Sorry, Amber and Avery wanted to come but they're not very well at the moment."

"Well I should go and see how they're doing?" I was about to tell Adrenous that I'm going to visit my cousins when my aunt grabs my arm and pulls me back.

"Wait until they're better. I don't want you getting ill in your condition," my aunt said. I stop in my spot and nod. I can't help but feel she's being a little off as she continues with, "How is the little one?" placing her hand on my bump. Just as her hand is on my bump she pulls away when the baby kicks aggressively, causing me to hiss in pain. That's odd. They've never kicked that hard.

"It's as healthy as can be." I answered, rubbing my bump gently. "Sorry, the pup's never kicked that hard before."

My aunt seemed to understand. "It's a sign that they're going to be really strong." *Perhaps.*

"I better get back but I'll speak with you later." I said before heading back towards Adrenous, Arif, and Rylan. I quietly groaned when I see that they're all talking with Victor.

Victor is the first to notice me, bowing his head. "My Queen." I appear to be the only one who noticed the hint of disdain in his voice.

"Victor," I said with an equal amount of disdain as I come to stand beside Adrenous.

"We've noticed an increase in rogue spottings," Victor said. "Now that you are queen, the matter calls for your judgment as well as the king's."

I furrow my brows and turn to Adrenous. "Have they been near here?"

"No." He shakes his head. "They've been spotted at a distance, never approaching my territory but they've been watching."

"We think they may be planning something." Victors adds, bringing my attention back to him as I try to think of another reason that they may be watching from a distance.

Perhaps they are planning something.

"I've only been queen one day, I think I'll leave the matter up to you, a more experienced person for the job." I remark, enjoying the surprised look on his face.

"Er, well yes, I suppose you're right my queen." I can literally see his arrogance growing and I had to stop myself from rolling my eyes.

"Good, I hope you'll have it under control." Adrenous adds In, causing Victor to frown.

Oh Victor, is it too much for you to handle?

"Relax Victor, I'm only joking." Victor sighs in relief and I can't help the smile planted on my face. "We'll discuss this tomorrow." Adrenous finishes before removing himself as well as me from the conversation. "How are you feeling?" He asks once we're seated at one of the tables.

"A little overwhelmed to be honest but I'll be fine." I assure him as I lean my head on his shoulder, inhaling his soothing scent whilst he places a hand on my abdomen, the pup kicking at the presence of their father's touch.

The action brings a smile to Adrenous's lips, his eyes flashing with love and excitement. "A feisty one already, just like their mother."

"And strong like their father." I add, smiling up at him. He dips his head down and captures my lips with his, a gentle kiss that warms my heart before he quickly pulls away at the sound of someone yelling and running towards us.

I narrow my eyes on a man dressed in armour who appears to be hurt. One of his eyes has been swollen shut and his clothes are ripped from top to bottom, revealing his wounds which resemble claw marks, soaking his damaged clothes and armour with blood. Blood is also trailing down from his neck, seeping out of what appears to be a bite mark.

Even I can tell the claw marks don't match the bite mark. It's clear it was two different creatures that did this to the poor guard.

He pretty much collapses to the floor in front of us but before he can hit the ground, Adrenous is out of his chair, holding the man up. Adrenous calls for help and it's Laurey who answers, placing Reagan in Rylan's arms before making her way over.

Adrenous lays the man gently on the ground. Many people are becoming worried, a crowd forming. "I need some room please!" Laurey rushed over. Arif, Hunter, and Titan help Laurey out, forcing the people back so that Laurey can do her job peacefully.

When Laurey is done assessing the wounds, she looks up at me and Adrenous with fear in her eyes. "This man was attacked by wolves and bitten by a Vampire."

Adrenous doesn't seem to believe it. It's obvious this has never happened before.

The man surprised us all when he jolts awake, his eyes filled with horror as his hand grips Laurey's wrist tightly. "R—rogues. Vampires. Together . . . on their way." His words are jumbled and most of it is hard to understand but the message is clear. "W—we were outnumbered . . . I'm s—sorry, my King. Forgive me."

The guard is close to taking his final breath but Adrenous is quick to correct the guard, "You did well, there's nothing to forgive."

The guard smiles weakly before his eyes shut for the last time, his hand going limp as it releases Laurey's wrist.

"Right," Adrenous's gaze shifts to everyone in close proximity, making sure he has their attention, "There are Vampires and rogues on their way here so Rylan and Laurey," they both look up at him, getting ready to follow his orders, "I want you both to round up the young and vulnerable, get them away from here as soon as possible."

Rylan and Laurey are already gone, going around to warn all the young and the vulnerable to exit the garden and make their way safely to the nearest town.

Adrenous address Hunter next. "I want you to scout the perimeter and detect how long until they arrive. Keep me posted."

"Already on it," Hunter answers, shifting while heading towards the surrounding woods.

Next is Arif and Titan. Arif is asked to gather all the soldiers whilst Titan formulates a tactical defence against the rogues and Vampires. Now that everyone is off to carry out their duties, that leaves me, Adrenous, and Raven who is making her way over after Adrenous called for her.

She stops in front of us and it appears she already knows what her job is, leaving me confused. I start to piece it together when Adrenous turns to me with a sad smile on his face. Before he can speak, I've already cut him off, shaking my head, "I'm not going unless you come with me."

"Ali." He gazes down at me, my heart aching at the thought of leaving him here when rogues as well as Vampires are on their way, "You're a queen now and being queen means you have to make hard choices for the safety of your people."

"B—but . . ." I realise deep down that he's right. My eyes watered as I reach up and kiss him. As I pulled away, I said, "You come home safe, you hear me?"

"I hear you, my Queen." He kisses the back on my hand, "I love you and our pup." He bends down and kisses my bump whilst rubbing it gently.

"We love you too."

My gaze snaps to the tree line when I hear howls and growls circle the garden, my eyes widen before I turn back to Adrenous who is now urging me to go with Raven, "Raven will take you back to the estate."

"B-but that's miles away." I stammer, not understanding how we're going to make it back there quickly.

Raven doesn't make time for my confusion as she starts to pull me in the other direction, "We're teleporting."

"Wait, what?" I try to pull back but she's not having any of it. I turn in the direction where Adrenous has been standing but he's long gone now, off to help the others. Please let him be safe.

I stop when Raven does, the both of us standing in the centre of the garden and away from everyone else. I capture Raven's gaze when she says, "I'm going to teleport us back to the estate but be warned, it's not the best form of travel for someone who's never done it before."

I'm not so sure about this.

"Will it hurt?" I ask just as she takes hold of both my hands.

"No," she grips my hands tighter as her palms begin to glow, a gust of wind forming around us as it picks up strands of my hair, "You may feel sick and a little dizzy afterwards."

Wonderful, you can already tick the first one off.

Just as Raven begins her chant, my hands let go of hers when I heard my aunt screaming behind me. "Alivia, what the hell is going on?"

I can see her running towards us, her expression contorted by fear and confusion. "Why aren't you with Rylan and Laurey?" I yelled at her.

She doesn't answer until she's next to me, breathing heavily, "T—they forgot about me."

That doesn't sound like them but why else would she still be here.

Fuck! I snap my gaze back to Raven, "Do you have enough power to transport an extra person?"

Raven shifts her gaze to my aunt, "I suppose but it'll drain more of my energy." Raven is a little hesitant but when she holds her hands out to both me and my aunt, I'm completely grateful, offering her a smile that shows her my deepest gratitude.

She begins her chant once more, the gust of wind forming once again, causing goosebumps to prick my skin. The wind, turning into a swirling vortex appears to swallow up the ground, my stomach doing a backflip at the weightless sensation. My aunt has gone silent and pale, clearly not liking this whilst Raven's eyes are still shut, her chant surrounding us like a soft echo.

Silence soon ensues, the ground forming once again, the swirling vortex still blocking our view of the room until the glow from Raven's hands dies down, the vortex disappearing as if it was never there.

Oh no.

I feel my stomach convulse, forcing me to bend over and throw up everything that resonates within my stomach. Raven is by my side, moving my hair away from my face and patting my back gently until I'm able to stand straight again. "Are you alright?" She releases my hair and allows me some room to breathe whilst watching me carefully, worried I'm going to throw up again.

"I'll be okay." I assure her, taking in a few shaky breaths before adding, "I'm more worried about the others."

"Me too." She admits.

We remain silent for a few moments as I wait for my stomach to settle before my focus shifts to the room we're in. It appears Raven managed to get us back to the estate and it seems we're in one of the lounge rooms but the room is shrouded in darkness. Raven takes note of this, flicking her wrist before all the candles on the walls ignite, casting most of the room in a warm glow.

It's only now that I realise my aunt has been really quiet. I find her near the wall with her back to me, "Helena, is everything okay?"

She doesn't answer me, both me and Raven now becoming worried when we exchange looks. Raven takes the initiative, approaching my aunt before placing her hand on my aunts shoulder, "Mrs Harmon, are you-"

She jumps back, removing her hand from my aunt's shoulder when the flesh on my aunts bones begins to shed. My eyes widen in horror, "What's happening?"

Raven is quickly in front of me, placing me behind her before forcing me to take a few steps back. "That's not your aunt."

I don't fully understand but she's obviously right. If this isn't her then where is she? Is she and my cousins safe?

My aunt's flesh is replaced with leathery, black skin. Her dress ripped to shreds to accommodate the body of a disgusting beast that now stands in her place. The creature's bones protruded from its form with talons instead of claws or nails. The beast turned around, staring at us with pools of blackness. My eyes grew wider. I'd recognise those eyes anywhere.

Tyke.

So this is a Rune's true form. Just as ugly as I imagined. It was the same beast that I encountered in the woods that day. The same one who watched over my mother and kept her in a cell. I can feel my claws elongating, the urge to slash his face dominant.

I go to step forward but Raven is one step ahead, stopping me from proceeding, "Don't be impulsive Alivia! Think about the pup."

Dammit, she's right. I have to think before I act.

Tyke grins maliciously, his eyes trailing down to my abdomen, "Another pup." He looks back up in excitement, "My master will be pleased to learn such news."

"Your master won't touch my pup." I growl, my wolf coming forward in anger.

Tyke tilts his head to the side, clearly amused as he takes a step forward, causing me and Raven to step back, "Stupid wolf, my master will have everything he's ever wanted, it would be foolish to think otherwise."

I don't believe him but there's something else that has me completely frightened, "Where's my aunt and cousins?"

Tyke sneers at me, tilting his head in amusement, "They're sleeping peacefully."

What the fuck does that mean?

"Where are they?" I snap, a growl resonating from my chest. I'm close to pushing Raven aside but I have to remain calm, especially for my pup.

"I already told you," he smirks, "they're at home sleeping." Tyke appears to enjoy the fear in my gaze, his dark eyes flashing with excitement.

"I've heard enough." Raven lifts her hand, ready to end Tyke but just before she's about to, a pair of silver cuffs with strange inscriptions carved into them appear around her wrists, causing her eyes to widen when Tyke is still standing before us with a smirk on his face, her magic having no effect on him.

"Long time no see, sister." A dark, familiar voice resonates around the room, causing Raven's eyes to drift from the cuffs around her wrists as she searches the room for the culprit.

I remain standing behind Raven as a man appears from nothing before stepping out of the shadows in the room with four Vampires, his eyes set on Raven and me as he tilts his head to the side.

Draven is just as I remember from Rylan's subconscious only this time his pale, white hair has been tied back into a ponytail and he's wearing a leather shirt and trousers that stick to his body like a second skin. He stalks towards us before stopping in front of Raven who is staring daggers at him. Raven steps back, taking me with her, "There's nowhere for you to go, dear sister."

Raven eyes flash murderously, the anger she's kept hidden for her brother surfacing. Before Draven says another word, Raven spits, "How dare you show your face!" She raises her hand, attempting to throw him across the room but it's no use. The cuffs around her wrists stop her from doing so as she looks back down at her hands with fear and confusion, "What the—"

"They're enchanted by me. Your magic is useless now." Draven taunts before Raven looks back up at him. The fear in her gaze takes me off guard, I've never seen her so scared before which has me equally frightened. Draven releases a dark chuckle. "I've learned a few tricks during our time apart." Raven's bottom lip begins to tremble, it's obvious she's never felt this powerless in all her life.

Satisfied with his sister's reaction, Draven turns his unsettling blue eyes on me, his lips twitching up, "Finally, young Queen, we meet in person. With how protective your king is, I thought this day would never come however, he was so busy protecting everyone during your coronation that he left his estate with only a few guards who were quickly overrun." Draven shook his head, laughing. "It's quite embarrassing how quickly his men fell."

You sick fuck! I stood there frozen, looking up at him with narrowed eyes as he continues to taunt me. "I have to add young Queen, you're very powerful. That day in Rylan's subconscious, I experienced just the smallest taste of your powers and it filled me with ecstasy."

"It was supposed to hurt," I jest as Tyke comes to stand beside Draven and it's only now that I realise we're surrounded by other Vampires and Runes, their eyes haunting as they look down at me and Raven.

Fuck.

Raven breaks from her silence, pleading with Draven, "Leave Alivia be, it's me you've wanted."

Draven clicks his tongue, shaking his head, "My dear sister, always trying to save others. On the contrary, it's the both of you I want."

"B—but I—"

Draven flicks his wrist at her, her head falling forward as she slumps back. One of the Vampires move forward, grabbing her unconscious body before she can fall to the ground. "She always did speak too much." Draven comments, the Vampires and Runes crackling with laughter in response.

I spit at him, my anger getting the better of me. Everyone stops their laughter as Draven goes deathly silent, my chest heaving up and down as I breathe heavily in anger.

He wipes the spit from his face, his eyes flashing with fury. "You're lucky my powers don't work on you." He taunts, gripping my hair back until I'm hissing in pain, "But there are worst forms of torture." I can feel my heart racing, my fear spiking. "For your pup's sake, I wouldn't do anything like that again."

I frown at his threat, glaring up at him when he releases his hold on my hair.

"Now," he addresses his men whilst looking down at me with a sinister smirk. "Let's get moving."

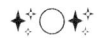

✦○✦

CHAPTER FORTY-TWO
Will You Help Me?

✦▢✦

Adrenous

"I can sense them. They're coming from the west, set to arrive in less than ten minutes."

"Very good, Hunter, make sure to keep an eye on them."

"Will do."

I remain hidden in the tree line, Arif and Titan close by with their own men to lead. We all keep our attention set on the west side of the garden. At any moment, the Vampires and rogues heading this way will break from the tree line not knowing that we're ready for them.

Half of the men along with Arif and Titan have shifted whilst me and the rest haven't. The shifted will go after the rogues while me and the others attack the Vampires.

They'll come into view in roughly thirty seconds.

I process the information Hunter is feeding everyone, all of the shifted wolves now leaning on their back legs, preparing to run out first. They'll be our first offence with Arif and Titan leading them out. Arif's men will be running out from the north and Titan's men will be running out from the east, completely surrounding them.

My nostrils flare, the wind heading downwind, carrying the scent of the rogues and Vampires but one scent seems rather familiar. Not long after, my gaze snaps to the first rogue that breaks the tree line. My eyes narrow on the wolf, my temper flaring when I recognise her.

Arif's men run out first, Rita's wolf's head rotating to see them coming for her. She remains still, seeming unfazed. I realise why when the other rogues come into view, running around her to meet Arif's men.

Arif's voice breaks through my anger. *"What the fuck is that bitch doing here?"*

It appears I'm not the only one to recognised the bitch. How dare she come back here after I had banished her from my land.

Titan's men are next, running out and attacking the rogues from behind when they are too distracted by Arif's men. A blood bath has begun, few of the rogues pouring blood, soaking the grass beneath them as they lay limp on the floor. My men are still far from winning.

In the next instant, Vampires appeared from the tree line, running at incredible speed and weaving their way through the battle and sinking their fangs into any of my men closest to them. Three of my men fall to the ground still alive, making it easier for the rogues to finish them off without a fight.

A growl reverberates from my chest, the sound tearing its way through the battle, forcing everyone to pause and look my way before me and the rest are breaking from the trees, surrounding the Vampires.

The blood bath ensues, my hand gripping a Vampire's neck right away, catching him off guard. My claws are already out, digging into his neck with incredible strength. He struggles against me but he's no match and soon the light has diminished from his eyes when I tear of his head, his body falling to it's knees before it slumps to the ground.

Few Vampires stop, looking my way to see me throw the head of their companion to the ground, my chest heaving up and down as I enjoy the anger in their eyes.

I ignite the fire in their eyes when I smirk back at them. One of them releases a painful screech before storming towards me, attempting to jump on my back and dig their fangs into my neck but I'm already out of their grasp. I turn in my spot to find them hissing at me, their fangs bared. "Our king will destroy all of you."

Before he can blink, I gripped his neck like I did with the other bloodsucker. I was seething, my eyes ablaze as I stare into his startled gaze, "Your king, like you, will die like the gutless fiend he is." He struggled to respond. I gripped incredibly tighter, tearing his head from his body and then turning to watch the rest of them retreat back. *Gutless just like their king.*

Now for my next line of business, I assess the bloodbath. Arif and Titan were holding their own. Hunter is also here now, using his gifts to sense the rogue stalking towards his back but before the rogues can strike, Hunter has already spun around, burying his claws in the rogue's eyes.

A dark chuckle reverberates through my chest at the sight. The blinded wolf releases a pained whine before Hunter silences him, his claws tearing out his throat. The wolf collapses to the ground, blood now springing from his neck until he bleeds out.

My eyes then narrowed on the one I was searching for, a new anger spiking within my chest at the sight of her here. She lead the rogues here and now she's about to face true torture.

Rita's wolf is still standing in the centre of the bloodbath, untouched as she watches her fellow rogues attack my men with joy. I storm towards her, making my way through the battle until her gaze snaps to mine. Within seconds, she's off, bounding into the woods with me on her trail as I run after her.

I pretty much sense the taste of her fear on my tongue, my eyes darkening with delight. *That's right, run from me. I'll soon catch you.*

She leads me further into the woods when my wolf starts to take over, his anger driving us both forward as soon as his paws touch the ground. A growl resonates from our chest, the sound startling nearby wildlife as it tears through the trees.

We propel forward, Rita now back in our sights as we charge, knocking her to the ground, causing her wolf to bark in anger. She snaps at our stomach with her jaw, her fangs sinking into the sensitive flesh before I force her head to the ground, my claws digging into her neck.

She pulls her head back aggressively, my claws dragging across her face, three claw marks now marring her wolfs neck and cheek, blood staining her blond fur. She backs up a few feet, furiously growling at me. I glimpse the movement of her feet and back as she prepares to attack me.

Someone's gotten brave.

My wolf barks, his nostrils flaring as anger consumes him. How dare this rogue think she can beat him.

She launches forward, attempting to claw at our throat. We duck down just in time, knocking our head into her belly, forcing her back to hit a tree behind her. We don't allow her to get back up this time, our claws sinking into her side this time. She gives up, submitting to me when she bows her head.

I step back, climbing off her wolf before I shifted back to human form. I stood over her wolf, my eyes ablaze with fury when I commanded, "Shift!"

The command is too strong for her to ignore and soon she's back to her human form, staring up at me with angry, brown eyes. She stands to her feet, not bothering to cover herself as she glowers at me. "The rogue king sends his regards."

I can't hold back the dark chuckle that escaped my lips. "I'm not surprised you sold out and joined him; however, there's one thing I want to know before I kill you."

"You can ask but I have no intention of answering." She bites back, glaring up at me.

My wolf comes forward, causing her expression to shift. The fear she's trying to hide surfaced. My wolf revels at the sight of her fear as I ask, "Why is Krellin and Marx working together?"

She shifts her gaze to the side, looking away from me as she refuses to answer.

Enough of her bullshit. I snap forward, my hand gripping her throat and squeezing tightly until she's struggling to breath. She looks up at me, beyond terrified as I sneered. "Fucking answer me!"

She claws at my hand but her strength in no match. Her eyes water at the sensation of her lungs constricting, the suffocation too painful. Finally she's coughing up. "M-Marx w-w-wants y-you d-d-dead."

After I released her, she bended over, coughing as her lungs begged for air.

"Why?"

She continuously coughs for a few more seconds before she's finally able to elaborate. "You may think you don't know him but the truth is . . ."

She stops talking, my eyes furrowing when her gaze shifts to something behind me. I turn in my spot, finding three Vampires baring their fangs at me. I turn back towards Rita when she smirks. "This is where we part ways."

You conniving little bitch.

I was about to snap forward and end her but the Vampires already made their moves. One of them buried their fangs in my shoulder and I groaned at the pain radiating from the point of contact. I elbowed the Vampire square in the face, knocking him back. Keeping my attention on the other two, I heard Rita giggle, her words causing my heart to stop cold. "Have fun with these while their friends take care of Alivia. You should have made sure to keep the estate protected . . ."

My eyes snap to her, seeing her wolf's back on me as she runs off.

She's lying!

"*Alivia!*" No answer.

The air is knocked from my lungs when one of the Vampires kicks my chest, knocking me back slightly. This time I was beyond angry. My wolf breaks through again, my bones snapping as he takes over. He wastes no time sinking his fangs into the Vampire's neck before shaking his head aggressively. My wolf bit down until the Vampire was no longer struggling. We toss him to the ground before glaring up at the other two. They shifted their gaze to their companion, their flight skills kicking in but I'm not letting them run away this time.

I chased the first one down, chewing a huge chunk out of his leg. He screeched in pain before I silenced him, clawing out his throat and then ripping his head from his body with my fangs.

The next one is just as easy. My wolf launched at his back, forcing his body to the ground. He manages to kick at my muzzle. My wolf enjoyed the pain, allowing it to feed his anger. The Vampire flinches at the look in our eyes, already knowing he's lost before I ripped into his chest. His pained cries bring joy to my ears. He's practically begging for death after I pulled his guts. It's only then that I give into his cries, biting into his neck before he ends up just like his companion.

I turn back to where I had last seen Rita but she's long gone, and so is her scent. *Fuck! I need to get back home right now!*

I run back towards the battle, my heart on the verge of collapse at the thought of Alivia. I've already tried to contact her and it's completely useless. Whatever they've done, they've blocked our connection.

When I exited the forest, I found Hunter, Titan, and Arif helping the wounded men. Most of our men survived with few casualties, whereas I can see many Vampires and rogues lying dead on the ground. That's the least they deserved for the crimes they've committed against us.

Deep down, this was all a distraction. The real crime was taking Alivia whilst I was busy dealing with these bastards.

Somehow they knew I would send Alivia back home, knowing most of my men would be busy in battle and she would be right there for the taking. *I fucked up!*

I make my way over to Arif. When he met my gaze, his eyes furrow at the devastation and anger mixed within my irises. "We need to get back, they've taken Alivia," I said.

"They've what?" Arif's features shift, his wolf coming forward at the news. "Raven was supposed to fucking protect her!"

"What's happened?" Titan questions when he hears Arif's outburst, walking towards us with Hunter next to him.

"Raven fucked up!" Arif snaps, no longer thinking clearly.

Titan and Hunter are more confused and I'm forced to take the lead before Arif snaps again. "Alivia's been taken and our connection has been severed."

I feel my chest tightening at the thought of what they could do to her and my pup. "Me and Arif need to head back, I need you to help the survivors and keep everyone safe while we figure out a plan." I announce, making sure everything else will be fine while I form a plan to get her back.

Hunter is the first to respond, his tone sympathetic when he says, "Of course, get her home safe, okay?"

Me and Arif set off, shifting as quickly as we can. It's almost dawn when I see the estate come into view, halting in our tracks when I spot a few of my guards slaughtered, their hearts pulled from their chests and thrown next to them.

I'm exhausted from running but that isn't going to stop me from killing any Vampire or rogue that may still be lurking.

My ears perk when I hear a male groaning, the sound leading me to a very beaten guard who has somehow managed to stay alive. Bite marks have marred pretty much every area of his body. His clothes have been ripped to shreds, covered in his own blood. I can see his chest barely moving, his breathing shallow as I make my way towards him. His eyes widen when he hears the sound of my paws against the dirt, his heart spiking before my scent reaches his nostrils and he realises who I am.

He looks at me from the corner of his eye, unable to move with the amount of broken bones in his body, forced to remain completely still. Arif walks around us, looking for any other survivors.

"Who did this to you?" I said.

His reply is delayed, the pain making it hard for him to concentrate. *"The dark Well . . . he was here with the Vampires. They took us by surprise, no one saw them coming."*

"Did you see the queen with them?"

"Yes, they took her and the light Well, who was unconscious, towards the mountains. The queen was screaming about her family, she wanted to know if they were safe."

Her family? He must mean her aunt and cousins back at the cottage. Why would they be in danger? I'll have to have Rylan check on them and make sure everything's fine. If Alivia was worried about them then there must be something wrong.

"I'm sorry I failed you, my King."

I shake my head, ready to comfort him when he takes his last breath, his eyes going dim as they remain open. I close his eyes gently, blaming myself for what happened to him. I should have sent more guards to protect the estate but I was more concerned with keeping everyone safe during the coronation. Now look where it's gotten me.

I need to think; they took Alivia towards the mountains. Every time I, or someone else, has searched for Krellin's hideout we always come up empty handed. There's only one person I know that can help me . . .

I quickly shift on the spot. "Arif!" I said. Arif catches my gaze, turning to face his wolf. "Bring Tristan to me."

He shifts back as well. "My pleasure." His lips turn up into a smirk, his eyes flashing when he heads towards the cells that are based in the centre of the woods.

Raven enchanted him so that her brother, nor any vampire, could track him so the chance is he's still there. He may be my only bargaining chip and the way he feels about Alivia, I can't see how he can refuse to help.

I head towards the estate, my nostrils flaring. I smell Alivia and Raven's scent along with a few unfamiliar ones. They all lead me to one of the many lounges. Like I suspected, nobody's here but my eyes do narrow on a pile of rotten flesh and a woman's dress. I bend down to examine it, realising it's residue from a Rune's shift.

The clothes amongst the pile carry Alivia's aunt's scent and that's when I piece it together. This is why Alivia was worried about her aunt. One of the Runes must have snuck into the coronation, posing as Alivia's aunt. That's how Draven was able to keep tabs on me and Alivia during the coronation.

I blow up, throwing a nearby table across the room. I take in a few gulps of air in an effort to control the ever-increasing fury battling its way through me. The anger makes me want to lash out until all my enemies are buried six feet under.

I sense Arif behind me. I turn to see Arif shoving a tied up Tristan towards me. His mouth is gagged so the only thing coming out are grunts and groans every time Arif shoves him. When they reach me, Arif forces Tristan to his knees before removing the gag from his mouth.

"What the fuck are you doing? Alivia said you wouldn't kill me." He hesitates, his eyes flashing with fear when he looks up at me. Alivia was no longer here to protect him. *Good for him, I need him.*

"Alivia isn't here so I'd be careful." Arif taunts, capturing Tristan's attention, a lump forming in his throat.

I shoot Arif a look, warning him to behave when I bring Tristan's focus back towards me. "Draven has taken Alivia."

Tristan's fear is replaced with confusion before he retorted, "How could you let that happen?"

I narrow my eyes, causing him to drop that snarky tone. "Believe me, it wasn't intentional." I stoop down to his level, my tone shifting when I add, "She's pregnant Tristan."

His eyes flash with surprise, his expression disbelieving. "She's pregnant?"

"Yes."

He's shaking his head now, tears clouding his vision. "She'll end up like her mother when my father finds out."

"I know." I'm completely terrified but I won't allow it to control me. I need to remain level-headed. It's her and our pup's only hope. "I need your help to get her back."

He stops shaking his head, looking up at me with wide eyes.

"Will you help me?"

✦○✦

CHAPTER FORTY-THREE
A Broken Man

✦☐✦

ALIVIA

    My eyes snap open, nothing but darkness fogging my vision. The air around me is stuffy, my breathing becomes laboured as my chest constricts around my lungs when the panic sets in, making it much harder to breathe. It doesn't help that the smell of the room is putrid, that alone pushing me to want to throw up. Where am I?
    I find myself curled up on a damp, concrete floor as I sit up and lean against the back wall. The noise of metal clanging against the concrete registers in my ears and it's only then that I feel a pair of steel cuffs around my wrists, connected to the wall behind me. How long have I been here?
    The last thing I remember was entering a dark tunnel down the side of a mountain before something hard hit the back of my head and I lost consciousness. A small whimper passes my lips when I place my hand against the back of my head, a dull ache now radiating from the giant bump that has now formed on my head. If only I knew who hit me . . .
    My pup?
    My hands instinctively gravitate towards my bump, a sigh of relief escaping when I feel the little one kick against my hands,

no doubt sensing my distress. At least someone's still fighting . . . if only mummy could do the same.

"Adrenous."

I call out to him but I can't get through, the connection blocked by the steel cuffs around my wrists no less.

I blink my eyes a few times, attempting to get used to the darkness around me. I place my hand against the wall, using its sturdiness to help me rise to my feet. The clanging of metal is very loud in my ears but I don't miss the sound of someone groaning right next to me.

"Raven?" I breathed out.

"Alivia?" she calls back, panic seeping into her tone.

"Yes it's me." I duck back down, not expecting the wave of dizziness to crash through my throbbing head at the action. I'm forced to relax for a second before I can continue to kneel down, placing my hands out in front of me so that I'm able to feel where she is. I close my hands around Raven's forearms and help her rest her back against the wall.

"Where are we?" I can hear the movement of her head as she looks around the dark space. "I can't see anything."

"It's some sort of dungeon from what I can tell." That's if the chains, the darkness, and that putrid smell is anything to go by.

"Don't you mean hell?" A dark, hoarse voice echoes from the opposite end of the room followed by a fit of coughs. His voice alone has sent horrible chills down the back of my spine which was in no way a good sign.

"Who are you?" Raven is the first to break from our previous shock. Neither of us expected someone else to be locked up in here with us. Her voice is cold and demanding as it echoes towards the unknown man.

It's a while before he responds, me and Raven listening to the sound of his chains rattling as he shuffles in his spot. "I've been here so long, I don't remember."

How long must someone be locked up before they forget something as easy as their own name?

I don't like the idea of that one bit.

But the more frightening . . .

"What did you do to end up here in the first place?" My voice echoes through the dark, empty space. To be locked up by Krellin, I assume the man isn't human considering vampires compelled and drank from them. He's been here for a very long time so he could be a Wolven that was locked up for Krellin's own amusement.

The man's next words sent chills to the bone and have me believing my assumptions were completely off. "I've done awful things. So many awful things that would give a woman like you nightmares."

My eyebrows furrow of their own accord, completely perplexed by his answer. After the man erupts into another fit of coughs, I turn to Raven and whispered under my breath, "Do you have any way of getting us out of here?"

I hear her bringing her hands up towards me as she shakes her head and whispers back. "I'm afraid not, not with these enchanted cuffs around my wrists. I've never known magic like this. I'm worried Draven has become more powerful than I previously thought," Raven said. Now I'm worried too.

I reach my hand out into the darkness, my fingers tracing the dents of the symbols carved into the smooth silver of her cuffs. How could these symbols hold enough power to make someone as powerful as Raven powerless?

I suppose everything has its weakness . . .

"Raven." I whisper-shout, an idea sparking my excitement as I grip Raven's wrists.

"Ouch." Raven whimpers at my grip on her wrists.

"Oh, sorry." I loosen my grip and continue. "If these cuffs are enchanted with magic, shouldn't I be able to deflect it like I did with your brother?" I know the idea is far-fetched but it's my only one. There can be no harm in trying, right?

Raven is unsure. "Enchanted objects are different, I don't know if it'll work."

"No one can escape hell." The unknown man releases a throaty chuckle, his words meant to taunt me and Raven.

I narrow my eyes in the direction of his voice, choosing to ignore him before I turn back to Raven. "What do we have to lose?"

"You're right." She exhales, placing her wrists on my lap. "Do it."

"Okay," I wrap my fingers around the silver before closing my eyes. I take a few deep breaths and focus all my energy on removing any power from the cuffs. When I opened my eyes again, Raven gasped sofly. I can see why, seeing my eyes glowing a bright blue in the reflection of the silver. I've never seen anything like it as I look at the two glowing orbs looking back at me. Are they really my eyes?

"Your eyes are glowing!" The unknown man mutters, sounding completely terrified. "Only my mother's eyes ever glowed." He continues to mumble under his breath. Some garbage about his mother before his words become incoherent and I go back to concentrating on the enchanted cuffs around Raven's wrists.

I can feel that wave of power slowly growing stronger, that glowing blue aura surrounding me, lighting up the dingy cellar before I'm able to harness it and send it towards the cuffs. I can feel the power of the enchantments, the symbols engraved into the silver glowing red, trying to keep my power at bay. In the background, I can hear the man whimpering, afraid of the blue aura surrounding me. I can hear his chains clanging when he shuffles back into the wall, trying to escape the light after being surrounded by darkness for so long.

I fight the urge to demand he be's silent and choose to concentrate on breaking the enchantments.

I'm so close . . .

The door to the cellar snaps open, shocking me into jumping back, my hands falling from the silver cuffs. Both me and Raven snap our heads to the door, our hearts beating erratically at the sudden interruption. My eyes are no longer glowing, the blue aura now gone as me and Raven look up at Tyke with wide eyes.

Fortunately for us, it appears he didn't see what we were doing as he nonchalantly strides into the room. He's back to his preferred human form, looking down at us with those pools of blackness, his black hair combed back.

A dim light coming from outside the door now fills the dark cell and I'm able to see more clearly. Tyke continues to walk towards me and Raven, the both of us pressing our backs firmly against the wall, trying to put as much space between us and him.

My gaze snaps to the unknown man when he begins to laugh hysterically. The difference is I can add a description to his voice and I'm horrified to learn . . . I recognise him.

He's obviously aged a good two decades but his yellow eyes are too distinctive and I'm a hundred percent sure it's him. He's clearly malnourished, his cheekbones protruding from his shrivelled skin, the result of not eating properly for several years, or should I say the last twenty years of his life. His dark hair is overgrown, tangled and filled with grime and dirt, not having seen a pair of scissors since he first laid eyes on this cell. His overgrown beard is in the same condition, completely covering the lower half of his face.

His hysterical laughter goes on, completely blind to the fact that I'm watching him with horrified, wide eyes. Raven see's the look on my face and I can tell she's comparing his characteristics to Arif and me when her eyebrows furrow, shifting her eyes between him and me before her own eyes widen, finally realising who this man is.

Tyke narrows his eyes, the continuous laughter driving him to the edge before he snaps. "Be silent, Alijah!"

Alijah's laughter dies down, only to be replaced with his muttering. "B—be silent . . . You'll become king if you do what they say . . ."

He's completely mad.

Tyke is before Alijah quicker than I could blink, hovering over him as he continued to mutter to himself. Alijah looks up at him, his eyes slightly unfocused. "I want to be king now."

I know I wanted the man to pay for my mother's death and Arif's mother's death but I never pictured anything like this. He's completely broken from the inside, making it harder to imagine him killing anyone.

Is this pity? I think so. How can I pity a man so evil? My humanity may be the reason. I wish I could be as heartless towards him as he has been toward others but that just isn't me. I'm nothing like him and I'm completely grateful for that even though a part of me is angry at myself for feeling sorry for him.

Tyke bends down, speaking to the man as if he is a child. I suppose mentally, he is. "Not today. How about the next best thing?" Alijah pouts, a strange image, seeing a grown man pout like a child. Tyke shoots me a look, his lips rising up to form a sinister smirk. "Your daughter is over there, little Alivia all grown up."

Why you—

Alijah's head snaps towards me, his yellow eyes igniting with excitement. "You've come back! You want to help your father become a king." How the hell do you speak to someone who's completely insane?

It appears that I didn't have to worry about that, Tyke beating me to it when he answers for me. "Yes! Little Alivia is back home where she belongs to do what she was born to do." Tyke continues to glance my way, enjoying how his words caused my hands to turn into fists, anger bubbling as I struggle to remain silent. "But sadly, for now, she will have to come with me. My king will love to meet her."

Alijah returns to his muttering. I'm not even sure if he was listening properly in the first place. Tyke begins his descent towards me, my eyes narrowing as I back up further on the wall. Raven attempted to crawl in front of me, placing herself in his way. "You're not taking her anywhere," Raven said, causing Tyke to look down at her with an amused grin.

"Tut-tut, little Well." He kneels down towards her, me and Raven watching him cautiously as he taps the surface of her cuffs and chuckles, "You're no threat towards me. Now move or don't, it's not an issue for me though, I would much prefer the latter. At least that way I get to have some fun with you."

I can sense Raven's bravery faltering, but she's still stubborn, attempting to stare Tyke down. I placed my hand on her shoulder. Her blue eyes flickered from Tyke's to meet with mine. She shakes her head, already knowing what I'm going to say. "I won't let you get hurt because of me."

Raven sighs softly, a sad smile tracing her lips, "That's my job Alivia. Adrenous trusted me."

"I know, but there's nothing you can do for me right now."

She frowns, knowing I'm right. She doesn't stop me when I stand from behind her, her gaze cast down. She wallowed in the vulnerability she still isn't used to.

Tyke smirks brilliantly at me as I stared blankly at him, watching him place his hand in his pocket before pulling out a silver key. He detaches my cuffs from the chain connecting them to the wall. They made sure to keep the cuffs around my wrists, weakening my wolf and preventing me from contacting Adrenous. I hate that these pricks are smart.

I walk past him when he steps to the side, giving me some space to walk towards the door. I stop once I was through the door, turning round to give Raven a reassuring smile before Tyke locks the steel door once again, drowning Raven and Alijah in the darkness once again.

Tyke leads me down a dark, narrow hallway. A few flickering candles barely kept the shadows at bay as he leads me up a set of stairs. He holds open another door for me, stepping to the side and smirking down at me. I shot him a look before sauntering past him.

I can hear him chuckling behind me. "Does no one teach manners anymore?"

"Manners are reserved for those who earned them." I can sense his displeasure with my answer but he doesn't say anything. I can't help but smirk slightly at the victory.

I can't tell what sort of building I am in but the interior is a lot fancier than I imagined. The ceilings are fairly high, the walls decorated with a dark green wallpaper and the floors made from a white marble. My heels echo off the flooring as I look around, my eyebrows furrowing when I can't find any window in sight. I suppose there wouldn't be any, the purpose being to prevent sunlight from getting in.

Tyke takes the lead, walking in front so that he can lead me toward a pair of double doors. He taps his knuckles against the wooden doors before a 'Come in' resounds from the other side. I take in a deep breath, watching Tyke open the door for me.

Just as I'm about to enter, a man and a young boy walks out. The man has dark, brown hair and extremely tanned skin, almost as if he doesn't originate from this area. My eyes widen in surprise when his brown eyes darken, his wolf coming forward to show dominance, scowling down at me before he's on his way. The dominance this man radiates is almost a certain match to the dominance Adrenous possesses.

I stare after him, his young son hovering a moment longer. He has the same features as his father but his brown eyes still have the innocence that comes with being a child. His eyes flicker to my bump, staring at it with curiosity.

"Torben!" He reluctantly scurries after his father when his name is called.

My instincts tell me that man was Marx.

Tyke shuts the door once I've walked inside and leaves me alone to step further into the fairly spacious room, my gaze falling on the big seating area. Sofas of various shades of different greens were centred around a giant fireplace. A fire was already roaring with life, licking at the blackened coal.

Draven was comfortably seated in one of the single sofas, taking a sip of some fine wine when his eyes flickered to my small form. The corners of his eyes crinkled with laughter when my eyes fell on Krellin and I froze.

In Krellin's lap was a young woman very underdressed, her breasts and private areas barely covered by two small pieces of leather. Her blonde hair was draped to one side, allowing Krellin to sink his fangs into her exposed neck and drink from her. Her eyes were closed as she moaned. *Was she really enjoying that?*

I quickly turned on my heels, wanting to run out of the room but was disappointed to find the door locked. I cringed when I heard Krellin address me. "Leaving so soon?"

I reluctantly turn to face him. He's wiping his mouth with a handkerchief, the girl now sitting on the sofa beside him, looking up at me with a nasty look in her hazel eyes.

I don't like how she is currently regarding me, considering her own situation however, I excuse her behaviour as a consequence of compulsion. I return my gaze back towards Krellin, his icy, blue eyes sending a chill right down the centre of my spine when they flash with excitement. He examines me whilst gesturing to the sofa on the other side. "Please, take a seat."

My nostrils flared. I have no intention of sitting anywhere near him. He placed his elbow on his knee and leans forward with his fingers grasping his chin, a twinkle in his cold eyes. They briefly flicker to my bump. I instinctively placed my hand on the bump.

The corners of his lips curve. "I must insist you sit. It would be in the best interest for you and the child." I can sense the threat in his tone when his eyes flicker to Draven, a smirk playing on Draven's lips when my attention is brought towards him.

Draven may not be able to use his powers against me, but I don't doubt he can hurt me.

I unwillingly take a seat opposite Krellin and the girl who continues to look down upon me. I chose to pay her no interest and blankly stare into the cold blue eyes staring back at me.

"I've been waiting a long time for this," Krellin muses, still analysing me. "You're a haunting reflection of your mother."

How dare he mention her. She would still be alive if it weren't for him.

He despised my silence but makes no comment on it and moves on. "Finally you're back where you originally belong, here to serve me and lead your mate to his death. It shouldn't be long. Adrenous will arrive with my son and everything that I've been waiting years for will follow on from there."

Adrenous is bringing Tristan here? Of course, Adrenous must believe he can use Tristan as a bargaining chip. Adrenous is smart, he won't openly walk into Krellin's trap.

"None of those things are ever going to happen!" I snap, glaring at him. I was ready to fly out of my seat and smash his head in but I restrained from doing so.

"Oh but you will, Alivia." His confidence causes my courage to falter, my expression dropping slightly. "In time you will."

Whatever you say.

"Who was that man?" I said, glancing at the door I'd come through and ignoring what he had just said.

Krellin's eyes ignited. "Coen Marx, I believe you may have heard of him."

So I was right . . . And now I know his full name. "What would a man such as yourself need with a bunch of rogues?"

Krellin chuckles. "That is none of your concern." He stands, bringing the young woman with him. "The only thing you need to be concerned about is playing your part in my plan." He glances at Draven. "Draven will take it from here."

Take what from here? My gaze lock with Draven's, my earlier resolve now gone as the look in his eyes takes me completely off guard.

"Showtime."

✦○✦

CHAPTER FORTY-FOUR
A Burst Of Power

✦▢✦

ALIVIA

"I hope you're not too uncomfortable." Draven smirks after connecting my chains to the concrete wall behind me. I had been forced to sit down in one of the metal chairs and believe me, it wasn't comfortable at all.

I don't answer him, narrowing my eyes as I watch him move around the small, dingy room that he had taken us to.

The small space consists of two metal chairs, including the one I've been forced to sit in, whilst the other remains next to me. A workbench is pushed against the left wall, filled with scattered books written in an unknown language with lots of different symbols. Many different liquids and other tools I don't recognise are also on the table, unorganised and placed in random places.

One thing that catches my eye is a knife engraved with strange lettering and made from gold. I don't know what the purpose of the knife is but I doubt it's meant for buttering his toast.

The door to the room is heavy steel and the walls a dark concrete. My connection with my wolf is very limited, weakened by the steel cuffs as well as the steel on the floor and ceiling. I can't tap into her strength, nor communicate with her. This the most quiet she's ever been and I don't like it.

I'm completely on my own. I've already attempted to communicate with Adrenous on multiple occasions and I come up blank every single time without fail.

I can't imagine what he must be going through.

Draven draws my attention back to him when he speaks. He has his back to me and his eyes set on a particular book. "How did you feel being reunited with your father?"

"He's no father of mine." I retort. Draven gives me a sideways glance, his eyes flashing with amusement before he goes back to the book.

"Why did Krellin lock him up anyway?" I ask out of pure curiosity. I neither care nor wish to break him free from his imprisonment. I just want to know the reason behind his sentencing.

Draven places the book down on the table and turns to face me. "Alijah offered Krellin you in exchange for power over the surviving Wolvens. Since Alijah's part was never fully delivered, Krellin took his rage out on him, blaming him for letting your mother escape with you."

I suppose that makes sense. I wonder what Krellin would do when he finds out it was his own son who helped my mother.

I lean back in my chair, my shoulders tensing up when Draven leans down towards me. He scans me with those icy, blue depths. I narrow my eyes, watching him warily. "You're no longer useful to Krellin in the way Alijah presented to him however, that doesn't mean you aren't useful to me."

"What's that supposed to mean?" I question warily, my anxiety spiking at that mischievous glint in his eye.

I'd wish nothing more than to hide the fear clawing it's way up my throat but I haven't got it in me to try.

Draven places his hand over mine. I instinctively try to pull away but he doesn't allow it. "You have no idea how powerful you are. I can basically feel the power radiating off of you," He runs his hand up my arm, sending a sinister chill through my body. "It's the only reason you're still breathing. Well that, and bait to lead Adrenous here."

I shrug his hand away, spitting. "You sick son of a bitch!"

He grins. "I agree, my mother was a bitch." His words made me glare at him as he rises to his feet and steps away.

My eyes land on the steel door when I hear it scraping against the floor. I furrow my brows when I see Tyke shoving Raven inside. Her cheek is slightly red, evidence of a slap. I'm unable to hide the anger when her watery eyes lock onto mine and they flash with relief before a small smile comes forward. She can see the anger that I didn't bother to hide as Tyke forces her down into the seat beside mine.

While Tyke connected her chains to the wall, Draven stepped forward, his gaze shifting between us before that dark glimmer lights up his blue eyes. "Finally, sister. After years of running from me, you'll finally meet the same fate as our parents."

Raven can't help the tears falling down her pale cheeks, her eyes locked onto his. Her voice draws at my heartstrings. The pain she's done well to keep hidden is completely surfacing. "How could you, Draven? They loved us! They loved you!"

Draven's eyes flash, a scowl pulling at his lips when he retorts, "That's where you're wrong." He turns to the table and pulls open a drawer. "Little Raven, always the favourite. It didn't matter what I did, I was never good enough. You were always more powerful and I was always seen as weak and incompetent."

"That's not true!" Raven snaps.

"Oh but it is. But you were blinded by the shower of approval our parents bestowed upon you." Draven inclines his head towards her whilst pulling something out of a drawer. "Do you know how weak and helpless I felt?" Raven doesn't answer, both our eyes catching the glimpse of something silver. Our eyes widen when we see the sharp point of a needle. "Well, you're about to." He chuckles before turning towards me.

My breath catches in my throat. I attempt to move back, the legs of my chair scraping against the steel of the floor, wanting nothing more than to put a good amount of distance between me and that needle. My eyes lock onto the sharp point meant for me, shaking my head. "Get away!"

His chest vibrates, a dark chuckle leaving his lips as he continues forward. Raven tries to break her chains from the wall, her attempts completely useless as she watches her brother stalk towards me. "Please, Draven. She didn't do anything to you."

Raven's begging does nothing to halt Draven's pursuit, his expression dark as he raises his hand holding the needle. "Remain still, it'll be less painful that way."

"No, no . . ." My body begins to tremble under his intense gaze. I've never felt so scared and as helpless as Raven must feel right now.

Adrenous!

The point of the needle in stabbed into my wrist, a cry leaving my lips at the sharp pain that travels up my arm. I instinctively try to pull my arm away but that only makes it worse. Draven quickly presses his thumb down on the pad of the needle, placing a strange liquid into my bloodstream.

He clicked his tongue. "If only you had just remained still."

Adrenous! Help . . .

I slump back in the chair. I could feel my eyes rolling to the back of my head. My body feels completely weak and drained. What's happening to me?

I can hear Draven snickering through my drowsy state. I blink up at him, my eyebrows furrowing when I see two blurred Dravens smirking down at me. "Liquid Silver does wonders."

Silver?

My senses are delayed and I was barely able to hear Raven beside me. "Stop . . .please," she said. It takes so much effort just to face her, and just like her brother, I see two of her staring at me.

The pain and hopelessness in her gaze doesn't help the panic setting in my breathing and beating heart.

All my focus is going into controlling my harsh breathing that I hadn't even realised Draven was now kneeling down in front of me.

Raven was still sobbing, her words incoherent as I lazily blink at Draven, my blurry vision hurting my eyes. It's a struggle just to keep my eyes open and focused on Draven's dark grin as he places his hands over my numb ones.

I can't feel his touch. My body and mind was completely numb, overwhelmed by the pins and needles that erupted across my skin. It's also fill my head. My ears perked slightly when Draven's mouth moves, his words following shortly after due to my delayed hearing. I don't understand the language in which he's speaking.

He chants the words repeatedly and I can feel a tightness form in the pit of my stomach. I squint at the blue aura beginning to radiate from my form, Draven's eyes flashing with awe as he continues chanting. I can see the reflection of my glowing eyes in his as he smirks up at me before his chanting changes, more words that I don't understand spoken.

My aura begins to fade, my power slowly draining as Draven revels the taste of my power that's entering him. No . . .no . . .no . . .

I felt a power shift before a scream tears from Draven's lips. The power tears its way out from his being and returns to me, his eyes widening with fear before shifting to anger. "What the fuck?"

I don't have the energy to react but I'm just as equally surprised. Draven looks at me suspiciously. "What did you do?" *What?* "What the fuck did you do?" He screams more aggressively, gripping my jaw to force me to focus in on him.

"N—nothing," I groaned, too tired to fight him or argue.

Raven is quick to my defence. "Her power deflected you, that's why it didn't work. It isn't her fault."

Draven doesn't even pay her a glance, his eyes staring into mine as if he's thinking of another way to extract the power from me. His eyes flash, an idea sparking in that cruel mind of his before his eyes trail downwards and lock onto my bump. *I don't fucking think so . . .*

"Get . . . away . . . from . . . me," I managed to get out, the liquid silver still in full effect.

Draven shakes his head, his eyes glinting with excitement. I lean away, trying to place my hands over my bump for protection but the chains limit my hand movement and I'm unable to. I'm afraid and it doesn't help that the silver had me unfocused and drained, unable to fight his pursuit.

My head swims as I try to focus on Draven, muttering for him to stay away but of course he doesn't listen. I struggle in my seat after he places both his palms against my stomach. The pup kicks at his hands, sensing my distress and causes Draven's excitement to grow. "Such a powerful, little thing."

"Adrenous . . . We need you!" I can sense my connection to Adrenous unblocked for just a split second before I was shut out again, the effort pulling on my drained state further.

I started to cry. I can't even protect my child, how can I ever be expected to protect a kingdom? My child doesn't deserve this. They're not even born yet and already they're being exposed to the harsh realities of the unkind world. I wish I had the strength to fight him but I'm too weak and vulnerable. He made sure of that. Mummy's sorry.

I'm barely able to pay attention to the words falling from Draven's lips. It's a similar chant to before but I'm certain a few words have been added or replaced. My child shifts inside my stomach, kicking me repeatedly in the ribs as Draven chants and smiles. All I can do is cry.

A red aura-like mist comes from my bump and flows right into Draven, his eyes glowing a dark, maroon red before it dies down along with his chants and he's left grinning with happiness.

"W—what did you do?" I demand weakly, my child now completely still inside my womb.

Draven is too busy focusing on the new power surging through his veins as a look of awe crosses his features. "So much power."

"Alivia, I'm sorry." Raven sobs but I'm in too much shock to make her feel better about this. I've never been so frightened, I can practically feel my whole body shaking. I don't even have the energy to continue crying. I'm also angry but it's not enough to accumulate the power and energy that's been taken by the silver.

Draven stands to his feet and grabs the golden knife from the table, causing my heart to beat erratically, "Please don't kill me."

"Don't worry, this isn't mean for you." He assures before turning towards Raven, "Are you ready to join our loving parents, sister?"

Raven drops her head, closing her eyes, the fight within her completely diminished. Draven stops in front of her, twirling the knife between his fingers. "But first, it's about time someone more worthy has that power of yours."

Draven kneels down and with his free hand, he captures Raven's chin, forcing her to look up at him. She stares at him blankly as he tilts his head to the side and asks, "What, no last words for your brother?"

"You're not my brother," she responds, her expression blank and unaffected by his taunting. He frowns at her words as she adds, "But don't worry, you'll get what's coming to you one day."

"Is that all?" He expected more from her but she had nothing else to say and nods her response. "Very well." He wraps his fingers around her wrists and begins chanting, Raven's power flowing from her being and entering Draven.

Soon he'll have everything he wants and we're too weak to stop it.

To my surprise, Draven's chanting is broken by Tyke's intrusion as he stands behind the half opened steel door, "Draven, Master demands your presence immediately." Tyke flinches when Draven growls and snaps his head towards him, clearly pissed off.

"Can't you see I'm in the middle of something?"

The liquid silver doesn't have as much of an impact on my senses this time and I can see Tyke clearly as his gaze flickers up, shifting between me and Raven, now understanding what Draven means by "something." He looks back down at Draven, his black eyes apologetic. "I apologise, but master did say it was urgent."

Draven growls in frustration but reluctantly moves away from Raven. He shoves Tyke out of the way and slams the door shut behind him, leaving me and Raven alone in the dark room.

I glance at Raven, her form shaking slightly. She's clearly still in shock, having her powers nearly taken from her. She's not out of the woods yet, It won't be long until Draven returns to finish what he started.

"Raven." My voice is hoarse and weak, reflecting how I feel. She raises her head to look at me and the pain behind her blue gaze has my heart clenching. "W-we need to get out of here-"

"It's too late Alivia." Her voice is cold and unsympathetic, her will to survive gone. "I've failed you. I failed your pup. And I failed Adrenous. I'd rather die here now than fail anyone else."

"Raven, please don't give up like this." I plead, reaching my hand over to place it over hers, running my thumb soothingly across the back of her hand. She doesn't react, her gaze plastered to the steel floor. I wish I could get us out of here. I feel a small spark jolt my hand when I briefly touch the engraved, silver cuffs around her wrists, causing me to retreat my arm back to the armrest of my chair.

Raven felt it too, her eyes snapping to the cuff around her wrist. "Liv did you just . . . ?"

"I-I don't know. I just wished I could get us out of here and it happened." I explain, hope simmering within my chest.

"Try again!" She encourages me, the fight in her eyes returning, chasing away her fear and hopelessness.

I still feel completely drained, physically and emotionally. But if I can just force myself to channel enough energy to free Raven from the cuffs for a second then I have to at least try. I owe it to my pup to try.

I poured any energy I have left into focussing on this one task, my eyes closed tight. My arms tensed as I draw on any power I can muster. I feel a tiny knot form in the centre of my stomach, my confidence in this working increasing. I can feel my eyes shift to that glowing blue and from behind my closed eyelids, I can see the blue light surrounding me.

Raven releases a breath, hope seeping into her tone. "I—it's working."

I open my eyes, my lips twitching up after I see the red glow of the engraved symbols dying out, losing their power that prevents Raven from using hers. The cuffs split down the middle, plummeting to the steel ground when they fall from around Raven's wrists.

Her eyes light up, feeling reenergised from her earlier vulnerable state. She rubs at the red marks left behind by the cuffs before she glances up at me concerned. "Are you okay?"

"Yes, just a little drained." Drained is a complete understatement but I don't need her worrying about me when we need to hurry up and get out of here.

Raven flicks her now free wrist, breaking my own silver cuffs along with the chains that were connecting them to the wall. I can feel a wave of depleted energy restore itself back within my being. I no longer feel as drained as I did before. My first thought is Adrenous but our connection is still blocked by the silver still running through my veins and the steel that surrounds me.

"Thank you." I smiled, rubbing my own sore wrists. We both stand but I wasn't prepared for the wave of dizziness that swam around my head. I staggered back slightly.

"Woah, careful." Raven quickly wraps an arm around my back. "Come on, let's get you out of here." I nodded my head as we start to walk towards the steel door.

Raven was about to pull it open when someone from the other side beats her to it, my eyes widening to see that Draven's returned. He's taken aback, not expecting to find us unchained from our seats. His eyes slowly darken before narrowing and he bursts with rage. "How the fuc—"

Raven quickly used her free hand to send him flying back, his head hitting the wall behind him. "Quick! We got to move." She walks us both past him and through the dimly lit hallway. We see a pair of stairs and quickly ascend them. When we reached the top, we found a wide open floor plan, a pair of double doors on the other side that lead to the outside.

Raven makes a beeline for them, bringing me with her as I struggle not to fall on the wooden floor. We come to a sudden halt when Draven suddenly blocks our path, my eyes growing wide when he stabs Raven in the chest with a golden knife.

No!

Raven stares wide-eyed at her brother. She's in too much shock to speak as Draven smirks down at her. Her legs gave out, her arm falling from around my shoulders. I quickly grab her, easing her to the floor. My own shock made it difficult for me to speak. The blood from her wound is staining her clothes and mine but I don't care. I feel as though someone has taken my heart and snapped it into two right before my eyes.

Raven holds my arm tightly, the light within her eyes flickering away as mine swell with tears. I hold her close, oblivious to Draven's presence. "Y-you'll be okay . . .Just don't close your eyes. Stay with me." My heart is pounding, a strong ache in my stomach at the thought of losing her. "J-just stay with me, okay?"

"I-I'm s-s-sorry." She chokes out, a sad smile tracing her lips as a single tear falls from the corner of her eye and trails down her cheek. "I—It's my fault. I'm s—sorry I couldn't help your pu—"

"No." I stroke her cheek with the back of my hand, trying to keep pressure on her wound with the other. "You did everything a friend should, none of this was your fault."

Raven smiles at me before her eyes flicker to my bump. She places her hand on my stomach, my brows furrowing when that warm glow illuminates from the contact. My pup moves for the first time since Draven touched my stomach and the action brings a second of relief to my eyes before the glow fades and I'm brought back to Raven in my arms.

She smiles up at me. "I-I can't br-bring back what was lost b-but at l-least s-she w-won't be a-alone."

"I-I d-don't u-understand." I sob, my efforts of keeping the pressure on her wound failing.

I'm losing her.

"I-I love you." She whispers, her words caressing me.

I force a smile, trying to hide the pain and sadness. "I love you too."

Raven smiles, her blue eyes beaming up at me with pure love and happiness before they start to close, my sobs growing louder as I watch the light within her eyes diminish. I release my hand from her wound, wrapping them around her to bring her body closer to me as the sobs continue to wrack my body.

My body freezes when a dark, cruel chuckle fills the air around me, my eyes snapping to Draven. "Don't waste your tears," He walks forward and smirks down at his sisters lifeless body in my arms. "She's with our 'loving' parents now."

Bastard!

My veins are flooded with white hot fury and I didn't even have to think before my eyes glowed blue. The aura surrounding me pulsed to life, giving me the energy that I didn't think I could have. For the first time, Draven looked worried and I watch him retreat slightly. I gently place Raven's head on the floor before standing on my feet to face the bastard who killed her.

"Don't do this, Alivia. You wouldn't want anything else to happen to your pup." He threatens me.

I hesitate for a split second and he uses that to fly forward, the knife soaked with Raven's blood, headed straight for my stomach.

I instinctively shove my hands forward, feeling a new type of energy crackle at the edge of my fingertips.

My aura pulses with electric before exploding out of me. I scream with rage, allowing the energy to take out everything in its path, including Draven. I watch as he's expelled from the room, sent away to who knows where and I don't care either. As long as he's as far away from the people I love as possible.

Everything that resided inside the room is now shattered or broken.

The burst of energy returns to my body but it doesn't disappear. My now empty blue eyes glowed in the direction of the doors that lead to the outside, their windows now shattered. I have no intention of leaving this place. Instead, I face another set of doors that leads back inside of the castle.

Time to make Krellin and the others pay.

✦○✦

CHAPTER FORTY-FIVE
A Fight Between Alphas

✦▢✦

Adrenous

"Fuck!" Arif growls. I turn to find him wiping his boot on the grass floor. "I've stepped in fucking deer shit." He grumbles, crinkling his nose at the stench that is now attached to his boot.

"You're not coming near me with that smell." Rylan grimaced, stepping as far away from Arif as he can. Arif growls, fisting his hands at his side.

I release a heavy sigh, shaking my head before turning back the other way. When will those two grow up?

About ten feet away from us is the ridge of a mountain, lots of trees and overgrown foliage covering most of its surface area. I can't see any evidence of life or indicators that show someone has been living within the mountains. It's just like all the other times I've searched this area looking for Krellin's hideout.

I face away from the mountain to face Tristan. He's laying low behind a few trees with the other men, all of them silent, following my order. There may be no signs of anyone lurking but that doesn't mean anyone isn't, which is why I have kept us a safe distance from the mountain, hidden in the treeline.

Tristan was squinting at the mountain when his green gaze was suddenly drawn to me. "Where did you say the passage was located?"

Tristan lifts his arm and points his index finger at a particular area of the mountain. I look at where he's pointing. My eyes narrow on a particular tree, it's roots and leaves overgrown, hiding the mountain wall behind it. "The roots and leaves cover a narrow tunnel that takes you under the mountain before it opens up to the other side."

Hmm . . . No wonder I have never found his lodgings. The tree completely covered the area and even with Tristan saying the tunnel is behind it, I still can't see it. Damn that fucking tree.

"Let's go." I order, waving my hand in the direction of the mountain. My men creep up from behind the trees. They remain low, the tall grass that covers the space between the treeline and the mountain giving them enough cover to stay hidden.

I remain slightly behind, scanning the area, including the cliff faces of the mountains, making sure there is no one hidden. I don't need anyone alerting our presence to Krellin when we're so close to getting my family back. If he's so much as touched a hair on her head, I will reign down fury on anyone involved.

When I get her back, she won't be leaving my side. Ever. After today Krellin will be as good as dead. Him and anyone else who poses a threat to my family.

I command my men to stop and get into position when we close in around the tree. Arif looks the tree up and down. Annoyance is clear in his tone when he snaps his gaze to Tristan. "You're telling me that because of a fucking tree, we couldn't find the bastards hideout." Tristan watches him warily when Arif chuckles but there is no humour in the action. "Oh, now I'm pissed.'

Pissed isn't how I would describe it. Livid. Now that's more like it.

"Tristan." Tristan shifts his wary eyes from Arif to me, the wariness not wavering in his gaze. "I need to know exactly who your father has watching his home."

"That may be a little difficult, I've not exactly been in the loop for the past few months." He huffs. I would have outed him for his attitude if it weren't for the current situation, but I have to admit the boy is right. I allow him to continue. "However, if my father's really made an alliance with the rogues, I think it's safe to expect both vampires and rogues keeping guard."

"I agree." The boy is smarter than I expected. I'll note that for the future. I turn back towards me men, all eyes set on me. "Your orders are to wait here until further instructions. Tristan, Arif and Rylan"—one by one, they perk up at the sound of their names—"we'll scout the tunnel and observe from the other side. None of you are to engage, am I clear?"

Rylan and Tristan nod their heads except for Arif. Instead, he narrows his eyes at Tristan. "I'm watching you, kid."

Tristan becomes defensive, a trace of hurt flashing in his eyes. "I want to help Alivia just as much as you."

"I doubt that." Arif scoffs. Tristan narrows his eyes at Arif, tension simmering between them.

"Enough." I demand, my eyes snapping at the both of them. "Arguing will not get my family back so I would advise you hold your tongues."

Arif grumbles, shaking his head but doesn't protest. Tristan sighs, crossing his arms across his chest and doesn't argue either. Once I'm satisfied they'll behave, I turn back towards the tree, moving the overgrown leaves to the side. I can see parts of the tunnel. It's dark and narrow but we'll fit through. I channel my wolf's strength, snapping the branches away and throwing them aside. I don't stop until the entire tunnel is visible and easily accessible.

I make the first move, ducking my head to avoid hitting my head on the roof of the cave. The other three follow my lead, crouching low in order to fit through the cramped space. The tunnel is fairly steep and it remains that way for at least a hundred yards before the floor evens out and a dim glow is visible a few more yards away. As we approach the dull light, it brightens and I'm relieved to see the opening which should lead to Krellin's estate.

Before I peak out of the opening, I turn to the other three, whispering, "Stay here while I examine the area."

Arif is the only one that is annoyed with that order, his bulky form uncomfortably squished between the hard walls of the tunnel. However, despite his obvious annoyance, I'm surprised he doesn't protest, allowing me to quickly turn back towards the opening.

I carefully step out of the opening and onto a short cliff that overlooks the land beneath it. Luckily for us, there is a narrow pathway that leads down the side of the mountain, making it easy to reach the ground. I crouch down, approaching the edge of the cliff in able to see what lays below.

Trees as far as the eye can see surrounds the small, open area next to the mountain. The trees a perfect barrier between the small space and the rest of the world. Just like the mountain protected them from me. The ground within the small, open space is covered in beautiful, green grass, professionally tamed and groomed. It's clear the vampires take care of the small living area they've dominated.

I noticed there are many rogues and vampires surrounding a building. They're dressed in armour, clearly prepared for battle. It's obvious they expect an attack from me, many paranoid eyes continuously scanning the area, including the cliff I'm leaning over. If it weren't for my quick reflexes, they could have easily spotted me by now.

I quickly lean back over when their eyes fall from the cliff. My attention is taken from the men to lock onto the giant, estate building they're protecting. The building occupies a great deal of the centre and gives of more of a castle vibe than a normal estate, the walls similar to mine though there are no visible windows. I suspected that would be the case.

Apart from having no windows it's almost as if he got the idea for this building from my own estate. There are also many sub buildings that branch off from this one, possibly living quarters for his people or cells for the humans he chooses to enslave and feed from.

Somewhere inside one of those buildings is where Krellin is keeping Alivia.

I'm close, little wolf. I'm close.

When I'm safely back inside the tunnel, Arif asks, "What did you see?"

"Mine and Tristan's suspicions were right, both rogues and vampires are surrounding Krellin's estate, all dressed in protective armour. They're clearly prepared for a fight so it will be difficult to catch them by surprise." A surprise attack would have been our best chance but it's clear they have the advantage in this battle. The trees are their defence in case they need to run away and our only access to Krellin's estate is through this small, cramped tunnel.

"Fuck," Arif growls, not happy with my assessment of Krellin's grounds and the difficulties we'll have to face in order to get his sister, my Ali, back. Arif's eyes snap to Tristan, his anger pushing him to become irrational. "We have his son, I say we trade the boy for Alivia."

"Arif." I warn but he carries on.

"What? The boy said he wanted to get her back to, let him prove it."

I'm about to snap at Arif when Tristan stops me. "Arif's right."

Arif's eyes snap down at him in surprise, not expecting the boy to actually agree with him. Even I'm surprised by the boy's boldness. Tristan uncomfortably shifts when he finds all of us looking down at him expectantly. He quickly said, "Those men know my father is the king, they'll immediately see me as one of them and try to save me in order to please my father. I propose, you take me down there as a hostage, they won't expect me to be on your side, giving us the surprise and the advantage."

Arif chuckles, patting Tristan on the back. "Way to go kid, you proved yourself."

Tristan rubs his back, unhappy with how Arif chose to praise him. "I just want to help Liv. This has nothing to do with me having to prove myself to any of you." Arif narrows his eyes at Tristan but one look from me and he shakes his head.

"It's a good plan, Tristan. It might just work." I offer him my own praise and he appreciates it more than he did to Arif's. Let's put this plan into motion.

We spend the next hour suiting up my men with sufficient armour as well as familiarising them with a tactical plan that will help us grab the advantage against Krellin's army. Tristan allowed us to tie his wrist with some rope which will help us fool them into thinking he's a hostage. At the same time, it can easily be broken when Tristan needs to fight.

I'm back to standing on the cliff that overlooks Krellin's estate, careful not to be seen just yet. Arif is behind me, a smirk on his lips as he holds and pulls Tristan's 'restraints unnecessarily harshly, causing Tristan to grit his teeth and hiss in pain.

"That's enough, Arif." I chastise him. Arif rolls his eyes but loosens his hold on Tristan's restraints. "Now come on."

My men remain close behind as we make our way down the path that will take us to Krellin's grounds. The second my foot touches the neatly groomed grass, I hear the rogues and vampires yelling to one another. Some men form a barrier with their bodies around the building whilst many of them run towards us. They halt in their tracks when I take Tristan from Arif, threatening them. "One more move and Krellin's only son will be harmed!"

Tristan pretends to be afraid, his eyes wide, frantically shifting between the confused and shocked expressions of the Vampires and rogues glancing at each other, not knowing what to do next. Even I'm convinced by his act.

One of the Vampires sneers. "You won't harm him, we have your mate inside."

My nostrils flare, fire crossing my vision and not even Tristan expects it when within seconds I'm holding the sharp point of a knife against his throat. This time he doesn't need to pretend to be afraid, fear and doubt flashing in his gaze, the vampires and rogues now hesitating, taking a slow step back.

"Perhaps this time you'll take my threat seriously. Now, where is my mate?" I'm in no mood for patience, the dominance seeping from my tone has the bloodsuckers' eyes shooting open with fear and shock. The rogues uncomfortably shift in their spot but it appears my dominance has no effect on them. How is that possible?

Unless . . . They have their own Alpha.

Rogues with an alpha? That's completely unheard of. They have a leader, that I know, but one with alpha status can't be possible.

"Where is she?" I demand, my wolf pushing towards the forefront of my mind. His wrath was more vengeful and destructive than my own. I doubt there is anything in this world he wouldn't do to bring her back to us.

"Woah, calm down, no need to do anything hasty." A voice calls from behind the rogues, all of them now moving to the side to make a path for someone, placing them in my line of sight. My eyes widen and my shoulders tensed. I feel as though I'm looking into the eyes of a ghost.

His dark brown eyes light up, amused by my confused and shocked expression when they meet with mine. His skin is darker than those around him, a trait that originates from the pack he was once from. I was certain my father had taken him, along with the Aibek pack, out of existence after his father committed a heinous crime. I'm fuzzy with the details but there is no way Coen could have survived and yet . . .here he was.

He's not wearing armour like the others, his chest visible along with a scar that runs down his right side, the rest of it hidden behind his breeches. He doesn't stop walking until he's a few feet away from me and Tristan, his eyes glimmering with amusement as they shift between me, to Tristan, and then his gaze locks onto someone behind me.

Arif is the first to speak, his voice dripping with venom. "You should be dead!"

Coen's eyes narrow on Arif, a smirk still playing on his lips. "I don't know about 'should be', but I can see why you'd be surprised to see me, considering what your pack did to mine." His eyes snap back to mine, silently making me responsible for the actions of my father.

"Stand down Coen, this is between me and Krellin." I warn him, my wolf coming forward as my eyes flash, challenging his own wolf when it makes an appearance too.

Coen scoffs, shaking his head. "That's where you're wrong, Adrenous. Think of it as revenge for all the lives your father took that day, including my own father's."

"Even you can admit my father's actions were just."

Coen shakes his head, a dark snicker resonating from his chest. "I'm afraid I don't agree with you."

"So now what, you'll help Krellin by allowing his only son to die." I threaten, the knife pressed against Tristan's neck now drawing a dribble of blood when I press down harder for emphasis. Tristan hisses through his teeth at the sharp pain. *Sorry, kid.*

Coen snickers again, his actions taking me of guard for a second before I realise he has no value for Tristan's life. "I'm sorry, little prince,"—Tristan sneers at the way Coen addresses him—"but unfortunately, my loyalties to your father don't extend to you."

So much for the plan. I growl in frustration before releasing Tristan. Within seconds he's snapped the restraints from his wrists, retorting "Fortunately, I have no loyalties towards you either." Coen's own guard drops for a second, him and the others regarding

Tristan as a traitor. It gave me the time I needed to signal my men to attack.

It appears this is the only moment of surprise we're going to get for this battle and my men take full opportunity. They striked at anyone close by as soon as the signal was given.

Me and Coen remain in the centre of a horrendous battle. Tristan is now sinking his fangs into the base of a rogue's neck, draining his life force. Arif and Rylan are back to back, punching and kicking Vampires that attempt to attack or slash them. The rest of my men are fighting one on one battles with either rogue or Vampire, few bodies from both sides dropping to the ground. The battle is equal, neither side winning or losing.

Coen's dark gaze locks with mine, the dominance radiating from the both of us. Coen takes a small step forward, his gaze never wavering when I make my own step forward. We each examine other, taking note of any weakness and possible strengths.

"You made a mistake aligning yourself with Krellin, Coen," I said as we circle one another cautiously, waiting for the other to make a move.

He narrowed his eyes, not caring for my opinion on his choices. "That's for me to decide. Unlike you, I've kept my pack strong, not allowing the likes of a girl, especially one that's only half Wolven, to weaken my men and cloud my decisions."

"You forget 'that girl' is my mate, and she is no weakness. She is my strength," I said. Coen has allowed himself to become unattached and cold, believing it is the only way to strengthen his pack. But he is wrong. Emotions and the people we care for are what gives us the strength to fight.

"My men, especially my son, will never let the likes of a girl weaken them. You and your mate are my example. You do nothing but prove my point," Coen finishes before making a move, his leg shifting forward as his right shoulder rolls back before he's throwing a punch directly towards my face. I dodge to the side. "I truly feel sorry for you if you believe mates are nothing but a weakness."

After Coen dodges my own strike, he retorts, "I don't believe, I know."

I exhale an angry breath, my eyes igniting with fire before my claws elongate and fangs protrude from their hiding place. My eyes flash, my wolf challenging him directly. Coen gets the message, agreeing to the challenge when he decides to bare his own fangs, slashing his claws towards my chest. I jump back, allowing his momentum to carry him forward before I kick out my leg, knocking the air from his lungs when my foot catches him in the ribs.

Coen growls. His eyes snapped back up to mine, but he doesn't allow his anger to control his next move, taking his time to assess me once again. "What's seems to be the problem, Coen?" I said.

His eyes flashed with anger, my plan to provoke him paying off, "There's no problem on my end, though I fear what your mate must be going through right now. Yet here you are, unable to run in and stop it."

I glared at him. It appears I'm not the only one who knows how to provoke their opponent. The only difference is he's right, my mate could be going through something awful right now.

And just like that... *"Adrenous... We need you!"*

Coen smirks when my whole demeanour shifts, desperation and horror contorting my expression as soon as Ali's world ring through my skull before utter silence ensues, leaving me no way to get through to her. *Fuck*!

Coen used the opportunity to strike me in the nose, a crack resonating from the action as blood drips from my nostrils. He then goes on to slash my chest with his claws, slicing deep through the flesh as I growl with pain. I shove my hands into his chest, propelling him back and away from me, his back hitting the grass floor. Now I'm desperate to get this fight over and done with. Alivia needs me.

Coen struggled back onto his feet as I stalk towards him, my eyes flashing with dark intent. Coen dashes forward, nearly striking me in the face with his claws. I quickly lift my arms, deflecting his fist before I quickly curve my fingers around his wrists, forcing his body toward me. I smash my head into his, full force. Coen grunts, his top lip cut open from being smacked into his teeth along with a bloodshot eye that he now struggles to keep open as he staggers back.

However, even with his now disorientated vision, Coen doesn't let up. His assaults become quicker and more aggressive as he flies towards me once again. Evading his movements and matching his speed, I throw a punch into his right shoulder, knowing that with his damaged right eye, his reflex will be slow and he won't be able to deflect me quick enough.

He's now off balanced, and I use this moment to bury my claws into his stomach, his eyes almost bulging from their sockets when that searing heat of pain travels up through his intestines. I curled my fingers buried deep within his intestines. "You made a mistake, Coen." His eyes flash with fear, "I'm sorry you couldn't see that soon enough." I tear my hand from his stomach, his intestines spilling into the floor as he drops to his knees.

I notice Rylan and Arif now standing close by, Krellin and Coen's men either dead or escaped into the woods like I suspected they would. Coen's flickering eyes shift between us as we watch him take in his last few breaths, unable to speak due to the blood spilling up through his airways and then dribbling from the corners of his mouth.

I furrow my brows at the sound of screaming. A young boy with dark eyes and hair that are similar to Coen's rushed towards him. The child's eyes are blurry with tears. Arif bends down and grabs the young boy before he can reach Coen. The boy kicks and screams, cursing at Arif and crying for his father. I order Arif to let the child go and he does so with great reluctance. The child deserves to say goodbye to his father.

The boy struggles out of Arif's grasp running towards his dying father. "D—dad?"

His father is unable to respond, choking on his own blood. No child should ever have to see their father that way but it appears this boy has most likely seen a lot he shouldn't have. He continues to sob, easing his father's body to the ground when his life source flickers out. The young boy closes his father's open and lifeless eyes before he unexpectedly rises to his feet and shoves his body into me, throwing his tiny fists into my stomach.

"You fucking monster!" Strong words spill from his lips. I made a move to contain his movements but he evades me and steps away, his once innocent eyes now flashing with anger that a child should never possess. And that anger's aimed at me. "I'll fucking kill you!"

Arif storms towards the boy but he runs away from him and into the dense woods. Arif runs after him, attempting to grab the child but he quickly ducks behind some vines making it difficult for Arif to grab him.

"Let the boy go, Arif. Getting Alivia back is the priority," I ordered.

He grinds his teeth in frustration. "Fine." He storms back towards us. "But I'm going after him later." Good enough for me.

We start towards the castle, my men taking the lead on this one, cautiously opening the doors and searching all corners for anyone living or dead. Once they signalled that it's clear, me, Arif and Rylan head inside. There are no windows, no lights apart from a few flickering candles barely keeping the shadows at bay. We storm the hallways, heading towards a pair of double doors at the end of the corridor, my instincts telling me that's where we'll find Krellin, and then hopefully Alivia shortly after.

When we burst through the doors, we find Tyke shuffling back, his eyes bulging as we made our way through the massive hall.

My eyes lock with Krellin's. He's seated in his throne that sits atop a podium with a human woman dressed rather inappropriately seated on his lap. Krellin's eyes snap toward our direction before shifting in his seat and sending the woman away. His eyes don't meet mine, instead they lock onto Tristan before narrowing.

"Tristan, what the fuck are you doing?" Krellin demands, his voice dripping with anger.

Tristan ignores his father's question. "Where's Alivia, Father?"

Krellin stumbles for a moment, speechless by the shocking revelation that his son is a traitor. He doesn't answer, snapping, "Why the fuck would you want to help that girl?"

"Easy," Tristan remarks, his eyes flashing with anger, recalling a memory from his past, "You killed my mother, used her to bear and raise me until you were done with her." Krellin is about to argue but Tristan doesn't give him the chance, "But not only did you kill my mother, Asmara was used for the same thing, and even after I saved her, you killed her."

Krellin's eyes flash with disbelief. "It was you?"

"I'm surprised it took you this long to figure that out." Tristan admits. The way he regards his father proves to me that Tristan doesn't care for him. "I won't allow you to do the same to Alivia."

Krellin shakes his head, the shock from realising his son is a traitor now gone. He surprised us all when a snicker escaped his lips. "Draven's already taken care of that for me."

"What?" I snap, my heart clenching. "You best be fucking wrong." I seethed, threatening him. "Now where the fuck is she?"

Before Krellin can answer, our attention was drawn to a pair of doors on the left side of the room when they fly of their hinges and splinter apart on the wall opposite. My eyes widen when Alivia enters the room, a powerful, static electricity radiating from her body, her eyes glowing with power but they're empty, completely cold. *Little wolf, what have they done to you?*

My heart plummets when my eyes snap to her dress. Her dress is coated in blood. I was so close to losing it until I realised it wasn't hers. Where's Raven?

"Alivia?" I called. She doesn't respond. She's completely oblivious to everyone else in the room apart from Tyke and Krellin, her eyes narrowing on the both of them as they cower before her.

Just one flick of her wrist and Tyke's flesh burned away, screams tearing from his lips as she forces him to shift back to the true, ugly monster he is. In the next instant, she's in front of him, kneeling down towards him. Tyke stares into her empty gaze with fear and what he sees has him whimpering. She wraps her hand around his throat, that blue static energy extending from her palm to wrap around his body.

His bloodcurdling screams echo around the room, the energy drawing on his life force until the screams stopped. She released his throat, his body slumping to the ground, dead.

Then her eyes turn to Krellin. Her next target . . .

✦○✦

CHAPTER FORTY-SIX
Come Back To Me

✦▫✦

ADRENOUS

Krellin stumbles out of his throne, cowering from a beyond pissed off Alivia. I don't know what happened to her but that wasn't my Ali I was staring at. This woman was cold and dead set on getting the revenge for whatever they had done to scorn her.

I feel my heart clench at the way Alivia still doesn't offer me a glance. The way she moves is slow, the energy around her reaching out and growing bigger, causing Krellin's fear to grow. Alivia doesn't even seem happy that she has Krellin cowering before her. She was walking towards him as if she has all the time in the world to get her revenge.

Krellin runs down the steps and toward the direction of my men. I suppose he deemed us a lot less frightening than Alivia as she continues her pursuit. Her aura continued to expand out, sizzling and crackling. Her eyes held no sign of emotion or even pain. Just plain emptiness.

Tristan and Rylan grab Krellin before he could run away from a fate he is going to receive either way. However, it won't be from my Ali. As much as I would love to watch her destroy Krellin, I won't allow it if it means she'll lose herself. I want my Ali back.

Tristan and my men kept hold of Krellin. Krellin doesn't struggle but he begs. "Keep her away from me!"

My men don't move or take him away, their eyes locked onto my mate as she moves towards them. Krellin isn't the only one afraid of her. My men are afraid because they know Alivia has one goal right now; to kill Krellin. If they remain in her way, what will she do to them?

Krellin will have what's coming to him, but I won't allow Alivia to be the one to do it. I have to bring her back to me . . .

Little wolf . . .

She's blocking me out and it kills me that I can't break through. She doesn't even bother to acknowledge me when I stride towards her. I would give anything to hold her, to know she's safe back in my arms, and to know our child is safe. But she clearly isn't safe through the blue aura. I can see her chest heaving, the energy she's exuding taking its toll on her. She continues walking but I block her path and for the first time her blue orbs flicker to mine. And nothing. No acknowledgment. No grief or pain., and no love . . .

What happened to you?

A part of me knows it must have to do with the blood soaking her clothes. I could smell Raven in it. Is Raven dead?

My eyes blazed when I snap my head 'round to Krellin, my voice reverberating through the room, shaking Krellin to his core. "What the fuck did Draven do to her and Raven?"

The sound of my voice is filled with so much anger and venom. It forced Krellin to shift his fear from watching Alivia to me. "I—I have no idea. He wanted their powers that's all I know . . . just please . . . keep her away from me," he begs. I'm almost embarrassed for him, a king begging another. Such a cowardly act.

It would give me pleasure to step aside and let Alivia have him but it means more to me to bring her back—to bring my Ali back. I turn 'round to face her and she begins her pursuit for Krellin once again.

I intercepted her path again and for a split second, I saw a hint of anger flash in those empty orbs. It was almost as if she deems me a nuisance rather than seeing her mate and the man she loves. I know the Alivia I love is in there somewhere. She has to be.

My eyes flicker to her bump, thinking of our unborn child and how I failed them as a father before I could even hold them in my arms. I won't allow our child to lose her mother on top of that.

Alivia's blue orbs narrow on me, tilting her head to the side as if assessing me. Wondering how far I'll go to stop her from getting to Krellin. "Little wolf," I start, her eyes remaining transfixed on me and I can only pray that my Alivia is listening. "Don't do this to yourself. Don't let Krellin take you away from me. Come back to me."

Her eyebrows furrow, trying to figure out what I'm saying. I attempt to move toward her . . . to touch her, but as soon as I approach that electrical, blue aura, I'm overwhelmed by its power. Her energy draws on mine, stealing my energy as her own, draining my wolf's strength. She watches as I fall to my knees, barely reacting to the pained groan that spills from my lips. Her attention falls back to her goal, her gaze flickering to Krellin and I can hear them shuffling back as she steps around me, continuing towards Krellin.

My body is so drained, the simplest movement feels as though I'm lifting steel. But like fuck will I let that stop me. I won't allow her to do this even if it kills me.

It takes everything for me to climb back to my knees. I quickly order my men. "Take Krellin outside while I'll deal with Alivia."

My men don't have to be told twice, retreating back out of the building with a relived Krellin, happy to put as much distance between him and Alivia as possible. However, Arif is hesitant, refusing to run away from his sister.

"Arif, leave." I warn him but he doesn't listen to me.

You stubborn bastard!

Arif is now the one standing in front of Alivia, his voice vulnerable, the most vulnerable I've ever heard it. "You're not going outside Alivia." He's obviously wary from his tone of voice. Alivia watches him, her eyes still an empty glow. Arif is unsure of his attempt to stop her but he finishes with, "Not as long as I'm standing here."

Alivia must have taken that as a challenge because in the next instant a burst of energy escapes her palm when she faces it towards Arif's chest and his eyes widen. Arif goes flying back through the doors that he was blocking, his back colliding with the hard floor as he slides across the ground several feet. Arif groans, pain and hurt flashing in his yellow eyes.

Alivia shows no remorse as she gets ready to walk through the now empty doorway.

"Alivia!" My voice booms around the building, bouncing of the walls, rage spilling from every syllable as her head turns towards me. At least now I have her attention. I storm towards her and take her by surprise when I wrap my arms around her form, locking them around her as I rest my head against her shoulder. "I love you Alivia . . . I won't lose you to this—whatever this is."

I hold onto her body tight, ignoring the pain as the energy that surrounds her now surrounds me too, stripping me down, making it almost impossible for me to remain on my feet. I kiss my mark that sits on the soft flesh of her neck, and I can feel her body shudder against my own.

Come back to me, little wolf.

I can now feel her struggling against me, her fists that are locked between our bodies, trying desperately to punch at my chest.

Get angry Alivia . . . Let it all out, little wolf.

I finally break through to her though it was costly. My limbs are now aching tenfold, my legs shaking and my wolf whimpering as his life force begins to strip away. Alivia's powers are killing him and it won't be long until I follow soon after.

We both collapse to our knees, me out of exhaustion and her from heartbreak. My wolf is hanging on by a thread but he holds no malice towards Alivia. If him leaving this world is the price he has to pay to bring her back, he'll happily pay that twice over with no regrets. That's how much we love her.

It hurts. The cord that connects my wolf's soul with mine was being torn apart. His energy draining away to fall in sync with the energy that surrounds our, little wolf. I can't help the sounds of pain that fall from my lips as I try to focus on keeping my arms around Alivia. My wolf quickly bids his goodbyes before our connection cuts.

Just as I believe he's going to be taken from me, Alivia's aura begins to die out, his light and spirit remaining intact with my own. I can't help but feel relieved, my wolf howling with happiness. However, I keep my arms locked around her. Her eyes return to their natural blue. That sizzling energy that once surrounded her has fused out and everything that she had put away, the emotions, the anger and the pain returned. My Alivia is back.

She screams in my arms, tears coating her cheeks, spilling onto my chest as I hold onto her, not letting her go for even a second. I allow her to aim her anger and frustration at me, words of anger and fury pouring out of her as she punches at my chest. "Why did you fucking stop me?" My heart skipped a beat at the pain seeping into her tone.

She continues to scream through her sobs. "You should have let me kill him! Raven would still be here if it weren't for that fucking asshole!"

I've never heard her swear so much but it matches the anger she's feeling perfectly. I make no move to argue with her, continuing to let her get it all out. We remain like this for god knows how long, my arms held securely around her body as she cries and cries, her screams of anger dying down to be replaced with the pain and grief of losing Raven.

Fuck! Even I'm pissed and hurt that Raven's gone. She was a good friend and we had known each other for so long. It's hard to come to terms with the fact that she's just gone.

It's another moment, possibly a few until those cries dull down and she's left breathing heavily in my arms. I pull away just enough to place a gentle kiss to the top of her head as she lays it against my chest. "Shhh . . ." I comfort her with my presence as much as I can, rubbing my aching arms up and down her back.

"H—he k—killed her Adrenous . . ." She breathes against my chest, recalling the nasty memory.

"I know." I twist her in my arms so that her legs can wrap around my waist, her head now resting against my shoulder. "You don't have to tell me anything right now if you don't want to—"

"N—no." She cuts in, drawing in a sharp breath. "But I'm sorry, I didn't mean to yell at you or hurt Arif."

"It's okay, I understand." I assure her as she pulls away, her liquid blue eyes boring into mine and this time there is so much emotion shining through her gaze. Especially the love she holds for me. "Do you want to tell me what happened?" I ask carefully. It's clear she wants to tell me something by the way her eyes hold a hint of fear.

What is she afraid of telling me?

She nods her head but her eyes glance away and she relaxes her head back against my chest, her voice soft as she said, "B—before he killed Raven he um . . . he tried to take my powers."

"And it didn't work." I assume from the obvious amount of power she still possesses.

She nods, her eyes tearing up. "But, because he couldn't have mine he took our pup's instead." Her arms fall to her stomach as she chokes up a sob. My blood runs cold at her words but it doesn't stop me from wrapping my arms around her tighter.

"It's my fault, I should have stayed with you." I murmured, keeping her close. "I'll make sure he gives back what he took, Draven won't get away with this."

She sighs gently, shaking her head. "I don't blame you, Adrenous. Besides, it's too late, I already took care of Draven. As far as I know, he's gone."

Draven's gone? Another person we don't have to worry about anymore. I would have like the pleasure of seeing his face when he realised it was all over for him but at the same time, I'm proud of my queen for handling him herself.

Alivia places her palms on either side of my face, the pad of her thumb rubbing smoothly against my skin. I found myself leaning into her touch. "Thank you for bringing me back," she said.

"Thank you for coming back." I chuckle and she rewards me with one of her beautiful smiles.

Then her smile drops a second later. "There's something else I have to tell you."

I'm apprehensive because it's clear it's bothering her. "What is it?" I ask gently.

Her expression shifts, trying to remember certain details. "When I held Raven in my arms and she was dying . . ."

"It's okay." I offer her the 'okay' to continue, kissing the palm of her hand as her fingers graze along my cheek.

"Raven did something for the child. She used her powers and then said, 'At least she won't be alone'. I don't understand what she meant." She explains and I find my brows furrowing. I wish I could ease the confusion for her but I have no idea what Raven must have done for our child but I'm certain whatever it was, it was a gift from Raven. But the word "she" ran through my mind.

Raven knew we were having a girl. The joy that filled me had me smiling. We're going to have a little girl!

Alivia tilts her head to the side, confused by the happiness that I'm exuding. "Our child is safe now," Is all I tell her, nudging her forehead with mine as our eyes lock. "whatever Draven did to her and whatever Raven gave her, we can figure it out together."

"Okay. Together." She smiles. She then exhales a long and tired breath, the exhaustion catching up with her.

"Is that everything?" I ask softly.

"No," she whisperers. I look down at her, her eyes looking up at me cautiously. "There's one last thing, but I'd rather show you then tell you."

I'm anxious to know what else there could be to show me but I oblige with her wishes. " of course." She smiles thankfully up at me. "Now, come on." I wrap my arms around her body, placing my hands under her thighs and then with great effort I lift her up and stand to my feet. "Goddess woman, did you have to drain me so much?"

She chuckles but whispers a "sorry." I smile and shake my head, getting used to the fact that my mate is truly powerful. I'm surprised it's taken her this long to use her powers against me. Goddess knows that I've angered her in the past.

Arif is standing in the hall when I walk through the door, rubbing his right arm. He must have hurt it when Alivia sent him flying. As I approach him with Alivia in my arms, his eyes uncomfortably shift to her. "Don't worry, she's okay now." I promise him.

"But I'm not," he replies grumpily.

Alivia shifts in my arms, a frown pulling at her lips. "I didn't mean to, Arif, I'm sorry."

He narrows his eyes at her suspiciously and for a moment we believe he's still hurt by her actions. "I forgive you." He finally sighs, a ghost of a smile tracing his lips, putting Alivia at ease so she doesn't have to feel more guilty than she already does.

"Are you alright to watch her?" I ask Arif.

Alivia doesn't give Arif the chance to respond, her arms wrapping around my body tighter, not wanting to let me go. Her eyes flash with fear. "Please don't leave me again."

"Shh . . . it's okay, I'm not going anywhere." I promise her, running my hands down her hair and then her back soothingly. "Arif's just going to hold and take care of you while I deal with Krellin, okay?" I press a kiss to her forehead. "I won't let you out of my sights again, alright?"

I pull away to stare into her eyes, letting her know that I'm being sincere. No way am I going to leave her alone again. Never.

"Okay." She finally agrees. Arif takes this as permission to wrap his arms around Alivia, placing his arm beneath her legs as the other wraps around her back. I place her into his arms with ease. Her eyes don't leave mine, making sure I don't leave her again.

"I'm right here, Alivia. I'm not going anywhere."

She nods, now resting her head against Arif's chest. "Now come on." I start towards the door, making sure Arif is following and that Alivia can see I'm staying close by

Time for Krellin to meet his fate.

CHAPTER FORTY-SEVEN
Dark Shadows And New Alliances

✦▢✦

ADRENOUS

The moment I exit Krellin's estate, I find him restrained to one of the many trees that surround the area. His hands are tied by metal chains that are then wrapped around the tree, reinforcing the fact that he's not going anywhere.

His eyes flicker from the men around him to me before he sees Alivia in Arif's arms as he carries her behind me. Krellin's eyes flash with fear, the sudden urge to want to get away as soon as possible becoming obvious in his demeanour.

"It's no longer her you should be afraid of, Krellin." I chuckle, my eyes flashing when his icy blue orbs return to my fiery gaze. "That's right, it's me you have to answer to."

Krellin sneers at me, a glint reflecting from his sharp fangs when they make an appearance. "Stay away, Adrenous. I still have Vampires out there who are loyal to me." Krellin appears confident that his threat alone is enough to keep him alive, a satisfied glint shining in his eyes. What a fool.

I stand a few feet away from him, crossing my arms against my chest. Krellin's confidence diminishes the moment a dark chuckle leaves my lips. The second I step towards him and my wolf makes an appearance, he realises he's completely and utterly fucked.

I don't give a shit about his bloodsuckers. Soon, when this is over, I have a plan for the rest of them.

And I have a feeling he won't like it.

I enjoy the panic that resonates from his core when he begins to struggle against the metal chains, fighting to break them apart and escape my wrath. I click my tongue at his useless attempts, my eyes flashing with dark amusement. "You aren't going anywhere, Krellin. It's about time you pay for centuries worth of mistakes that you've made towards my family. And let's not forget the pain you've caused my queen and unborn pup."

Krellin seems perturbed by my response to his threat. Realising that I'm not going to back down, he turns his attempt to Tristan. "Don't let them do this Tristan, tell him what will happen if he kills me."

Tristan arches an amused brow. "They won't do nothing Father, you're forgetting most of them follow you out of fear.". Krellin narrows his eyes as his son continues on. "Most of them won't miss you, including me. You really were a terrible father and an even worse king."

"You pathetic, little prick!" Krellin spits, his temper flaring. "I should have killed you along with your pathetic whore of a mother!"

Within seconds, before I can fully process what is happening, Tristan is in front of his father, aiming his fist at the right side of Krellin's face and hitting his target with so much force that the sound can be heard at least half a mile away. Krellin releases a pained scream, his right eyebrow now split open, blood oozing from the cut, dripping down his face and onto his black shirt.

Even when Tristan has his fist back to his side, you can see his body trembling, his knuckles red from the force he'd used to punch his father. "You are the pathetic one. My mother is the one who deserved to live, not you and for that, I'm going to allow Adrenous to torture you any way he likes."

Tristan is breathing heavily when he finally walks away from his father and towards the side where Arif is sitting on the grass with Alivia on his lap. I can hear Alivia trying to comfort Tristan as I return my attention back to Krellin. Time for Krellin's torture.

I've been waiting so long to do this and it's obvious in my gaze when my eyes flash down at Krellin and he coils into the tree.

I want him to see just how deadly I can be. My wolf wants it just as much but he's afraid it'll scare Alivia. She hasn't yet seen his true power, let alone the form that comes with it. I assure him, she'll be fine, our little wolf can handle anything.

But first things first. "I'd like a knife." I call to my men but towards no one in particular. I can see Krellin's bleak and hostile expression from the corner of my eye as I grab a knife from the hand of one of my men.

I twirl the small, but incredibly sharp, dagger between my fingers. The shiny glint of the silver catches Krellin's eye and I'm certain I heard him gulp at the sight of it. I can practically smell his fear and it excites my wolf, causing our lips to curl upwards.

Krellin reluctantly shift his eyes away from the knife to look at me when I demand his attention. "I'm going to enjoy this," I said. Krellin barely had a chance to respond when I threw the knife at him. A bloodcurdling scream claws its way up Krellin's throat when the knife buries itself in his left shoulder.

Alivia cringes at the sight, burying her head in Arif's chest whereas, Arif and Tristan don't tear their eyes away, their lips curled up with enjoyment.

"Is Alivia okay?"

Arif responds to my question whilst nodding his head. *"She's fine, keep going."*

"Oh, I wasn't going to stop."

I pluck the knife from his shoulder when he's no longer shaking with pain. I can see through the now ripped fabric of his shirt, his wound slowly healing. The blood staining his shirt and shoulder is the only evidence left behind from the wound.

His healing ability is what's going to make this torture process slow but fun for me. No matter how much I hurt him, it will heal and then I can do it all over again.

Krellin ducks his head down, now staring at the ground through his watery gaze. "Look at me." I demand, my tone withholding a dark threat. He lifts his gaze, afraid I'll do something cruel and unimaginable if he refuses. I'm going to anyway but I want to see the fear and pain in his gaze every time I punish him. I want to make sure he pays for every problem he's caused me, Alivia, our pup, and everyone else I care about.

Krellin cringes when my lips curl up wickedly, the ruby colour in my eyes shimmering.

His eyes snap to the silver dagger, now stained with his blood, when I bring it towards his face. "Tell me, Krellin, what part of your body should I slice first?"

Krellin shakes his head. "D—don't . . ."

He trails off when I narrow my eyes disapprovingly. "Choose or I will," I beamed.

Krellin grinds his teeth in fear and frustration, his body slumping against the tree in defeat. "My chest," he muttered.

"Are you sure?" I press, my eyes flashing darkly. "There's so much surface to slice on the chest."

"Then I suggest you get it over with." Krellin snarls, too proud to go back on his answer.

As you wish . . .

I slash across his chest with the dagger, his shirt ripping open. A nasty gash spewing blood can now be seen across his chest as Krellin grinds his teeth, trying not to scream or groan In pain. Before the gash can heal, I slash across his chest in the opposite direction, the two gashes forming a bloody "X" on his chest before they heal.

Krellin writhes in pain, his skin now coated in sweat as he struggles to remain stood, the tree being his only support.

"Any more requests?" I mock, my brow arched when his eyes flicker back up to my own.

"Do you enjoy hurting a man who can't defend himself?" Krellin retorts, his voice hoarse from all the screaming. "It's not merely a challenge."

My wolf perks up at the idea of fighting Krellin on equal grounds. The challenge excites him. "Oh, so you'd like a fair fight to see which of us is truly better?"

"Exactly."

"Don't Adrenous!" Alivia's voice slices right through my skull. My eyes meet with her cobalt gaze from across the field. I can see she's afraid.

"Don't worry, little wolf. He won't be going anywhere. This is merely just a game he has no chance of winning. Do you trust me?"

Alivia's eyes flashed with concern but she nods her head. I do know what I'm doing. Krellin won't be going anywhere.

Before I even think about removing the chains that have Krellin Trapped against the tree, I barked at my men. "Men, take form around me and Krellin." My men follow my order, surrounding me and Krellin in a circle and leaving enough space in the middle for us to fight. I gesture to one of my men closest to where Krellin is restrained. "Release his restraints."

Krellin's eyes remain locked onto my own whilst his restraints are removed and even after he's free to move away from the tree, he stays. He's still weak from his wounds, taking a moment to regain some strength whilst using the tree for support.

"Please be careful, Adrenous."

"I will be, little wolf."

Alivia's still unsure about me accepting Krellin's challenge. I can sense her fear through our bond, my eyes meeting hers, reassuring her with a smile. She smiles back though it doesn't touch her eyes whilst she rubs her bump for comfort.

This is for Alivia and our pup. Krellin is about to see just how evil and frightening I can be. Sadly . . . Alivia will see that side of me too. I can only hope she understands it's necessary for all the pain and grief Krellin has caused us.

My wolf is still uneasy about the idea. We haven't shown our true form in such a long time but that's about to change.

Krellin moves away from the tree, now relying on his own two feet to keep him from collapsing to the ground. His cold, undead eyes scan my form, contemplating ways he could overpower me or even kill me. Unfortunately for him, I have the upper hand. Alivia has never seen my wolf's true form and luckily, neither has Krellin. But it doesn't mean I'm not going to have some fun with him first. The thought causes my eyes to flash with excitement, Krellin's eyes shifting to mine seeing the excitement in his eyes before he frowns in response.

Krellin steps to the side, I follow the action, hoping he'll make the first move. My wish comes true when he lunges forward, striking me in the stomach. I allow him to hit his target, the force causing me to stagger back. I can hear Alivia in the background gasp before becoming confused when a chuckle reverberates from my chest.

Krellin doesn't know what to think of my response to being hit by him. It's clearly not the response he wanted. Krellin bares his fangs, moving at incredible speed until he's behind me. I feel him jump onto my back, burying his fangs into the skin of my shoulder.

I merely shake him off me, like a person would an Insect, forcing him to dislodge his fangs as he crashes down to the grass floor. I feel the drizzle of blood as it makes it's way down my chest, my eyes glancing down at the blood as I touch it with my fingers, assessing it before my eyes flash down at Krellin, a dark smile making its way onto my lips.

"What's so amusing?" Krellin bites whilst climbing back up to his feet within a second. His features contorting angrily, annoyed that I find his offences amusing.

I don't answer. My wolf comes forward, narrowing his eyes dangerously, putting Krellin on edge.

Krellin cringes when the sound of bones snapping can be registered through his ear canals. My dark, red irises shift from a ruby red to a burgundy red, remaining transfixed on Krellin's wary form. Dark, black shadows begin to surround my form, flickering away from me until all anyone can see are my burgundy eyes shining through the shadows. The shadows shift and take form around me, my wolf now claiming the shadows that spew from his body.

Krellin coils away from me, his eyes frozen with fear, looking up at the shadowy beast that now stands before him.

My wolf turns to look at his mate and instead of Alivia, we're met with her wolf shining through her gaze with a look of awe and fascination. We expected to see fear and pain like everyone else who sees this form for the first time but Alivia seems to be taking it rather well.

"Adrenous, wha—How?"

"This is my wolf's true form. Did you think you were the only powerful one?"

"N—no. Why didn't you show me?"

"Because my wolf wouldn't allow it. He was afraid you'd run away from him or reject him. He didn't want you to fear him as a monster."

Alivia frowns.

"I could never reject him. I love you both no matter what."

"We love you too."

My wolf relaxes, knowing our mate loves him just as much as she loves me.

Arif smirks our way, he knows what follows whenever my shadowy beast makes an appearance. He'll enjoy watching this.

Tristan on the other hand, has his mouth wide open, unable to tear his eyes away from my beast.

I love it when people see him for the first time.

Our focus shifts back towards Krellin, finding him having taken a few more steps back while we were talking with Alivia. Is the little bloodsucker afraid of a shadow? My wolf's shadowy paws move forward, Krellin flinching away whenever shadowy wisps come close to touching him. A growl emits from my wolf's throat, his top lip reeling back to show solid, sharp fangs that could easily rip Krellin to shreds. He's going to regret challenging me.

My wolf lunges forward, Krellin quickly darts to the side but my wolf's shadowy wisps snake around his form, trapping him in the shadowy circle. Krellin panics, attempting to run through the shadows but they take on a solid form when they push him back in, keeping him in place.

My wolf inclines his giant head towards the disgusting bloodsucker, licking his sharp teeth with his tongue as we stalk towards him. Krellin trembles beneath my wolf's heated gaze and when my wolf snaps at Krellin's right arm, he releases a haunting scream, one that echoes through all of us. My wolf releases his arm and allows the shadows that surround Krellin to pull away from him.

My wolf doesn't want this to be an easy kill. Krellin wanted a challenge . . . My wolf does too.

Krellin runs away from us when he realises he's free. He attempts to get past my men that surround him but that desire is quickly tarnished the moment one of my men knock Krellin back a few feet, sending him on his back. My wolf shakes his head in disapproval, our burgundy eyes flashing with excitement.

Krellin isn't escaping us.

Realising he's trapped either way, Krellin forms a protective stance, preparing to fight my wolf rather than submit to a more humane punishment. My wolf has no desire to go easy on

Krellin. He's going to regret everything he's ever done in his existence.

"What are you waiting for?" Krellin snaps angrily as my wolf patiently watches him.

For you to make the first move.

Krellin's had enough of waiting, moving swiftly around us until my wolf can feel Krellin sinking his fangs into one of our hind legs. My wolf shakes his whole body, kicking Krellin away. We quickly turn round to face him and my wolf crouches down, making sure our head is level with Krellin's body before we run, full speed, towards him. We knock him back with our muscular head, hearing his ribs snap on impact before he crashes to the ground.

Krellin struggles to stand, holding his broken ribs whilst he waits for them to heal. My wolf however, doesn't wait. He snaps his solid, sharp fangs at Krellin's left leg, shaking his head aggressively when we have a tight grip on his thigh. Krellin's continuous screams bring my wolf joy. My wolf is reluctant to let go of Krellin's leg but eventually he does and we watch as he breaks down, sobbing.

His leg is badly mutilated, our sharp teeth having torn his flesh right down to the bone. His clothes are soaked with blood as well as torn from my wolf's many attacks.

"P—please . . ." Krellin begs before choking on his sobs. "Y—you win."

My wolf's ears perked up, the sound of Krellin submitting to him gave him a sense of satisfaction.

Everyone watches as my wolf's giant form disappears behind the shadows. He shrinks until it's my body stepping out of the shadows as they disappear from behind me. One of my men instantly steps forward with a white robe in their hand, passing it to me before I place it around my naked body.

My eyes then flash down at Krellin's broken form. "Are you admitting that you're weaker?"

Krellin struggles to breath, his mangled leg only just beginning to heal. "Y—Yes." He croaks,

"Now please, just get it over with and kill me."

A smirk graces my lips, putting Krellin on edge once again. "Not so fast"—I take a few steps towards him—"there's just one more thing I wish to do before I kill you."

Krellin snaps. "What more could you possibly do to me? Just fucking kill me already."

"Tristan," I called, ignoring Krellin's narrowed eyes before they flash with confusion. Tristan walks warily towards us.

"Yes?" Tristan's brows furrowed as he looks at his father.

"When your father dies, you will become king—"

"What?" Krellin bellows.

Angered by the interuption, I bend down towards him and bury my fingers into his mouth, forcing him to choke up before I grip that annoying muscle and rip it from his mouth before throwing it to the ground. Krellin tries to groan and scream but without his tongue, everything is muffled.

Satisfied, I turn back toward a shocked Tristan who's gaze is staring at Krellin's tongue with revulsion. I can also see Alivia cringing at the side with Arif chuckling at her reaction. She glared at him before smacking his shoulder. I find the sight amusing as Tristan's green eyes return to me when I look back at him and continued. "You are going to be the next Vampire king, in charge of your father's old subjects. Since I can't possibly kill all of them, I want to make an alliance, a chance for peace between Vampires and Wolvens. We can't have a repeat of your father's mistakes."

Flabbergasted, Tristan struggles to process my words. Warily, he asks, "You mean you're going to allow us to live openly. You're not going to attempt to kill all of us."

"No. I believe that like you, some Vampires hold the potential for good. And unlike you . . ." I offer him a knowing look before elaborating. "I expect you to kill the ones that aren't like you. However," I quickly add, my tone firm. "I intend to keep the humans safe, so if you wish to live openly, you can't feed from them against their will. They can either consent and donate or animals it will be."

"That's reasonable," Tristan said, a genuine smile forming on his lips.

In the background, I can still hear Krellin's muffled protests, no longer able to voice his displeasure. Turning to Krellin, I ask, "I'm sorry, do you have an issue with your son becoming king?" Krellin growls. "Is that a no? Wonderful. See Tristan, even your own father supports my decision."

Tristan shakes his head, chuckling.

"I'm done with you Krellin, any last words?" I chuckle darkly, grabbing a scythe from one of my men.

Krellin grinds his teeth in frustration, my taunts infuriating him. Well, he won't be infuriated for long. In one swift motion, I slice the scythe through Krellin's neck like butter, severing his head. It thuds onto the ground and rolls a few feet.

I hope he has a nasty fate waiting for him on the other side. Rest in peace.

✦○✦

CHAPTER FORTY-EIGHT
You're Not Worth It

✦▢✦

ARIF

"It's this way." Alivia guides us through the dark, narrow hallway, one flickering light casting dark shadows across the walls. The sound of our footsteps are eerie as it echoes off the concrete floor. There is also a putrid smell in the air, mixing with the humidity that surrounds us. It causes me to gag slightly as I continue to stomach the foul smell. What could be lurking down here that Alivia is dying to show us? If anything, I hope it's not the source of that smell.

Me and Adrenous follow Alivia closely behind, not sure exactly what it is she wants to show us. She preferred for us to see for ourselves as she put it. As much as she wants to show us, she appears worried and anxious by the prospect. Without asking her, me and Adrenous are aware we're not going to be pleased.

Alivia comes to a halt when we arrive at a steel door, Alivia's 'show and tell' waiting on the other side.

Alivia doesn't attempt to open the door, turning to me. "Do you mind?" I glance at her before realising the door is locked and that she's asking for me to break it down. Easy peasy.

"Step back." I instruct them before allowing a minute for Alivia and Adrenous to move away from the door before I stand in front of it. I channel my strength, turning my hands into fists, power surging in my fingertips before I pull my arm all the way back and then forward with great force and momentum. The steel door goes flying of it's hinges before smashing into the back wall. A loud 'clang' resounding around the room as the concrete wall that absorbed the impact of the door, cracks from the force. The cracks branch out as dust falls from the ceiling.

I turn to Alivia with a smirk on my face, gesturing to the dark cell that appears completely empty. "After you."

She gratefully passes me to enter the dark space, the putrid smell more concentrated in this area.

Eh . . . I was hoping that smell wouldn't be part of it but I guess I'm not that lucky.

Adrenous is next to walk inside, leaving me the only one left in the hallway. I'm reluctant to enter, the smell pushing me to turn back but I force myself inside. The room is too dark to see anything, forcing my wolf's eyes to come forward, his sense of sight allowing me to see past the darkness.

The cell is made up of dark, damp concrete with no source of light except of that shining through from the hallway. There are metal chains dangling from the walls, used to keep prisoners locked up with no light or warmth.

Alivia leads Adrenous towards the far right of the room where now, for the first time, I see a man curled up in a ball, shaking for dear life, his hands and feet shackled to the wall behind him. I narrow my eyes on him before glancing back up at Alivia, Adrenous asking the question we both want the answer to. "Who is he?"

Alivia takes in a shaky breath, her eyes uncomfortably shifting to mine when she answers, "Our father."

"What?"

Alivia cringes and looks away when I snapped. I can't believe that this man huddled into a ball and shaking is the same man that terrified and beat me and my mother. "You're mistaken," I said. That's the only way her answer can make sense.

Adrenous watches the man curiously, appearing in thought when he crouches down and grabs the man's upper arm. Instantly the man comes out of his crouched position, his eyes wide open as he stares back into Adrenous's red gaze that has now shifted to hot fury. Like me, Adrenous instantly recognised those yellow eyes similar to mine. Alivia wasn't mistaken.

My hands automatically curled into fists as my body fill with tension. I don't move, my eyes narrowed on Adrenous and my father.

Adrenous's pent up aggression drives his actions when he automatically backhands my father across the face. My father groans, Adrenous spitting. "Alijah." The name rolls uncomfortably across his tongue as he glares daggers at him.

"You're supposed to be dead," my father mumbled. "Are you a ghost?" He holds his cheek, his eyes still wide open as he stares at Adrenous, believing he's hallucinating. "Krellin . . . he was supposed to kill you."

Adrenous narrows his eyes further, his jaw clenched. We both thought my father would have more to say than that but clearly he's been kept in this cell for far too long that his brain is fucked. "No," Adrenous growls. "Your plan never worked and you will never be nothing more than the bastard who stabbed both my parents in the back."

Again, Adrenous couldn't control himself, gripping my father harshly by his collar before bringing him to his feet and slamming him into the wall. My father is beyond scared, unable to control his bodies constant twitching. Adrenous suddenly wraps his hands around his neck, strangled noises now passing from my father's lips.

Being strangled by Adrenous isn't exactly fun. As someone who's been on that side of him, I should know.

Alivia quickly grabs Adrenous's arm, her voice pleading. "Stop, he doesn't even know what's real and what's not. He's insane and no longer a threat."

"So I should just let him live and get away with what he did to my parents?" Adrenous's voice is dark, his eyes still on my father as he grips my father's neck harsher. I make no move to stop him.

"No." Alivia shakes her head, her hand still gently holding onto Adrenous's arm. "We'll keep him locked up here. That's far worse than allowing him the sweet kiss of death. At least this way, he will suffer longer."

My sister is right. Adrenous reluctantly releases my father's collar, my father dropping to the ground in a fit of coughs. Adrenous takes a step back, Alivia quickly wrapping her arms around him. "Alijah will spend the rest of his life paying for what he did to all of us." She breathes into Adrenous's chest. "I promise," she said.

Adrenous takes comfort in Alivia's embrace, his arms wrapping around her small form tighter. "I believe you."

They break their embrace when my father's voice resonates around us. "You . . . too weak. I should be king."

I can see Adrenous tense up all over again, resisting the urge to snap as his wolf comes forward. I quickly step in. "You two should head home and get some rest, you both need it. I'll take care of everything here before I leave."

"What about Raven's body?" Alivia asks, the hurt lingering in her gaze.

"I'll ensure she has a proper burial." I assure her, a comforting smile pulling at my lips before it's gone and I turn to Adrenous. "I also need to track down Coen's son. Perhaps it'll lead me to the rest of the rogue's hideout."

Adrenous nods his approval. "Thank you."

"It's my pleasure," I said. "Now take my sister home and make sure she gets some rest."

They both say goodbye to me before exiting the cell, leaving me behind with my father and the disgusting smell lingering in the air.

I exhale a sharp breath before turning back to the man that dominated my nightmares as a child. I crouch low in front of him, Alijah barely looking my way as he mutters incoherent words. "Alijah." I say his name, refusing to openly call this man my father.

He lost that right a long, long time ago.

My father's yellow irises briefly flicker to meet mine before he's cowardly huddling into the damp concrete wall for dear life, his chains rattling in the process. "Your eyes . . . Son . . . get away!"

Well, at least I know he recognises me.

"LOOK AT ME!!!" My words cause the room around us to shake, dust falling from the ceiling as Alijah finally looks at me in fear, his yellow eyes wide open. For years, I wanted the reasons behind this mans hatred for me and my mother. And now that he's here in front of me, I won't be denied that closure.

"You know who I am so you know what you did to me when I was a boy, don't you?" The question is rhetorical. I don't actually expect an answer and my father doesn't offer one as he watches me raise a finger to the scar on my eyebrow. "You did this to me. I was trying to protect my mother from one of your beatings when you threw me across the room and I hit my head on the edge of the table and passed out." I don't even want to think about what I saw when I woke up.

Alijah shows no recollection, but he does study the scar I've pointed out to him.

The force in which I had hit my head that day knocked me out. I then woke up to find my mother's lifeless body, her face and body coated in blood from his countless beatings. That was the last day I had seen my father. It was the same day he killed Adrenous's parents before he disappeared for good.

And now here he is . . . practically brain dead, unable to comprehend or even process what I'm telling him.

Alijah's eyes are almost unseeing as he stares into my yellow eyes, almost as if he's not actually looking at me but rather through me. He points at the scar on my eyebrow, my eyebrows furrowing when he whispers, "I . . . did that . . ." He continues to ramble on until I can barely understand him.

"Yes, you did." I nodded, my wolf's anger building the longer I remain in my father's presence. "And this"—I point to the scar that ran across my jaw—"this was way before that. You did this when I attempted to fight back for the first time. You decided to teach me a lesson by slicing my face with a sharp blade, do you remember?"

It kills me, having to remember these memories after I spent years trying to forget them. Because of my father, I feared I would end up like him, that I would turn against my mate and children but I didn't. I love my mate Sylvia and our children, Alex, Kieran, and Cammie so much. They're what kept me strong and happy for so long. I would do anything for them in a heartbeat which is why . . . I don't understand why my father couldn't be like that for me.

What did I do to make him hate me? Was I really such a terrible son? And what about my mother? She did everything for us. She loved us both so much even when he would take his anger out on her. She tried to be the best mate to him, I watched her cry so many times when she thought I wasn't watching. She would blame herself for his actions, thinking it was her fault. I wish she were here so I could tell her how much I loved her, how much she meant to me and what an amazing mum she was. But he took that chance away from me.

When my father says nothing else, I grow impatient and snap. "Why did you kill her?" My voice is filled with the hurt and guilt that arose from my mother's death. I should have been able to protect her from this monster but I couldn't. "And you destroyed her by raping Alivia's mother . . . why?" I need to know. My mother never deserved what he did to her. Why the moon goddess gave her such an insufferable mate is beyond me and I want the answers I've been denied for so long.

My father begins to fiddle with his beard, pulling at it relentlessly as words begin to spill from his lips. "I want to be king . . . Camille and son only make . . . me weak . . . Kill them . . ."

Is that it? He thought we were weak so he treated us like shit. My eyes blaze with fury, unchecked rage battling its way towards the surface when my wolf suddenly takes a front row seat the moment my mother's name left my father's lips.

My claws elongate as I climb over him, pounding my fists into his stomach. I listen as he cries like a child, begging me to stop. It only enraged my wolf more. I claw into the flesh of his arms, legs and stomach, enjoying the torturous cries that pull from his lips, the sound bringing a serene noise to my ears.

"Is that all you wanted? Power?" My anger took on a new turn. "We made you weak so you punished us?"

My beatings and the anger I've held for at least twenty years of my life continued to roll out of me wave after wave. It's not until I look at a very battered and bruised face that I reel my wolf back in, halting my fists in the air before drawing them back to my sides. My father is just about breathing, his eyes swollen shut as sobs reverberate through his chest.

There's no ounce of sympathy in my gaze as I stare down at him. "I should kill you right now. You don't deserve to live for another second after all the pain you caused but . . ." I wiped the blood from my hands before standing on my feet. "You're not worth it."

He's a vile, disgusting being who's actions were solely for his own selfish gains. It was never mine and my mother's fault and it's about time I stop blaming myself for his actions. He's not worth the anger and pain I've felt for so long and it's about time I realise that.

I turn away from him and walked towards the cell door. I offer him one last glance before I seethed. "You don't deserve to have my anger, my hatred . . . I hope you enjoy rotting away in this cell for the rest of your miserable life." I leave the room, letting go of the fear, the anger, and the hatred that man caused me for so long. He will no longer dominate my life. He doesn't deserve that from me anymore.

When I finally breach the exit, I see Tristan and most of Adrenous's men still lingering about. Most of them are picking up the dead bodies of the few who didn't make it out of the battle. I bow my head in the direction of the fallen Wolvens, giving them my respect. They all fought well and will not be forgotten.

My eyes snap to Tristan when he takes it upon himself to walk over to me. I narrow my eyes on him when he eyes the dried blood on my hands and trousers before asking, "Is Alijah still breathing?"

"He'll live," I respond bluntly. Tristan furrows his brows, nodding as I continue with, "I want you to make sure he remains locked up. He's to never leave that cell, do you understand?"

"Like I'd release him." Tristan sounded offended, causing a humourless, dark chuckle to reverberate through my chest. He narrows his eyes, now on the edge. Good, he should be on edge.

"I still don't trust you, kid. Just because Adrenous allowed you to take up your father's position doesn't mean I won't be keeping an eye on you," I said, making it clear to him that I'll make sure the Vampires remain in check.

There are many of them who won't be happy with Tristan as their king. If he doesn't fix that problem then I'll happily step in without a moment's thought.

"It was foolish of me to believe that after everything I've proven, you still refuse to trust me." Tristan shakes his head, not at all pleased with my attitude towards him. Like I'd give a fuck.

"You have a long way to go before I'm even close to trusting you, kid." I turn away from him before he can respond, calling over my shoulder. "Make sure Raven's body is taken back to Adrenous's estate, ready for burial."

Tristan watches me walk away as I head towards the surrounding woods. "Where are you going?"

"To find Coen's bastard son."

Hopefully his tracks will lead me to the rest of the rogues. I still have some pent up aggression which I wouldn't mind taking out on them.

✦○✦

CHAPTER FORTY-NINE
Never Again

✧□✧

ALIVIA

I curl up into Adrenous's strong chest as he carries us all the way up to our bedroom. I allow his scent to envelope me, bringing me comfort and security.

He pauses a second to pull open the door handle before strolling inside our room, making sure his strong arms are securely wrapped around me. He doesn't stop in our bedroom though, continuing towards the door that leads into our wet room. He stops a second to open that door too before steam suddenly encases my senses, the warm air wrapping around my skin like a cozy blanket.

"You and the pup will benefit from a warm bath," Adrenous says, placing me down onto the floor as my feet touch the cool surface.

"Only if you join me," I plead, blinking up at his red orbs.

Adrenous smiles, gripping my shoulders gently to turn me around. He runs his hands down toward the knots that keep my dress together. He wastes no time untying them before I feel the filthy fabric falling away from my skin, piling up around my ankles. I step out of the dress and turn back towards Adrenous in only my underwear.

My cobalt eyes stare intently up at him, not once wavering as I begin to remove my underwear myself. Adrenous's hot gaze admires my bare flesh, my swollen breasts begging for his touch as my nipples harden at the cool air.

Adrenous steps forward, causing my breath to hitch as he runs his hands up my arms before grazing his fingers across my chest, taking one of my breast into his giant hand. I release a soft moan, his hand massaging my breast softly. He suddenly bends down so that he's on his knees, now taking my nipple into his warm mouth, his tongue flicking across the sensitive nub.

"Adrenous . . ." I moan. I feel his lips smirk against my flesh, his tongue continuing to tease my nipple until it's completely hard. He groans against my nipple as he sucks it through his teeth, causing me to gasp and moan.

He pulls away, leaving my wet nipple exposed to the cool air and a whine of frustration to leave my lips. I gaze into his heated gaze as he rises to his feet, his hands travelling to the hem of his shirt before pulling it up and throwing it to the floor. My eyes now trailed over his rippled, hard abs. I lick my lips, enjoying the view of his bare chest. Adrenous chuckles, drawing my gaze back up to meet his as he removes the rest of his clothes.

Adrenous strolls past me towards the bath, stepping inside. His body is now below the hot, steamy water. He offers me his hand, inviting me to join him. I take his hand gratefully, placing my feet into the warm water before bending down to rest my back against Adrenous's chest, my head lulling back to lay against his shoulder.

Adrenous places his hands on my swollen stomach, his fingers moving soothingly against me skin. The pup surprises us both when she kicks at her father's hands, bringing a smile to both our lips.

"I'm so happy you're both safe." Adrenous whispers against my ear, placing a gentle kiss to the sensitive area behind my ear.

"I'm happy you are too," I tell him softly,

He placed my hands over his as they rest against my stomach, our pup still kicking gently. "Arif told me that you killed Coen?"

"I did," Adrenous confirms. "I found out he was a Wolven from a pack that my father had punished because of a crime his father committed. For a long time, I thought he was dead but he was building up the rogues, naming himself king. He's gone now, but his son and the others are still out there. Arif told me he's already on his way to track them all down."

"Do you think Arif will find them?" I anxiously fiddle with Adrenous's fingers as the question passes my lips softly.

"I can't be sure as of yet." Adrenous admits, sighing.

"And what of our pup? I'm scared, Adrenous. I know Raven did something good for her but we have no idea what Draven did in the first place. I have no idea what to expect when she's born," I said. I'm constantly afraid now and it's taking its toll on my mind.

He takes his hands from my stomach to grip mine firmly, rubbing the back of my hands with his thumbs. "I promise you, whatever it is, we will handle it together. Our daughter will be just fine, I'm sure of it."

"How can you be so sure?" He just sounds so confident and I wish I could believe him but my thoughts are still raging, my anxiety wrapping around my chest. It'll take a lot more to convince me for my anxiety to release its grip.

"Because she has a strong mother to guide her and a father who would do anything for her. She will be fine."

"You're right," I breath, feeling only a fraction of worry leaving my body. I relax further into Adrenous's chest, allowing the warm water to numb my mind.

I sigh happily when Adrenous begins to press light, hot kisses against the skin of my shoulder. His lips against my skin brings a welcome distraction and I fall into his embrace, allowing his touch to erase the tension in my shoulders.

Adrenous takes a bar of soap that was rested on the side of the bath before bringing it to the skin of my chest, massaging my breast with the lavender scented soap. The smell tingles my nose as a smile pulls at my lips, Adrenous's lips continuing to press kisses along my neck until I'm subconsciously moaning, the sensations causing my body to relax every single muscle.

Adrenous places the bar of soap down once I'm completely relaxed against him. He rinses the soap from my chest with the water that is only now starting to become slightly cold. I shiver in his hold and that's when he decides it's best to climb out of the bath.

"Let's get you into bed." He whispers into my ear once we're out of the bath, the cool air causing goosebumps to prick my skin.

Once we're both dry, we climb into the soft covers of our bed, the sheets soft and inviting. Adrenous wraps his arm around my body, bringing my back flush against his chest. He lightly kisses the area starting from my neck down to the skin between my shoulder blades. My soft moans echo through our dark bedroom when his lips make contact with his mark at the base of my neck.

I turn in my spot, wanting to face him. There's still some things I need to get of my chest. His gorgeous, ruby eyes are staring down at me with so much love that I'm almost overwhelmed. "Adrenous." I whisper, Adrenous frowning at the worried undertone in my voice. "Promise me that you'll do everything in your power to remove the rogues as a threat."

"I'll do my best, Alivia, that much I can promise."

"Then I will promise the same thing. If I have to, I will kill them myself. I won't allow them to threaten us again, not anyone," I said. Adrenous furrows his brows at my words. "I'm done being weak. If I've learned anything, it's that I'm capable of so much more than I thought and I won't let anyone hurt my family if I can help it."

After what Draven did to me and to my unborn daughter, I won't allow anyone to have that sort of control over me ever again. Anyone who hurts Adrenous, our pup and anyone else I love, they will know my wrath and they will perish.

"Alivia don't lose yourself because of what Draven and Krellin did otherwise, they win and you shouldn't allow them to. I already almost lost you once, don't let it happen again, I wouldn't be able to live without you." Adrenous warns me softly, his eyes pleading me to listen to him.

I take his hand, assuring him with my touch as my thumb rubs soothingly against the back of his hand,."You won't lose me Adrenous, but I'm not going to let anyone make me feel vulnerable and helpless ever again."

"You're are anything but that, little wolf."

I smile at his words, knowing he means them sincerely.

I mean what I said. Anyone who comes close to threatening my family, my pack, my kingdom will have to face my judgement. This with Krellin, Draven, and Coen will be a warning to anyone else who has the same goals and agendas.

Never again will I be seen as weak and vulnerable as I was. Never again.

✦○✦

EPILOGUE

Six years later...

ALIVIA

I've learned in the past few years that being queen isn't easy but it is meaningful and extremely fulfilling.

I love ruling by my mate's side, Adrenous valuing my thoughts and opinions above anyone else's. Our kingdom has grown exceptionally, both Wolvens and Vampires living in peace since the alliance between both races was made.

Tristan has become a remarkable king, the Vampires giving the utmost respect since he brought them out of hiding. They no longer have to fear Wolvens unless they take blood from an unwilling participant. Any Vampire that goes rogue, breaking the laws set by both Tristan and Adrenous, is either punished or killed depending on the severity of their crime.

The alliance is a success, the human village very safe now that Vampires aren't allowed to kill on will. It has given my aunt and cousins a chance to move back now that the threat to their lives has passed. It turns out that when Tyke posed as my aunt at my coronation, Draven had casted a spell on all of them, placing them in deep slumber. When I blasted him away, that spell was broken. They were pleased to move back home and didn't neglect to visit me regularly.

I'm happy with the alliance. It helps to keep my family safe but it still doesn't seem to have the approval of my brother. He's still on edge, not so easily taken with the Vampires who can now roam free. He has however, grown to trust Tristan individually. They have even teamed up to track the remnants of rogues that followed Coen, including his own son after Arif was unable to track them down.

As of yet, they haven't had such luck but with my constant pestering, I haven't allowed them to give up. I won't allow any threat to remain now that my children are in my life. My loves.

Adrenous rests on the couch, his eyes closed whilst he snores in his sleep. He holds our youngest in his arms who's also fast asleep as he cuddles up against his father's chest. Wyatt is only four and named after Adrenous's father. He's adorable, his black curls falling over his forehead. Wyatt has cobalt irises, hidden beneath his closed lids, which are vibrant and filled with so much happiness that a little boy could possess.

Wyatt loves his father and Adrenous already has him training with the other pups. He wants our son to be prepared for anything no matter how old he is and who am I to prevent him from doing so. I too, want our son to be ready for any and all obstacles.

I'm currently curled up against Adrenous's side, my legs bent on the sofa cushion with my nose buried in a book. The fire that crackles from the fireplace illuminate the pages of my book and sends warmth to the surface of my skin.

"Mummy?" I glance up from the book, Asmara calling me as she steps into the room.

Asmara is only six, being born just two months after Adrenous killed Coen and Krellin. She was named after my mother of course. It felt right to name her after the woman who helped me have the life I do now, without her, I would have been left to the mercy of Krellin and my father.

I stare into her gorgeous red irises that remind me so much of her father except for the fact that hers are currently sad and filled with so much innocence. She shuffles her feet from side to side, her fingers clasp together in front of her black dress as she glances up at me.

"What's wrong, baby?" I place my book down on the arm rest and sit up, holding my arms out to her.

She strolls over to me, the flames from the fireplace shimmering off of her dark brown hair as it falls down her back in gorgeous curls. I gently place her on my lap as she shuffles in order to get comfortable before telling me in a small voice. "The other pups were making fun of me again."

Oh boy . . . I frown. "What did they say this time?"

"They said I couldn't keep up with them, they're too fast mummy." Her words sadden me and it hurts that I can't ease the sadness lingering in her soft gaze. "I'll never keep up with them."

Ever since Asmara turned three it became clear to me and Adrenous that she wasn't like the other pups her age. She has always been delicate and doesn't have as much strength and stamina as she should. I know she's come to realise this too and it breaks my heart.

It doesn't help that I believe it was Draven's doing that's behind it. If I didn't know any better, I would say my daughter is human. I pray I'm wrong . . . It shouldn't be possible but we won't know the truth until her first shift is due.

Even so, my baby has so many strengths. She's very smart and perceptive for her age and she loves to read and explore the outdoors. I only hope she comes to realise her strengths rather than focus on her weaknesses. Everyone has them, including me and her father.

"It's okay not to be the fastest or the strongest baby," I said. Asmara gazes up at me, her brows furrowing at my words. "As long as you try your best and do everything with a heavy heart, that's all anyone can ask of you."

Asmara doesn't know how to process my words, doubting them because of what the other pups have said to her. "B—but the other pups say that a Wolven isn't allowed to be weak. We have to be strong, and if I'm not strong then am I a bad Wolven?"

"Of course not." I wrap my arms around her tightly. I won't allow her to believe that for a second. "You have mine and your father's blood and with that, our strengths. That means it's impossible for you to be a bad Wolven."

She smiles at my words, her eyes brightening instantly. "Thank you, mummy," she said. I place kisses all over her face, causing her to giggle in my hold. "Mu—mummy!" she laughs, trying to wriggle out of my hold.

"Mara." I stop and look up to see Rylan's son, Reagan strolling into the room. Reagan is a year older than Asmara but he's very taken with her and they've been good friends for three years.

Reagan has taken on all of his father's features, from the brown hair and green eyes to that cheeky smile and the need to make everyone feel better with jokes and laughs.

Asmara turns in my spot to look at him. Reagan is uneasy and uncomfortable now that we're watching him, averting his green eyes to the floor, mumbling "I—I just wanted to make sure you were okay."

Reagan is so adorable and it warms my heart that he's worried for Asmara. I know he likes her, the two of them inseparable half the time, enjoying to play and spend time together whenever they can.

Asmara climbs out of my hold and walks over to him, wrapping her arms around Reagan, surprising him. "I'm okay, thank you."

I smile at the two of them, Reagan now reciprocating her hug when his arms wrap around her in return.

When they pull apart, Asmara turns to me. "Can I go back outside to play?" She pleads me with her eyes and it makes it almost impossible for me to say no.

"Okay," They're about to run off when I quickly stop them in their tracks. "But only for an hour."

Asmara agrees, nodding her head. "Thank you mummy." She runs out of the room, heading back outside.

"Thank you, Queen Alivia." Reagan calls too before running after Asmara.

With a friend like Reagan, my baby will be just fine, I'm sure of it. I can only hope that the other pups stop being so hard on her, my baby is trying her best and will make an amazing Wolven.

Whatever happens and when it finally does become clear what Draven and Raven did to my baby, we will figure it out together.

But if anything, Asmara isn't weak, that much is clear.

✦○✦

Do you like fantasy stories?
Here are samples of other stories
you might enjoy!

Luna Catherine

Yolanda Jolante

CHAPTER ONE

He had taken everything from me yet I'm still here. My own brother, Ronan.

Ronan lost himself a long time ago, and selfishly enough, he dragged me down along with him. I was of pure innocence, and he corrupted me. He made me bear witness to the most heinous of crimes, filling my mind with nightmares. I watched him in silence as he went down a black hole, returning to be what he secretly feared the most—a man with a dark soul.

He's claimed to not fear anything; a rebel who lives off instilling fear into others. He feeds off the control he has, the adrenaline rush he gets when a life ends by his hands. He can be irrational at times, a loudmouth, cocky, stubborn, dark, and twisted, yet still, he can't control one thing.

His love for me.

In his own twisted way, he loves me. He's done so much hurt and pain. He's been cruel and left me bare at such a young age, but still, he keeps me close. He feeds off my strength and breathes calmly in my silence. Now that he's grown, he can't find it in him to destroy me any further than he already has.

A murderer, a selfish and cruel man, and many more titles to everyone else but a frightened, confused, and an out-of-control little boy in a man's body, right in my view.

A storm is brewing, I can feel it. He knows it too because I told him before. He's tried so many times to ignore me, but today, he can't because, like always, I'm right.

A crash sound comes from the living room. He's breaking stuff again. He's earned everyone's attention, all movements still, in his outburst.

I watch him silently by the doorway while he loses his cool once again. He throws a glass to the nearest wall and makes one servant gasp in shock.

"Everyone, out!" he demands.

Not needing to be told twice, every present person scurries out of there, leaving us alone. Right after everyone has gone, he walks over to the drinks cabinet, pulling out a bottle of brandy.

I finally enter, walking over to stand by the large windows, not even sparing him another glance.

I hear him shuffling close, then the sound of liquid being poured before glass is slammed hard against the wooden table.

He loudly gulps down his drink. He's frustrated, I can feel it.

"Be careful, brother, before you kill yourself," I say.

He growls in answer, wanting to ignore me but he can't. I know he wants to have another, and if he does, he might lose his senses. That's never a good sign, especially today. A drunk Ronan is the worst Ronan.

"You've done wrong, brother. Now, you just might meet the outcome of your actions," I tell him calmly, like always.

"Shut up!" he growls in warning.

I do.

He paces up and down now.

"Damn troublemakers."

More like you, I want to say.

A cold, icy chill runs down my spine, and my body tenses in the process.

"The storm is coming. The storm is near."

I hear a growl before I'm spun around to face him, and his brown eyes darken. I don't even wince when he tightens his grip on my arm.

"Stop talking gibberish and say what you mean!" he seethes, his alcoholic breath fanning my face.

Like a lightbulb clicking in my mind, a certain wind washes over me. It's them. They are close. I don't know who they are, but they come with a mission.

"Be prepared . . . for just about anything," I tell him.

He growls in anger before he backhands me across the face, sending me flying and landing hard on the floor.

"If you have nothing better to say, then shut the hell up!" he shouts, leaving the room.

He has listened.

I close my eyes for a minute, blinking back tears and softly rubbing at my burning cheek.

"Oh no, miss!" Cara—one of the omegas—says, rushing over to help me up. "Please sit and let me treat you."

"There's no time. Please take care of the glass and then go into hiding."

Her eyes search my own until she gulps in realization of the situation. "Trouble is coming once again," she mumbles.

All I do is stare at her.

"You've always been the calm one out of everyone here, and the most truthful. Ha!" She sighs. "I will do as you say, Luna."

I close my eyes, holding back my tongue from telling her to stop referring to me as Luna.

Leaving her alone to attend to the scattered, broken glass, I decide to leave and go to my room, wanting to treat my cheek and to try to look presentable because I know Ronan wouldn't be pleased with me if I wasn't.

Coming back down the stairs in a long black jumpsuit with ballet pumps, I feel them really close, though I may not see them. It's a matter of time before they appear. I remain in the living room with half of my body visible through the window.

His footsteps echo as he appears, looking cleaner in dark jeans and a white shirt that hugs his muscles. I can feel his gaze on me.

"What the fuck are you wearing?" he shouts, and I almost jump out of my skin.

I turn to face him, opening my mouth to say something, when the cold chill comes at me like a bullet going through my chest.

"You have visitors, brother," I tell him, turning to face the window.

I hear his footsteps come closer.

"Shit," he curses before storming out of the door.

Ronan with his styled, cut, light-brown hair appears into view, standing on the front yard with about ten to fifteen men. A few minutes pass and no one shows up, making Ronan glance over his shoulder at me. His eyes narrow and I notice him try to fight off a smirk.

This is a promise that there'll be consequences if I'm lying, but I'm not. He's doubting me yet again.

All too soon, a group of tall men appear from the forest. Ronan's demeanour changes and his body tenses when he turns back front. Amongst the approaching men, I notice the one in the middle—the leader.

He is the most muscular out of the men; he's breathtakingly handsome with his midnight black hair, striking emerald-green eyes that meet mine, a strong jaw, and sculpted blank face. He shows no emotion to the onlookers, yet I can sense him. I'm stronger than him in this.

He is feeling everything, and he thinks I can't. His scent is of fresh pine and woods—earthy and pleasant to my nose.

I know without a doubt that he is my mate, the one I'm destined to be with, my soulmate. Yet what he represents, what he stands for, his views on mates, and all he's been till now forms a defensive shield against the bond.

He is just like my brother.

I sigh and slump in disappointment and defeat.

I watch the interaction between my brother and my mate. It's intense and doesn't seem like something good will be concluded. It's been a few minutes now, and I hold no hope for what may be.

Turning away from the window and meaning to walk away, I stop in my tracks when I sense it—a strong and intense gaze. I glance over my shoulder at the precise moment he nods my way. My heart flips at his intense eyes.

He has just caused the first real reaction from my already still heart.

When Ronan glances over his shoulder, I'm suddenly grabbed by arm and dragged out of the house, earning frightened eyes from pack members and hard ones from my mate's company. I'm shoved hard towards the ground, only for someone to grip my arm strongly to prevent me from going down any further.

Sparks erupt throughout my body, and I gasp at the contact. It's him, my mate.

I almost whisper it out but bite down on my tongue, not wanting to expose anything. Being pulled up, I sneak a glance to my mate. My breath hitches at the sight of his beautiful green eyes. I notice a small but deep and permanent scar on the side of his face; it still doesn't take away from his captivating looks. His scar is a sign of things he's gone through and conquered.

He catches me looking at his scar, and that makes his eyes harden with anger laced in them. I'm spun around to face my brother whose eyes are trained on me.

"So are we talking now?" My breath hitches when something sharp is pressed hard against my neck.

My eyes are only on my brother.

"What do you want, O'Connell?" my brother grunts, clearly annoyed by the situation we are currently in.

"You know what I want, Black. It's been long overdue now. Give me back my beta."

"Dead or alive?" Ronan arches his brow.

"Don't play games with me and give me what I want." My mate's deep voice sounds calm but deadly.

"Or what?" Ronan asks, clenching his hands into fists.

"Do you really want me to answer that? Alright, let me demonstrate." Without any warning, the sharp object is shoved into the side of my neck and pulled out. I'm immediately thrown across the yard, my body slamming hard against a nearby tree.

Growls erupt, bones crack, and bodies collide. I glance up from the ground to the horrific scene in front of me. Werewolves are everywhere; there's so much blood and fighting between my brother's wolf and my mate's right in the centre.

Pack members scream and run around, trying to get to safety.

Pain erupts from my neck and reaching up to where I was stabbed, a wetness coats the wound. Soon, I'll be bleeding out.

My attention diverts when I sense it, my brother's life is hanging in the balance. I sit upright, pressing against my wound and facing what now looks to be my mate's dark-gray gigantic wolf standing over Ronan's midnight-black one. My mate's eyes connect with mine just as he digs his teeth in my brother's wolf's neck.

My heart hammers hard against my chest. He won't hesitate to kill Ronan, but his eyes tell me that I've only got one chance to do something.

He's daring me to do something.

"Stop! Stop please!" I plead, struggling to rise on my feet.

I stagger close to them. A few of my mate's men remain, looking rather threatening.

"Alpha, I have a proposal. Let him go please." My brother's eyes narrow in threat, but I avoid his eyes, looking at my mate's.

I'll deal with my brother's wrath after. Right now, I need to manage the situation. Though it may be my first time being given the platform.

My mate doesn't let up. He puts pressure on my brother's neck, earning us both a growl and whine from my brother. Time is of the essence; I can almost hear him say.

"Your beta will be released, so long as you release our own." I take a ragged breath. "I will take upon any punishment and everything your beta endured in time of his captivity. I will accept with no argument or fight. The length of time he stayed here is the length of time I'll remain there."

I gasp when I feel myself really bleeding out now. I watch my mate's eyes take notice of this before he growls and takes a step back, loosening his grip.

"Please, release my brother. Brother for a brother." I gulp though I choke a bit.

My mate shifts into his human form, and I look away from his nudeness. From the corner of my eye, I see one of his men take a pair of grey sweats to him.

I'm getting dizzy now.

"What. Do. You. Think. You're. Doing?" my brother growls, his body shaking in anger. He is injured but I know he'll heal soon.

"I'm doing what's best, brother. You might not agree but it is. I-I will take my punishment once I return." I wish I didn't have to say this out loud, but it's for Ronan to clearly hear me and understand.

Ronan grunts before instructing one of his men to fetch the beta.

I sigh in relief for that—knowing a person will get to go home to his family. I stagger back due to the dizziness and almost fall, but my arm is gripped hard to the point of pain by my mate's men.

I mistakenly whimper due to the pain, but then, there's a growl. The grip on my arm is loosened and is being replaced by pleasurable tingles that I almost sigh out in relief.

The beta is soon brought out, beaten and bruised yet still standing. His fellow troops help him to one of the cars. I take a much-needed breath in preparation of me looking like him when I return. Well, if I don't die out due to all the bleeding.

Maybe I might just die here. That'll be fine with me.

"My beta," Ronan grunts.

All too soon, his beta is thrown at his feet, being helped up and taken in the house probably to the pack doctor.

I can't even watch anymore. My vision gets blurry, and my body weight takes over. I feel myself falling, only to land in someone's arms. The sparks give it away.

Before I can slip into darkness, I hear the parting words between my brother and mate.

"You know that I'll come back for her. She belongs here."

"No. She's mine now."

If you enjoyed this sample, look for
Luna Catherine
on Amazon.

AMBER LEE

THE
RUN

CHAPTER ONE

The recognizable smell of the lake fills her lungs. She can feel the water, lapping around her waist and cooling her overheated skin. It's such a warm day and after being outside for most of it, the family has decided to jump in; clothes on and all. She can hear her siblings giggling and laughing as splashing and half-hearted threats fill the air around her.

She spots a duck, one of the many who calls this lake their home. They often don't hang around when she and the family come to the lake, scared off by the threat that they presumably pose, but this duck has stayed. Its small black eyes, meeting her own gaze in near defiance. Then, it parts its bright colored beak and lets out a shrill loud noise.

She frowns, confusion setting in. That isn't the sound a duck makes, is it?

Again, it makes that offending noise. Then again and again and again.

Rae's fist hits the top of the alarm clock as she groans and rolls onto her back, staring up at the patchy white ceiling above. She contemplates how long she'll get away with just laying here this time. One mississippi. Two mississippi. When she reaches a new record of twenty-four mississippis, three knocks sound on the outside of her door. *Huh*, she thinks, it must be a slow morning for everyone.

Every damn morning is like clockwork.

"Rae, Cassidy won't let me in the bathroom." Her nine-year-old sister, Poppy, calls through her door. "Can I use yours?"

Not wanting to get up, Rae just yells back, "Did you bribe her?"

"Yes. She said she won't come out, and I really have to pee!"

"Did you ask Jace for help?" She calls back, referring to their sixteen-year-old brother.

"He said to ask you."

With a groan, Rae sits up and runs a hand through her chin-length blonde hair, getting her hands stuck in a knot. Sitting on the edge of her bed, she stretches her toes until they crack—a habit after years of ballet—and manages to find the will to get to the door. Opening the door, a blur of blonde hair and gray long Johns goes flying past her before her bathroom door is slammed shut behind it.

Well, Rae thinks with a yawn, *guess she really did have to pee.*

Heading for her dresser, Rae picks out her work clothes and throws them on her bed, waiting patiently for Poppy to finish. When she hears the toilet flush, she leans against the doorframe with a raised brow. Poppy reemerges from the bathroom looking a little embarrassed and a small smile in place.

"Good morning," Rae greets.

"Good morning. Sorry about that."

Rolling her eyes, Rae ruffles her sister's already rat nested hair. "No worries, kiddo. You sleep okay?"

Poppy grins and nods, making her glasses bounce a little. "Yup. I had a dream the moon was populated with unicorns that mined skittles with their horns."

"Sounds like an awesome dream."

"It was. Hey, Rae?"

"Yeah?"

"Can I have skittles for breakfast?"

"Not in your life. Now go get ready for school."

Poppy pouts at her. "Will you braid my hair?"

"Sure, but you're going to have to make it quick. I already told Cassidy last night I'd braid hers too."

"Okay!" she shouts before running out of the room and down the hallway towards her room.

Rae rolls her eyes and is about to shut her bedroom door so she can get dressed when she hears her sister shriek. This one is her seventeen-year-old sister, Cleo. Since hitting the teen years, Cleo has been a handful, but the older she gets, it seems to Rae that she only gets worse.

"Cassidy, get out of the bathroom now!"

Cassidy, their six-year-old sister, opens the door to yell back at Cleo, "No! Go away!"

Deciding to just let them deal with it, Rae shuts her door and locks it before heading back towards her bed. Stripping off her nightclothes, Rae replaces them with her cleanest pair of jean shorts and her white button up short-sleeved work shirt. The words 'Peter's Patties' is written on the back and left breast with red lettering.

Rae corrects her collar and straightens out the gold charm necklace around her neck. It was a gift from her mother on her fourteenth birthday, the year of Rae's first shift. Rae, like her father, is a werewolf and up to this point, the only one of her siblings able to shift. Her mother gifted her a gold moon charm to go along with the four-leaf clover she gave her on her birthday. Before she passed, she also added a heart to remind her of the love in her life.

Rae lets go of the necklace and gets back to getting ready, not wanting to dwell too much on thinking about her mom. It's been three years since the six Applebee siblings lost their mother to brain aneurysm and their father to grief, but none of them have been able to get over it. Losing your parents in a one-two punch is never easy, especially when the youngest is just three years old, and the oldest, Rae herself, was only sixteen.

Despite the hard times, Rae has pulled her family by bootstraps and made sure they stay together, no matter what. It is what Rae knows her mother would have wanted, and Rae plans to keep that promise she made on the day of the funeral. She would keep them together no matter what.

Parting her hair down the middle, Rae puts her pink-tipped hair in twin low pigtails and puts on her watch. Grabbing her fringed brown leather satchel and black beaten down converse, she goes through a mental checklist to make sure she's got everything. She's pretty sure she does, but her track record isn't so good.

"Rae, I'm ready!" Poppy yells through the door.

Unlocking the door, Rae opens the door to see both Cassidy and Poppy, this time ready to have their blonde tangles tamed. Poppy with her large blue eyes, glasses, and blonde hair looks a lot like their father while Cassidy, also blonde, has their dad's brown eyes. Whistling, Rae moves towards the stairs, grabbing the brush and hair ties in her hands as she passes the girls.

"So you girls excited? It's almost the fall equinox," Rae asks as she walks down the stairs.

"Fall what?" Cassidy asks, screwing up her face adorably.

"Equinox," Poppy tells her slowly. "It means that there will be equal parts of night and day from now on. Usually, the pack does the celebrations, you know the ones when we're stuck with Hudson for the night while they all go and party."

"We do not go out all night and party. We just do the rituals of the pack, Poppy, you know that," Rae corrects, but it falls on deaf ears.

"Hudson is so boring, though," Poppy whines. "He doesn't let us do anything!"

"That's not true," Hudson's voice objects from the bottom of the stairs. Hudson is the semi-middle child in the Applebee clan at the age of fourteen, and with his brown hair and brown eyes, looks the most like their father. "I let you watch those stupid *Twilight* movies."

"They're not stupid!" Cassidy yells. "Edward is my boyfriend!"

Rae winces at her volume, but it's Hudson who speaks up. "Cassidy, you're too little for boyfriends."

"I am not!"

"Jacob's my boyfriend, and I'm not too young," Poppy adds.

"Yes, you are," Hudson tells her. "No boys until your both thirty."

"Rae!" Both girls shriek.

"What the hell is going in here?"

Rae slaps her hand over her face as her brother Jace gets into the mix. Jace got the quirky genes in the family, giving him red shaggy hair and freckles along with their mom's blue eyes. With the small black gages in his ear and lip ring, Rae can't help but think he looks adorable. He hates it when she says that, but she can't help herself. In her mind, he'll always be her baby brother.

"Hudson said we can't have a boyfriend until we're old and gross!" Poppy tells Jace.

Jace's eyebrows shoot up, and he gives Rae a "what the hell" look. Rae just shrugs and smiles at him. She really has no words to go into why two young girls shouldn't even be interested in boys, let alone a sparkly vegetarian and a giant whiny puppy. When she was Cassidy's age, all Rae liked was eating mud and throwing sticks at the ducks in the pond.

"I don't know why you'd want to like boys, anyway. They have gross germs."

"No, they don't," Poppy denies but sounds unsure.

"They do," Jace insists with a nod of his head. "Every boy who is related to you has these gross germs that can only affect you. They make you sick, make your stomach hurt, and can sometimes turn you into zombies."

"And that's where I'm going to stop you," Rae says, suddenly clapping her hands. "Come on girls, you gotta eat."

"I'm not hungry," Poppy says, holding her stomach.

"Me neither."

Rae gives Jace a dirty look which he only shrugs at. Rolling his eyes when she gives him a silent warning, he sighs. "I made chocolate chip pancakes."

"I call the big one!" Poppy yells before running for the kitchen, only to have Cassidy run after her.

With both the girls gone, Rae gives Jace a flat look. "Zombies? Really?"

"Hey, it'll keep them away from the boys," Jace states with a shrug.

"Keep who away from boys?"

Jace, Hudson, and Rae all look up to see Cleo walking down the stairs and grimace. Today, she's dressed in high-waisted red shorts too short to be legal, a white half shirt, and a leather jacket. Her shoes are black platforms, and she's wearing a daisy tattoo choker on her neck which Rae is pretty sure is attempting to hide a hickey.

Cleo has been dressing more and more provocatively lately, and from what Rae's been hearing, it's not going to waste. She's just happy they got Cleo on birth control at fifteen and had "the talk." At this point, Rae is pretty sure that's all she can do without making her run away again, claiming Rae is "stifling" her. Maybe she is, but Rae would rather stifle her sister than have her sister knocked up and running off with some jerk off boyfriend.

"Nothing," Rae dismisses, deliberately not reacting to her sister's behavior as usual. "Jace, do you need a ride today or are you good?"

"Actually, Shane, and Connor are going to pick me up today."

"Hudson?"

"I'll take the ride."

Rae nods before turning to Cleo. "How about you?"

"Ride in the Scooby Doo van with you? No thank you." Cleo scoffs.

"Suit yourself." Rae sighs before waving the brush and hair ties in her hair. "Now, if you'll excuse me I have some hair to tie into submission."

She's about to move towards the kitchen when Jace grabs her arm and stops her. Speaking lowly, he tells her, "The alpha called this morning."

"What did he say?" Rae asks past her dry throat.

"Said he needs you to stop by before you go to work today."

"Did he say why?"

Jace shakes his head, "No, but with the equinox coming up . . . I'm sure you can guess."

"But . . . I can't do it this year."

"Rae, you're nineteen," Jace says sadly. "You were exempted last year due to our circumstances, but he's not going to let it slide this time. We all have to do it; it's just a rite of passage."

Rae hangs her head and grunts, "I don't want to."

"Oh, come on, it's not that bad," Jace says, hitting his shoulder with hers. "It's just a chance for people to find their mates, Rae. There's no guarantee you will so why not just go on with it, have some fun, and make the alpha a happy man. He'll be off your back, and you'll be off the hook another year. Besides, Phillip went last year, and he found his mate. She even accepted him, poor woman. So I'm sure your mate will look past your ugly face too."

Laughing a little, Rae punches his arm. "Ass."

"You love me."

"Like a rash I can't shake."

"Why would you shake a rash?" he asks, faking stupid.

Pushing his head, he chuckles as he goes towards the kitchen to eat with their other siblings. Rae pinches her lower lip between her fingers and thinks over everything Jace said. *He has a point,* she realizes. *If she just goes to the damn Run this year, the alpha will let it go, and she can just go on with her life.*

But what if she finds her mate? She thinks faintly.

"No," she mumbles out loud to herself. "That'll never happen."

Shaking her head, Rae heads into the kitchen, ready to start the beginning of what is sure to be a very long day.

If you enjoyed this sample, look for
The Run
on Amazon.

ISABEL WOLF

INTO THE WOODS

BOOK I OF THE HELLHOUND SERIES

PROLOGUE

Once upon a time, there was a little girl whose mother always told her bedtime stories before she went to sleep. Stories about the big red-eyed black beasts that walked during the nights, where they would destroy villages and kill people in an effort to find their lovers. *Soul mates.*

Lovers to whom they would be bound to until death separated them apart.

I never thought that every story she told me would end up being true. Hell, I never thought that someday, in just a matter of seconds, I would become one of those girls—the ones who were bonded to a beast.

-Elizabeth

CHAPTER I

"Everyone needs a fresh start in their life,
An adventure that they seek."
-Elizabeth

ELIZABETH

Leaving the place you grew up in was always hard to think about and even harder to do so.

I would miss Stockholm.

I would miss its coldness and the people who I grew up with and, over the years, became my second family. I would miss the Stortorget—the oldest square in the city with distinct red and yellow buildings—and the small coffee shop where I spent most of my time with my closest friends.

I would miss exploring the secret gardens of the Tantolunden park. The green gardens that gave me peace and helped my mind become clear whenever I needed it.

Most importantly, I would miss my mother; my butler, Wilhelm; and even my annoying best friend, Anastasia. I never thought that I would have to leave the town that was so full of memories and the stupid mistakes I made in the past, and the university where I worked so hard to get into to fly over ten thousand kilometres to Canada, to my aunt, Lena, and her husband, Louis.

The people who knew me all my life never thought that I—Elizabeth Zemerlöw, a twenty-year-old girl who never cried—would actually cry right in front of my friends at a local bar where we always hung out.

"You better call and message me every day." Anastasia cried hysterically against my left ear. She held me so tight that I could barely breathe.

"Let her go, Nia. She is barely breathing." Jack laughed as he took his glass and drank the entire vodka in one sip.

As if she didn't hear a single thing he just said, Anastasia simply squeezed me tighter against her body. At first, I thought she was just joking about not letting me go, but now that it was getting too hard to even breathe, her claim wasn't as funny as I thought it was.

I tried to push her away, but it was difficult to make her budge.

"Seriously, Nia. I can't breathe." I sighed.

After realising I was serious, she finally let me go.

"I'm sorry, Ell." She hugged me again, but this time, she gave me a hard kiss on the forehead.

"Yeah, she's drunk," I said to the rest of my friends.

Anastasia moved away from me, her focus shifting to a blond guy behind us.

"What are you doing?" Chris asked her but Anastasia, being Anastasia, just walked over to the blond guy, clearly not caring that the redhead girl next to him might be his girlfriend.

"She won't remember any of this tomorrow," Hana said.

"I know." I took a sip of my water. "It's such a shame that I won't be here tomorrow to see her face when you tell her. Actually, do me a favor and record it," I said a little louder.

The music in the bar got louder than before, causing several people to dance like crazy on the dance floor. Many of the men were grinding themselves to several girls's asses. Some of them, and by some, I mean Anastasia, was already perched on one of the guy's shoulders, screaming incoherently at the DJ.

"She's crazy," I said, still looking at her.

I will miss this. I will miss her and her psychotic nature. I will miss my crazy best friend.

"When are you leaving?" Hana asked.

"Tomorrow. I mean today at 10 AM."

"That's less than ten hours," Hana said. "Aren't you gonna be tired?" she asked.

I shook my head. "I have twelve hours to sleep on the plane."

"So how is it like there? I mean in Canada?" Chris screamed as the music started to get louder.

"It's good. I've been there a couple of times, and it's really beautiful." I smiled. "My aunt already did all the paperwork for the university, and she already found me a job at some local library."

"Which university? Are you taking the same courses or . . . ?" Hana placed a lock of her hair behind her ear.

I shrugged. "They are the same ones. Ancient history and English literature." I bit my lower lip as I tried to remember the name of the school. "I believe it's called Nightclaw University. I'm not quite sure."

Chris and Hana glanced at each other. Their eyes widened as they looked over to Jack who was looking directly at me.

"What?" I asked as I started to get nervous. Their moods seemed to change quickly the minute I mentioned the name of the school.

"Haven't you heard about the curse?"

Oh no, not them too.

"What curse?" I hoped it wasn't the same curse my mom told me about.

"About the beasts walking at night. I heard the Nightclaw family owned a few of those monsters," Hana said.

"Yeah, I also heard they kill people at the university, especially young girls." Chris threw his hands in the air before he let out a ghostly sound.

I started laughing. "Where did you hear those stupid things? My mom told me some stories, but yours . . . I can't even." I rolled my eyes and looked at them, but they weren't even laughing. In fact, they seemed pretty serious about those stories.

"They are not just stupid stories, Elizabeth," Jack told me. His blue eyes stared into my green ones.

"Remember my cousin Monica? Well, she goes to that university. She told me what happens to the people who go there. They all die, Ell," he said.

"Okay." I raised my hands. "I think I know where you got these stories from." I remembered telling it to Jack before I moved my attention to both of them. "The only question is who told you?" I asked both Hana and Chris.

Hana shrugged. "From Jack."

I sighed. "Okay, if it makes you feel any better, I'll try my best to stay away from anything that can kill me."

Chris leaned forward and placed a hand on my shoulder before he spoke, "I have to go now." He nodded over towards Anastasia. "I have to drive her home before she does anything stupid," he joked.

"Yeah, I'm gonna leave too," Hana repeated.

Bastards. They just want to leave Jack and I alone.

"You promised me that you'll drive me home," I told Chris.

He shrugged and a devilish small smirk appeared on his lips.

"I'll drive you," Jack said.

I looked at him for a moment as I tried to decode the meaning behind his sudden offer.

"Then it's settled." Chris clapped his hands. Both him and Hana moved closer before they gave me one final hug as they left the dance floor.

"Good luck. Be safe."

*   *   *

A deep silence settled between Jack and I during the drive. It almost seemed like we didn't even know each other at all. He was focused on the road while I was looking at my phone, answering my mother's ten missed messages.

"So this is it?" I froze at his question. I bit my lower lip, locked the phone, and turned to him as I noticed the way his jaw clenched.

"I don't know what you are talking about." I leaned on the seat and closed my eyes for a second.

"You know what I mean. I didn't want to make a scene in the bar, but now that we're alone, I want to talk about it." His voice was like a whisper that broke the silence in the air. I had been actively trying to avoid this conversation ever since we broke up, but now I realised that there was simply no way around it.

"I know. It's just that we won't work out, Jack. You . . . I . . . what you did . . ." I saw my house from the corner and immediately turned to him.

"You can just drop me here. Thank you for the ride."

He slowed down the car, and before he could completely stop the vehicle, I opened the door and got out of there quickly.

"Elizabeth, wait!" I heard him call my name from behind.

As soon as I got into my house, I immediately slammed the door shut and locked it.

"That was a close one," I said to myself.

I turned around and peaked through the window as I watched him drive off.

"This is a new start, Elizabeth. Everything will be okay."

* * *

"Did you pack everything you need?" my mother asked while she drove me to the airport. It was the seventh time that she asked me that in the last thirty minutes.

"Yes, Mom," I told her. Even our butler, Wilhelm, smiled at my answer.

"I called Lena, and she'll wait for you at the airport," she reminded.

I nodded and looked outside of the window as I subconsciously tried to memorize the entire scenery, including every person and brick in this beloved town of mine.

The car stopped and I knew that this was the last time I'd ever see my home before I go.

"Honey." A soft voice interrupted my thoughts. I turned around and saw my mother's crying face. Her green eyes were red and glassy looking. She opened her arms for a hug, and like always, I gladly took it. After I undid the seat belt, I moved closer to her and buried my head against her neck.

"You know, you could have taken your father's offer and went with the private plane. At least, you would be here for two more days."

I took a deep breath.

I know.

"I'll call you all when I land or at least send an e-mail when I settle down," I said as I tried to change the subject.

I turned around and glanced over to Mr. Wilhelm in his black suit. Yes, he was our butler, but sometimes, he was more of a father to me than my actual biological one.

He smiled at me. "I will miss you, Miss Elizabeth. Don't forget to send me a postcard."

I laughed at his comment.

"I won't. I promise."

* * *

The whole flight was pretty much okay. Somehow I managed to sleep through the entire journey. When I woke up, the plane had already landed in Canada, where the blonde stewardess had to wake me up.

After I mumbled a quick thank you, I grabbed my backpack and started heading out of the plane.

"Thank you for enjoying our flight," another stewardess said. I smiled at her as I climbed down the stairs.

The first thing that caught my eye was the sky. It was grey, but it wasn't as cold as it was in Sweden during the first days of September.

"Excuse me, can you please tell me where the exit is?" I asked an older man. He smiled at me, and I guessed he understood English.

He turned around and pointed at the exit sign. I had no idea why I didn't see it before.

After I grabbed my suitcase, I started to search for my aunt. My mother told me she would wait for me next to the H12 exit at 11:30 AM. Now it's 11:45 AM. She was fifteen minutes late. As I waited for her arrival, I stood at the exit sign with a heavy backpack and suitcase, feeling like a complete idiot. Eventually, a few people started staring as if they had never seen a tourist before in their lives.

"Are you searching for someone?" I jumped at a female voice that spoke up behind me.

When I turned around, I saw my aunt Lena stand in front of me with her arms open. I immediately dropped everything that I was holding and hugged her, although not completely. Something wasn't letting me hug her properly.

"I waited for you for about fifteen minutes," I mumbled into her ear as I tried to hug her tighter. I hadn't seen her and Louis since their wedding.

"Well, this baby isn't going to feed herself."

Baby? I moved away from her, and my eyes immediately landed on her round belly. My eyes widened in response.

"Mom didn't tell me a thing." I was still in shock. How could she not tell me about this?

"I wanted it to be a surprise." She smirked and wiggled her eyebrows.

I laughed. She always found a way to make me laugh.

Out of the corner of my eye, I watched Louis walk towards us with a phone over his ear. He hadn't changed a thing. He still looked young for a thirty-three-year-old.

"I have to go now. My niece just arrived. I'll give you a call when I get home," he said before he hung up.

I had to admit, back when he first started dating Lena, I didn't really like him because there was always this dangerous aura around him. Nowadays, that feeling I had was long gone. He made her happy and seemed to always do whatever it was she asked him to, something I didn't really see in a lot of men.

"Hello, Elizabeth," he greeted me.

"Hello, Louis." He placed his hand around Lena's waist and pulled her towards him before he gave her a small kiss on the nose.

"I see you hadn't changed a thing. Are you ready for your new life in Shadowrose?" Lena asked as she returned the kiss.

"I am," I answered with confidence.

"But are you ready for the beasts?"

I laughed and walked next to them. Louis threw an arm around Lena's shoulder and held her close to him while we walked through a bunch of people.

"You mean the stupid stories that people keep telling me?"

"You know they aren't just stories," Lena said in a serious tone. Louis looked serious too.

"What do you mean?"

"There are wolves walking at night. Big black wolves, Elizabeth. They aren't something you want to deal with."

If you enjoyed this sample, look for
Into the Woods
on Amazon.

ACKNOWLEDGEMENT

I would like to thank my family for all their support and my boyfriend, Luke, who has encouraged me to write every step of the way. This book wouldn't exist without any of you. I love you all.

AUTHOR'S NOTE

Thank you so much for reading *The Wolven King*! I can't express how grateful I am for reading something that was once just a thought inside my head.

I'd love to hear your thoughts on the book. Please leave a review on Amazon or Goodreads because I just love reading your comments and getting to know you!

Can't wait to hear from you!

Chelsea L.L. Bones

ABOUT THE AUTHOR

Hello, my names Chelsea, the author of 'The Wolven King' amongst other things that I'm currently working on. I love to write, ever since the age of fifteen when I realised how much I enjoyed it. I love the way my work effects my readers, whether that be heartbreak or love, it's all intentional with the words I write. Of course, writing is a big part of my life, and when I can't write, it's because I'm working. I work full time Inside a dental practice with a team I really enjoy working with.

For those who are interested in my likes, I really like to relax after a long day of work and read a book. Reading inspires me to continue writing and one of my favourite books to read at the moment is the ACOTAR series by Sarah J Mass. I love a bacon and cheese burger when I go out for a meal and really enjoy spending time with family and friends. My family, friends, and my boyfriend Luke all support and encourage me day-to-day to write and follow my goal of becoming a successful author. Not to mention, my massive following of readers who enjoy my work and keep me going, too. I thank you all so much! And I love you all!

Printed in Great Britain
by Amazon